Praise for SNAKE ROPES

Richards's debut is a cornucopia of secrets and surprises, ritten in a bright, sassy style. The author is exuberantly inventive in creating a bitter-sweet world of magical transformations.' *Independent*

A terrific story, quirky and wildly original.' Joanne Harris

ichards handles her ambitions with aplomb. SNAKE ROPES is partly an extended meditation on trauma and healing, nd the trauma is handled so well that the reader is exactly as upset as she needs to be to follow through . . . SNAKE ROPES reminds us that the act of storytelling is in itself a form of resolution.' *Guardian*

'Richards skilfully alternates between Mary and Morgan nd their stories, touching on themes such as the transmission of folk wisdom, the creation of myths and violence against women.' *Financial Times*

'From the islanders' subtle creole to their myths of sea and sky and earth, Jess Richards has nurtured a remarkable community, their home glimpsed in the sea-mist like a new Avalon. Angela Carter or Laura Esquivel would have been proud of this.' *We Love This Book*

'A mystical book where a harsh self-sufficient lifestyle meets myths, legends and magic . . . an unusual, haunting debut novel.' thebookbag.co.uk

Jess Richards was born in Wales in 1972 and grew up too fast in south west Scotland, where she lived with her English parents and three brothers, watching the ferry boats going to and from Northern Ireland. She left home at 17, went over the border to England and lived for a year in Carlisle before moving to Devon. She gained a first class degree from Dartington College of Arts when she was 21. After brief stints busking and carrying on in both Leeds and London, she moved to Brighton aged 23 where she has grown up a bit more slowly, and has lived and worked ever since. SNAKE ROPES is her first novel.

www.jessrichards.com

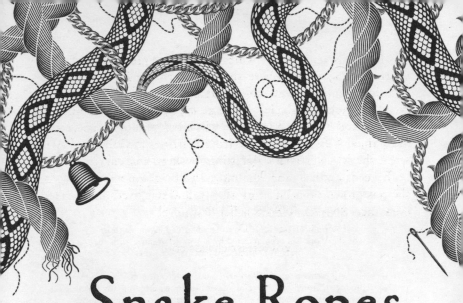

Snake Ropes

jess richards

SCEPTRE

First published in Great Britain in 2012 by Sceptre
An imprint of Hodder & Stoughton
An Hachette UK company

First published in paperback in 2013

1

A CIP catalogue record for this title is
available from the British Library

Paperback ISBN 978 1 444 73785 1
eBook ISBN 978 1 444 73786 8

Printed and bound by Clays Ltd, St Ives plc

Hodder & Stoughton policy is to use papers that are natural, renewable
and recyclable products and made from wood grown in sustainable forests.
The logging and manufacturing processes are expected to conform to the
environmental regulations of the country of origin.

Hodder & Stoughton Ltd
338 Euston Road
London NW1 3BH

www.sceptrebooks.co.uk

For Kate,
because she makes up words:
Mitt nitt jub.

and

for Mr Blight,
who lives in the Thrashing House:
a man I've never met.

Mary

The tall men in boats are coming. I see them through the window, close to the beach. My little brother is sat on my lap. Him puts hims hands on the table, leans round and looks up at me. Hims brown eyes have my reflection inside.

I smile at him, stroke the curls on the back of hims head where them need a wash. I say, 'Sorry Barney. I've got to get you hid, them're coming.' Him grips on my neck hard, buries hims face in my hair and I carry him across the room. Him is so warm and I want to hang on to him, but I put him down by the cupboard door, and hims face trying to look all angered makes me want to laugh, but I dun.

I hide him in the cupboard behind the boxes. Give him a blanket to keep him warm. Tell him, 'Shush now, and dun even breathe if them opens the cupboard door.'

The tall men are all skinny and pale, with long dark coats and black hats with big brims on them. Them give us goods for our stuff. Trade them calls it. Da says it be more like theft and if we lived on a main land we'd get a lot more than what them give us. We've got to survive on what we can get. No one here goes to the main land, and no one wants to. Our boats aren't strong enough, we dun know the way, them can't understand us, we're fine as we are. We have so many reasons; them stretch as wide as the distance to cross to take us there.

I stand at the window watching. Nine boats long and thin, like the men. Two in each one, rowing with long oars. I sort the piles of broiderie, put the ones them will like best on top. Da's left the fish out in the cold room, ready for the tall men.

Barney grumbles loud in the cupboard so I call out, 'Now dun fret, you'll not be shut in the dark for long, it's just till them've gone.'

The tall men dun move to speak to one another. Silent as shadows, everyone says, but when the tall men do speak, them pick the words what'll get what them most want. Not like us folks what live here, we sometimes chatter out whole bunches of tattle. Perhaps we should lock just a little behind our lips, then we'd get more back.

I've got to be watchful with Barney. Three boys on the island were took in the last three months. Three men what go drinking with Da, each of thems sons are gone. Dun think them've got blown off the cliffs, we all think it were the tall men what took them.

Since our Mam died we struggle to get by. Da gets fish from out the sea and I do broideries for selling to the tall men. My broideries are lovely, everyone who sees them says so. I do all the flowers what grow in the summer before the wind sweeps them away, and all the butterflies. Mam left boxes and baskets full of threads and linens. Them said at her funeral that she were the best broiderer this island's ever seen. She taught me some before she died but I got better quick; Da said we'd be eating grass and drinking air if we were to live off just hims fishing. Him says now I'm sixteen, I'm old enough to trade with the tall men alone.

I did well last month – the batch I'd stitched raised the tall men's eyebrows and got us more goods from them than the month before. The colours sang in the sunlight on this table, as if my hands had stroked them into the fabric, rather than jabbed them through with the needle. Some pictures are more difficult to bring to life than others, pulling and drawing, pulling and drawing.

Not a sound from the cupboard. For a three-year-old, Barney is good and quiet for me, when him knows I mean it. I cross the room, whisper at the door, 'Them're coming. Keep quiet, good boy.'

'Dun like it in here, is dark and smelly.' Him snuffles.

Hims bunny doll lies on the floor next to the cupboard door. I scoop it up, open the door a crack; hims brown eyes are all teary behind the baskets of linens. Him reaches out hims hands.

'Here's your moppet. Just stay put. I'll cradle you when we're done.' I close up the door.

A few women have brought thems trade down to the beach, and are handing over woven rugs and baskets to a pair of tall men what're stood by the boats. Fourteen of the tall men walk up the beach in pairs, them head to the path what leads up the cliffs, to other homes of folk what do trade. One pair of tall men come towards this row of cottages. Them need the agreement of two to make the decision of one. Just as we're suspicious of them, them dun trust us not to argue, especially where thems goods are concerned. Thems coats might be covered in seaspray and salt when them have crossed the surging waves to get here, but them are well stitched, as if somewhere on the main land there's a great old woman who sits there with needles for fingertips, stitching in straight perfect lines, with the threads tucked away so them will never escape.

The knock, four raps on the door. Four raps again.

I open the front door.

3

'Miss Jared,' says the tall man in front. I swallow a laugh, everyone here calls me Mary.

'I've got the broideries ready.' I step back and sweep my hand towards the tabletop by the window. I wish the sun would shine in and make the broideries look alive. Today them look dull and faded.

Them lean over the broideries, long pale fingers fondle them. I wonder why them dun take the girls, only the boys. Something boys can do what girls can't. But what that could be I have no idea; everyone knows boys are only of use if them take to farming or fishing.

One has a pair of glasses balanced on the end of hims nose and I wonder if him wears them out at sea. Him glances at me over them, without a squint. Can't be that bad sighted then.

'These are quite . . . elaborate.'

'That's what you wanted last time.' I bite my lip.

'Slightly overexpressive,' mutters the other one, hims eyebrows raised.

'You said . . .'

'Not *this* extravagant. Not what was meant.' Hims voice is low and steady.

'Just tell me the price you're suggesting.'

'The women won't like the more . . . elaborate ones. It's the simple ones we can sell.'

'The ones you passed over last time?' My voice sounds shrill and both the men straighten up, near enough hit thems heads on the beams.

'We are at the behest of fashion, Miss Jared. We can give some as tokens, as gifts, if women choose to buy the plain ones. They want rustic.'

'So you're saying last month them wanted drama, now them're wanting dull?'

4

'Precisely.'

'Well, I dun know how them can change fashion faster than I can make them. Why them can't just stick with thems likes from last month for a few weeks more.'

A thud from Barney, in the cupboard.

I stamp on the floor.

Them dun notice.

I fold my arms. 'So, how much?'

'Ten units for the lot,' says one, hims lip twitching.

'Well, I think I'll hang on to them till them come back *in* fashion.'

Him breathes in like I've just jabbed hims chest with one of the needles.

I stamp to the front door and open it. The wind blows in the smell of the sea. I stare at the floor, twirl a strand of my dark hair around my finger and pull, hard.

'Twenty, then. You wouldn't want to be seen as a charity case, I'm sure.'

'Dun care about being seen as a charity case, we've got to eat.' I glance up at hims cold blue eyes and swallow hard. 'Thirty.'

'Twenty-five, final price.'

'Take them.' I smile. 'Do you want to do the fish? It's out in the cold room.'

We go around the side of the cottage, and the cold room door sticks – the wooden door is guarding the fish. I can feel the tall men's eyes on me. My hair, my waist, my backside as well, no doubt. Them're all eyes, the tall men, each and every one.

I yank at the door as hard as I can, it whaps against my boot and springs open. In the dark, the dead fish eyes ogle me from the half-cask barrels. It's so dark in here and I'm shivery just stepping inside. Ash, soot and straw are spread all over the walls to keep the ice frozen. It works. Da's left the fish sorted and packed in the barrels I wrench out of the ice in the floor. Five heavy barrels and them dun even offer to help.

Pulling the last barrel out, I hear the back door slam and glance at the side of the cottage. 'So then.' I glare at the two tall men. 'What am I getting for this lot?'

Them move further away, so them can see the whole lot of fish all together. Them hiss prices back and forth and glance up at me every so often. Taking thems time, as always. Just want to get a good long stare at a single young woman. The wind musses my hair up and I dun bother getting it off my face. I wipe my pink wet hands on my dress. I stink of fish. Good.

Eventually a trade is offered, I needle them up a little and settle. It's a good job Da's got a daughter, for the tall men offer far more for what girls and women make with our hands than what fishermen drag out of the sea.

I've got enough sense to do the best trade I can, and also enough sense not to help them once them've paid. The tall men take the broideries and go down to the boats. When them come back, I get them to put all our goods on the path by the front door. I count them up while the tall men come back and forth to drag the barrels of fish down to thems boats.

I take some of the jars and cans of main land foods into our cottage and put them just inside the front door. The jars and cans are worth one unit each. I go outside to get more of the goods. There's a box with the words *exotic fruits* printed on the side.

'What's this meant to be then?' I call out to the tall men who've just grasped another barrel of fish.

The tall men look up. 'Five units.'

'But it's strange-looking things I'm sure can't be eaten.'

'Happy enough with them on the mainland,' says the one with the glasses.

'Joyful, no doubt, to send them to us,' I mutter.

Them carry on hauling the barrel, and I knock on a yellow thing shaped like the sun, but squashed. 'What's this then?' I hold it up.

'Melon,' calls out one, and them both stare at me like I'm simple, so I take the box indoors, put it on the table by the window and go outside to get the rest.

There's a tin of varnish and a pot of white paint worth three units each, seven boxes of matches and two packets of fire-lighters. There's a small sack I've never seen them bring before. It's got red words on it, but I dun know what's inside, for the words are in foreign. Dun ask them about that one. Maybe the foreign will make sense later, when I've opened up the sack.

The three units of ice are in great sacks made from the clear shiny stuff them call plastic, thick layers of it. I put it in the cold room and kick the door shut behind me. I watch the two tall men emptying the last of the barrels into the crates in thems boat. The tall men never forget the ice, for it's needed to keep the fish fresh. Still have to trade them for it, but. Main land folks must stink of fish. Whole lot of men here do fishing, and there's a fair few cold rooms on the island, as well as a smoke-house. But the fish is all traded, for none of us like the taste.

I think the tall men must have one great huge boat what picks up all nine of the oar boats. Them keep it just over the edge of the horizon. For if them dun have a quicker way to get from the main land to here than just oars, then the ice would melt on the journey.

Not that I'd say anything to the tall men, for however them do it, them're the only folks what bother to brave the distance to us.

Back inside, I watch the tall men roll the empty fish barrels back up the beach to the cold room. Them leave them stacked up outside, so the other tall men know them've got our trade and dun come knocking twice.

I call, 'Come out Barney, them're done.'

No answer. Him must have fallen asleep in there, or be messing with me.

I cross the room, open the cupboard door. The moppet sits on top of a basket, its ears askew.

Barney's blanket lies there rumpled, without him on it.

My head goes bang bang with the throb in it. I open the boxes at the back, pull Mam's linens out of the baskets. No Barney.

I tear through to the bedroom, look under hims small bed, under my bed, rumple up the bedclothes in case him is hiding. In Da's room, I rummage through the wardrobe where Mam's clothes still hang, but there's no Barney. Back in the main room I check the cupboard again and under the table.

I open the trapdoor in the floor and climb down the ladder into the storm room. Light a candle and check in the shadows. Nothing. I slump down on the floor.

Barney's mine. Him can't be took like the others. Him is too young.

If Mam were still alive she'd be shouting about this. She shouted so often, even when Da gave her a bruise for saying Barney were hers but not hims. Them shared me. Dun know why she wouldn't share Barney as well. Maybe she thought Da dun bother enough with me, so a son would be just another thing for him not to bother about. Or she could have loved Barney best.

I loved him best.

8

I want to shout like Mam would've done, only I've got all the shouts stuffed in my chest and them dun want to come out. Barney's been mine since Mam died. Da said after her funeral, 'Him is all yours Mary, through an' through. Nowt to do with me, so you got to work hard, do a lot of broideries to keep him fed.'

Always has been my arms Barney wanted.

I've always wanted him in my arms.

In our bedroom, I stuff the pillow from Barney's bed in my arms and squeeze, hard. If I squeezed him this hard I'd stifle the life out of him, but my arms need to do something. Tears pinch up in my eyes. I dun have the time for this, got to move, else there'll be no chance to do anything – the tall men will be gone and there'll just be a blank hole in the world what Barney's fallen through.

I dun know what to do.

What did Annie next door do, when her Kieran got took? I must have known. Weren't long ago. Kieran, fourteen years old, nose thick with freckles, just like hims Mam. What happened then, what did Annie do?

The front door thumps and rattles.

Da's voice hollers, 'Mary, where are you?' all gruff. Him is back much earlier than usual.

I've got to get out before Da sees Barney is gone and decides Barney being gone is all for the best. One less mouth to gannet down not enough food.

Hurling down the pillow, I run to the kitchen, click the latch and get out the back door, around the side of our cottage and down to the beach where the tall men are loading crates and boxes onto thems boats.

My boots slip on the shingle, get tangled in the spiky grass, sand gets in the holes and near trips me. I get close enough to one of the tall men, grab hims wrist as him is picking up a crate of ropes, wearing black gloves. Hims cold wrist feels like him is dead though him is up and walking. Touching hims skin sends a judder right through me.

Him drops the crate. We both jump back. Him turns and glares at me.

I yell at him, 'My brother, give me him back! Him is only little – what use is him for you? Him is mine, the only one I've got!'

Him leans forwards. 'We don't have him. We don't have the others either. If your parents can't afford to feed you, we can't be answerable for their actions, or their blame. We're here for trade as we always have been.'

'We have to go,' says one, shadows in hims eyes.

The tall men load up thems boats, like I'm not here. I clamber over the boxes and check each boat, all the baskets, every sack. There's nothing being loaded but fish and flour, brown boots from the cobbler, horseshoes and birdcages from the smithy, weavings, woollens, tapestries, stitchings, broideries and ropes. Clothes and cushions for the fancy women's houses what them must change as often as thems fashion.

No brother.

All the crying what's stuck in me finds the blank place in the world what him has fallen away through. I fall on the sand, can't see a thing through the tears. Been looking after him so hard since Mam died, I feel like hims Mam myself. I draw my arms around my chest, only there's a hollow where him should be. Tears fall into it; him is not there to cradle. I want to be strong for him, only I can't when him is not here.

A tall man leans over me. Him has brown eyes, not like the others. Him looms against the grey sky, like a giant gravedigger. I grasp a stone lying in the wet sand and raise my fist, to hurl it at him.

Him grips my wrist. I try to shriek but my throat's stuck. Hims touch sends shivers all up my arm and I can't move my hand. Him pinches out my fingers. It's a big white shell what's in my palm, not a stone at all.

Him lets go. 'You can't hurt me with *that*.' Hims voice is low and cold. A glimmer of gold flecks around the pupil in hims right eye. Puts me in mind of the gold flecks in Barney's eye. Him smells of salt and dust. Something in the smell makes the sky blink dark for a moment. Then it's grey again. A sharp pain cuts through my belly.

Him turns and walks away. The tall men are done with me. Done with all of us till next month. Them push the boats off the beach and the long oars stir up the waters.

Barney is not in the boats.

Not in our home.

Not in my arms.

My throat gets unstuck and I howl and scream like my heart will clean break out of me. So loud Da comes out of our cottage.

Da gets to me and I feel a sharp bite on my shin. A thick rope lies next to my foot on the sand. It's moving, twisting, glints of teeth woven through the strands. Da pulls me up on my feet and I punch hims big chest and bury my head in hims neck.

'Barney's gone!' I shriek. 'Him's been took.' And everything goes blank and dark.

*

Da sits beside my bed on the wobbly stool. Slumped over, wearing all greys, him looks like an empty canvas bag.

Him says, 'You've got a fever, Mary. Been talking strangeness what makes no sense. Brown eyes and blue eyes and bruises. Ropes tied all over you an' the whole island. You know where you are?' Hims tired eyes look at me like I'm going to be gone any moment.

I roll away, face the cracked grey wall and whisper, 'Want him back.'

Da's voice sounds loud. 'Him is gone, Mary, and it's not your fault.'

I know it *is* my fault. Shouldn't have let him get away from my eyes, not for a moment, not even to be hid where I thought him'd be safe.

The ropes come up over the bed. I'm tied to the island and all twisted. I scream and here's the blank dark place again.

I hear my voice . . . 'Da, find him . . .'

'Him is gone . . .'

In the blank dark, blue eyes are everywhere, staring at me.

I shout at them and ask them and cry at them, for Barney.

The back door to the cottage slams.

I'm carrying a fish eye out of the cold room on the tip of a broiderie needle. I grip the needle with all my fingertips to hold the eye steady. The eye blinks. I judder and the eye falls off the needle into a barrel filled with ice. My head is burning hot. Someone wipes a cold cloth over my forehead.

The back door slams in the distance.

'Mam,' my voice says, 'can you see Barney?'

Da's voice is loud in my ear, 'Mary, you're in a fever. Mam's buried.'

'No . . . no . . . no.'

Mam's voice is here. 'This fence is made of threads. Woven with broken lost things. Everything they want to forget.'

'Dun tell me to forget Barney!'

Something cold on my face. A hand, a cloth, a piece of ice . . .

Da's voice, 'Shush up Mary, you're shouting . . .'

I call out, 'Mam, can you see where him is?'

Da's voice says, too loud, 'Mary stop it, it's a fever you're in. Mam's gone. Settle now, settle.'

Mam's still talking. 'Forgotten things *will* make a person sick . . .'

I'm crying.

She's gone.

Da wipes the cold thing over my face, says, 'Have a drink, come on, there's meadowsweet in this water.' Hims arm holds up my back, tilts a cup to my mouth. I clench my lips tight shut, water rains all over me. Wet all over . . . Da bangs the cup down, and says, 'You dun even *want* to get better.' Him lets go of my back, I fall. Down through cloud, rain, fog . . .

Hands reach out from the sky, hold out food, bowls of soup, plates of steaming vegetables, stew, I'm getting fatter and fatter from eating and I punch my huge belly. It unravels, like stitches on a broiderie. All the stitches twist, wriggle like maggots, twirl and squirm themselves into the shape of eyes.

I'm in a tunnel of blue eyes.

The back door slams.

Da's voice calls my name from the day Barney got took, calls again. Over and over, 'Mary, where are you? Mary, where are you? Mary . . .'

Him never called Barney's name.

The blue eyes blink.

Him knew Barney weren't here . . .

Da puts hims cold hand on my cheek. 'Come back Mary, come home, come back.'

*

This morning the sun is bright. Da opens the curtain so the light gets in. I sit up slow. Him looks like someone I dun even know.

Da folds hims arms. 'You're through the worst of it. I need to go fishing so we can eat – the tall men'll be coming back in a week or so. Is tha' all right, but?'

'Aye Da, you go, I'll be fine right here.'

Him is polishing a battered compass with hims jumper sleeve. Hims eyes are so tired. Like them've seen a thousand monsters just sitting here with me. But Da knew Barney weren't here . . . the day him were took.

'Go Da. I'll be fine. Da?'

'Aye, Mary?' Him puts the compass back in hims pocket.

'I'm sorry about Barney.' I watch hims face. It dun change.

Him picks at a hole in hims jumper. 'Aye,' him says, quiet. 'So am I.' Him gets up, stretches, cracks hims neck and goes. Him dun mean it. Hims life will be easier with just us two working, with no boy he dun love, to teach to catch fish.

So the tall men are coming soon. I've been in bed for over two weeks.

Days and nights and days of fever.

Dun believe I've lost this much time – Barney missing, with me not able to look for him. I want to cut and rip and unpick all the days what've gone, thread them back together so them're made all over again, but I can't feel my hands.

Nights and days and nights of not looking. Of no one looking.

I try to stand but the floor shifts around and my legs trip me back on the bed. I try again. And again till I'm all stood up. It takes a while, but I get over to the bedroom door. I go through to the main room with the cupboard with Barney in it, only him isn't in there. I open the cupboard and look at all the boxes and baskets full of threads and linen. It's dark in there.

Blank dark.

Ice in barrels. I blink, and it's just the cupboard and all the broiderie stuff Mam had. All the hoops and frames. All the linen she never put pictures on. That's what I do. I make broideries on the linen and the tall men come and take them away. Them take a lot of things away. Them dun take my brother, though that's what everyone'll say, but I know, because I looked.

On the floor by the cupboard, there's a white shell what looks like something I should remember, so I pick it up. I grip hard on the shell. I remember the eyes of the tall man who pinched out the fingers of my hand when Barney were took. Brown eyes. Not like all them others. The gold flecks around the pupil in hims right eye. Just like Barney. Maybe Barney got took into hims face somehow and kept hims own eyes. The smell of the tall man fills my nose. Salt and dust. I snort it out.

I put the shell to my ear.

Listen close; the sea comes in, so close, like it's in the room with me, so close, like it's in my head, filling it with waves.

Barney's voice speaks inside the shell, 'Mary, where's moppet?'

Just hearing him I cry out.

This shell is precious.

The floor goes crooked. The wall hits against me. I go into our bedroom. Barney's moppet lies on hims bed, its long ears unravelling, one eye hanging off and a squinty mouth.

I bring it to the table in the main room by the window and sew on the eye, only it seems even more wonky.

Getting my broiderie scissors, I cut the whole belly open down the middle. I take some of the stuffing out and put the shell inside. Stitch it up again, like a surgeoner.

Secret now.

I put my ear to it and hear Barney's voice in the shell inside of it. 'That's better Mary,' him says. 'All better now.'

I want to speak back, only my voice is gone.

Too secret to speak of.

I lie down on Barney's bed, curled up with the moppet next to my ear, hear Barney's voice sing la la la like the baby him still is. I listen close, hims voice talks and I hear a dreaming place of Barney's. Not the blank dark place in the fever – Barney's dream is all light and the wind blows us up in the sky like butterflies.

Barney's dream is in hims voice:

In this place you an' me dun have to be big or growed up acause we're small like flutterbees. We both little up in the sky. Mam and Da is big. Them creeps out of a tunnel in the grass.

Them runs round round round looking for us, we doing hidings in the sky. Them looks up high and sees us. Them pulls fishing net out thems hair. Them doing chasings after us. Me and you, Mary, we got our own flutterbee wings, real ones.

We go up in the clouds acause we doing laughings what makes the wings flap hard.

Mam and Da is leaping – jumping up and up to catch us in nets. Them sees us with brave wings, an' shrieks in thems mouths so loud thems eyes roll around and all around.

We laughing Mary, doing laughings so loud.

Mam and Da is leaping higher and higher, eyes all big mad. We not afeart; we know them can't catch us.

Morgan

Mum has emptied her plate of parsnip stew. She looks at me with narrowed eyes across the kitchen table. 'Why aren't you eating?' she asks. 'Is it an attention thing?'

The twins watch her.

Dad eats painfully slowly.

'I'm not hungry,' I answer.

Mum says, 'Yes, it was like that when I cooked too. This is why I prefer eating. Cooking's awful. I eat it through my nose, just smelling it I get the taste, and by the time it's ready, I'm full.'

'Yes, it's like that,' I reply. But it's *not*. After I'd called them the first time, then finished cooking, I dished it all up and ate mine. I called them again, waited for them to come. Emptied their plates back into the pot, warmed it, sat and tapped on the table and dished it back onto their plates when I finally heard their footsteps coming along the hallway.

Mum stands up. She says, 'You like me again,' as she walks out of the kitchen.

Dad glances at me, nods just once, chewing.

The twins scurry out after her. 'Mum, can we—'

'—have a story tonight?'

'The one with the flying rats . . .' A door bangs shut and their small feet run up the stairs.

I clear their plates and put them in the washbowl. Dad sits at the table, still slowly chewing, his curly grey hair tied back in a black bow. He looks like a pirate, but smells of cologne.

'Dad, they're *my* books, they're the only things I . . .' I turn to face him.

He stares into his plate, his eyes like marbles.

I pull out the chair next to him and sit down.

'Dad, if she reads one of my books to the twins, will you make sure I get it back?'

'What?' He swallows almost painfully and shakes his head. 'Oh.' He looks surprised I'm here. 'Yes, it's very good. More peppery than usual. I'd prefer even more, next time. But yes, very good. Thank you.' He puts down his spoon though he hasn't finished his meal. 'Right. You're all right?' He glances at me and back at his plate. 'Good. I'll go and take over from your mother with the twins.'

'Thanks. But Dad, could I talk to you—'

'Good. Very good.' He doesn't look at me as he leaves the kitchen.

I put on a block of peat, stoke up the fire in the range.

Pick up a bucket and go out of the back door to the well in our garden.

And back into the kitchen and pour
and pour
back to the well
back to the kitchen
and pour –
fill four huge pans with water.

Put them all on the range together.

When they're boiling, I get all the small sacks of rice out of the cupboards.

I put the rice in the boiling water.

When the rice has puffed up, thickened and starchy, I go outside, put a bath towel over the drain by the back door and strain the rice.

Haul the rice back into the kitchen, wrapped in the towel.

And again. And again.

I cover the whole table in rice, a glutinous thick layer and I stand in the corner of the kitchen and watch the steam coming off it.

When the steam has gone, I get a wooden spoon and a mixing bowl and stand on a chair.

I scoop out the rice so the table shows through where I carve the words into it:

I AM HUNGRY BUT
NOT FOR FOOD

Mary

Somehow time has passed. Nights have washed through the sky like a dark blue dye, and rinsed out into days. The broiderie needles feel like them're covered in salt. So do the linens and the threads and the table. So does the washtub, my blankets, Da's fishing nets, the tatties and Barney's bedsheets. Salt is used for the fixing of dyes, but I dun want the world to be fixed like this.

While Da is out fishing, inside this home I have to somehow keep, somehow live, no one else breathes this air, no one else eats or sleeps. No one stares from the window, washes or cleans, makes messes or broiders, loses or finds things, mends broken torn dropped things, cooks or tells stories, smiles, shouts or curses, unless it is me.

Barney's toys are faded, bleached and pale from missing hims touch.

About one hundred and fifty people live on this island and if I have to ask every single one of them if them know where Barney is, I'll lose my voice and my legs'll fall off from walking to them all.

So I'll have to do it a bit at a time.

This morning I can walk better, so I leave our cottage, turn left and walk as far as the furthest cottage on this row.

Rap on the door.

Chanty answers. 'What you knocking this early for?' Her hair is curly on one side and flat on the other. She's got the Thrashing House key on a chain around her neck; it's her turn on the bell list so I've got to talk nice to her today.

'Excuse me, Chanty, for interrupting your sleeping. Thought I'd get your Mam. Have you seen or heard anything of my Barney?' I ask, my arms folded.

'Course not. You still sick? Been took. Tall men dun it. Ask anyone.'

'I'm asking you. Please.'

'Ah, get gone. Got too many things to do before the bells.' She shuts her door.

I might have to talk to her polite, but I can think whatever I want. Bloody rude cow.

I hammer on the next door.

Beattie's got her sleeves up. Her arms are red.

'Have you heard anything of Barney?' I ask.

'You've been in bed the longest time. All right now? Come in, I've got eggs and tattiecakes on the go. You look like you could do with a bit of mothering.'

'No, you're all right Beattie. You heard any talk?'

'No doll, no talk of the boys. Or nothing new or for certain. Get back indoors, it's going to rattle down any moment.' She peers up at the thick grey clouds.

It dun rattle down yet.

I bang on the next three doors.

Merry is sat just behind hims front door on a wooden stool, sharpening the paring iron and slane what him uses up the peat pits. Him dun bother answering me as him is old and miserable. Him dun ask folk questions anyway, so him won't have been told.

Jek's fixing hims fishing nets and asks me how come the women have took to putting buttons on the necks of the jumpers, and him shows me how easy them get caught in the nets. I tell him it's probably to do with main land fashions, for Annie told me a few years back that the tall men wanted jumpers full of holes called the grunge, but now them want cable or ribbed.

Old Nell's walking stick is leaned against Camery's door, so she must be visiting her. I can hear them inside, arguing. Nell's saying, '. . . them're a danger to us, could've killed her. We *have* to keep getting them took . . .' and Camery's saying, '. . . so them're a danger to folks further away? Well, why are we not bothered about them? Just because we dun know any main land folks, it dun mean them're any less . . .'

I knock and Camery answers her door. She cries out and tries to hug me, but her pale ragged shawl stinks of chicken shit, so I get clear fast.

The last door is Annie's cottage, right next to mine. If anyone'll talk, she will.

She opens it before I get near enough to knock it. Her three great black dogs charge out and one thuds me spinning. Annie kicks the front door shut behind her, sweeps her frazzled hair off her face.

'Oh Mary, come on. Glad you're better. Gave me a fright you being sick so long. Let's us two walk on the beach, the dogs need it.'

'You're all right, Annie, my legs'll not do more than what

22

them've done this morning. You heard anything about your Kieran yet, or my Barney?' I lower my voice. 'What are them saying in the Weaving Rooms?'

'Shush now. I'm not telling you Weaving Room talk. Look, whoosh! Them're off!' She strides after the dogs down the beach, her brown coat swashes in the wind. She calls over her shoulder, 'I'll pop round yours later, Martyn's fixing up our new cottage at Wreckers Shore. Him'll be gone all day.'

'You're moving Annie?'

She turns round and smiles. 'Aye, but it's lovely. More space all round it. We'll grow tatties and onions and kale, it'll be perfect. Dun be sad! I'll still visit you. You get indoors afore the rain.' She strides away. She could do with one of Beattie's breakfasts – she's just as skinny as me, and twice as tall.

I go back indoors to our cottage, sit down and let my head unravel in Mam's old rickety chair. The rain rattles down on the roof and makes the beams seem too low. I'm too small to see anything, to find anything so little as Barney, when there's this huge sky what takes over the whole island by hurling down all this rain.

So none of my neighbours know anything about Barney.

Or no one's saying anything at any rate.

*

I keep the moppet hid from Da. The moppet fills a small part of the gap what Barney's left, for it gives me hims voice. Not always; sometimes it's just the sound of the sea, but sometimes it's Barney's baby talk I hear, before the waves wash hims voice away from me. I ask it over and over, every day, 'Barney, where are you?' But hims voice always says, 'It's dark.' That makes me cry more than anything else.

Da dun speak about Barney. I keep asking him questions, I know him has got an answer somewhere hidden in hims head, only him won't tell me it. I dun like it here with just me and him. Him is out at sea all day and some of the night, thinking solid thoughts what always draw him back to land. And when him comes home, him wants me to fix the fishing nets while him eats dinner, then him washes the smell of sea and fish off himself and goes to sleep on Mam's side of thems bed.

Each morning Da says, 'It's best to carry on as usual,' before him takes up the nets and leaves. I wait for him to say something different, but him dun.

Tonight, Da comes in, pulling the smell of the sea behind him.

I say, 'Tell me what happened to Barney.'

Him dun speak.

'You just want me to broider. You never cared for Barney and you dun want me to find him. You . . .'

Him takes off hims coat and thrusts it on the hook behind the door.

'You know something, but you dun want to tell me it, because we need less to live on, now him is gone.'

Him folds hims arms and says, 'It's best to carry on as usual.' Him goes to the kitchen, picks up a bowl, ladles in the chicken stew, sits down and fills hims mouth with it so there's no room for any answers to come out.

*

I've thought really hard about how to get an answer out of Da's head and I think I can do it with just two words.

Da is going to be home for the whole day today, for him says the waves are white and high, which means the sea's too full of wind and danger for fishing.

I practise while I get dressed and while I wash my face and tie back my hair, and the more I say it I know I can keep saying it because I dun think I can stop. In the kitchen I make our porridge and say it while I stir the pot.

Da walks in and I feel hims eyes on me.

I say, 'Tell me, tell me, tell me, tell me . . .'

'Stop it, Mary.'

I keep saying it.

Him takes hims porridge into the main room, sits in Mam's rickety chair by the empty grate and ignores me.

I eat my porridge in the kitchen and between mouthfuls keep saying it.

When it comes to mid-morning, him shouts, 'You're driving me mad! Shut your bloody sodding mouth up!' Him glowers at me like him wants to stick a fish hook in my lips, so I whisper, 'Tell me tell me tell me,' all the afternoon, all the while him goes in and out of the kitchen through the back door, and all the while him tidies up out the back, and all the while him gets water from the well and washes down the kitchen floor, and all the while him cleans and oils our boots, even Mam's old ones she'll never wear again, and all the while him shuffles in and out of the main room, all the while I try to teach my hands to broider again, all the while I peel potatoes and chop leeks for soup, and all the while I sit opposite him and watch him eat it without filling the empty bowl I've put in front of me.

Him gets up from the table, hims hands thump down.

I look up at him, say it louder, 'Tell me tell me tell me.'

Him leans over me, says, 'Forget Barney and get on with your broideries. What's wrong with you? You're skittering in some kind of madness and you'll *not* be pulling me in there with you!'

25

Him gets hims coat and stamps off outside, hollers that him is off to the peat pits to do something useful, and the door bangs shut behind him.

Even without him here I keep on saying, 'Tell me tell me tell me,' because now I've been saying it all day long, I really *can't* stop. The words are in my ears and my mouth and my head.

I keep saying it and the bells ring out, but Da still isn't back. I say it at the moppet but it just stares back at me, all wonky and silent. I put the moppet on my pillow. The moppet rushes the sound of the sea into my ear, but I keep whispering till I fall asleep.

Morgan

I'm locked in my bedroom, being punished for the rice.

Mum said, 'I would never have dared waste food. Never.'

I said, 'It's not a waste. There's always loads of rice because someone keeps leaving it outside our gate and you let Dad out to bring it in, but we never talk about it. I ask, but you won't tell me.'

She said, 'I don't want to talk about rice, and you, you're giving me a headache – what do you mean, hungry? *I'm* hungry, my family only had two rooms, between six of us – no room in there for me, not for anything I might be *hungry* for . . . broken hand-me-downs—'

I said, 'I'm not a child. You've moved the age. It was eighteen. I *am* eighteen.'

She said, 'It wasn't. It was *always* twenty-one. You're too immature to leave home. You're making me feel nauseous. Is this what you want? That rice is disgusting. Congealed. I feel sick.'

How often she tells me how I make her feel.

She yanked me into the kitchen, handed me a bucket and a cloth and walked out. I cleaned the rice off the table and it took a while because it had set like glue. I wasn't sure what to do with it all, so I took the grille off the drain just outside the back door and pushed it down there. It filled up the drain and there was still some rice left. So I filled the bucket from the well and poured it in. It glugged through the rice, which sunk a bit in the drain. Not enough. So I wrapped my hand in a towel and pressed it down to make room for more, and the towel felt like a slug. I poured more water in, and more rice, more water and more rice, till all the rice had gone.

The drain might be blocked.

Mum came back into the kitchen with Dad when I was looking at how shiny the table was. Neither of them spoke. They both hauled me up the stairs, one arm each, pushed me into my bedroom and locked the door.

I didn't speak either. Because it doesn't matter. It happens all the time.

I stare out of my bedroom window. On the hill in the distance is the tall building with the bell tower. Sometimes it seems newly constructed, perfect. Other times, when the wind blusters and the sky turns charcoal, it's more like a ruin, the ghost of a house.

My bedroom is the smallest room in our house. There's nowhere to hide things, even if I managed to steal anything of use. In here, I have: my books, a single bed, one table, one chair, my old dresses of Mum's that she's taken in, my rags, a tiny pair of nail scissors and a hairbrush.

Other rooms, I'm kept away from. The room Mum builds furniture in has hammers, saws, screwdrivers . . . all the tools she needs to create furniture of beauty and function, but the same tools I'd use to break my way out.

The high fence outside, the fence that runs all the way around our house, has only one gate. The gate is kept padlocked. And

Mum has the only key. It swings from an old charm bracelet that she never takes off her wrist.

She said for years I could have my own padlock key when I was eighteen. That she'd get Dad to go to the smithy and get one cut for me. And I've counted the passing of years and months and days, imagining my eighteenth birthday, when I'd walk to the gate, my hand outstretched, my fingertips clasped on the key, unlock the padlock and walk away.

But my eighteenth birthday was three months and twelve days ago and I still haven't been outside. Because Mum changed her mind. So she told me she'd never made that promise. She said, 'I just wouldn't. Doesn't even *sound* like me. I'd worry too much. You don't want me to worry, it fills me with . . .' She held her chest, as if she couldn't breathe. Then she narrowed her eyes and said, 'You wouldn't want to make me feel like that.'

After her mind had changed, and my birthday had gone, I tried to dig my way out under the fence with a bread knife. In five weeks I'd only dug down about a foot, a tiny bit at a time. I hid the hole under a plant pot.

Then a stormy wind blew the plant pot over and the knife went blunt and my mother found the hole and cried and raged in her room and my father disappeared in there with her, and when they came out they hid the knives till they realised that meant I couldn't cook, so they gave me just the one, watched me chop vegetables with it, and then took it away.

By the time they trusted me enough to give me back the knives, or didn't want to watch me making their meals any more, I'd decided to steal the padlock key when she was sleeping. The night I made my first attempt, their bedroom door was locked.

It was locked the next night, and the next, and the next.

The night after that, I tried again, but a small square of white paper was pushed out under the door, and it said in her hand-writing: 'I'm cleverest.'

I realised then, she'd decided to think of everything.

One night last week, I saw my twin sisters steal down the stairs to the basement. The next night, I went down the stairs. At the back of the basement are three rooms: one for the coffin-building, one for the office where my father writes all the deaths in his book and the other for the preparation of bodies. In the coffin-building room there was a hole that the twins had started to dig in the back wall. It had been boarded over, roughly. My mother's handwriting was smeared in pink paint over three planks she'd hammered across it: 'Morgan. You will never think one step ahead. I know you better than you think.'

I didn't bother telling her it was the twins. When they were really small, the twins joined in my games. Before they learned that they could play more interesting games when alone with each other. The babies they'd been when I carried them, one in each arm, the toddlers they became, one attached to each of my legs, have now become inseparable. In my parent's eyes, they are obedient little girls. In mine, they are far too quiet, and they tell one another's lies a little too well.

I went into their room and asked them about the hole in the basement. They gazed up at me, holding hands, and said in rehearsed voices, 'It was a tunnel. For *you*. It was meant to be a surprise.' When I told them I didn't believe them, they looked at each other's eyes in silence, the kind of looking that they can get lost in for whole days, or until they get hungry.

Since then, I haven't thought of another escape plan to try.

Other than the one I've got now.

The one where I annoy my mother so much she'll *want* me to leave.

But I can't annoy her tonight because I'm locked in my room till my family get hungry and remember that no one else wants to cook. I don't mind being in here, because my books are locked in with me.

I am reading reading reading, locked in the stories.

I'm a wicked daughter, a drunken witch, a terrible scientist, a king with a severed hand, a resentful angel, a statue of a golden prince, the roaring wind, an uninspired alchemist, a fantastic lover who has only one leg, a stage magician with glittery nails, a shivery queen with a box of Turkish sweets, a prostitute wearing poisoned lipstick, a piano player whose hands are too big, a raggedy grey rabbit, a murderer with metal teeth, a spy with an hourglass figure . . .

I am eighteen years old and my real life is here locked inside these books.

My pretend life is here, locked in, with my family.

I breathe on my bedroom window and write in the condensation:

WITCH REQUIRED,
PREFERABLY WITH BROOMSTICK.
ENTRAPPED FEMALE IN NEED OF
ESCAPOLOGY LESSONS.
PLEASE APPLY WITHIN.

Mary

The tall men are at our door and I've little from my hands. Just a few thin white pockets I've broidered with grey rabbits. Them dun say anything about why there are so few broideries. Them hold up the pockets and one says, 'Good size for mobile pouches, but they'd prefer owl motifs.'

I take what the tall men offer, which isn't a lot.

Them give me another box of *exotic fruits* and some ice.

I dun tell them that one box of fruits isn't enough to trade on for what we really need: all the milk, eggs, meat and vegetables what we get from the farms.

I say, 'What're them dried maggots you gave me the last time – what're them meant for?'

The tall men look at me blank, so I show them the small sack.

'It's rice. From China,' one says, like that should mean something.

Them heave the two barrels of fish down the beach to the boats. I put the ice in the cold room. Them bring back the empty barrels and leave them outside.

I go back into the cottage and the front door closes behind

me. In the box, there's a great rough fruit with spikes of leaves on the top of it. It smells sweet enough but I dun know how to crack it open or how it should be cooked. And these small fist-sized fuzzy things again. Them have small round labels what say kiwi, and the picture of a fat bird. Dun think them're eggs of any kind, but. I've still got some of these from last time, and them've just wrinkled up and stank the cottage out with the smell of piss.

*

Through the window I watch the tall men loading the boats. The crates of ropes are out there on the shore, the tall men pick them up, wearing thick gloves, and put them in thems boats, careful. The ropes are left on the edge of the beach before the dawn breaks. No one talks about them. Mam wouldn't tell me – I asked, only she said, 'Dun ever, *ever* touch the ropes – them've some bite in them.' And she laughed like she dun mean it. Even when I've been up early, I've never seen who brings them, but the tall men always take them away.

There's poison in the ropes. Them look like snakes with no heads, and them move, twist and coil. Little glints of sharpness are tangled through them, like teeth, but not shut away in a mouth where them belong. My shin is still bruised from where I got bit.

Some of the women are on the beach with baskets and boxes of cloths and linens, knits and weaves. Camery and Chanty carry a rolled-up tweed fabric them must've made in the Weaving Rooms. Chanty's not long twenty-one, so she's done well to learn that quick to make it. Or stuck out her lip and whinged enough to get a whole lot of women to help her with it more like.

Jek's caught eight barrels of fish and him helps the tall men drag them down the beach. Him passes my window, carrying a great sack of goods back to hims cottage. Camery follows him with a smaller bag, she pulls out a great big can with a blue label and shows it to him. Dun know how she's going to get that can open. Never am sure about cans. I hardly ever open the ones I've got in the cupboard, unless we're low on food, and I've sharpened a knife. The knife goes blunt getting just one open. Sometimes I'm not sure that what I find when I've opened the can is worth eating, for them've got the strangest foods on the main land. Chanty stomps past the window, carrying a small box of fruits.

Some of the tall men head to the path up the cliffs, off to the folk what dun come down to this beach. So everyone else is still getting thems trade done. I think of the tall man with Barney's eyes. The salt and dust smell of him sticks in my nose. There's something locked in the smell.

I get the moppet from the bedroom and go back to the window. Holding it up to my face, I stroke my cheek with its scratchy paws. I say, 'What should I do?'

Barney's voice speaks, 'Tall man took me.'

I grip the moppet, hard. 'Which one?'

'Brown eyes.'

'But I looked in the boats the day you were took and you weren't there. Barney?'

The sound of the sea in the shell washes hims voice away.

I hug the moppet to me.

It can answer questions. So it's real.

I pull at the front door, only it wants to stay shut. It's all jammed up so I try the back door. I tug and kick at it but it dun want to let me out. I hear doors slamming and put my hands over my ears, only I can still hear them. I climb on the

34

table, open the window and jump out. I push the window shut.

Annie's talking outside her cottage next door with one of the tall men. She looks like she's been crying, only she's stood up straight and sure enough with her jaw out. Her three black dogs stand behind her, them dun leap at him. The tall man gives her a hessian sack. She must've done a lot of knits this month. She's still talking, like she does.

The tall men are shifting boxes and crates onto the boats. A stack of handmade paper, a small gate from the smithy, a basket of woollens. Everyone says the tall men all look the same as one another, but I can see thems faces are all different. I get closer, but not too close. I want to see thems eyes but my legs feel like them're wading through thick water.

I blink hard, for the sky seems full of creases. I'm still too sick from the fever to be here on the beach. Lines of clouds on the horizon spread and split like strands of thread. The sun shines bright.

A sound of wings flapping. I look round and a barn owl is coming right at me. Usually barn owls fly silent, but this one is blustering, buffeting like it's learning how to fly. Only as it gets closer I see its face. A woman's face. Round like the moon, but angered and bruised, thick with frowns. It flickers and changes, like light jumping on the waves from the sun. An owl's face. A woman's. Owl's.

I blink hard. My eyes aren't right. I'm skittering back into the fever place again.

An owl's face. Her head turns and her vicious eyes stare at me, like I'm an insect she's hungry for. She hovers above me. I fall back on wet ripples of sand, my head too hot, my heart thud thud thud.

She swoops down so her face is close to mine.

Her white and golden feathers, hair, feathers, is all in tangles.

She screeches.

Her eyes burn. The sun shines white, too bright.

I shout, 'Are you real?'

A couple of the tall men glance over at me but I dun think them can see her.

Her shriek is a tearing sound. Her woman's face is cloudy and blue-grey, covered in bruises, or maybe that's the colour of her skin. Can't see her face for bruises, and it keeps flicking from owl to woman.

She lands on the sand next to me. Her breath stinks of blood. There's a rattle in her throat what sounds like tiny bones breaking. She flicks her talonclaws in and out. She looks at me with longing . . . or hunger? She breathes so hard, the light feathers on her breast quiver. She's searching for someone . . . not me. My hand reaches out to touch her feathers and I pull it back . . . she's just an owl. Her voice screeches like it could tear the fur off mice. She leaps up into the sky and flies off, a flurry of pale wings, out to sea.

I'm breathing too hard. Two tall men carrying a heavy hessian sack walk up the beach towards me, heading to the path up the cliff. I scramble up, my dress soaked, my legs shaking with cold.

One of them is the one with Barney's eyes. Him trails them eyes down my body. I wrap my arms around myself, step backwards into a deep puddle and the sea soaks into my boots.

I stutter out, 'You—' I try to say something else but my mouth won't speak.

Him glances down my body again and says, 'This one looks just like her dead mother.' Him stares right at my eyes. I look away.

So him knew Mam.

'Leave this,' says the other. Them walk away up the beach. I wonder if . . . I wonder if Barney . . . I watch them struggle with the sack to the foot of the path what leads up the cliff. I wonder if Barney will ever be a grown-up, and look *just like him*.

But Mam can't have bedded him. She couldn't want to bed a tall man. Not Mam. Not ever Mam. She were a broiderer. The best broiderer. Everyone says so. If she'd bedded him, them'd never speak of her at all. Mam and Da fought sometimes, like any other pair, but them loved just as loud. Da would've smelled that tall man on her, for him stinks. Da would've smelled him and turned from her. But though she's dead, Da loves her still.

Seawater soaks up my dress. My boots are full of freezing water. I stamp out of the puddle and onto the sand.

The other tall men are emptying barrels of fish into the boats – them never even saw the owl woman. Mam did a broiderie of an owl with a woman's face, screaming. It were fearful. That broiderie is stuck in my head, twisting around. No real owl woman. Just a barn owl.

But that tall man's eyes are really Barney's. I watch him and the other tall man carry the sack up the path to the cliffs.

*

I dun look up at the Thrashing House while I pass it, dun breathe too loud neither. No one's been put in there since I've been alive, but we all know to be careful. I keep following the two tall men south, along the cliff path.

Them turn off the path by a crumbling drystone wall. I follow them down the slope and up the next hill to the stone track, past a cluster of cottages and barns. Them are going to the track what leads to the smithy, the cobbler's and the glass-maker's cottage and barn, where the furnace chimney blusters smoke into the sky.

As I walk, my damp dress sticks to my legs. I practise saying, 'You . . . took Barney. Did you bed . . .' But my throat's closed up tight. I try, 'Tell me tell me tell me,' for I know I'm good at that, but I can't speak louder than a whisper.

The tall men rap on the door to the cobbler's and Moira opens it, her dark hair under a brown woollen shawl. She sees me and calls out, 'Mary, you're drenched, get yourself home – you'll catch your death!'

The tall men put the sack down by her door. It has the word *lime* printed on it, and I've seen them sacks at Dougan's furnace, so I think it's for glass-making. Them'll be going to Dougan's barn after Moira's done her trade. One of the tall men glances over hims shoulder at me, shakes hims head and turns back to Moira. She lets them in and shuts the door.

The wind blows against me and I'm freezing from the waist down, like there's half a ghost living inside me. The chimney at Dougan's barn is smoking. I walk over and bang on the barn door. Dougan screeches the door open, a rush of warm air floods over me.

'Can I stand by your furnace? I'm soaked.'

'C'mon then.' Dougan wipes the sweat off hims bald head, steps back and I go inside. It's all dark apart from the fire from the huge furnace. Him scratches hims grey beard and draws a chair up next to the fire. 'Set yourself down there, I've got to get on, but.' Him heaves an open hessian sack, which has the word *silica* printed on it, across the rough floor.

There's a row of small glass squares on the table next to me. I say, 'You're making the windowpanes thinner, but the ripples are still there.'

Dougan says, 'Takes years to learn to get the glass this thin and them're still not even. Still like water, whether them're thick or thin. My Dad never could get them all smooth, though him tried for near on forty years. Your panes holding firm Mary? Not had your Da round, not since the last storm.'

'Them're good strong windows at ours, the glass is thick.' I look at hims big belly. 'Dougan, Da is my Da, right enough, you never heard any of the men talk of it being . . . someone else?'

'Now what'd make you say that? You know your Da's your kin. You got it in your head you dun look like him or what?' Him drags another opened sack of silica across the floor. 'I should make you a proper mirror, girl.'

'You're all right, I've got a little mirror of Mam's. But listen, there's more women than men what live here – how do we know each Da is our own, for all of us? What if there's not enough Da's to go round?'

'What've you gotten into your head? You got soaked down that there beach and come wandering – you getting all feverish? Just more women, for women have more daughters than sons is all. Heard you were sick. Should be in bed.'

'But is him mine?' I ask.

'Course hims your Da, daft one.' Him drags another open sack across the floor.

'What about Barney?' I ask. 'Is him Barney's Da too?'

Him lets the sack drop, the fine sand spills onto the dirt floor. Him stretches hims back, comes over and frowns at me. 'Now what's got you to thinking like this? What's rattled you? It's sad Barney were took, but what—'

'Nothing.' I pick up one of the windowpanes from the table and look at him through the ripples.

Him takes the glass from my hand, puts it back on the table.

'Something's done the rattling, not every day a girl comes round asking if her Da's really hers . . .' him says, quiet.

'Think I'm seeing things. Now I'm sat by your fire, it feels like it were all in my head.'

'Seeing things is it? My, you're still sickly, but. Here.' Him goes to the corner, snatches at a pile of cloths, comes back and throws a thick woollen checked blanket at me. 'Wrap up in this and get yourself home. Your Da should get Valmarie to check on you. Get you some of her herbs.'

'No, I'll be right.' I wrap the blanket around myself. 'You getting a sack of lime from the tall men? Them're next door.'

'How d'you know it's lime?'

'It's got *lime* wrote on the sack. Like them ones over there.' I point at two other sacks of lime leaning up against the wall, both opened. 'And the ones you've been dragging've got *silica* wrote on them. Looks like a kind of sand to me. If you look at the letters, you'll get to know them're different without opening the sack before you need to use it. I could show you—'

'Aye. Well. Best see about this lime then.'

'You remember I broke that windowpane at home, the moment you'd just fixed it in.'

Him smiles. 'Little 'uns throw things all the time. You just had a better aim than most. Now, your Grandmam it were, set you off hurling things that day, if I remember right.'

'You must've had to trek all the way back up here to get another pane, then bring it back to fix it again.'

Four raps on the door. Four raps again.

Him says, 'Well.' Him goes to the door. 'Dun break anything while them're here. Got to keep an eye on you.' Him looks round at me, a spark in hims eye, and opens the door.

With the light behind them, the two tall men are like shadows. All three wander off to talk. Dougan looks simple in hims waistcoat and baggy trousers next to the tall men's clever long coats and hats. I fold up the checked blanket, put it on the chair and stand in the doorway. The tall men have thems backs to me. Dougan leans on the drystone wall. I go outside and pretend to trip over the sack of lime them've left lying in the grass. I curse, loud, and rub at my foot.

The tall men glance round. Dougan winks at me and him goes off around the side of the barn to hims cottage.

The tall men stand waiting. Them're talking to each other, quiet. I'm staring at the one with Barney's eyes and thinking Mam must've shut her own eyes so tight and pretended him were Da, but I dun want to think about that, so I think about him taking Barney, and how him could've done it without me seeing, when I searched all the boats. I dun want to say anything till them've finished the trade, for I dun want Dougan to hear.

All the same, I step towards them.

But Dougan comes round the side of the barn, frowns at me and strides over to them. Him is carrying a white bulging pillow-case. Him says to the tall men, 'My Nell says you can take these as a trade for the lime. One sack this month and two next. Them're well hooked, you'll see that.'

The tall man with Barney's eyes pulls out a crochet bobble hat. Him nods, puts it back in and says, 'Till next month.'

'Fine,' says Dougan. 'You be fair over it – bring me something you think'll be good for my Nell an' all, since that there crochet took her some time, and her eyes is going.'

Nell leans round the side of the barn and calls out, 'Mary, come here.'

'You're all right, Nell, I'll be off.'

She hobbles over to me, leaning on her walking stick. 'I said, come.' She pulls her black shawl away from her chest. She's wearing the Thrashing House key.

'All right.' My head bowed, I follow her round the side of the barn towards her cottage.

At the cottage door, she turns, 'What's this about you thinking your Da's not really your Da?' She taps her walking stick on a stone. 'Doug tells me you're still sick, and talking nonsense. Now, I knew your Mam, and I were there not long after you were born. Your Mam were in a state, for she were so young, and dun know what giving birth were to be like, but your Da were acting like any new father. You're your Da's daughter, through and through.'

'But what of Barney?'

'Never saw much of your Mam round then. But it's like to be that she were scared right through with another baby coming. It's no good you thinking like this. Barney's took. You and your Da got to stick together Mary, you only get one lot of kin in this life, and it's looking like for you, your Da is it. Dun be casting him off, not when him is the only belonging person you got left.'

'Da dun miss Barney, not one bit.'

'Well, for sure hims like to be acting like that. Him might be cutting off hims feelings so him is not full of missing him. Men're just like that.'

'No, it's not like that. Him really *dun* miss him. Not at all.'

'Well, it may be that's the way of it, and you know your Da the best, I'm sure. And if hims not missing him and you are, that's like to be hurting you now. But not one boy has come back. Your Da knows that. Dun be seeing blame where there's none.' She frowns.

'Have you ever seen this thing, a white owl with a woman's face? Mam did a broiderie of her, and I saw her, like a real thing, on the beach.'

She stares at me, her mouth wide open. 'Them've done it,'

she says. 'Mary get yourself home. Get your Da indoors.' She pushes me away.

'So she's real?' I gasp out.

'Doug!' Nell shrieks, her eyes wide. Then she says to herself, so quiet I almost dun hear it, 'I've got to get the key to Valmarie. She's on the bells tonight.'

'I'll take it to her.' I reach out my hand.

She starts. 'No you will not.'

Dougan comes round the side of the barn. 'You all right Nell? Mary, not troubling her are you?'

'Get indoors Doug. You done with the tall men?'

Him walks up to us. 'Aye, them're heading off. But I've got the furnace still blazing – I'm not done in there.'

Nell grips Dougan's arm. 'Leave it to die down. Get in.' She shoves him through the cottage door. 'Mary, get your Da indoors. Go. Now!'

I say, 'But Da's out on the sea—' but she shuts the door. Her and Dougan bicker behind it. Him is yelling at her that him dun want to be shut indoors and she's yelling back that him should be grateful to her, but she's not going to tell him why. The next thing I hear is a wallop what sounds like one of them has clanged the other over the head with a pan. There's a crash and it all goes quiet.

I'm about to look in through the window but Nell opens the front door, comes outside and locks it behind her. 'You still here? You never heard none of that Mary Jared, get off home. Get your Da indoors.'

'Why?' I call out, but she scuttles away around the side of the cottage. I follow her but she's gone over a stile, and hurtles off, scattering brown sheep through the field in the direction of Valmarie's house. So she can walk fast enough even with her walking stick, when she's got a purpose.

I go back to Nell's cottage and listen at the door. Dougan must be still out cold. Nell's left the cottage key in the front door so I draw it out. It sings in my hand as I shove it in my dress pocket. It's mine now.

*

The two tall men walk towards the cliff path.

I call, 'Wait – you've got to tell me—'

The tall men turn round.

I choke out, 'You took—'

One of them says, 'Nothing that wasn't traded.' Them turn and walk away.

'Wait—' I walk after them. 'What's—'

The one with Barney's eyes stops again, turns to face me.

The other one says, 'Leave her, Langward. Got to get on.' Him walks away.

I say quiet, 'That your name then, Langward? And is that the name my brother should've known as hims real father?'

Hims lips draw up in a smile what dun reach hims eyes. 'So, has your brother been found?'

'You're saying you dun know where him is, then?'

'Not yet.'

'But you *do* know – you took him!'

Him leans forwards. 'I don't have him. I want to find him too.'

'So you *are* Barney's Da!' I cry out. 'But how can you be – Mam wouldn't have . . . not with you, not with any one of you! But you took him.'

'You searched our boats.'

'You could've hid him, then put him in your boat when I were crying – my eyes blurred with tears, couldn't see. Give me him back!'

44

'I said, I don't have him.' Langward glances at the other tall man walking away and says, 'Don't work yourself up to another fever. I heard your father was very . . . attentive. But there's only so much time he can spend nursing. I assume you need to trade *something* to survive.'

'Folk'll be so mad if them find out you've been with a woman from here!'

Him glances after the other tall man, still further away, then back at me. 'Then don't tell anyone,' him says. 'You seem to be good at keeping secrets.' Hims eyes look cruel for a moment, not like Barney's at all. 'Your mother wouldn't have bothered about searching for him. She'd just have let him . . . drift off.'

I dun know what him means. Telling me how to think. Him is messing with my thoughts of Mam.

'You're so like her. So much anger . . .' Him reaches out a pale hand towards my face.

I step away. 'Shut your stinking mouth up!'

Him glares at me. 'So, where can I find my son?'

'You can't have him for a son.'

'My blood . . .' him says, flexing back hims wrist so the blue veins rise.

'It's *me* what loves him. *I'll* find him. Blood's just blood. Nothing more.' I stamp away towards the cliff path, turn to the south, and dun look back.

Morgan

I'm lost somewhere between this wooden spoon and the stew I'm stirring in the pot. I add pepper. And more. And more. My abdomen cramps. I'm the one on the rag, but Mum's the one who's sulking. I can feel her heavy sulk all the way through the ceiling, from the room above this kitchen.

My parents aren't even trying to fit in. The height of our house – two floors above ground – makes it too exposed. It creaks in the winds. Our house was built by my parents, with wood salvaged from a shipwreck. People must have died in that wreck. My parents didn't care; they just wanted the planks. The people who live on this island must have wanted the planks too, but they will all get good solid coffins – and Dad will provide them with decent burials, given time.

Dad dragged the wood here, plank by plank, up the hill from the shore. As always, he was wearing his suit. Mum waited for him with me, in the shack they'd made next to the foundations of this house. It was so cold in there, I didn't even find any spiders. No one who lived on this island came to visit us in the shack. I thought I heard whispers, but each time I said so, my mother croaked. That scared all the whispers away.

Croaked like a toad, hunched her back, but kept her eyes fixed on me.

I slice up an onion and four cloves of garlic and throw them in the bubbling pot. I'm cooking in the wrong order today. I chop up the chicken meat. The smell of the flesh makes my stomach clench. Does marrow need to be salted? I can't remember. I look out of the kitchen window. The tall fence blocks out any kind of view. All Mum said when she built the fence was, 'I've always wanted a picket fence around my home,' and got on with it. I remember her hammering the slats deep into the ground.

That's a bitter taste.

More flavour . . . I slash parsley with a gleaming knife.

I've heard people on the other side, laughing at it as they pass by. Why wouldn't they? It's ridiculous, but Mum thinks it's the best thing that's ever been made. This was my mother's dream, the home she'd always wanted. A picket fence was the final touch, and it was the final touch that sealed us in.

Mum built her picket fence thirteen feet high. And painted it bright pink.

I draw bread from the oven and it fills the room with the smell of warm yeast. It collects Mum's sulk from the air in this kitchen, pummels it down and flattens it on the floor. The tiles feel damp under my bare feet.

I open the kitchen door, call out 'Lunch!' The cramps in my abdomen almost buckle me over.

No reply, and Mum's sulk is still thickening in the air out here in the hallway.

I go back into the kitchen and set the table for five. Lunch isn't really anywhere near ready yet, but no one ever comes when I call, and they'll be longer than usual, when they've got to pass through the remainder of Mum's sulk.

I go out of the back door into the garden, draw a bucket of water from the well and carry it to the door. I lift the grille off the drain, pour the water in and it flows away. The rice has gone down. It's not blocked. Another day, I'll block it up. Stuff something thicker than rice down there. A bedspread, maybe. A tablecloth. Some of her clothes. Or his. Not the twins'.

Another day soon, I'll annoy Mum much harder. Get her to *want* to unlock the padlock and send me away. But not today. Not with these cramps settling in. I put the bucket on the floor in the kitchen, stand at the back door and look at the pink paint peeling on the fence.

Mum stood in this garden and stared at her fence when she'd finally finished building it.

Dad said to her, 'Come inside.' He waited. He touched her arm.

She didn't move.

He put his hand on her shoulder.

She didn't speak.

The stars came out.

'You're safe,' he said. 'Please stop running now.'

The moon shone down.

'I'll go to bed,' he muttered, and disappeared into the house.

I stood here in this kitchen doorway and watched her. She stood there and the sun rose. Dad came back, watched her for a while, made himself some tea and went away. The sun set again and still Mum stood there, her back to me and her face to the fence. The wind blew, her brown hair whipped into tangles, but still she said nothing. Not a word, till the moon was at the highest point in the sky, and she finally spoke: 'That's just perfect. Just right. I think I'll have a nice cup of tea. Can someone make me one please? I have blisters on my hands.' And she pushed past me into this kitchen, blisters outstretched and sat at the table to wait for the tea to be put down in front of her.

Of course, I made it. Just the way she likes it. Nettle tea. Three spoons of honey, not too strong but just strong enough.

I wrapped up her hands with an oatmeal poultice and white linen bandages.

She said she didn't like the colour of the bandages and tore them off.

I don't like the colour of my rags either. Blood on bright red cloth is difficult to see to soak off. Mum gave me these rags, after she'd finished building the fence. When it was just the two of us in the kitchen in the middle of the night, drinking tea in silence.

She glanced at me. Nodded. Stood up, went off to another room and came back in with the red squares of fabric flapping in her blistered hands. Her cheeks were almost as pink as the fence. She said, 'Stuff these in your knickers and keep yourself clean.' I hadn't started my periods yet, I was too young. But I knew about them. My parents brought a lot of books with them. I read about mythology, psychology and biology, as well as picture and storybooks. I've learned what I need to. I know that snails don't have periods, nor do young girls or old women, toads or moths or spiders.

I asked her, 'Does it hurt, bleeding?'

She told me about her first period and how she'd come home from school because she'd been in so much pain she thought she was dying. Her mother had said that all wounds bleed, and she must shake off the pain and get back to school. Mum said she thought she was wounded then, that she had to bandage it and not let the pain show. She said, 'I felt so much, so much . . .' She searched for the word, her eyes wandering over her blistered hands. I said, 'Shame?' and she flashed her sharp eyes at me and said, 'No. Not that, never. I was *never* ashamed.'

49

I didn't believe her. After a long glaring silence, her eyes were shining and she said, 'Even now, my periods aren't any easier.' I swallowed hard. She glanced at me and when she spoke her voice was quieter. She said, 'You're pale. Yours won't be as sore as mine. Mine were always the most painful, more than anyone else.' I felt hopeful, because I thought she'd noticed I felt scared. I wanted to have my period then and there all over the kitchen chair, just so she might keep noticing how I felt. I thought if I was an adult, a woman like her, with pain to bind us, she'd know how I felt. But I checked, and there was no blood.

Soon I'll be out there, on the other side of that fence and across a long stretch of water, in a place I can call home. I'll hang my red rags off some other washing line, with no pink fence to hide them from view.

Mary

I've come down to the south cliffs, and I'm looking out to sea at the three ancient cliff stacks called the Pegs. Them've stood there, just off the edge of this island, forever. Da always says, 'Down the south and past the Pegs' is the way him rows to fish, but I can't see hims boat on the horizon. I want him to come back to shore now. If him could see on my face that I know about Mam and Langward. If him could catch at the tangles all stuck in my head, and know the right things to say. If him could . . . only him is never sure what to say when I'm brooding. Him gets to working rather than asking: him'll wash down or mend, sandpaper or hammer, fix or get rid, anything to busy hims hands. We're a silent pair, when I'm all in knots.

The Pegs are five hundred feet high or more. Home for fulmars, not long back from the south, bougirs what're gone till the spring and all kinds of small chittering birds. The Pegs look like giant pegs on a washing line, only the line them're pegged on is deep down under the sea.

I look straight down. The sea sucks and crashes, laps, then tongues, then slaps the bottom of the cliff. It's a long way down, and so fast to get there. I step back. I wrap my arms around myself. This is where the gales blow the hardest. Sheep and cows have been blown off these cliffs, when the winds rage high. This cliff is where –

Dun want to think about that.

I remember seeing Mam and Da go off for a walk on Da's birthday one year, them walked away side by side, touching at each other's fingers. For hims birthday she'd told him to put down the nets. She said there were to be a day of no work, and there were a wind blowing her hair when she said it. Him liked her to wear it down. Them were gone for near on the whole day and I stayed indoors, playing with Grandmam.

Out there the sea's too deep, too rough by the Pegs where the currents are thick. The waves swash round, pitch and surge. Folks say that a huge drowned dress is pegged to the bottom of the seabed. When Grandmam were alive, she told me the dress belonged to Sishee, a giant who were pegging it out to dry, years and years before the sea were even there. Sishee were singing a song made of pictures and no words.

My head is murky, thick with Mam and Da and Langward and Barney. Langward saying Mam wouldn't search for Barney means I've got to think even harder about what she were like, so my memories of her dun get stained. Or dun get *more* stained than them feel right now. I can remember Mam brushing my clean wet hair, holding it at the roots and brushing the ends so she dun tug and hurt me. She loved me. She loved Barney. She *would* have searched and searched for him. She'd have known the right questions to ask and the right folks to answer, and she'd have been better at it than me. I saw how swift she could unpick her threads when she'd used too many colours in a broiderie. She'd find the stitch just before she went wrong and start again from there. She would have found Barney by now.

Everyone here thinking the tall men took the boys means no one does any looking. But now there's me *and* that stinking tall man looking. Dun want to think about him, but I have to. Because what if him finds Barney first? I've no boat to follow him and I dun know the way.

The clouds stretch out like threads and I dun know if it's just my eyes getting strange from this cold feeling unravelling in my belly, or if it's real. I reach in my dress pocket, pull out the moppet and whisper to it, 'Barney, you said the tall man took you. But him can't have done. For him wants to find you. But dun let him. Let me.'

The moppet curls up in my hand.

I ask it again, the question I've already asked it over and over, 'Where are you?' It dun speak, not even to tell me again that *it's dark*. I put it back in my pocket.

The sea looks like it's panting with all its rising and falling. The owl woman screeches but I can't see her – that sound must be real, if nothing else is. This white sky, so bright my eyes water. The Pegs flicker like them are shedding pale feathers, like them're breaking apart, going to come off the line under the sea, and let Sishee's drowned dress float up. The air feels so thin, the whole sky is going to tear open.

*

Nell's crouched next to me, leaning on her walking stick and shaking my shoulder with a wrinkled hand.

My head thuds. 'It were here Mam died, weren't it? Right here on this cliff.'

'Home. Now.'

I scramble up, look out to sea, say, 'That's Da – down there!'

Not far from the Pegs is a man in a small fishing boat. It's Da for sure, in the brown tattered coat I've stitched up for him so many times.

'Asylumfodder . . .' says Nell, getting up, slow. 'That's what them do to mad folks on the main land. Look at him.'

Da sees me and Nell up here on the clifftop. Him is waving from the boat. Only I look harder, and him is not waving – him is throwing hims arms around like something's attacking him. Something's flying around in the air, tormenting him. Only there's nothing there. Him looks like someone I dun know. Him is angered, afraid, laughing, crying.

Nell nods down the cliff, says, 'Him'll be towed back in.'

Jek is there, in a small fishing boat. Him gets closer to Da's boat and reaches out a chain to hook the boats together.

I grab Nell's arm.

'Da . . . is him – what's happened to him, Nell?'

'Come on Mary. You look a wreck.'

'What you said at yours, about the owl woman – you said *them've done it*. What them, what've them done?'

She pats my hand and I let go of her arm. 'Weaving Room talk. Can't say. Come on.' She hobbles away, her grey wool coat blusters in the wind.

I call after her, 'Why are you here?' I have to walk fast to keep up with her and her mouth is set on staying closed. So I ask her over and over the same questions, faster and faster, but she's still not speaking, so I change what I'm asking and ask her if she gave Valmarie the Thrashing House key.

Nell says, 'She were coming for me as I were heading for her. Met her halfway, and she fair snatched it off me and took off. That's not how it's meant to happen, but I suppose she thinks she can do what she likes right now.' She huffs out breath. 'Never said that, all right?'

I ask Nell over and over if any of the women have said anything in the Weaving Rooms about Barney. She keeps her lips tight shut.

54

'Nell, what *are* you doing here?'

'Saw you heading this way. Weren't having you coming here alone when I know it were on these cliffs your Mam died. Bloody diamondback addersnakes. Look at you, shivering all over. Come on.'

Jek is towing Da's boat north towards Traders Bay, to the beach right by our cottage. I say, 'If Da is mad – is him gone, but still here?'

'Keep walking.'

*

We're climbing down the steep path from the cliffs to Traders Bay. Nell's staggering to stay upright and she steps sideways, leaning on her stick so she dun fall. It's near on dusk, but the tall men are in thems boats, waiting, the oars still, just out to sea.

Them should've been long gone by now.

A skinny woman on the beach waves both her arms at me. It's Annie, with her three black dogs bounding round her. Her husband Martyn knows Da so well. Them could help me nurse Da, them might know best what to do. Or him could stay with them for a time when them move to Wreckers Shore, away from hims boat and all the things hims hands get busy with at home. There, him could be cosseted, wrapped in Annie's soft knitted blankets – with thems son Kieran gone two months, them have a mattress gone cold.

Annie rushes to the bottom of the path, her dogs barking. 'Mary, where've you been?' she asks, shrill. Her hair is more of a mess than usual, and her eyes are like poached eggs, them're that puffed up.

Nell sits herself down on a rock at the bottom of the path, breathing hard.

I say, 'Look Annie, Jek's bringing Da back in. Him is—' I run to the edge of the sea, Annie right beside me. Her dogs bark at the boats coming in.

Jek splashes out of hims own boat and ties it to the cleat post. Him heaves and tugs Da's boat up onto the sand. Da's eyes roll in hims face.

'Not him an' all!' Annie cries, and I see in her eyes she's been here on the beach, waiting and watching for a reason. 'Martyn, Clorey and Bill are in this state an' all – Martyn dun want to leave our home this morning. Only I made him. Said him were being lazy, that I needed him to do hims job so I could get to mine. Him knew something bad were to happen to him today, thought him were safer indoors. Only I never listened, I forced him to go out. If him'd only said—'

'There's others, all like this?' I gasp, watching Jek yank at Da's arm to try to get him out of hims boat.

Annie says, 'Martyn were found on the north shore. With the poisons in the sea there, him could've killed himself. Clorey and Bill were found hugging each other in the graveyard, talking crazed – tattling what made no sense. I been searching for your Da's boat since them took Martyn. Everyone knows.' She stares at Da.

'Everyone knows *what*?'

Da can't see Jek trying to get him out the boat. Da's eyes roll and hims head jerks like a puppet. Like someone else has hims strings, and them're going to make him stand up.

'Him'll be put in there too.' Annie grasps at my shoulder. 'You think him is back, but him is not. Not in here.' She taps the side of her head.

'Everyone knows *what*, Annie?'

She's shaking her head, watching Da, her hand over her lips.

Jek struggles with Da, pulls him out of the boat. Jek staggers and Da slumps on the sand. Da has a long line of drool coming from hims mouth and soaking in on hims coat. I look up the beach at our cottage. A light flashes from the end of the row of cottages, pointed out to sea. One, two, three flashes. 'Annie, look—' I point over.

'What is it?'

'A light, but it's gone.' I ask her, 'Where are the other three men, where's your Martyn?'

'Oh Mary,' she whispers. 'Them've all been took to the Thrashing House.'

It were Grandmam what first told me about the Thrashing House. She said:

The Thrashing House has its own decisions and thoughts, its own judgment and consideration of what's right and wrong. It'll beat the truth from a liar. It'll beat the vanity from a mirror and the sting from a grain of salt. We dun know what happens to those what gets put in, only that them never come out.

'Them're coming for your Da,' Annie says, nodding up at the cliffs.

A stream of people run along the cliff path carrying burning torches. Nell stands at the bottom of the cliff. She's calling up to them, pointing her walking stick at Da. About seventy folks, more women than men, charge down the path. Them're shouting and angered.

I want to get indoors and hide, but Da is dribbling like a baby. I hear Grandmam's voice in my head . . . *them never come out.* If Da could get to the main land . . . What did Nell say, about asylumfodder . . . it must be . . . what the owl woman's done to him. Anything could happen on the main land in grand houses. Them might have a clever surgeoner what could open hims head and mend it. Them might make him learn to write, so him could write me a letter. Send it to me with the tall men.

Mam told me that folks we'd barely ever seen would come from all over the island if someone were to be put in the Thrashing House, but she never said how fearful them would sound. Only one way to get him away, with an angered crowd clashing and shoving, the air thick with thems yells and hollers all heading straight for Da.

But out to sea, the tall men's boats are further away. So the light flashing near the cottages were a signal, to tell them to go.

I yell out to sea, 'Come back! Take Da to the main land with you!'

The tall men keep rowing away.

I shriek, 'Him has some chance with you, none at all here!'

The crowd are coming down the path.

'Come on Annie, help me!'

She backs away from me, shaking her head.

Jek stares at the crowd coming for the beach. Stumbles away from Da.

I grip Da's shoulders. 'Why are them after you? Tell me what you've done!' I shriek over and over in hims ear. 'If it's about Barney, tell me where him is! Please, Da, just one word – anything – get up!' Him struggles and I drop him.

'Jek, help me!'

Jek legs it away up the beach.

'Annie!'

Tears run down her face. 'No Mary, them've took mine. I'm not putting my neck out for this one. I'm not any part of saving someone else when mine love's gone.' She backs away, sits down on the sand, covers her mouth with her fingers and watches me struggle with Da. Him won't get up.

The crowd are on the beach.

Folks all around me shove and push me away from Da, there's flashes of scarves and coats, sharp nudges from elbows.

Some of the women have got hold of Da, him is pulled up and I yell, 'Da, tell me what you've done!' but him can't hear me. Them drag him along, hims arms flop over thems shoulders, I elbow my way nearer, but I'm shoved further away. Them're pulling him to the path up the cliffs.

Nell is next to me, she grips my arm and says in my ear, 'Sorry Mary, it's the same for all. Him has to be punished if him is guilty.'

I pull away. 'Guilty of what?'

She pulls me back, says, 'Ask that pair. Them're calling the tides of us all tonight.' She's looking at Valmarie and Kelmar, who stand watching as Da is pushed and shoved and carried up the path by a wave of folks.

Them're taking him to the Thrashing House.

I'm shoved closer to Valmarie. I elbow through about five folks and yell at her, 'Dun put Da in there – him has to speak!'

Valmarie says, 'The others have spoken enough. Your father, her Martyn,' she nods over at Annie, who lies face down on the sand, her shoulders shaking, 'my Bill and Kelmar's Clorey. They took and traded the boys, not theirs to take. A price has to be paid, a judgment made.'

I shout, 'How do you *know*?'

Valmarie talks loud – she's telling all of us, 'Because we called her up. Me and Kelmar called for justice. *For times when you don't know who is to blame.*' She sounds like she's singing a song. Her eyes shine like black glass. 'We called her up, set her on whoever took our sons. Thought she'd go for the tall men; we even timed it for when they were coming. Only she knew. She went for the fathers. Sent each one mad. And they'll be punished. We're the mothers. We have the right.'

Kelmar's voice hollers, 'We made Bill, Clorey and Martyn talk before we put them in. Admitted it, all three – gabbled out the truth. The fathers of our boys took them from us. Traded them with the tall men. Our sons are lost to the main land.'

'No!' I yell. 'Them dun take *Barney*—' I'm shoved further away from Valmarie and Kelmar, between pushing shoulders and nudging elbows and all around me voices are shouting and fretting.

A voice close to my ear says, 'You're so like your mother.' I spin round and it's the tall man, Langward, here in the crowd. Someone pushes me, I shriek out, 'Why're you here? You've got a light to flash, call back the boats! Get gone!' but I can't see him.

I see Nell and call out, 'There's a tall man still here!' but I'm shoved away from her and she's lost in the crowd again.

Valmarie and Kelmar see Langward in the middle of the crowd, hims arms outstretched like him is set to walk into the sea, not drowned in a crowd of angered people. Them charge in, shrieking like the owl woman. Them drag him towards the path what leads up the cliffs to the Thrashing House.

At the bottom of the path them turn and face us all. Valmarie's black hair beats against her pale face in the wind. Langward looks blank, like him has got a mask of hims own face on. The two women hold him firm, though him dun move.

Valmarie's mouth is a sneer. She calls out, 'This one,' she yanks Langward's arm, 'doesn't belong here. And look out there.'

She points a pale hand out to sea, 'The others were waiting for him, and yet he doesn't go!'

Voices in the crowd murmur, 'Thrash . . . thrash . . . thrash . . .'

Valmarie stands tall, her voice a bell, 'Staying behind, thickened with guilt. His guilt forces him to stay. Was it his idea, did he talk the fathers into trading our sons?' Shouts and cries shriek all around me in the crowd.

I'm pushed closer. Kelmar shouts, 'Him is called!'

'Thrash . . . thrash . . . thrash . . .'

I shout, 'So take *him*, but let Da go! Make Da talk!'

Valmarie reaches in and pulls me towards her. She hisses, 'This is justice. All four sent mad. All four to be thrashed.' She grips my arm hard and I'm too close to Langward, I flail and scratch her face. Someone tears me away.

Blood runs from the scratch on Valmarie's cheek.

Her coat falls open and the Thrashing House key hangs from the chain around her neck. I stagger away from her, trembling. Her eyes spark, like there's some kind of animal living inside her and it wants to bite me. She changes her mind, looks away.

Kelmar stares at Langward's eyes. Him smirks like this is a game. Kelmar's mouth opens wide. She says, 'Mary—' and stares her moon face at me. She frowns, closes her mouth and grips hard on Langward's arm.

Her and Valmarie march Langward up the path to the cliffs, towards the Thrashing House. The rest of the crowd follow, Nell, Moira, Camery and Chanty among them, Jek's joined them as well. Even Merry and a crowd of farmers, other fishermen Da knows. Thems voices low. 'Thrash . . . thrash . . . thrash . . .'

I kick at the wet sand. There's a soft creamy owl feather tangled in my hair. I put it in my pocket.

I walk to the edge of the waves. The tall men's boats are still further away. Langward must have shone that light at them to make them leave. So him wanted to stay *here*.

To look for Barney.

But Langward dun know what goes on in the Thrashing House, else him wouldn't have let them take him there.

I take the owl feather out of my pocket and put it in the foam of the smallest wave.

'Bye Da,' I whisper. 'Wish I could miss you as much as I should. When you get thrashed, try to turn into something what'll tell me what you've done to Barney, and I'll be able to miss you a lot more. But if you've hurt him, then I'll smash my way into the Thrashing House, and asylumfodder the ghost of you.'

Morgan

Through a window upstairs in the corridor I watch the sea in the distance. The night sky blurs in the ripples of the windowpane like deep blue waves.

This corridor is the biggest space in the whole house. I'm pacing. I breathe condensation onto the window, and hide the sky. I walk along the corridor, along the black and white squares that Mum painted on the floorboards, past the closed doors. Mum is in the bedroom behind the second door on the right. Her mood is damp. Doldrums damp. It seeps out from under the door.

I reach the end of the corridor and breathe on the other window. I can blot out the whole island with just five inches of fog.

Stopping outside Mum's door I listen to . . . nothing.

I walk with tiny steps, the whole length, and the whole length back. Cover these black and white squares with paper footprints, curled like autumn leaves . . . like somewhere *outside* might be, thick with an autumn that has no walls. I look down at my toes on the black and white painted squares.

Mum always says I'll never be able to find my way back to the mainland.

I step on a black square. Both my feet fit inside it. I step onto a white one, balance on one foot. My game of three choices. Forwards, backwards, sideways.

Mum says I wouldn't know the direction, which way to turn. What to do. Step on a black square. I'll know when the moment comes for me to spring forwards.

Step back.

I walk forwards, black, white, black, white.

There's a chill on my ankles as I pass Mum's room. Whenever I ask her why we left, she says different things each time: 'The wind blew us here,' or 'It was your father's work,' depending on what mood she's in. For years I wished, on the fog I breathe on the windowpanes, for the wind to change and blow us back again, but it never did.

In our home on the mainland, when I was little, I was allowed to come and go to the nearby school. Mum didn't trust people easily, and she didn't like to go outside.

Some days she said I wasn't to go to school, because, 'It doesn't feel like a safe day.' On her unsafe days I'd stay indoors and keep out of her way. I'd play *three choices*. I made up this game after reading one of my storybooks alone, and then hearing Mum read it to me, and listening to how she changed the words. In the real story, the clever daughter always got three choices. My game started with flipping coins, where I'd give myself three things to do. One head and two tails meant I had to do the first choice, two heads and one tail meant the second and any other combination meant the third. I was never good at sums.

Once, on one of her unsafe days, the three choices I gave myself were:

1) stay in bed and read all day,

2) go into the back garden and collect up all the insects that live behind the nettle patch,

3) fan my face with the front door and talk to people I don't know.

The coin flip got me the third choice. So I stood opening and closing the front door, watching strangers pass along the pavement. I flapped the door, singing *Come in, we're friendly and we don't bite; Come in, we're friendly and we do bite;* and *Come in, we're not friendly and we bite.* Some of the strangers smiled as they passed, but no one came in. I played that game all afternoon. Then my teacher stalked past on her way home from school, glanced at me, then at the window and shook her head. After she'd gone, I tiptoed outside down the marble steps and looked up through the railings at the window. Mum was standing there, her arms folded, her expression frozen; but her eyes moved, following me. That evening was the first that Mum locked me in my room.

A day or so later, Mum received a crisp white letter that she read, showed Dad and locked away in a drawer. She made a phone call and within a week my parents told me they'd told 'the relevant authorities' that I was to be home educated.

Mum was best at teaching maths and art, so on her safe days we'd paint pictures and measure the depth and resonance of the colours and calculate the proportions of positive line to negative space. On her unsafe days we'd sit at a table with one piece of paper and a pencil. On these unsafe days, she'd show me long division. Tunnelling down, she called it, the way her head drooped closer and closer to the tabletop. When her cheek rested on top of the pencil in her hand, I'd gently take the pencil away, make her a cup of tea and be quiet for the rest of the day.

Dad was best at biology and literature. He often took me into the overgrown back garden at dawn before he went to work, to examine varieties of insects. We'd make lists of adjectives to describe each specimen. He described butterflies as ambitious, disillusioned, eager and brave. Spiders were painstaking and possessive. We laughed together, when he decided that earth-worms were merely discreet. I liked collective nouns, and I remember shouting, 'A clutter of storm clouds, a rehearsal of thunder and a rampage of rain!' as we both ran indoors to get dry.

But I missed the chatter of other children, the games in the playground, the different colours and smells; coat pockets with secret supplies of fizzing neon sweets, toy mice made from real fur, and more than once, a live earwig. Looking in lunch boxes was like peeking into kitchens. Curry or white bread sandwiches, pasta, buckwheat or noodles, yellow cheese, biscuits, oranges and apples. Once there was a lime. We'd made a hole in it and took it in turns to wear a green nose.

After not going to school for a while, I realised I should have been more careful when I picked what the three choices were. I decided to make sure my future choices didn't involve anyone else, definitely not strangers, definitely not teachers passing by. I learned to stop flipping coins, give myself three choices and just pick the best one. This is how I've learned to trust myself.

In this house, I used to scrunch up my toes and fingers and claw my way around my bedroom and imagine being old Nogard – a dragon who walked backwards. As a young teenager I'd play with my hair. I'd become a garden witch – my hair backcombed with chives woven through it, a prancing prince with a neat ponytail and a pigeon-toed walk, or a queen with a high fore-head who wore her fingers as a flexing, creeping crown. I played sleeping games and tried to fall asleep for a hundred years, but with my eyes open wide.

The last time I asked Mum, a few days, weeks ago, whenever it was, why we had to leave the mainland and come here, her reply was, 'All the doors slammed shut.' When I asked her what she meant, she said, through thin lips, 'I didn't say that. Wouldn't have done. There are no doors.' But this house is full of doors, and all of them are closed.

Mum tells me I've forgotten the journey here, made up some distorted memory of it. She's also told me over the years:

I don't remember, so you can't remember,
your memories are dreams, but my dreams are real,
the only real place is where we are now, because
everywhere else is just somewhere else.

She says these things to make me believe I can find contentment in the life they've chosen for me. She says these things to make me believe I could never find my way back home. She says these things to make me believe that she has a great, but contained, wisdom, and this is the only place in which she can overflow . . .

I used to believe this.

But now. A travesty of wisdoms. I still like collective nouns. An ambush of memories . . .

Memories are frozen moments, paragraphs cut from different books and shifted around. Us and our possessions, a truck, a cart, a train, then roads and boats . . . getting as far away from the city as we could. Sleeping in barns across the countryside. A travelling circus, a woman in a frilly skirt juggling paper hats to make me laugh. Bankers with gold coins piled on trays in cities. Windows in skyscrapers that changed colour with the sky. Highwaymen setting fire to barns, freeing the horses. More cities; eating chips and brown sauce in cafés with waitresses in blue shoulder pads and baby-pink aprons. Advertisement signs the colours of emeralds and rubies, strings of lights like pearls, factories where silent women made the same dress, over and over and over again. Uniforms and bandits, bikers wearing angel wings. Spidery eyelashes, underground hospitals where people could buy new faces.

I don't trust these memories are real, though they're as vivid as a picture book.

But I do remember the coast, and the trader men in long coats and strange hats, with their great old steamer ship, loading our boxes and crates as I stood and looked at their smaller oar boats trussed to the rails.

They said, 'We'll take you as far as you can go,' when they saw how much my parents were willing to pay. These men took the banknotes my parents offered and gave us safe passage through rough waters and remote cliff stacks, passing a surging of seals, a flicker of gannets, a huddle of puffins and a melancholia of cormorants standing on black rocks, drying their prehistoric wings through uncounted nights and days.

On the steamer ship, passing an archipelago of islands, the last tiny island I remember passing was called Hirta, and the men in strange hats said it was so remote that it had been evacuated years ago, because it was too hard to survive there.

They said, when Mum offered them yet more notes, that they were taking us to another island, even more remote, where some of the ancestors of people who'd lived on Hirta had disappeared to, generations ago. They told her that on this island, there are no clocks, that time is measured by the passing of seasons.

Mum said, 'That sounds perfect – clocks, ticking, are only a measure of the length of time between birth and death, and after all, what are heartbeats for?' And she threw her watch overboard.

The trader men said that no one but them knew that these

people lived here, and they took care not to introduce too many customs of the mainland, because that's how colonies were destroyed.

My parents stared at one another for a long time when they said that. Some silences are best left alone, so I watched the wash at the back of the ship and tried to remember the journey, to fix it in my mind so I'd never forget how to return. And I thought about clocks. Without clocks I might not know how old I was or when it was my birthday. I cried a little and asked one of the trader men what the date was, so I'd be able to count nights and days and months and years.

In my bedroom I pull the atlas from the shelf above my narrow bed. Flick through the pages till I find the one that shows the direction. A map of a small country, with lines that divide it. All the tiny islands to the north and the west. Even Hirta is almost off the edge of the map, and this island which has no clocks isn't there at all.

As far as we could go. So here we are. As far as we can go, unless we go back to the start. That is how I read my books. This is how I will also have to live my life.

A heartbeat of ticks. A limitation of maps. A circumference of stories.

Mary

Annie lies face down on the beach, like she's waiting for the sea to come in and carry her off. Her dogs sniff and nudge her head, her legs.

I kneel down and lift her face.

She pulls it away, her eyes tight shut.

'Come on, come home with me.' I touch her hand, but she slaps mine away. 'Annie, you'll freeze, you're no good for anything if you stay lying here – all you're doing is soaking up salt out of the sand.'

She groans, rolls her face towards me. Her eyes, half shut, are fit for dreaming.

'Come on,' I say, firm, like I'm older than her.

Her eyes open, but she dun really see me. She lets me take her hand. I lift her arm around my shoulder. She leans on me, hard. We stumble up the beach to my empty cottage. The door lets me open it, and we walk through.

*

Annie's dogs lie by the fire in the grate. The smell of peat fills the room. I've sat her in Mam's rickety chair. She gazes at the fire.

I kneel in front of her, hold out a bowl of potato and beef stew. 'Eat this Annie, you'll feel better.'

She reaches out her spindly hands. 'Ta, pet. You're right good, like your Mam were. You got any of that sickly clover wine of yours an' all, just a small one?'

I fetch it and pour her a large one. She knocks it back. I pour her another. I get my stew and we eat together. Annie gannets hers like she's not eaten anything for days.

'What did the four men do to the boys, Annie?'

She looks away. 'Traded them.'

'Why?'

'Tall men said them'd have a better life on the main land.'

'Martyn told you this?'

'Him always talked things through with me. Always has done what I've told him to.'

'You knew—'

'I weren't *meant* to know. Valmarie and Kelmar dun know—'

'—and you never told me.'

'I never told *anyone*. It were the men the tall men went to. Knew mothers wouldn't agree to it, like as not.'

'Neither would I.'

'If it worked out well enough and no one figured what were going on, them were going to ask more fathers for thems sons an' all. But if anyone ruined it, we'd get nothing for them. Couldn't do that to Martyn. Not when him shouldn't have even told me about it.' She drains her glass. I fill it again. 'Always have known when there's something on Martyn's mind. Can't keep secrets from me, gets all tongue tangled, knocks things over an' all sorts.'

'So *you* think the tall men have Barney on the main land.'

'You couldn't look after him right, could you?'

'Always have done, since Mam died. Hims been mine all this time.'

'You're too young. And your Da dun bother with him, Mary.'

'But—'

'My Kieran—'

'You let them take your own son, now how come—'

'Him'll be taught to read and write, take pictures with a metal thing of what him sees. Write on a board made of keys. Them said them want boys on the main land. That's what Martyn were told. Them said there's a whole bunch of other things him could do, what him can't learn here. There's a future for boys on the main land. None for him here. All we've got for them is the work of thems fathers, year after year. But Kieran never took to fishing. Never took to anything at all. Tried him with Dougan, glass-making, but him only lasted a day. Smashed too much. If him dun have any skills in hims hands, what else is there for him here?'

'But Barney—'

'See, Mary, tall men say we're wrong in not teaching the boys to read or write. Now we've always been this way, but the tall men said we're letting them be no more than useless. No future in useless. I dun agree with them at first, but them talked Martyn into it, an' if there's other things him can learn . . . we had to think of our boy.'

'Barney's too little for anything like that.'

'Them must've had a reason. Nothing to do with my Martyn. Tall men would've talked it over with your Da. Dun know what were said.'

'If I tell you something about Mam, you'll keep it to yourself?'

'Aye.'

'For you were close with her, for her sake you will?'

'Always.'

'That tall man what'll be thrashed, him were Barney's real Da. I saw it in hims eyes.'

She nods, slowly stroking one of her dogs. 'I've seen hims eyes.'

'Annie, I dun want anyone thinking bad of Mam. But Kelmar saw it. Should've seen the way she stared at me when she saw hims eyes. You knew Mam the best, did she tell you about him?'

She puts her spoon in the bowl, drains the wine, puts her bowl on the floor and all three of her dogs leap forwards, but there's only room in the bowl for one dog's tongue. It growls and the other two back away.

Annie dun notice, she's fixed on the fire. She whispers to herself, 'Won't be able to move house now. Not without Martyn. Have to stay here. The new cottage. All gone. It were so lovely. I'd knitted new blankets. Can't move now. Not without Martyn . . .'

'Please, Annie.' I put my hand on her arm. 'I dun remember everything – some of it's gone, worse since Mam got deaded. It's all got tangled. Tell me about Mam.'

Annie's dirty grey dress is still damp. I put a blanket on the arm of her chair, top up her glass and she drains it again, her cheeks flush. She covers her mouth and mutters, 'Your Mam never said anything to me about a tall man. But I weren't in a good way. Mightn't have listened if she said anything when Barney were born. I'd just lost another baby.'

'I'm sorry.'

She wipes a tear from her eye. 'No more after Kieran. Loved him too much. Not enough love in me for any other. The unborn know. Them just . . . slip away . . .' A sad smile closes her voice away from me. Her eyes stare off through the fire.

Annie glances at the front door and leans forwards. 'My Mam told me about a kind of punishing ritual. She said it used a real bird, with the instincts of the bird freed up. Something to do with calling up the spirit of one of the dead, putting it inside the bird and letting it loose. She said the spell needed earth. From a grave. It makes me shudder.'

I shiver. 'So if the bird were an owl, it would have the ghost and the owl's hunting instincts all mixed in together?'

'Mam might've been scaring me. Like that, she were.' Annie shivers again.

The fire crackles loud, we both start. She shakes her head and gulps more wine. 'My Kieran liked you, Mary. If you'd only have noticed, him might've tried harder to be good at something. Not just gave up.'

'Never thought of him that way.'

She glares at me like I've just called him useless.

'Him were nice enough, but I dun ever want him to . . .'

The firelight glints on her hair. 'Well, him won't *now*, will him?'

My face is burning. One of her dog's tails wags so hard it thwacks on my leg. That'll bruise.

'Oh, come on Mary. Come here.'

I lay a brick of peat on the fire and sit down on the floor next to Annie's feet and lean my head on her knee. She puts her hand on my hair.

I say, 'That tall man thinks Barney's still here. That's why him stayed. To look for him. So them might well have the other boys on the main land, but them *dun* have Barney.'

'Your Mam never told you about Kelmar?' she hiccups, puts her hand over her mouth.

'Kelmar? Mam dun let her in our home.'

'Right.'

'And Valmarie, Mam said her eyes weren't right in her face. "Some kind of strangeness in her . . ." That's what Mam said.'

Annie talks slurred. 'I heard Valmarie eatsh fish. Can you imagine?' She takes a glug of wine, to take the taste away. 'Both them couples were always fighting. Not like me and . . . Martyn. Loved him, I did. Still do. Martyn's more easy swisher-swayed into things than your Da, *an'* Bill *an'* Clorey.' She sighs. 'Maybe I'm too easy swayed an' all. Not so shtrong in here.' She pats her hand on her chest.

I get up. 'We could try to get the men out before the thrashing starts? Take Da's axe?'

'You dun go near the Thrashing House. It's kept locked for a reason. You get inside that place, you'll not be coming out.' She slumps back in the chair and I catch the glass before she drops it.

She gasps, 'Dun even think about it Mary, I'm not shpeaking of it. Can't bear to think . . . of Martyn . . .' Tears dribble to the end of her nose and hang there. 'I can't get him out. There's not a way to do it, I'll . . . end up . . . in there . . .' She sobs into her hands.

Opening the drawer in the table, it creaks as I pull out a hankie. I think of Grandmam and what she said about the Thrashing House:

So if you were ever put inside of it, what truth would it thrash out of you? If you know what that is, feel it glow bright inside you. Be true to who you are deep down, whether that's a do-gooder, or a thief, and that will be the end of that, and there will be no cause for worry.

I pass Annie the hankie, it's got a rose broidered on the corner. One of Mam's, finer than any I've ever made. It must have something of Mam still in it, as Annie stops crying as soon as she wipes her eyes. The bells ring out and she leans back in the chair. Like someone's stroking her hair, she goes all limp.

Annie dun stir, so I cover her with the blanket. One of her dogs is watching me as I close the curtains and go through to the bedroom and close the door.

*

I stare at Barney's empty pillow on the small bed opposite mine.

I can't go to sleep, though the bells are still ringing out. Valmarie must've been distracted with putting the men in there, so though she's ringing late, she's making sure everyone goes to sleep, by ringing for longer. My head feels like it's made of twisted threads. But there's one thread I dun want to cut. The one between me and Barney.

I get out the moppet and lie it on my pillow. I ask it again, 'Where are you?'

Barney's voice whispers, 'It's dark. Tell me story.'

My eyes blur with tears, to hear Barney's voice, so close. I lie down and stroke the moppet's stitched-up belly. I think of the story of Sishee that Grandmam told me when the bells had rang out, but I couldn't sleep. Da had bashed hims knee, and him and Mam were in thems bedroom – she'd made him a poultice with some herbs she'd got from Valmarie, but him were groaning, and I could hear him through the wall. Grandmam told me to hop in with her, so I got in her bed, curled up next to her and listened.

Sishee's story is of the dreams we give away. I still half believe in Sishee, because half of me feels like a child. We've

76

been told this story as children, and we still believe it in our hearts.

I tell it to the moppet:

At night-time on this island, when the bells ring out, the giant woman, called Sishee, comes alive, treads soft over the island, looking for her drowned dress. Sishee is old, older than anything else what exists here, but she is sound in her footfall, and silent as air in an empty jar.

She is naked, apart from a necklace she wears around her neck. She wears shadows over the parts what are secret. The necklace shines out like the moon. She gathers up all our dreamings, all our thoughts and hopes and night-time terrors and collects them in a glass jar.

Our dreamings want to be took, so we are contented when we wake. Them want to be seen by someone what wants them, not folks what want them to go away, like we all do.

When she is near, the dreamings rise up to meet her, float and curl and twist themselves out of our heads, out of our rooms, up into the night sky, and them twirl around the clouds, waiting for her. If them stay within us them are frightening or confusing, but when them leave us, them turn into something beautiful.

She collects all our dreamings in case she can find something what will tell her about her dress. She's still got hope, even after all these years. Her dress is drowned so deep below the ocean only she could ever reach it, because there's nothing too far away to reach if you want it bad enough, and know where it is, and how wet you have to get to find it. Sometimes when you look for something so hard, you look in the wrong places.

You must never dream of her dress; if she sees that dream, she'll find it, and she'll not come back to take our dreamings away again. Some say if she did find it, she'd pick up the Pegs, and without them the whole island would slide into the sea. Others, more sensible folk, like me, know that's a load of old rot. The island's not pegged to anything, it's as solid and sure as all old things are.

So when you're in bed, you've got to stay put and not disturb anyone else what's trying to sleep in your home. If our dreamings dun get took, we'll all go mad, some quick, some slow, for the dreamings will latch onto us like limpets.

As the dawn breaks, Sishee stares through her glass jar, holds it up to the horizon to see the light come through. Searches deep inside each dream to see if she can spy her drowned dress; the thing she wants the most. Then she shakes her head and lifts up the graveyard hill to put the jar away beneath it. Under the gravestones all our dreamings die down to nothing, leaving her jar empty for the next night.

Morgan

I love the sound of these bells that ring out each and every night. It's been a way of counting time, when I could so easily miss a whole day passing. They ring all the way from the bell tower, and tonight the tall house on the hill seems like a twisted ruin.

I curl up and hug my pillow to my belly. The bells ring on and on, reminding me that I'm not alone. That time does pass here, not just for me, but for the people who live here. There are no clocks, but these bells measure days. They remind me that time does move forwards, and it won't always be just me and my family, that there are people living all around us who I've never met.

The night is where the banished hours live. Sometimes I stay awake all night counting, just so I can check that seconds, minutes and hours are still moving forwards, and the moon and the sun work like the hands of a clock, arching over the sky.

Often, through my bedroom window, I catch a glimpse of people in the daytime. Women in shawls and thick coats, men in baggy working clothes, herding the brown and cream sheep and muddied black cows to the fields in the morning and back to the barns at dusk, as the sky fills with funnels of chimney smoke.

In the summer the men pick handfuls of brown and cream sheep's wool off the bushes where it gets caught. They wash the sheep in the brook that crosses the field. They send sheepdogs to catch them, shear some of the sheep by hand, collect their wool in baskets and leave the bald sheep to roam. In winter, the sheep are thick with dirt. Time can be measured by the seasons, by migrations, by the thickness of the coats of sheep, the stages of growth in plants and the weather. There's always weather.

Sometimes when I see people out in the fields I wave from my bedroom window. But whether the sky is dark grey and clouds thicken and rain pelts or when the sky shifts colour and the sun shines out, or there's nothing but white sky and a whistling gale, no one waves back. Whatever weather the sky brings, it must be reflected in the windowpanes, so no one can see me.

I've found the present Mum gave me for my eighteenth birthday, instead of the padlock key. The book of blank pages and the pen that I'd hidden under my mattress and forgotten about. The padlock key would have been freedom, but this book is both freedom and a trap. There would be freedom if I could write in it. Write memories down and keep them safe. But it's a trap for my thoughts; if I write them inside it, they will be caught.

I open the book. Stroke the first blank page.

Anything I write will be found and read. That's the whole reason Mum gave me it. But what she doesn't know, is that I *realise* it's a trap.

The pages are so clean. An invitation to choose what I want Mum to read. Pick a memory. One that will annoy her. One that she wishes she could remove like a splinter. Three choices. Counting days and time and writing about ticking clocks might annoy her a little, or writing about her promising to give me a key and then changing her mind might be an irritation, but neither of these are enough for her to want me to leave.

I could write down a phrase from my psychology book, but I don't know if she'd understand what I meant by writing it. I take the book from the shelf and find the page that speaks of narcissism. How strange that a beautiful flower has the same name as such an ugly disorder. This page describes exactly how my mother behaves. This page speaks of things that I can't. Whenever I'm angry, with her, or my father, I read this and think it must be so hard for her to be like this. So hard for him to care for her. Reading this page dulls any anger I'm feeling. Reminds me that it must be much worse *being* her, rather than living with her. My mother, reduced to a list of symptoms. Lack of empathy, intense mood swings, controlling behaviour, self-importance, fear of change, compulsive self-preservation . . .

My hand takes the lid off the pen. This feels cruel.

This page shouldn't be one of the three choices. I can't quote it because I can't tell how she might feel, reading it. It might hurt. It might make all of her symptoms real to her.

So. Three choices. Write about: 1) Ticking Clocks. 2) Broken Promises. 3) Ghosts.

It has to be ghosts.

Those are the memories she really hates me to talk about. Especially the memories I have of my best friend, Anita, who lived with us in the house on the mainland. I think about her all the time. And Mum locks me in my room whenever I mention her.

I pick up the pen and write:

List of Leaving:
I was seven.
Mum wanted to leave.

I'd watched through keyholes.
She built emotions up inside her like a storm,
kept them stored in her mouth.
She exploded, threw a milk bottle full of dirty paint water
at Dad.
He thundered, locked me in my bedroom, before returning
to her.
Anita hovered, transparent.
She flitted between floors.
Listened in. Came back and told me:
'She's scared. Wants to run. You're leaving with them.
Leaving me.'
We both cried, but she still wouldn't let me hug her.

*

I breathe fog on my bedroom window, draw Anita's face opposite mine.

I left Anita behind. She was the best friend a little girl could ever have. A ghost child only I could see. After Mum had stopped me going to school, I'd thought about other children all the time, and I'd watched them from the windows, going to school in colourful huddles. The first day I ever saw Anita, she was just there at the window, beside me, watching them. I wasn't frightened. She'd talked about the children, what they were wearing, what they might be saying, what they would have in their lunch boxes and pockets. Anita said she'd been there in our house all the time I had, but she wasn't sure I'd want to see her. I said she should have let me see her before, because I wanted someone to play with. She'd smiled and said simply, 'Well, here I am then.' And until our family left, we were rarely apart.

We used to sit in the corridors of our house. On creaking

floorboards we'd catch insects together, keep them in glass jars, feed them on ivy leaves. She wouldn't ever let me touch her, she said she didn't know what would happen if the dead touched the living; to her, it felt wrong. But we talked about everything, there on the floorboards in the hallways, peering at magnified insects.

She flitted in and out of other rooms. She often said, 'You should ask your parents where their money comes from,' but I didn't want to know. I was more interested in our captives, the insects, though we'd always set them free. My parents told me she wasn't there; while she was sitting next to me at the kitchen table, the plate I put there for her was never filled. I tried to feed her my own food, but she said I needed it more than her. I ate each mouthful for her as well; somehow when my own belly got full, I could fill hers. I wonder if she's still there. She never changed; I got taller, while she stayed exactly the same.

At first, when I talked about Anita, my mother would leave the room, her hand over her mouth, her face pale. My father would stay behind. Watch me, take notes, ask me where Anita was, he'd squint at the corner of the room, the sofa, the chair next to me, usually just slightly to the left of wherever she really was. He would never see her. Never asked what she *said*. I liked him asking about her, liked being alone with him, liked his interest in someone who I'd learned to love so easily.

But he lost interest in Anita when he realised how frightened Mum was.

Not long before we left, I was waiting for Anita under the elaborate mahogany table. I had a magnifying glass in one hand, and my other palm gently hugged a clothes moth. My parents came in and sat down. I heard Mum whispering to Dad, 'What if they *know*? You should have thought of that. Your plans only included the living, but what about the dead . . .' And just a moment later, she found me under the table. She pinched my shoulder and snarled at me, 'You're nothing special, if there really are ghosts, they'd want to talk to *me*.' I crushed the clothes moth in my palm, and when Mum had stamped out of the room, I opened my hand. The moth was still alive, but I'd broken one of its wings. I blew on the broken wing for ages, to see if air could make a flying thing mend. It didn't.

I still insisted I could see Anita. Dad was no longer interested, he and Mum seemed joined together like paper dolls. They were adamant that Anita wasn't real. They got angry with me when I cried and screamed and sobbed when we left; they couldn't understand my grief at leaving her behind. But she couldn't leave that house.

She said to me, 'I belong to it. I can't move, not like you.'

Anita's condensation face runs in streams down my bedroom window.

With my tiny nail scissors, I cut out the page I've written the List of Leaving on. I fold it over and over and clip out a series of paper dolls. Girls in skirts and boys in trousers. Over the faces of the skirted dolls, I draw a happy mouth, an angry mouth, a frightened mouth. I leave the boy faces blank. I hide the paper dolls under my mattress.

I know Mum will find them.

Mary

Something taps on the bedroom window. I bundle up with the moppet under the blanket, and keep still.

A low voice hisses from outside. 'Mary, it's Kelmar.'

Mam never let her come round.

She taps again, whispers, 'It's important.' Tap tap tap on the window.

I cover my head with the pillow.

Hold my breath till I can feel she's gone.

Mam must have not liked her for a reason. Kelmar's the only midwife, so Mam must've had to let her birth Barney. Kelmar's seen Langward's eyes. So if Kelmar's here to tell me Da isn't Barney's father, and Langward is, well. That I know already.

I lie in bed thinking, no, dreaming, no, thinking of Mam, broidering the diamond markings of the diamondback addersnake what killed her. I say, 'Mam, broider me a picture of Barney . . .'

Mam's sat at the table in the main room, I'm in bed smelling the lavender sachet under my pillow, but I'm stood right next to her as well.

She's whispering, whispering, I lean in close but can't hear what she's saying. I feel my pillow on my cheek, but it's not the pillow, it's her hair against my skin. She sits there stitching by the window . . . her breath smells of lavender. Her eyes stare out of the window.

'Mam, can you see where Barney is?' I ask. My cheek presses against the pillow, I'm lying in bed and I'm standing next to her, I watch her stitching.

I ask her, 'Would Da've given Barney to someone?'

The fabric she's stitching stretches out of the window, all the way up to the sky. She's lost in the stitches.

'Please Mam, *who* would Da have given Barney to? Who would hide him from me?' She dun reply. 'Mam, if I dun know *who*, I'm going to have to search every cottage on the whole island . . .' She's using every colour of thread that she left behind her. Stitching diamonds full of secrets.

I start. I wasn't asleep. Next to me on my pillow is a broiderie of Mam's.

Threads tangled and knotted together on the back. I spread it out; the back of the picture is like a map. Threads lead everywhere, tangled together in knots and frays. I turn it over. It's the broiderie she did of the owl with a woman's face. The feathers are delicate and soft; shades of white, cream and honey-coloured threads. But her face is screaming, jagged black lines come from her mouth.

I roll it up and whisper, 'Mam? Dun scare me . . .' I listen, like she'll speak, only she dun. The thought of Mam's ghost being here makes my palms sweat though my fingers are freezing. Grandmam once told me ghosts could step inside the living and nudge the living person out. Though she made me scared of them, I still remember what she said:

Ghosts come after the living so them can possess us, step into our skins alongside us, breathe on just our in-breath, borrow half of our heartbeat, tangle half of our thoughts and choose from half our choices. But ghosts are greedy, them wants all of us. Ghosts dun get contentment with just half, them miss stupid things like thems own favourite foods, or the way them did thems hair, imagining it were better than anyone else's. Ghosts dun want to share. If one side of a person's face gets kissed and likes it well, what if the other side wants a kiss an' all? Imagine if the side what got kissed was your face, and the ghost side of your face got jealous. What kind of a fight do you think that would make?

Like enough you'd never get kissed again, neither side of you.

Dun want to share my body with a ghost – the feeling of anyone, even Mam, just stepping into me makes my skin prickle, like my body could be haunted without me even knowing.

Sometimes my body dun feel like it's mine. It gets numb or I get an itch and dun feel how bad I'm scratching it, or I get a bruise but never felt the blow what put it there. Grandmam never meant to scare me, for she told me this story to get me to stop being grouchy. Her moral were all about folks being happier in our own skin.

From the outside, if a living person has got a ghost in them, them'd still look the same, as them're sharing the same skin. Skin is important to ghosts, as it's part of what them misses; to be touched. No one would notice, while them're sharing nicely, for the ghost learns how to act like the living person them're inside of, only once them gets the hang of it, them can just nudge the living person out.

And no good can come of that.

I put the broiderie of the owl woman in my drawer next to my box of keys. The box rattles. I take it out and put it on my bed. I pull Nell's key from my dress pocket and it hums in my fingertips, sings with the feeling of her touch. I hear her voice in it:

This thing won't go in the houses. Too wild for the indoors. Dun know how I know that, just feels right in my cockles, whatever them are. Doug'll be angered when him comes round, only I've got to get him safe `.` . . . that kind of wildness, it'll tear at anyone in its path . . . not just the guilty . . . not just the tall men . . .

Nell's key can't tell me anything I need to know about Barney. Just Nell worrying over her Dougan, and thinking the tall men were guilty, as she were when she last touched it. I close my eyes and think of Barney, to make sure the metal hasn't caught her thinking about him. But it's blank behind my eyes. I put the key in my wooden box.

I've got the key from Chanty's, but Annie never locks her door, nor Beattie, nor Jek. Them can't think them've anything worth stealing. The keys in this box won't tell me anything about Barney. But anything metal that folks have touched *since* Barney went missing, the metal will know. I need to get front door keys and listen to what them tell me. Keys will have all been touched often, and recent. And if someone has him hid, them'll be locking thems door. So I've got to steal folks' keys.

The floorboards creak as I stand up and push the moppet into my dress pocket. Dun want to sneak past Annie, so I pull on my boots, throw a thick shawl around myself and ease open the bedroom window. I climb out, drop down on the spiny grass and climb up the path to the cliffs.

I can hear the clicks, the whirrs, the creaks of the Thrashing House, only I know it's inside of my head I hear it, like the thrashing is about to begin. It sounds like the beating of wood on stone. No. It's my heart beating. Thudding and thwacking like there's a judgment on *me* all the way from the Thrashing House. Is this how it calls, through a heartbeat? My heart thuds and thwacks as I climb the path and try not to slide where the soil is loose. I wonder what it feels like, to have truth thrashed out. If it hurts.

*

The smithy's cottage windows are dark. I try the door, and it's locked. There's nothing by the door, no pot to hide a key under, so I go to the barn where him works, and listen. Nothing. I turn the handle and the door creaks open. I step inside.

The barn smells of burned saucepans. My eyes get used to the dark. In one corner is the forge, the great anvil stands next to it and I try not to trip over the tools with long handles him has left leaned up against all kinds of old blocks of wood. There's a new birdcage hanging on a hook from a beam, all coils of metal and I think them've got great huge birds on the main land for the gaps between the bars are so wide. Unless them wear the birdcages like hats, for I never can tell which kind of fashion is going to take them all over from one month to the next.

On the ledge of the forge I find a box of matches. I strike one and walk back to the door. There's no key in the lock. There's wrenches hanging from hooks, sledge hammers leaned up against the wall. The match burns my fingers.

I drop it on the stone floor and light another. There's a small set of drawers, the top one is full of nuts, bolts and hinges. The match burns my fingers again so I shake out the flame and light another. In the next drawer down, there's a clutter of chains. I spark another match and rummage in all the drawers. No sign of hims key.

Another match. There's a box of tacks on top of the drawers. Underneath is a key. I pick it up, blow out the match and close my eyes. The smithy's face swirls up, hims cheeks red from the fire. So this is the right key to hear hims voice in. I put the matches and the key in my pocket, creak the door open and go outside.

I walk up the hill to a long low cottage that old Jessup and her man live in. I look through the window next to the front door. A small room with a couple of stools, a great basket of raw wool, carders and a spinning wheel by the grate. I look through another window at the kitchen. There are milk pails on the table and ridged butter hands in a small washbowl. I try the front door, and them haven't locked it. The key's in the lock on the other side, so I put it in my pocket and close the door, quiet.

I pass a barn, the cows moan, thems hooves shuffle. Chickens squall and a cockerel shrieks and joins in, so I leg it back down the hill, past the well them all share and dun stop till I'm at Dougan's barn. I lean on the wall till my breathing slows down, and walk, quiet.

Moira the cobbler, she's not locked her door. Just behind the front door is her workroom. All her shoe trees with half-finished leather boots, a whole load of her tools laid out on the table, the awls what she stabs the holes in the leather with, her stretching pliers and the hammer she uses to bang the nails in the heels. She's got leather strips piled on a shelf, and though the leather is from the tanners it's lost the stench, for it's been cured. But I can't see where she'd put a key. I go through the doorway at the back of her workroom and I'm in her kitchen. It's all quiet. On the right of the kitchen there's another door what's open a crack – there's just the sound of her breathing. In her kitchen, I strike a match. There's a hatch to her storm room in the floor, so I open it and hold five lit matches down. There's a stack of leather cut-offs in the corner and shelves with jars of pickled onions, cabbage and eggs. The steps on the ladder are dusty, so she's not been down here for a while. She's nothing to hide. I dun need her key.

Outside, I walk back towards the cliff path to go home. I'll go out and get more keys tomorrow night.

I walk along a stone wall, there's about nine dead moles hanging on string along the top. The farmers kill them and put them there, to show all the other moles what them're up against. But moles are blind. That's why them keep getting caught.

*

The Thrashing House looms tall and dark. I get nearer, and stop, dead.

It's thrashing inside. Clicking and creaking and whirring and beating. It's come alive with the thrashing. It's made of dark wood and it stretches so high the sky spins. An owl hoots and I near scream out. It's a pale barn owl, high on the roof. It swoops over me, wings spread wide. I turn, watch it circle over the beach and it flies off into the dark.

I take a step towards the Thrashing House, and another. This place is ancient. The arrows carved in the door point up, and down. The sounds punch through the air, it judders through the soil under my feet, the sound thwacks and beats and whirrs and creaks like wood and I run to the top of the path what leads down the cliffs and I hit the top of the path too quick and

I trip

slide

fall,

catch my leg on a rock. Earth and sand fall away down the cliff. It's a steep drop, right next to me. I pull myself away from the edge through damp earth, my heart thud thud thud against the soil. The soil thud thud thud against my chest. I feel with my hands, where folk've left footprints, for the crowd what put Da inside were stood right here. The Thrashing House creaks, groans, thwacks, but I pull myself towards it and slump on the ground. I push myself up and my fingers touch something metal. A heavy chain. It sings in my palm. There's a link missing, the welding hasn't held.

Something's fallen off it.

I drop the chain and scrabble around in the footprints with my hands. The Thrashing House creaks and cracks and whirrs. My fingers find something else, cold and metal. Much heavier than the chain. It hums right through me. I sit up – it's cold in my hands. This metal is strong. Old. I blink and the metal shows me a picture behind my eyelids.

I close my eyes, and see . . .

A tussle, the shoves and sounds of a crowd of people wash around me. Murmurs of 'Speak. Speak. Speak,' from voices of old and young, men and women. Annie's husband Martyn's voice. Slurred, confused. 'No future here . . . not for Kieran . . .' Another voice, Clorey's, muttering over and over, 'Better life than mine.' Bill, Valmarie's husband's voice, sharp as slaps, 'Jealous. Yes. No. Wanted her back. Got him gone . . .' A picture of the Thrashing House, clicks of a lock, the door creaking open. Darkness inside. An angered shriek from a woman, the woman wearing this key. Valmarie. The crowd pitching, pushing and shoving the men through the door, Bill's face, turning, eyes wide, mouth like a cave . . .

The Thrashing House creaks and clicks and thuds.

The metal shows me a dark sky. Flashes of faces, shawls and brown boots, angered voices, the smell of trampled earth, the sea, the flames in the torches, the Thrashing House towering above, a wash of faces, colours behind my eyelids. Trapped in a murmuring crowd, elbows, knees, pushing and shoving . . . pushing, then . . . falling onto earth. Still. Silent.

This metal were dropped in the crowd what were stood here tonight.

I look up at the Thrashing House – it creaks and cracks and whirrs and it's battering inside, so loud that I know it's too late for all the men inside it. Too late for Da.

But I've found the Thrashing House key.

I shouldn't even touch *this* key till I'm twenty-one. I lean close and look at the maze of shapes cut out of the bit that would unlock a door. Like a part of a puzzle. The bow, the part held in the fingertips, it's got a design made of arrows carved into it, one pointing up and one down.

I swallow the sickness down what's in my throat, wrap the key in my skirt, tie a knot in the fabric, so it's hid and I'm not touching the metal.

This key will have passed through the hands of all the women when them've took thems turns on the bell list. The women's voices will all be stored in the metal of this key. So I won't need to take any others. This is the only one I'll need. For women know everything what's going on. I've got to get this key home, and get it well hid.

*

This morning the early sun shines as I open the curtains of the bedroom window. All seems still outside. My cottage is full of creakings and footstep noises and nothing making the sounds.

Something small and grey moves on the floor.

It's the moppet.

It crawls out from under my bed. It crawls awkward, its arms and legs aren't the same length so it moves like it's drunk. The moppet's head is sewn on straight up, so as it crawls it can't see where it's going. It faces the floor, with its raggedy ears dragging on the boards. It reaches my feet, sits back and looks up at me.

Barney's voice says, 'Mary, I tired. Stay home warm.'

I pick it up and sit down on Barney's bed. Tears make me not see right. I hold the moppet in my shaking hands. Dun want it to be able to *move*, not if it's going to make me fearful. But I look down at the squinty mouth what should be Barney's mouth, the raggedy ears what should be hims curly hair. And I dun mind if it scares me, for it's got the voice I love the most. I even miss wiping hims snotty nose and washing off the dirt behind hims ears.

I want to ask it the question I should have asked it already. The one I've been too afraid to ask. So I do.

'Barney, are you dead?'

Before it can answer, the sobs shake so hard in me I can't stop them up. I wish I could unspeak it. Dun want to hear the answer. I bury the moppet in Barney's blankets.

*

A clatter from outside the bedroom stops up my tears. I crouch down and look through the keyhole. A wide eye looks back at me. I fall on the floor and bang my arm.

Annie curses on the other side. 'Thrashes been, Mary! You gave me some shock there.'

I scramble up and wrench open the door.

Her hair frazzles around her face, a pink smudge on her cheek from where her face rested on Mam's chair. 'I were only seeing if you were still asleep or no. I must have nodded off. Dogs woke me up knocking over the stool. Best get going home.'

'Annie, stay a while.'

She puts her hand on my shoulder. 'Oh Mary, what we going to do? We lost too much too quick 'ent we?'

I nod.

She takes my hand and we sit by the empty grate. She says, 'Ah, you poor thing, me in such a state, you must have been feeling right bad about your Da, only you managed to get both of us warmed and fed. You just got to take care of yourself. Feeding one is easier than two or even three. You're still young, you'll get through.'

'So you're saying I should forget Barney?' My voice cracks.

Annie says, 'I'm feeling a whole lot better, after a good sleep in your Mam's chair.' She whispers, 'Tragic what happened to her. Your Mam, my friend. Beatrice.'

It's a pinprick in my belly, to hear her name. Everyone always calls her 'Your poor Mam', or 'Remember Mary's Ma?' Sometimes I forget she were ever called anything else.

I say, 'With the amount of diamondback addersnakes folks say we've got on the island, you'd have thought someone could have come up with something in time.'

Annie starts, eyes wide. 'No Mary, it were a deep, deep bite, she never even saw that diamondback. She were filled with the venom so fast she were out cold in a heartbeat.'

'Well, you'd best get back home to feed your dogs.'

Thems tails thud on the floorboards as Annie stands up.

I smile at her. 'I've never been alone here. Not proper alone. Even with Barney gone, when Da were fishing, I knew him'd be coming back.'

'If your Mam were here, she'd tell you to get to doing your broideries. So I'm saying it for her.' She squeezes my arm.

'Ta, Annie. I wish . . .'

'I know, pet. Me an' all.' She wipes her eyes. 'Dun tell folks I knew about the boys being traded. I'll not say anything about your Mam and that tall man. Stick together, we should.'

I nod but dun look at her.

'For your Mam's sake, Mary. Stick with me.'

'Aye. All right. For Mam.'

We walk to the door and I'm thinking about what Grandmam said:

The Thrashing House beats the truth out of a person and turns it into some small object what can be seen and held. These objects are kept safe inside a glass cabinet, in the Weaving Rooms, where only the women go, and when you're of age, you will be able to go an' all.

'Annie, you'll go to the Weaving Rooms soon? You'll get to see what the objects are what come out the hatch – will you tell me what object comes from Da?'

'No, Mary, I will *not* speak of Weaving Room talk. And you've got to get on, keep going.' Her eyes shine with tears. She runs her thin hand across her nose. 'If I think about Martyn, I'll want everything to stop. There's no good can come from that kind of thinking. Right.' She steps forwards. 'I've got to get these dogs out before them piss all over your floor.'

Right enough, as soon as we look at them, the dogs all clatter over to the front door and scratch at it to get out.

Annie kisses my cheek. 'I'll check on you later. You'll have a lot of broideries to do if you're to keep this cottage on. I'm sorry Mary, sorry for us both.' She opens the door. The dogs lurch out and head straight for the beach. Annie follows them. The wind blows her hair, it looks like golden smoke.

*

I make grey porridge, it glugs in the pot. I sit at the kitchen table and eat it on my own.

I get the buckets and go out of the back door. I walk along behind the row of cottages and up a small track to the well these cottages share. No one else is out back, but Camery's chickens chatter to be let out of the hut. Beattie's left her washing out on her line all night, her big white drawers and yellowed pillowcases sag. I fill the buckets from the well, take them home and slosh the water in the biggest pots on the range, go in and out with buckets, till I've filled the washtub in the kitchen. I lock the front and back doors, close the curtains up and use the copper jug to wash my hair and scrub the rest of myself clean till the water's gone cold.

After I've dried off, I bind my breasts flat with a damp roll of bandage. Been binding them for a long time, and I dun remember when I started. Mam must've gave me these bandages when them started to grow. A blank in my memory. Mam never bound hers, and I dun think other women do, but the bindings make me feel stronger. It's hard to breathe when I've bound them too tight, as I do often. As the bandages dry, them get tighter and tighter. I change my vest, drawers and socks and put on a clean grey dress.

I put dried heather in the grate on top of half a firelighter, spark a match, light the twigs and blow on them to get them burning. I put a brick of peat on and get the fire built up. Grey snakes of smoke rise up the chimney.

In the bedroom I reach under the mattress on my bed and

97

get out the Thrashing House key, wrapped in the broiderie of the owl woman.

I've put the other keys that I took last night in my wooden box. Dun need them, but them're mine now. Them'll manage fine without them.

But no one'll manage fine without this one.

Even wrapped in fabric, the metal of the Thrashing House key pulls at my thoughts. I sit in Mam's rickety chair by the fire.

The key is made from a strong old metal. It's gathering a sense of me, so it knows how to talk back when I touch it. I want to get at the stories caught inside it. But it's pulling at my thoughts, not giving the stories up.

It's trading for memories.

No other metal has ever wanted anything back from me. Just given up what it knows at the first quiet touch.

The smell of peat fills the room. Outside, the waves swish swash along the shore. I unwrap the edge of the broiderie and hold my finger over the bow of the key. It hums, pulls at my fingertip. It makes me think of Grandmam, we're curled up in her bed and I'm fidgeting with her hair. It makes me think of Mam, watching her carry Barney down the beach to show him the sea. And Da, grinning so proud, when Mam told him how much she'd got from the tall men for one of the best broideries she'd stitched – a picture of red poppies, the petals blowing off in the winds.

I think about when I'm grown to be twenty-one. Then I'll get given the Thrashing House key for my turn on the bells. It won't be hid here in my cottage with me. A woman will walk up to me and put it, on its chain, around my neck. Everyone'll talk nice to me for the whole day while I wear it, and I'll go up to the bell tower that night and ring out the bells.

There's a separate door to the bell tower, though it's attached to the Thrashing House, and it's this same key what unlocks both doors. The bell tower has just one flight of steps all curled around, no doors inside it that go into the main building. Ringing out the bells must be like reaching up to the stars to pull them down and sew them together, and tucking up the whole island under a bedspread made of stars.

Mam told me, once, when she'd been up there for her turn on the bells, 'It's like the Thrashing House were pulling at me through the walls. I were in the bell tower, but the pull of the Thrashing House made me jittery. I could have left the bells, gone downstairs, outside, and found myself going through the great front door. I felt it was gathering a sense of me so it could call me, make me do just that.'

I were sat up in bed, couldn't sleep. Barney must've been crying.

She whispered, 'I could hear clicks and whirrs in there; the Thrashing House were trying to figure me out. Trying to listen close, to the truth of me.'

Mam said, 'You dun think bad of me, Mary, do you?' She looked stricken.

I said, 'No, Mam, I dun think bad of you.' Though I dun know what she were talking of. I felt freezing, when she said that. Her eyes were wide and scared so she put her arms around me. I wanted to touch the Thrashing House key then, and I reached out for it, but she took the chain off from around her neck and gripped me tight again. It felt like she were tangling me up in blackthorn branches instead of her arms, but I let her hang on till she were calm, for she seemed so upset.

*

99

Remembering made me fall asleep. The morning has gone. I build up the fire again, keep all the curtains closed up and make kale and tattie soup.

Back in the main room, I sit by the fire. Unwrapping the key from the broiderie, I lie it on my lap and hold my hands over it. It pulls. The air between my palms and the key buzzes.

Think of Barney. Who knows where him is?

But the key wants more memories. It's still trading. If I let it take what it wants, it will speak back. It chooses this memory . . .

Grandmam came to live with us before she died, when I were about seven. Well before Barney were born. Mam said she were too old and crazed to live in her own cottage.

She dun like it here at first, ran around our home with bare feet, spitting curses at all of us. She saw us like something else, not the belonging people, the family we were. Kept pulling at our hair, mumbling that *five* were a bad number of folks to have living together, though we were just four. Mam said Grandmam'd never got over her husband, Mam's Da, taking off to live with some other woman. Mam said best not to ask Grandmam about that, for as she'd got older her mind were crumpling. Grandmam sometimes thought him were stood right next to her, like the ghost of a living man.

Grandmam rambled about all kinds of things: outsiders and insiders, marriages shipwrecked, the locked-up pink fence on the other side of the island, the Glimmeras fighting. Said we were all cooped up together like chickens peck pecking at each other. Well, her and Mam pecked hard enough at each other for sure.

She dun have to broider or mend or stitch, as she told Mam, 'I'm far too ancient to be using up the last snippet of my eyes on the needles and pins.'

Mam weren't best pleased, but she broidered more than ever.

Me and Grandmam used to play together like she were a child. It seemed sometimes to me like we were the same age on the inside. Though on the outside her wrinkles creased her face up, to smiles or tears like tracks in the sand.

We used to trade secrets, I'd tell her about the things I'd done and pretended I hadn't, like when I ran away to see the pink fence when the chalk flowers were drawn on it, and then ran right back home again. Grandmam said, 'That were a good one, take me along when you run away the next time.'

She told me the secrets of when she'd pissed where she shouldn't have, and she'd laugh so loud Mam'd dash in for them secrets, like she could smell them. Truth is, she probably could.

It were when Grandmam were telling a story that she'd sound her age. The part of her what were the same age as me would sometimes play with the stories, find different morals and meanings from what were meant. Some of the morals she played with made more sense from her lips than the morals other folks would've come up with.

Grandmam lived here with us, sharing my room, for only a few years before she died. Them years were the most I'd laughed and fought and been afraid and felt like I were with someone who knew everything, but knew how to play all at the same time. My job was 'Look after Grandmam', and it were the best job I've ever been given to do.

I looked after her so well, I got her laughing till she coughed, not caring how loud she snored, eating the butter cream cakes Mam baked before anyone else had one, breaking things deliberate and helping me steal keys for my collection.

But she would never have let me steal this one.

Grandmam loved tangling up Da's fishing nets when no one were watching. She had a child's heart, so my job to take care of her were easy. I kept it beating so hard in her she lived longer than them said she would, but I had no games in me to fight against death; not playing with her, listening to her stories, cooking her broth or warming her with fires or soft blankets could look after her from that.

In the last few days I had a Grandmam, I saw death, a shadow with no face, waiting in the corner. Only it weren't going to let me bring it into any game, fight it for Grandmam and win, and by then, Grandmam were propped up on cushions and weren't able to play, other than with how fast or slow her breathing went.

Sometimes Grandmam's breath stopped for a moment, I'd call in Mam, we'd watch her, then she'd breathe again. In the gaps between breathing not me or Mam would breathe them breaths for her, lest we took the life out of her before her time. But that shadow with no face were stood there in the corner, and it must have breathed for her, even without a mouth, for Grandmam died anyway.

'She were old,' Mam said, and hugged me. 'It were the way of time.'

I told myself Grandmam's stories over and over again after she died, so I'd never forget them. I can still remember the stories in her exact words. I'm warm now, even in my hands, thinking of her fireside voice.

The key wants me to remember Grandmam's stories for comfort. So I'm calm when I listen to what it tells me. I put the key on the floor, for I want this memory just for myself.

Grandmam told me about the Glimmeras, and she would moan and groan, tug at her hair when she spoke. The story of five old women what live on a tiny rocky island just to the north of ours. How them got there, Grandmam weren't sure. She said them'd been there forever.

This is what she said:

Be mindful you never become like them, for though once them must have been like normal folk, them are not like us any longer.

The Glimmeras are a family to each other. Five of them, all old, all ancient. Them are mothers or sisters or daughters or grandmothers to one another. Them have been alive for so long that no one remembers. Each one has a different colour of hair: red, gold, grey, white and black. Them have claws for hands, and them eat only dead fish, for that's all them can get.

Them always used to bicker. Each believed herself to be better than the others, to be the greatest of the five: the queen, the leader, the priestess, the witch, the boss. One day a rare thing happened, and all of them agreed on something. The thing them agreed on was that them would have a competition that would decide, once and for all, which one would be the best of the five: the queen, the leader, the priestess, the witch, the boss.

The competition was called 'The Thronebuilding'. Them were all very excited about the idea as this were the most important thing ever to happen on thems tiny island. It were the first time them all agreed on anything. Them made sure each understood the terms before them began.

Each of the five was to build her own throne using only the rocks on the island. The competition was held on the tallest part of the island, so them could all see the thrones that the others were making, so them could see what them were competing with. It dun matter who finished first, but them agreed that the winner would be the one with the grandest throne. The one who won would make all decisions and settle all arguments.

All agreed with each other that the winner would have the final say on everything.

The Glimmeras set to work. Each tried to make her own throne grander than all the others. But because them all could see what the others were doing, every single good idea worked on the thrones was copied. No one wanted to lose, so them copied each other, stone by stone, rock by rock, pebble by pebble. When them finished, all the thrones stood along the pinnacle of the top of the tallest part of thems island, all lined up next to each other.

When it was time to judge the winner of the competition, them all stepped back and looked at the thrones. Them roared with anger and flew at each other, lashing out with thems fists and teeth, as all the thrones, while very grand, looked exactly the same. No one could win.

Them fought and fought till all were exhausted. Them slumped down all cut and bruised, each in thems own throne. A whisper started between them about having a new competition. Them argued and hissed and cursed and swore at each other while the sun rose and set and rose again, but them finally agreed on the terms of the new competition: the one that could sit on her throne for the longest time would be the queen, the leader, the priestess, the witch, the boss of all the others.

The whole thing was, there only ever were them five what lived on that rocky island. Them could only ever rule over one another. Perhaps if other folks, not related, lived there, the Glimmeras would have saved themselves from thems fate by bossing everyone else around. But there never were any other folk, so that never came to pass.

The Glimmeras sat next to each other for a week, arguing the whole time, then a month passed and them scratched and screeched at each other. Of course them were all soiling thems clothes, sweating in the sunshine and shaking in the icy winds of night. Not one would budge. The whole place smelled rank.

Them stewed in thems own filth, screeched and argued and fought and scratched and wriggled and snarled at one another for so many years while thems hair grew long, then longer and longer still. It got all matted together.

Now them can't move away from one another or thems thrones unless them all go, thems hair is so tangled and tousled and woven together. Them look like them are one body with five faces, all joined together, covered over by hair. Them must still have thems own arms and legs and bodies beneath it, hidden away.

Thems hair coils and twists, in parts like a woven rug, in other parts like a tangle of bushes or a whisper of light. In the sunshine the whole mass of hair glimmers, shines back up at the sun like it's competing with its brightness.

The hair covers the whole island; nothing can grow beneath it, as it blocks out all the sunlight. When them walk around thems stony island, them all have to decide when to go as them have to walk together.

If one trips and falls into the sea, them all fall into the sea.

If one has a nightmare, them all have a nightmare.

If one gets sick, all get sick.

If one is hungry, them all have to go to the sea and snatch at the dead fish: only them hate doing anything together almost as much as them hate each other.

Them fight all the time, pull out chunks of each other's hair, trying to break free. Thems fights cause storms. In the winter blizzards the snow is the dandruff from thems heads where them pull and tear at one another, trying to break apart.

We know this is true because the snow here is warm.

*

The fire is glowing, so I lay on another block of peat. Grandmam wouldn't tell me the moral for the story of the Glimmeras herself. She'd ask *me* for it. I'd say something different each time, so she'd get mad like a Glimmera and chase me around the cottage, tugging at my hair. I said the moral were:

dun fight if you can't win, or

dun argue with someone if you dun want to get stuck with them forever, or

if you want snow what isn't cold, dun wash your hair, or

if your family stink, stay on an island together so no one else can smell you.

That last moral were always my favourite, as she'd go for me then and we'd knock chairs sliding and rugs flying, chasing after one another. We broke Mam's mixing bowl, skidding into the kitchen table.

Mam told Grandmam off, said, 'You're acting more like a child than Mary does.' Me and Grandmam both sat in the corner on the floor, plaiting our hair together so our heads were all joined up.

When Mam called us for our tea, we played a game where we would only speak if we could both say the same words as each other, loudly, at the same time. We only ate when we raised our spoons together. Soon we were feeding tattie soup into each other's mouths. Made a right mess.

I know some of the stories Grandmam told me over and over could be just stories, but all stories have some truth in them. The snow here has always been warm since Grandmam told me it were. And there are other reasons I know this story must be true, because from the north shore, where no one lives, we can see a small rocky island with a mound on the top far away in the distance. A glimmering comes off it, like it shines the sun right back at itself.

The men dun go to the north of our island to fish, for there's something in the sea what makes it shine too bright. It looks like stringy seaweed, but we know it's the Glimmeras' hair. There's some kind of poison what fizzes and burrows all the way through it. Whatever it is, the fishes can't swim, can't even live, it's so choked up. It creeps closer when folks step too near the water, so we keep well away.

If the Glimmeras' hair crept up from the sea and covered over our island, we'd get deaded, choked in it. It never has happened yet. I think someone cuts it away from the north shore with a knife. Only there's so much of it, it'd take a boatload of knives to do the job.

I stand up and stretch. Make a cup of mint tea and stir in a little honey. It's getting dark outside. The whole day has gone so fast. Remembering makes me feel more tired than anything else. The key's making me remember things in the time them really took, not like a quick picture memory, or one of the blanks I've got where a memory should be. Dun remember Barney being born, but Mam always said I were terrible sick around then and she had to keep me in my bedroom, so I dun make her get sick and hurt Barney when him were still in her belly.

If Grandmam had still been alive, she'd have nursed me, and I might've remembered that, for she were never patient when I were sick. She were always prodding at me, saying I had to get better and play with her. And them prods of hers did make me get well faster than any kind of tincture. It's comfort, like warm snow, remembering Grandmam. Warm snow makes me not mind so much about being alone.

I take the tea back to the fire, sit down and blank my thoughts. Just think of Grandmam saying 'warm snow'. Not hard to do.

Just blink, make my mind blank. Refuse any other thoughts before them twist in and unravel.

My thoughts are still. I'm blank enough to listen. I pick up the key. It's cold in my hands. Not pulling at memories. So I've done my part of this trade.

Now it will speak back.

Morgan

My parents are behind some door or another, the twins in their bedroom. My book of blank pages and pen have gone. The paper dolls under my mattress have been taken. But it wasn't as I thought it might be. I'm still here. And there wasn't an argument or a fight. It was worse.

No one has looked at me all day.

The twins were in their playroom downstairs this morning, and I went in and they were sitting cross-legged on the floor in the corner, tying their four hands together with a red ribbon. They were staring into one another's eyes. They never hear me when they're staring like that. I saw them again later, scuttling into their bedroom, just along the corridor from mine. I knocked on their door. They didn't answer. I tried the handle but they were holding it on the other side so it wouldn't turn.

I tried to talk to Dad when he came out of my mother's workroom, but he kept his eyes on the ceiling as he walked away, murmured 'Later . . . later . . .' and shut himself away behind another door.

We've eaten three meals together and though our mealtimes are mostly silent anyway, none of them looked at me. Dad didn't even come to the kitchen for the last meal. Mum, Hazel and

Ash ate quickly, I watched their plates till they were empty, and so did they. Then they went away.

So Mum's told everyone to ignore me with their eyes, as a punishment.

If there was a wicked stepmother who lived here with us, she might tell me to sweep the floor and polish the cutlery and do the dishes and clean out the firebox and scrub the range. I could dance with her while I raged and swept, throw ashes at her while she shouted. I could battle with her, disagree, rage and be transformed. We could fight *really* hard but talk about it afterwards. She'd be wicked, beautiful and have a knife-sharp wit. I'd secretly love her, because when we'd fight, she wouldn't cry or sulk, she'd match my angry words, and I'd match hers. I wouldn't have to surrender in order to protect her from how she *feels*, as I do with Mum. I know from all the storybooks that wicked stepmothers are to be avoided if you wish to remain good or pure or ignorant. I really want one.

There isn't a wicked stepmother telling me to punish myself with housework. But I have my real mother, who tells me it's my job to look after everyone else, thinks that housework will keep my feet on the ground and stop my imagination taking over.

But if they're not looking at me, they can't see me. If they're not seeing me, they won't guess what I'm thinking. So for now, I can let my imagination do whatever it likes.

It's almost night and this day has made me feel so invisible, the light has moved across the sky outside slowly, slowly.

My head is full of thoughts and languages and my imagination thinks that all the stories have gone wrong.

I've been dancing in ashes for a hundred years with a frog that has turned from me, kissed a prince and become a toad. I'm meant to have been a much loved daughter made from snow but my parents used icing sugar so I can't melt and leave them thinking I was always perfect. I've developed a fear of enclosed spaces, so I don't want arms around me or a ring on my finger. I'm not hungry for an oven-baked witch, I'm not laughing at an empress who wears the skin of her fattened emperor as her brand new clothes, I'm in a corner, watching the ice queen who is worried about eating rich foods for a feast in her honour, in case she gets heartburn. I'm so tired, but I don't want to sleep for decades to give *anyone* a kiss they've wanted for only a moment.

I need to be lifted out. Picked up, and put down somewhere else. I write on the window:

ANY LOCAL WITCHES, YOUR PRESENCE (WITH BROOMSTICK) IS STILL MUCH NEEDED. WICKED STEPMOTHERS IN POSSESSION OF AXES OR HACKSAWS OR NON-ELECTRICAL POWER TOOLS MAY ALSO APPLY WITHIN.

I lie on my bed, close my eyes and think of our own story. All families must have one. Some are spoken of, and some need to be remembered in fragments in order to be pieced together. I think of Mum in the days after she'd built the fence . . . dressed in magenta overalls and an orange shirt, her hair twisted away under a bright green scarf. She drew roses, sunflowers and violets all over the inside of the fence in coloured chalks. She drew flowers all over the outside of it as well, but I didn't see them. She said, 'Now, *that* shows everyone my talent. And it will wash away in the rain.'

She put the padlock on the gate to keep everyone who lives on the island out. On her charm bracelet, the key to my freedom still clanks and clunks.

When she'd locked the islanders out, and us in, she told me, 'I've met some of the women, they're all mad, they think your father is some kind of deranged man, because who would want to be an undertaker?' She sobbed, 'I'm not like the women who live here and they laugh at my voice because I speak properly. I *won't* be laughed at.'

I said, 'Are there children I can play with?' and she said, 'Where do you keep your loyalty – in your little finger?'

Mum settled into building our furniture once the chalk flowers had been rained away. We were eating lunch on a picnic blanket spread on the kitchen floor. Mum told Dad that she was going to make all the furniture we needed for our home with her own hands. The beds, chairs, shelves and tables. She told him, 'It will all belong to me if I make it.' She glared at him, 'No one else could ever claim it was theirs.'

Dad put his radish sandwich down and stared at it for a long time. He doesn't like us to talk at mealtimes, because he has to concentrate so hard on eating. He didn't always find it hard to eat; in our house on the mainland, he was a lot wider. He used to go out and eat fine food and drink fine wines. But since we've lived here, he chews slowly, never clears his plate and finds it hard to swallow.

I wipe my bedroom window, breathe another fog on it and write:

I HAVE TO LEAVE

If I stay in this locked room for much longer, I'll destroy all the books – tear out the pages and rearrange the paragraphs. I still have my small nail scissors. Little use when it comes to picking a lock, breaking down a fence or digging a tunnel, but they can cut up the pages of a book and make up a new story.

I take down some of the storybooks, the atlas, the mythology, psychology and biology books. I pick up the scissors, and put them down again because if I can't get away from this house, these books could be the only books I ever have. I open them at random pages, move my finger over the words and point at different sentences.

I say aloud . . .

The match girl . . . danced with . . . Medusa . . . her psyche was disturbed by . . . photosynthesis. Travelling to Atlanta . . . she married . . . a wooden spoon. In the snow-capped mountains, carrying . . . fungicides . . . she dissected . . . the Furies. They were diagnosed as . . . lampyridae. The girl had . . . a psychotic episode . . . of the . . . tentacles. She ran away with the travelling . . . metatarsals . . . she wore . . . a golden fleece . . . and lived with seven small . . . ladybirds . . . in the . . . barrier reef . . . she was jilted by her most beloved . . . bipolar . . . bear.

Dad knocks on my door. It's his quietest knock. He opens it and comes in, says gently, 'I'm sorry. She was very upset. She's shut herself away downstairs now. Drawing, I think.'

'And I'm not upset?'

'I didn't want you to be in here alone, angry or tearful.'

'Well, I'm not angry or tearful.'

'That's good.'

'I'm invisible.'

'You aren't. I promise.'

'Don't go. Can I talk to—'

He shakes his head. 'I promised her a cup of tea, so I'd better go and make it. Think about something you like, to make you feel more . . . visible. Collective nouns. You used to like them. How about a symphony of starlings?'

'An unkissablement of toads.'

'That's good, if nonsensical. A . . . twilight of candles.'

'Ah. An infestation of rice.'

'Hm.' His mouth looks stern, but his eyes smile as he closes the door.

Mary

Across the palms of my hands the key hums.

At the touch of it I feel old, because the key is old. I could sit by this fireside for years, holding this key, hearing the memories of the women what've touched it; the stories locked inside its metal. I could sit here for the rest of my life . . . but I need to find the right touch, the right memory, so it'll show me who knows where Barney is.

It's usually the most recent touch metal remembers first. But sometimes it's not just the most recent touch, but an older one, the one the metal itself remembers the deepest – the moment the person holding it felt something them're trying to hide and the metal caught the feeling and stored it up inside itself, because all things metal can keep secrets.

The feeling of the key confuses me; it's been touched by so many. It shows different colours, different sounds – hammering on metal, a band playing an old tune on fiddles, the sound of the sea, all tangle and tilt around my thoughts. Smells of moss, lavender, seaweed, metal smelting at the smithy, yeast, leather, birdskank, rosemary, sage, burning peat, clover wine, frying onions. It has inside it something of all the hands it's been through. Like a riddle, where I've got to work out who's left thems imprint the deepest on it.

The key rings in my hands, is ready to speak. I've got a whole list of questions to ask. It hears this thought and rings hard, sends a judder through my palms. It throws my questions into a blank place: I can't think what them are. The key pulls a picture from me – it rises up through the tangle from other people's hands, the twists of colours and sounds get dull, the smells fade away.

A memory of the first time I felt the secrets kept in metal. I'm small, wandering on the beach. A ring glints in the sand. I pick it up. As soon as I ask it who it belongs to it tells me. Valmarie's wedding ring from Bill. I see her pale face, black eyes, long dark hair, her full lips.

I take it to Mam, tell her, 'You can't have it, it's Valmarie's.' Mam dun believe me, but I tell her over and over that it is. She takes me to Valmarie's house, says on the way, 'That'll show you, you're wrong,' for she wants to trade it.

But Valmarie says, 'Yes, it's mine,' and takes it back. She slips it in her pocket. She's stood there in her doorway with her arms folded. She's interested I can hear her voice in it. Asks me sharp questions. Mam wanders off, picks leaves off her bay bushes. I want to follow her, but Valmarie's talking to me:

'All metal or just rings?'

'I think it's the metal, if I listen close.'

'*Just* metal – or can you hear the call of other lost things?'

'Just heard the song of the metal and your voice when I touched it.'

Mam came back and said to Valmarie, 'Just let her alone. She's got the hands of a broiderer, just like her Mam.'

Valmarie never asked us in.

When we were home, my hands dun know what to do. Them were restless, like them missed the metal of the ring. My fingers kept twitching and I dropped near on everything I picked up.

But Mam must have been watching my hands. She said, 'Set yourself down by me, Mary, and I'll set them wrong fingers of yours to right.' She began to teach me to broider, just the two of us, sat by the fire with the flamelight flickering on the threads. And each stitch I made, though to me them seemed wonky, she looked at them close, nodded and told me I were stitching the best stitches she'd ever seen.

*

'What do you want to tell me?' I listen to the sound of waves from outside.

The key hums, comes alive in my hands. This is the question it wants. It picks up the wash of the waves and the salt water is in this room with me, swirls around me in circles, starting at my feet, rising over my belly, up to my shoulders. Grey, blue, dark, drowning in air, then breathing underwater. Plunging down. Twisting. Dark. Cold.

The waves swash around me.

'Show me.' My hands frozen. A feeling of gulping for air, of limbs thrashing, of salt water, filling my eyes, my mouth.

'Show me.' The key pulses in my hands – it's pushing off the cold with some warm heartbeat deep inside its metal.

Not pushing – a pull, a twist, longing. The deep ocean surges in the key. It's a ringing from one of the women's hands, a yearning the key has locked away. The touch of a woman, weeping for cold. For the taste of salt and the dark of the deep ocean. Transformed, tricked or trapped here. Her secret is here in the key: a woman who used to have a different shape, a Silkie;

117

a seal on the outside, a woman on the inside. The skin of a seal and the heart of a woman. On land, she has the skin of a woman and the heart of a seal. Never content, never at home. A Silkie with a lost pelt is tied to the land in human form, till she can find it and go back to the ocean.

Her face flashes into the dark place behind my eyelids, a pale outline growing brighter.

Valmarie's voice speaks:

Dry people live on dry land breathing dry air in dry homes. On land, they love fire. Their homes are full of fire and flakes of dry skin they can't even feel scratching off. Salt is for jars, for food, for preservative, while fish are sent away to the mainland to be eaten after they have been decayed, rotted, drowned in air.

The room with a candle lit is where the heart beats in each home. I have seen into the heart of every home on this island and taken the things I want. Called a vision to me, and then the desire comes – to hold whatever I want, and make it mine. I am from the water, so my powers lie in fire. People believe me to be powerful, so I have become powerful.

Belief is an infectious disease.

No one would understand if I were to speak of how I miss the pull of the ocean's currents. They would say I should accept this woman's body. No one knows how it feels to have been something more instinctive, more vital.

They can see I am different, so they call me witch, but it is instinct that calls me, even on land. To become powerful, believe it, and others will follow. To fall into love: fall out of yourself. To become the best at anything: be the worst at something else. To feed others: starve. To punish: make some guilt.

*On land, I still have traces on my body of the seal I was.
The paleness of the moon reflects in my face. My hair is as
black as a thickening of water. This land-mirror-beauty is
nothing compared to the beauty in movement, in strength and
power, the love and the ache in the wide black eyes of a seal.
And yes, power. There's power in beauty, whether the woman
wants to be beautiful, or not. Without my sealskin, I am trapped
here being beautiful. Always searching, trying to find something
more.*

*Something in one of these rooms shimmers at me. I see what
I want, I take it. I go to their home when they are sleeping and
steal it.*

Then I don't want it any more.

*What is a diary, a letter, a child's toy, a box, a necklace,
a coin or a flower when what I really want is my home.
What good can come from the theft of someone's hope, their
secrets or their love, someone's grief, when I can't get what
I need?*

*Each night I dig the graveyard as if my hands have claws.
How can this be allowed to happen, that dreams die down, rot
among the corpses, to nothing? Look underneath the soil, where
the roots hang down, tangled in bones. Where earth rains from
my spade.*

Out in the graveyard, buried among the dead, is my sealskin.

I try to move my hands, put down the key. It freezes. Heavy on
my palms. I open my eyes, the room is full of seawater. Pebbles
are scattered across the floorboards. A herring flicks past my
face. In the fireplace, tendrils of seaweed stretch up the chimney.
I'm like a rock, fixed, not able to move.

Valmarie is a thief.

I ask, 'Has she got my brother?'

The key pushes the question away and a bell sound clanks, muffled, underwater.

My eyes close.

This is not the end of Valmarie's story. The air in this room feels dry in my throat, and my feet sink in cold sand.

Valmarie's voice speaks low:

My sealskin was stolen when I was seventeen, washed up in a storm. The man called Bill found me. I fell out of my sealskin, and lay as a woman, trembling and naked on a rock on the shore. My sealskin lay beside me, though I didn't yet have the strength to climb back into it. He said my eyes were stars, my hair the night, my skin smooth as cream. Some such falseness. He couldn't see I would have been far more beautiful inside my sealskin, that the light from the sky bounced off the fur, that the curve of my back met the shape of the waves, that the surges and ripples of my muscles inside it could twist and turn my whole body spiralling through currents, into the depths.

I reached for my sealskin. Bill's eyes burned me. He picked it up, said he'd take me to his home to recover, said that later he would help to get me back to the ocean again. My sealskin was soft and delicate, its fur dark and silver-tipped like glints on ice. He threw it over his shoulder. It was nothing to him, but when he carried me up the hill to his house, I stroked it on his shoulder with my fingertips.

I never saw it again.

My sealskin was my strength. The only way I could get back home. Inside it I was myself.

The thief Bill carried me home, dosed me with some bitter herbal tea to soothe my drying throat, night after night. Stole my memory. I forgot all of who I was, lost myself in Bill's words. Hung onto them as if they were ropes thrown from a ship, and

I would drown if I let go. Bill and this island claimed me as a possession. He told me his story. I was born on this island, I knew him all my life, loved him and only him. He hid my sealskin and married me. When I stopped drinking the tea, and my memory came back, it was too late.

I tried everything to get him to speak of it. To tell me where it was. He said he didn't want to lose me, he couldn't remember, he was drunk when he hid it. It was stolen, someone tore it up, it was destroyed. I seduced him, flattered him, cried for days, fed him, starved him, shouted, begged, tore at my hair. He'd never say.

I realised that a part of me still carried it with me – a fragment of it shielded my heart. It kept the coldness safe deep inside me, where it could never be touched. This coldness spread, for the currents of the sea still surge in my blood.

He followed where I led him. Took favours granted as signs of hope or love, some such gifts. His hope allowed me to lead him into the worst kind of currents – the ones of self-deception. From those currents, sooner or later, there are no ways to journey back.

I let him believe I loved him, showed him by lying with my body. He got me pregnant. The young nearly tore me apart clawing his way out of me, yet I loved Dylan from the moment I melted into his black eyes. Bill watched me with him, said I spent too much time feeding him. I saw jealousy in his face.

But at last I had someone to love.

I stopped speaking to Bill. Stopped dreaming, wouldn't look at him when he came home, was never in his bed.

After a time, Bill said, 'You're silent like you're already in your grave. I've lost you and no one is mourning but me.'

After years, he told me, 'Buried your sealskin somewhere in the graveyard. It's been there, rotting all these years.'

Fragments, pieces that were once a part of me.

Dylan disappeared the day after Bill told me where he'd buried my sealskin, when I finally knew. My Dylan, my young. Not long turned thirteen. I left him lying on his bed in his room, went outside to stare at the graveyard. When I went back inside, he was gone.

I said to Bill, 'Another piece of me has been taken.'

Then I cried.

This loss is as deep as the loss of my sealskin. All losses open doors into older grief.

Bill took my hand. He said, 'Now you're in tears, showing me this, I feel closer to you than what I ever have.' I snatched my hand away.

Naked and stolen all over again.

I told Bill how much I hated him. Told him I never loved him, and shipwrecked his self-deception as he buried my hope.

My sealskin's fate, but not yet mine. I want justice.

Kelmar's son gone, then mine. Then Annie's son, and now Beatrice's. With Beatrice buried, and Annie devoted to Martyn, it's down to me and Kelmar to call up the help we need. Take whatever truth it brings.

Morgan

Mum unlocks my bedroom door, comes in, folds her arms and says, 'You haven't washed up. There's a stack of dishes left, I can smell them from here.'

Her voice doesn't belong here.

I put down my book. 'How can I wash up, when you've decided I need to be locked in my room and don't even . . .'

She glares at me. Taps a finger on the door. Strokes a whorl in the wood. Waits.

'All right!' I push past her, stamp down the stairs to the kitchen. There's a cold cup of tea on the floor in the hall, so I take it into the kitchen.

The washbowl has dirty plates stacked in it. I go out of the back door to the well in the garden, and like an overworked kitchen girl, I sigh as I fill a bucket with water, bring it in and pour it over the plates till the washbowl is full. I plunge in my hands and it's freezing cold. I'm a serving girl in a grand castle, seeking something precious to steal that will buy me my freedom.

On the mainland, our house was full of everything we could ever possibly want, but none of it felt like it belonged to us. I watched Mum pace the rooms while Dad was out, spied on her as she stroked the grand piano that none of us could play; she opened a rosewood trunk and lifted out a beaded wedding dress that she'd never worn and wouldn't fit her; she fingered the embossed spines of a collection of antique hardback books, printed in a language that none of us could read.

I pick up a plate gently, run my fingertips over it and pretend it's made of ivory.

Mum comes in. She leans against the solid kitchen table; it creaks under her weight. I feel her eyes like a scratch on the back of my neck. 'Don't leave the kitchen in such a mess next time.'

The room fills with her heavy thoughts.

I'm not a serving girl any more.

'What is it?' I ask.

Her eyes watch my back. 'I saw what you wrote on your window. *I have to leave.*'

I wipe another plate clean, turn away from the washbowl and put it on the kitchen table, get a dry cloth and put it next to the plate. I pretend I'm a queen and Mum's my servant. I announce, 'You should dry,' and go back to the washbowl.

Mum doesn't notice I'm being a queen. She says, 'Writing things down doesn't make them true.'

'Stealing things from under other people's mattresses doesn't make them yours.'

'What about me?' I know she's squeezing tears up in her eyes. 'I can't breathe . . .'

'You're selfish, Morgan. You know, there was a time I couldn't breathe. Giving birth to you – do you think I could breathe then? Your father didn't have to go through that. You've been talking to him, haven't you? What have you been saying about me?'

I'm not a queen any more. I say, 'You *chose* to give birth to me . . .' I put another plate on the table.

She says, 'When you talk about leaving here, do you think *I* can breathe? Who'll look after the twins? And do *this* . . .' She waves her hand at the clean plates. 'I'll shrivel. Is that what you want?'

I wipe another plate and wonder what shrivelling might feel like. But I say, 'The twins are fine, they're so . . . involved with each other, they don't need anyone—'

'You're weedy. I don't like looking at you.' She folds her arms and the table creaks.

The washbowl looks far away. My arms seem really long. I watch my tiny hands scrub at a fork. Three choices: Angry. Silent. Walk away.

She says, 'At your age girls think they know everything. You're wrong. You wouldn't survive anywhere else. You're too sensitive, you'd get hurt. You'd have an accident. Someone would kidnap you. They like long blonde hair, they like thin women because they fall over easier than fat ones. Can you imagine how I'd feel, you not here, worrying about you, all the horrendous things that can possibly happen, I'd think of all of them, every single one, I'd never stop worrying, never sleep for caring. It would cripple me. You couldn't find a job. You're all book talk and attention-seeking. The only thing you're good at is reading, and no one gets paid to read. We shouldn't have taught you. You read too much, all those words have got stuck in your head, making you think you could belong anywhere but where you're standing. It's ridiculous.'

A hammering of words.

I spin round with the fork in my hand. 'Mum, the only place I'm ever standing is at this washbowl. I could stand at a washbowl anywhere.' I gesture through the window at the fence outside. 'Nothing happens. Nothing but the paint chipping, and the whispers on the other side.'

'Put that down.' She points at the fork I'm pointing at her. 'What whispers? There are no whispers! I'm protecting you from them!' she shouts, her voice is a knife. 'They wouldn't understand you – and they'd say hateful things about me to you! I can't trust you not to listen to them, not when they're telling you lies about me, and then where would I be? A daughter who hated me, that would be terrible.'

I put the fork on the stack of clean, dripping plates. I say, 'They call us three "the hidden daughters". I've heard whispers on the other side of the fence.' I wash up a handful of spoons.

'When will you stop making up stories about yourself? Hidden daughters. One day I'll tell you about hearing voices—'

'You *have* told me about hearing voices! You've told me that you don't, but that you're special and you'd be the one to hear them if anyone could. There aren't any voices in this house, not the whisper of a ghost. Even if there were, you wouldn't hear them, because you don't listen!' I crash the spoons on top of the plates.

Her hands shake. 'Stupid girl!' She bangs her fists on the kitchen table and I hear a clank of metal. 'You belong with us.'

I turn back to the washbowl. A silver knife gleams under the water. I wash the surface with a cloth, the silver glistens. I say, 'I don't belong *anywhere*,' and slice my thumb. The scarlet blood seeps out. I put my thumb in my mouth.

Mum walks out of the kitchen. I run the cloth over the knife and wipe it clean.

Mary

I heard women passing by earlier, talking of the Thrashing House key. Annie called round again, said she'll keep looking in on me. She's fearful about Valmarie and Kelmar calling up the owl woman. Says them dun know when to stop.

I lean the moppet on my pillow under a blanket with its face poking out of the top like it's really Barney. Tell it, 'Go to sleep, little one. It's got dark quick. Not long, before the bells ring out for the dreamings.'

But them can't.

The Thrashing House key sings in my hands when I take it out from its hiding place. I wonder whose turn it should be to ring the bells. Camery's face is there behind my eyelids when I blink. If the dreamings dun get took, folks might just have to hang onto all the dreamings and thoughts them want to get rid of. It might mean that some folks get to talking more.

I wrap a warm blanket around me and sit on my bed next to the moppet. I hold the key in both hands and close my eyes. The key hums, almost hurts my hands. Like it wants to be held, but it's full of a cold gale. It wants something what can really touch it, but it could just blow away, for the winds are too strong.

This key is different to other metal. Other metal just gives up what I want to know, gives me a face or an answer like it's glad to. But this key is so old, and it's used to the touch of so many hands, it feels like I should do what it tells me, and not the other way round.

The next question gets blown into my head: 'Who's watching me?' It's not what I wanted it to be. I try to change it, to ask about Barney, but the question's linked itself to me. This is the question the key wants asked. It holds me locked, the gale blows my hands, them clasp on tight, the key grasps my hands back. The question won't let me go.

So I ask it.

'Who's watching me?' Behind my eyelids, darkness shifts around.

A feeling spreads out of the key; arms reach up to clasp around me, the arms dun hold me, them pass right through. I try to open my eyes but the key blows a gale over my face. My hands are blown onto the key, the key is blown onto my hands. The wind dies down.

The face is blurry and faint. Mam's face, behind my eyelids. Her dark hair like mine, her face pointed, circles under her eyes what stare off to something distant. The key rings out her voice from the past.

Tears soak my face as I listen:

I want this child I'm heavy with to come out. Too heavy for my back. It's funny to think of me being someone's Mam. Ned as someone's Da. Him will tell this child stories of the sea . . .

It's my turn on the bell list and I'm so heavy I dun know how I'll make it up all the steps. Shouldn't have to go there yet. It should be someone else. I've only been of age to go to the Weaving Rooms a week, and it's my turn already.

So here is the key around my neck. Them say the list's always the same rotation, dun matter whether I'm ready for it or not. All this secrecy, and perhaps I'm not seeing it the right way, but what if it's all just a load of fuss over a matter of bells and sleep?

If this key were to unlock my belly, that would be something. Unlock me, let the baby come out gentle.

Ned says him will catch as much fish as him can, and I've done so many broideries that the pictures got strange. Some of my mother's stories crept into my hands.

Unlock a memory . . . the north shore. The sun shines. Then it were dark. Too dark.

I were a child.

Lost. Couldn't believe how far back the tunnels in the caves went till I were caught too deep. I found a drawing of this key on a cave wall. I'd never seen this key then, just thought the drawing must mean a door were close by. I got afraid.

Mam were outside, under a grey sky, looking to the north. 'Strange winds blow down from the Glimmeras,' she said, when I finally found my way back to her. She said nothing about me being lost. Like it was only a moment I'd been wandering, far inside the caves. If this baby is a girl, she'll never let me be so lost. Not like my own Mam did. I need a daughter to love me.

My eyes flood tears over my cheeks. I want to keep this key forever, so I can call up Mam's voice, this moment, years ago when she first held this key in her hands and left her imprint in the metal. She's left a hole in the world what's Mam-shaped and no one else fits in it. Not even Annie, though she loved Mam so she's always been good to me. Not Beattie or Nell or any of the women I know. Because Mam brought me into the world and there's no one can replace someone what's done that.

Mam sounded like she wanted me to love her more than Grandmam did. Dun think I did that enough. When Grandmam lived with us, Mam often got me to come away from her, wanted me to do something with her instead. But I loved playing with Grandmam, so I were grouchy with Mam when she wanted to teach me how to bake cinnamon biscuits, or to learn a new stitch. I never told her I loved her. Never knew she'd not be here till she weren't. I wipe my eyes on my sleeve. Now I can't tell her that ever.

If she were here, I'd say: I loved you because we were belonging people and you made me, cooked me up in your belly, didn't throw me out cold before I were ready. You made me live when you could have let me die, and babies *can* die, so easy. But I dun, for you must have kept me warm, loved me even when I screamed you awake.

Only a week in the Weaving Rooms and her first turn on the bells. Too young to have heard much women's talk. That tells me why every year on my birthday she looked at me like I'd hurt her. She'd say the right words and give me a gift, a new toy, a coat or a new downy pillow or the wooden box I keep my keys in. Her eyes were telling me how much it hurt her, bringing me out of her and into the world. Only I never knew it then. I'd smile at the gift she gave me, eat the cakes she'd bake, but as soon as I could, I'd get away from her eyes, curl up in bed under my blanket and try to sleep the rest of my birthday away.

I pull the blanket tight around me. She dun look at me like that the rest of the year. Dun have to remember her eyes like that. I can blank out anything I dun want to think of. It's easy. I just blink, and think of something else. Mam fed me soup and honey tea when I were sick. She taught me the letters and numbers when I were so little, Annie said I wouldn't take to it yet, but I did, because Mam believed I would.

On Barney's first birthday, Da went off fishing and Mam went off somewhere early that morning. When she came back in, I were sat on my bed, holding Barney. I were gazing in hims eyes and him were staring back, like him wanted a proper look. Mam smiled at us, said she'd been out to pick me some flowers, 'For you're always picking flowers for me.' She gave me a posy of violets and took Barney out of my arms.

Memories dun have to be real, them're just pictures, like broideries. Just got to make the memory strong enough, the picture real. Stitch it so fine that the colours gleam. Think of it over and over, pass my thoughts through the eye of the needle, make the threads hold firm, like a herringbone ladder stitch, get the split stitches with the needle right through the middle of the thread, till it looks just the way I want it to.

Or if it dun come easy, cut it all away and stitch something different.

The question I asked the key were: who is watching me?

So it's Mam.

Mam holding the doors shut when she wants me to stay home. Mam putting her broiderie of the owl woman on my pillow.

The windows rattle in the wind. Nothing here but me and a draught. And this key I shouldn't have. A cold breath on my cheek. Not really. Just a draught. I need to piss. I get out of bed, wrap a shawl around me, go out the back door to the outhouse, freeze my backside, come back in through the kitchen, get the moppet and go into the main room and get under the table.

The table is like a house indoors what gets no weather. I feel younger, smaller than I really am. I can pretend I live down here with Barney, in our house under the table. I whisper to the moppet, 'Where are you?' but it blows back the sound of waves in the wind.

Outside, a gale picks up. It wails around the cliffs.

I hug my knees to my chest.

Rain raps hard and the window rattles. I crawl out from under the table and stuff a cloth along the edges of the window to catch the leaks. The sky is dark, thick with black clouds. The wind rages, the waves crash, froth and roar like them're being chased.

There's three women with dark shawls over thems hair coming along the beach through the rain, and the women have seen me. One raises a hand but I can't see who them are, for the ripples in the windowpanes blur with the rain.

I hide the moppet in the bedroom.

A loud knock on the front door.

I put the Thrashing House key up the chimney, on the ledge where the flue twists back, wipe the soot off my hands onto my dress, go to the front door, twist the latchkey and call out, 'Come in.'

Them open the door. It's Chanty, Nell and Beattie.

'Come in, you're drenched.' I smile at Nell and Beattie.

Nell says, 'We're not here for long. Got others to see, unless—'

I gasp out. 'Is there news of Barney?'

Beattie says, 'The key's gone.'

'What key? Come in, you're soaked.'

Chanty says, 'Look, Mary, we all know you're in the habit of thieving keys. You were round Nell's and she dun find hers since she left you stood by her front door. Had to break the window, and though you'd think Dougan wouldn't mind putting a new window in—'

Nell says, 'Him'd walloped hims head on something, and

weren't feeling up to it.' She glares at Chanty. 'Anyway, hims fixed the window, and there's no real harm done.'

Chanty says, 'And—'

I say, 'I never took anything that's not mine.' Nell's looking at me like she's being kind and she's about to stop. Rain streams down her face.

Beattie says, 'It's the Thrashing House key. Valmarie had it last, and it's gone. We need it back. Now, we're not blaming you, we're doing the rounds. If you got anything to say, you'd best say—'

Chanty butts in, 'Folk'll be worse angered if *someone* turns out to have lied about it and made all us women go out in the rain, instead of being indoors.'

'Well, I'm sorry you're wet, Chanty. I have asked you in, but you're not wanting any warm from me. Funny that.'

Nell says, 'Settle, you pair.'

'I dun know anything of the key.' I scratch my cheek. 'If Valmarie had it last, you'd best be going to her. She might've hung onto it. Want to use it to call up something more fearful than the owl woman.' I nod at Chanty. '*You'd* best watch out.' I glance up at the dark sky.

Nell says, 'Is Annie indoors? Does she—'

'She's not said anything to me.'

'Keep your ears open. The bells need to be rung.'

'I'll say if I hear anything.'

Beattie says, quiet, 'Do that, Mary. Soon.'

Chanty turns to Beattie and moans that I stole her key five years ago, and she had to trade for a new one from the smithy by doing a lot of stitching, and that her Mam said she were careless, but she knew it were me, and she says how she felt terrible – and poor her, and her poor Mam . . .

'Oh, dun wallow in it,' says Nell.

I fold my arms. 'Chanty you're half drowned. Best get indoors or you'll get *full* drowned. That'd be a shame.'

Beattie steps away from the door. 'Chanty, you're of age. Act it. Come on. Annie's next.'

Them walk away towards Annie's cottage. I pull the door shut and lock it, quick. Can't keep this key. But . . . if the bells ring out, them'll think the key's been found and I can keep it for longer.

For them're right, the bells still need to be rung.

*

No one is up here on the cliff path. I walk around the side of the Thrashing House, the wind tangles my hair. I unlock the bell tower door and step inside. The hinge on the door creaks as I close it behind me and lock myself in.

There's a curved wooden staircase, the steps worn from women's feet. A box of matches and a jar of candles at the foot of the steps. I light a candle. The walls are curved, made from wood, but all in one piece, no joins anywhere. There are pictures of women painted on the wood, the colours faded. The pictures show women climbing the stairs, each holding the Thrashing House key. All different women – a bride, a pregnant woman, a dancing woman, a woman with a spade, one with a spindle, another at a loom and a stooped old woman with an axe. The staircase curves around and I touch my fingertips on the cracked face of a young pregnant woman, clover flowers painted on her dress over her bump.

A groan, from inside the wall. I climb faster, my boots stamp too loud. A creak. The pictures look angered, dark red eyelashes, all the painted eyes of the women can see me, too young to be here.

I stop and hold the candle to the nearest picture. A drip of sap comes out of the corner of one of her eyes. Mixes with the red paint. She's crying blood.

I spin round and crash down the stairs, the candle goes out and I drop it and run so fast I wallop into the back of the door. I unlock it, take the key from the lock, get outside, away, slip and slide on the grass, get to the top of the steep path what leads back home.

*

Back in my cottage, breathing hard, I put the key on the table and loosen the bindings around my chest. Through the dark, through the wind, the bells ring out. I dun lock the bell tower door behind me. That's all it is.

Someone's gone in there and is clanging out the bells.

The rain rattles down on the roof and I get under the table and put my hands over my ears, and even when the bells stop, I stay here, listening to my breathing.

Someone knocks on the door.

I call out, 'Come in!' Scrabble out, see the Thrashing House key lying on the table and put a cushion over it as the front door opens. I spin round. It's Beattie, her hair still wet, clinging to her plump cheeks.

I say, 'The bells rang – someone must've found the key.'

'We looked – no one were ringing them bells.'

'How—'

'Mary, I'm done in. Dark in here, but.' She glances around the room. 'I've got to get home. Sleep. But the women are pointing the finger at you. Chanty's stirring.'

'I dun ever take—'

She sighs. 'See, Mary, old Jessup says her key's gone as well, and she swears she left it in her door, on the inside. So folk're talking.'

'If the bells ring by themselves – what does that mean?'

She shudders. 'Dun know. But the bell tower door were *open*. Camery's gone off, says she knows where she can get a strong plank to hammer it shut.'

Morgan

Tonight, my bedroom door isn't locked. I look out of the window. A woman wearing a pale shawl thrown around her head and shoulders is surging forwards through the fields in the dark.

I wave.

She doesn't see me. But she's coming this way. Moving like the wind is blowing her here, the rain, lashing her face. She's still closer, and disappears behind the fence.

I tiptoe out of my room and downstairs, turn the key in the front door and dash outside.

My bare feet are cold in the wet grass.

She stands by the gate, I can see her between the slats in the fence. I put my eye to a gap.

She's got red fingers and they're clutching a small sack of rice.

I ask her, 'Have you come for me?'

'No.'

'Are you a witch?'

'No.'

'Well, what do you—'

Dad is right behind me, in his satin dressing gown. He pulls me away from her. 'Quiet, child.' He asks her, 'Has someone died?'

Her voice shakes. 'None are dead. But we need a plank. Just one. Need to seal up a door.'

'A door?' he asks.

'Can't say more, but it's to be done tonight. Now. Look, I've brought you another sack of this stuff.'

I press my hands on the fence and look at her between the slats. '*You've* been leaving the rice here – is it some kind of message?'

Dad pulls me away, frowning. His face shines with rain. He says, 'Morgan. Indoors.'

The woman says, 'It's forwards trade, I want a good coffin box, solid, polished wood, flowers and everything, but if I can have a plank, I'll ask the tall men for another sack of this stuff, and bring it the next time . . .'

'No, don't,' Dad says, glaring at me. 'We don't have any use for it.'

Pulling Dad's sleeve, I say, 'Get the padlock key from Mum, let me get the plank, I'll go with her – she'll need help to carry it.'

'Dun need help,' the woman says. 'Only a plank is all.'

'Dad?'

'No. You can't. Indoors,' Dad says. 'Now.' Rain drips from his nose. He glares at me.

My soaked hair sticks to my face as I walk to the side of the house and watch him from the corner. I listen. He says to the woman, 'I'll get you one if you take it quietly, and don't come back for another. My wife's asleep – I don't want her disturbed. I'll pass it over the fence. You're strong enough?'

'Aye.'

He glances up at the windows and goes indoors.

I go back to the gate. 'Can you get me out? Can I stay with you?' I whisper.

'Got no room at mine. Can you stitch?'

I shake my head.

'Knit? Weave? Spin?'

'No.'

She steps towards the fence and looks closely at me between the slats. 'Any good at hooking?'

'What?'

'Crochet.'

'No.'

'Well, what *can* you do then, hidden daughter? What're them doing, keeping you indoors, wrapping your soft toes in petals?' She comes still closer to the fence and her eye stares through the gap at my bare feet.

'I can read, cook, sweep – I can tell stories, I know *some* things – I've read—'

'You'd need to trade.'

'Trade?'

'Trade with your hands. Or have your belonging people,' she nods at our house, 'let you grow with useless fingers?'

'They've taught me all kinds of—'

The front door opens.

Back at the side of the house, I watch Dad lean a dusty plank of shipwreck wood up against the thirteen-foot-high fence. He lifts it and tilts it over with a push. The woman must have caught it as the end of the plank rises, then slides down, disappears on the other side.

She says to Dad, 'I'll leave this here anyway.'

'No,' he says. 'We don't need any rice. Tell me, is there news about those men?'

'Ta for this.' I hear her dragging the plank away through the grass.

Dad glances up at the windows again and goes back in through the front door.

I'm feeling too useless to find any choices at all, so I stare up at the dark sky and let the rain soak my face.

Mary

'You're different to my other keys. I'm *borrowing* you. I might sound mad and crazed talking to you but it helps me think and no one's listening. So this is what you've done.

'You've made me remember Grandmam's stories for comfort, so that makes me think there's something bad I'm going to find out.

'I know that Da took Barney, and that's why him were sent mad.

'But I dun think Barney were took to the main land by the tall men like the others, for Langward were searching for him here. So Da must have given him to someone.

'And you've told me Mam's watching me.' I swallow, hard. 'Is it *that* I were meant to hear?'

The key lies there, silent.

'Look, I know I've got to give you back.'

Think.

I stare at the key. 'What do I need to know from this whole day you've made go too fast? Memories and stories and voices . . .'

Think.

Mam in the caves on the north shore. The loneliest place, furthest from all our homes. Caves and tunnels what stretch back so deep under the island, no one knows how far. That would be the best place on this island to hide someone, if you dun want them to be found.

Think.

Da went up to the peat pits not far from the north shore near on every week of hims life. If I were Da and I dun want to hurt Barney myself, but I had to hide him so well him would *never* be found, that's where I'd choose.

*

My belly feels hungry-sore. I rummage in the kitchen cupboard and cook up some kale and onions in butter. Kale's good for strength and I'll need that if I'm to go up to the caves. I throw an egg in the mix and the smell of it makes me shake I'm so hungry.

As soon as the food's ready, I sit on my bed with a spoon and the pot, like me and Barney did when Da were out fishing, and gannet it all down. The moppet lies on the blanket next to me. It dun move and won't talk. There's not even the sound of the sea inside it. On the blanket is a small light coil of hair like the finest thread. One of Barney's. I put the pot on the floor, pinch the hair off the blanket and twist it around my thumb.

Someone taps on the window.

'Mary? It's Kelmar again.'

'Get gone.' I whisper. I put the hair under my pillow.

Kelmar taps again. 'It's important.'

I scrunch down under the blanket and shut up my ears with my hands. Mam were important. Mam dun talk to her, and I've got to have one belonging person I can trust, even if she's deaded. I push my hands even harder over my ears and close my eyes.

*

I start awake, see the moppet's raggedy face on the pillow. Dun mean to fall asleep.

The bedroom door rattles. I hurl myself out of bed and swing open the bedroom door.

In the main room the curtains blow up. The window is open. There's a lit candle guttering on the table. Valmarie's been here. The room looks the same: Mam's chair, the empty table, the worn rugs . . . the tongs on the hearth . . .

I put my hand up the chimney and run my fingers over the empty ledge. I put my hands over my ears and crouch down on the floor. Groan so loud it echoes below me through the floorboards, comes back up at me from the storm room.

The Thrashing House key has gone.

I get a bag and put in the moppet, a blanket, a sharp knife and a small box of broiderie threads and needles of Mam's. Dun want to be away for long without something of hers with me. I blow out the candle, put my coat on and sling the bag over me.

I try the front door, but it won't open. I whisper, 'I know that's you holding it shut Mam, stop scaring me.' I make sure it's locked, take out the latchkey, climb on the table and get outside through the window.

I take the latchkey to the cold room. I close my eyes to the dark and the ice and the barrels and whisper to the latchkey, 'I'm leaving you here, for I dun know how long I'll be away for. But if I get lost in the caves, and if Barney's found by someone else, be here for him. Let him safe into our home.' I put the latchkey on the ledge near the cold room door.

I'm going to thieve the Thrashing House key back and go up to the caves on the north shore. Because if I'm wrong about Da hiding Barney in the caves, I'll still need the key and all the women's voices in it.

I'm going to burglar Valmarie's house.

*

It's a long climb up the path, and in the dark after the rain the grass and rocks are all streaked with silver and shadows. The night makes everything different colours. Puts me in mind of a broiderie of Mam's. Stars up above and all these dragonflies skittering around green and grey flowers, what grew and stretched towards the moon.

I bit my lip and told her, 'The colours are wrong.'

She said, 'It isn't wrong, it's just different, for there's a sliver of a moon throwing shadows around.'

I thought hard about it and decided she meant that the moon is like a fisherman, up there disguised in all that deep blue, catching stars in a net. Only it catches shadows as well, and throws them back down to us.

From the circle of boulderstones, I can see the graveyard hill. Starlight glints on the granite headstones. Mam's buried in the graveyard, a headstone with her name, Beatrice Jared, and mine and Barney's names carved below it. When Barney and me die, the deadtaker will score out our names from Mam's grave and we'll get our own graves.

I remember the coldness of Mam's skin in her coffin box. I kissed her brow to say goodbye, and she were covered all over in sea thrift with pink flowers. The flowers seemed so alive, though them'd die all over her when them were sealed up and under the soil. I felt sorry for them flowers.

A sharp wind whips my hair across my face. I crouch in the

wet grass next to one of the boulderstones. I can feel the cold of the stone on my cheek. Just below the Thrashing House, with a clear view of the graveyard hill, Valmarie's house is tucked in a hollow.

My hands look like white gloves. I cover my fingertips with my mouth, breathe on some warm. Closing my eyes, I think of the Thrashing House key. Just to be sure. I think of its shape, the heaviness of the metal, the pattern of arrows in it. And it *is* Valmarie's face what swirls up behind my eyelids. The key is back where it belongs and perhaps that's where it should be, so the bells get rung, so the women can pass it between them, night after night after night, and everything can be as it always has been . . . but the palms of my hands feel empty. My hands still want the stories trapped in the key.

I look down the hill at Valmarie's house. A candle sparks alight in her window. She's not asleep.

Morgan

A cough. I wipe my eyes and look up. Dad stands in the dark at the other end of the kitchen table. He says, 'I didn't hear you go back to bed.'

I say, 'You look like a ghost.'

He says, 'Light a candle.'

'No.'

'Don't tell your mother—'

'I don't tell her anything.'

'—that I gave away a plank.'

I push my hair back and smooth it down neatly. I choose to try being a psychologist. 'You don't want her to be disturbed.' I put my palms together.

'No.' He sighs.

Psychologists make people talk. I wonder if he will. He isn't looking at me. I say, 'Does she think there would be damage if we weren't so trapped?'

He sits down opposite me, puts his elbows on the table. He glances at me, and away. He looks like he's been caught. He says, 'She wants to live like this.'

'It's some dream, to know no one.'

'She can't cope with other people's emotions.'

I nod, wisely. 'I've noticed.'

'She finds them unsettling.'

'It's unsettling that we're alone and you're talking like her.'

'What?'

'There's a word for that – mirroring? It's in the psychology book.'

His voice is louder. 'It's not an appropriate word when she's not here to mirror. So you've read a book and you think you can diagnose her?'

We stare at each other in the dark.

I look away. 'I don't want to.'

He says again, 'You think you *can* diagnose her?'

Outside the window, I can see the pink fence, dim in the dark. I say, quietly, 'Have you heard of narcissism?'

Now he's looking at the fence through the window. He says, 'You'd do better just to see her as vulnerable, in need of our care, rather than fitting her to a list of symptoms. She needs empathy.'

'*She* needs empathy?'

'What point is there in analysing her?'

'I need a case study. Our family might be my only one. If it is, I won't be a very good psychologist.'

'We don't need one.'

I lean forwards and he looks back at me. I say, 'Did she ever see a *real* psychologist?'

'She wouldn't have wanted to. She doesn't want to be . . . dissected. Sampled or discussed.'

'Well, she's probably deeply happy that we live on an island with no psychologists. Unless everyone who lives here is a psychologist. But then, I wouldn't know, would I?'

'She has every right to expect our understanding.'

'And I don't?'

'She needs to feel safe.'

'If I was a real psychologist, I'd say, *there's no danger.*'

He pauses. 'Don't attempt to diagnose her. It won't do her, or you, any good.'

'Has she always been this focussed on herself – is it her ego—'

'Her ego?'

'—or her id?'

'What about them?'

'That make her this . . . emotionally—'

'I don't want to discuss her like this.'

'But we never discuss anything.'

'We're talking now.'

I stare out of the window again. 'So, this is you, speaking to me. And you're still not telling me anything.'

'She's become more . . . fragile over the years. Her emotions have been jarred, become set at some young age when she was too often left alone. Some parents are more . . . attentive than others. These things are learned through generations.'

'So, what is she passing on to me, and Hazel, and Ash – that parents should have temper tantrums whenever their children do anything that upsets them?'

'You could at least try to understand her.'

I sigh. 'I am trying. She felt unloved. Is she loved enough now?'

'We bring towards us, so often, that which we are most afraid of.'

'Is that a quotation?'

'I don't remember.'

'You asked that woman, the plank woman, about—'

'Don't tell your mother that either. She'll find it . . .'

'Disturbing. That someone wanted something from us other

than burial. Disturbing that you know something that's happening here. So tell me. I won't be disturbed.'

'They don't teach boys to read here. Your mother finds that idea threatening. She thinks that if men are treated like simple beasts, that's how they'll behave.'

'Has she ever encountered a simple beast?'

'In her nightmares.'

'She has nightmares?'

'Always.' His eyes stare at his hands. His fingers drum on the table.

I ask, 'What do they do?'

'Who?' He raises his eyebrows.

I spread out my palms in a psychologically open gesture. 'The beasts in her nightmares. What do they do?'

'Turn their backs—'

'That doesn't sound like a nightmare, it sounds like body language.'

'—because they want to eat her up, but they don't love her enough. They would rather die of hunger.'

'Are you saying she wants to be eaten?'

'Have you ever had a dream where you're shouting and screaming for something you desperately need, only to find that all the people turn away, and their backs are hairy, ridged, frightening to you?'

'No. There's no point in analysing my dreams. They're all the same thing happening over and over again.'

'Until you do, you won't understand her.'

'Do you?'

He shudders. 'She says our dreams are tied together.'

'And are they?'

He meshes his fingers, glances up at me. 'What?'

'The men who live here. The men who can't read. Are they

really like beasts? When you bury them, are their backs hairy, from a lack of literacy? Is there a collective noun for men with hairy backs?'

'Keep your voice down. Not that I've encountered.'

'In the garden at home. Our real home, do you remember telling me that earthworms were . . .'

'I may have said they were cautious.'

'You said they were *discreet*. You've forgotten.'

'You're testing me.'

'I'm just confirming whether your long-term memory is working or not. Or perhaps testing my own. I was trying to ask, what were you saying to the plank woman about some men?'

'The drain was blocked.' He pauses.

I tap my fingers on the table.

He says, 'Your mother sent me out to the smithy – she needed a rod to unblock it. The smithy talked. And I've overheard passers-by, whispers—'

'So *you* don't deny the whispers are there?'

'She says the people on this island don't understand her. She believes *we* don't listen. No wonder she needs this safety. Can you imagine how it must feel for her, believing no one ever hears her?'

'But she talks all the time. *She* doesn't listen, so she can't tell when we hear her.'

'Give her time.'

'How many years does she need?'

'As many as it takes.' He slides his chair out and stands up. His dressing gown is still wet from the rain.

I say, 'Aren't you cold?'

He says, 'I *do* understand how you feel. It might not always seem that way, to you, but—'

'It doesn't. You side with her. Is there a shadow side of both of you – has her shadow put yours in a corner, to play with?'

He stands in front of the kitchen doorway and I can only just see his face. He says, 'You *have* been reading that book, haven't you?'

'Devouring it.'

He glances over his shoulder at the doorway, coughs and says, 'In the past, I persuaded her into situations I shouldn't have. As a child, my family had nothing. I saw opportunities and was blinded by my own . . . greed. The outcome was . . . she became . . . terribly frightened. Fear can become trapped within someone who is already vulnerable, even if the actual danger was eradicated, by us leaving the mainland.' He nods at me, 'And yes, sometimes feeling this amount of guilt is not unlike having a shadow.'

'I think I *would* be a good psychologist. Thank you for telling me *something*. What situations did you persuade her into?'

His face fades into the darkness of the hallway and his feet creak away up the stairs.

Mary

There's a small willow tree next to Valmarie's back door. I crawl under the lowest branches, wriggle back in the leaves. The door is open as wide as my hand. Inside her house footsteps thud on a wooden floor. Chairs scrape. I tuck my feet in tight underneath me.

Valmarie's voice speaks; there's someone with her.

'—but what came out?'

'Stone from Clorey. A stone with a hole through it.' It's Kelmar's voice. 'Sounds right to me, like that *were* the truth of him. For hims stone voice banging on relentless with no bloody substance were all I ever got from him. Not like you . . .' Her voice trails off.

I hunch back under the bush and listen as hard as I can.

'Bill, what came out of him?' asks Valmarie, sharp.

'Well, that were strange, that were a pile of dark, dank earth. Like him buried hims truth, or hid something true deep down underneath the earth. Or it could mean that him died in hims heart, that him were already as good as buried.'

'So it's true.' There's anger in Valmarie's voice.

Kelmar's voice says, 'What's true, Val?'

Her voice is sad. 'He buried something true in the grave-yard . . .'

Valmarie coughs and asks, 'What truth came out of Annie's Martyn?'

Kelmar says, 'A question mark made of glass. Something him wanted to know, only the answer would've shattered him?'

Valmarie says, 'A secret from Annie, or her from him? I'd be surprised. Annie hopped around after him like a hare. And he thought her the most beautiful woman on the island.'

'Can't see it, can you? Skin and bone, and that tangle of hair. Takes all sorts. Mary's Da were an old worn boot, just the one, and cracked. Felt all kinds of uselessness.'

I've got a pain in my chest, thinking of Da feeling useless.

'What of the tall man?' says Valmarie, sharp.

I listen, hard as I can.

'That's what were the strangest. Nothing left of him at all. No trace, not a shadow. Do you think him were a ghost, so him vanished himself?'

Valmarie says, 'Seemed real enough to me when we took him there.'

'But just vanishing. Do you think we missed it? It could've been so small we never got it out the hatch. A grain of sand. A speck of dust.'

So Langward's truth vanished. I shiver so hard the leaves rustle.

Kelmar keeps talking, 'Do you miss Bill, Val, even a bit?'

'Not after what he did. Nothing can replace . . .' She sounds tearful. 'You're not acting like you miss Clorey.'

'I'd not miss him any more than I'd miss breathing if I woke up dead.'

Footsteps thud, there's a clang of pots. Must be the kitchen behind that door. Just thinking of Langward makes my belly twist. The smell of him – but salt and dust aren't bad smells anywhere but on him. Spending so much time on boats him would smell of salt, and him could just have musty clothes.

Even so, hims smell is haunting me.

The wind blusters through the leaves of the willow, twigs catch in my hair. I crawl out, listening close. Valmarie and Kelmar are too quiet. Maybe them can sense I'm hid out here. Some kind of knowing them've got . . . I hunch down under the kitchen window, right next to the open door. There's a candle burning on the windowsill, so them won't see me past the reflection.

Inside, Valmarie's stirring one of the pots on the range.

Kelmar's at the table chopping herbs. She says, 'There's too many things unpunished. Small things, mostly – thieving and suchlike what dun warrant a thrashing. But some crimes are never punished, because none will speak. We should have a way that someone can speak out just to one person, not to all. If them'll not speak out at the Weaving Rooms, or are too young to do so, then them get no justice. None are took to the Thrashing House and there's only silence. I wonder sometimes, what of the men? If them're hurt, them dun tell any of us. Just sort it between themselves.'

Valmarie shakes her head and smiles at Kelmar. I've never seen her smile before. She says, 'Women don't have to resolve everything for everyone.'

Kelmar says, 'Some crimes are unheard of for years, some are never spoke of, because the folks concerned can't go to the Weaving Rooms to talk of it, or the crimes what are the worst – them dun want *all* folks to know.'

My throat's thick, stuck. There's something in Kelmar's voice what makes me want to walk right into that kitchen and just cry. Fill the whole kitchen with tears till she has to swim to get me, and gather me in her big arms. But I dun even know her. Dun want to. I wrap my arms around myself, tight.

Valmarie leaves the boiling pot, puts her hand on Kelmar's shoulder and says, 'You've been told something—'

Kelmar shakes her head. 'It's not about our sons. Not for the chattering of neither, it's just . . . some folks dun feel able to speak.

Valmarie goes back to the pot and says, 'Well, if they won't speak out, that's their business. The Thrashing House feels to me like it's made from the worst parts of us all. All brought together in one place.'

Kelmar picks up a bowl and stands next to Valmarie. She pours chopped leaves into one of the pots and says, 'What'd you mean, worst parts of us?'

Valmarie says, 'No, no – stop – that's enough sage.'

Kelmar puts down the bowl and gets a wooden spoon. 'I'll stir it.'

Valmarie nods, steps back and wipes her brow.

'Worst parts, Val?'

Valmarie watches her stir. 'All of our angry vengeful thoughts, all the guilt, the blame, the sadness, jealousy. Well, that's what it feels like, walking past it. It's pulling those feelings in, soaking them into the wood. Anyway, I've never known how it came to be there. It's ancient, isn't it? Did your ancestors build it? It *felt* ancient when we unlocked that great front door, pushed the men through. Ancient and hungry.'

Kelmar glances at Valmarie and says, 'The Thrashing House isn't made from any part of *us*. It's made from just one tree.'

Grandmam never told me about *this*.

'Here,' says Valmarie, patting Kelmar's arm. 'I'll take over now. Crack the willow. It would have taken more than one tree to build the Thrashing House.'

Kelmar goes back to the kitchen table and breaks a chunk of bark into small pieces. She says, 'That's not what I mean. The tall trees what used to grow here were cut down long before you and I were alive. My Nan's Grandma told her the Thrashing House *grew* itself. That it were the last remaining tall tree. It twisted out its branches, dug in its roots and grew so big that none would go near it to cut it down. Then it made itself into the Thrashing House, twisted and flattened out the walls and the door and the bell tower. In the top of the bell tower the bells grew like flowers, and them grew into the bells we ring out. The key grew like a fruit and it were picked by a woman on her twenty-first birthday, so that's how the women've come to have it and the age of being a woman were decided.'

Valmarie says, 'Well, we've got the key back. Not before time. That girl is a liar and a thief. We should—'

Kelmar says, 'Pass it to the next on the bell list tomorrow.'

'Do you believe that's how the Thrashing House came to be?'

Kelmar says, 'Well, if it's true or it isn't, that's what's been talked of in my family. I think the Thrashing House *calls* the folks what are needed here to this island.'

'What makes you think that?'

'I think *you* were called. For you're needed, and the tall men are needed for the trade, and the few other folks what've ever found their way here – we needed someone to bury our dead, dun we? Him knows how to prepare the dead. She makes good solid coffin boxes. We need them, whether we like it or not.'

Valmarie says, 'Well, it's a good job we don't have to like them. I didn't hear any kind of call . . . I was *made* to stay.'

Kelmar says, 'But you're needed. You learned skills with herbs what none others've ever had before you. You can see right into a person and know just the right dose, and the herb what's needed. You've got this whole house full of herbs, the tinctures you've made, and folks come to you to talk of what ails them, but you'll not tell others what's not for thems ears.'

A pot boils loud and rattles the lid. Valmarie says, 'You're wrong. I've learned things because I've had to. I needed to stop feeling like driftwood.'

Kelmar puts her arm round Valmarie's shoulder and says, 'You *are* needed here, Val. Dun matter *how*, just matters that you're here. Well, that's what I think. But the Thrashing House dun call the men to be put *inside* it. Your husband. My husband,' she spits out the words. 'We took them there ourselves. Maybe *we* wanted them gone. We should at least be honest with each other – we did want rid of our men. Come on. You never loved Bill.'

Valmarie says, 'You're talking as if we *named* the four men.' She clatters on a board with a knife. 'But we didn't. If we were acting on our own feelings, no other men would have been put in there. Just Bill and Clorey.'

Kelmar speaks slow, 'Maybe the Thrashing House wanted that tall man. Him went in without a fight. You know, I think it really *were* calling him. Perhaps *him* needed to be punished.' She comes nearer the window, reaches up and gets a jar from a shelf. She goes back to the table and says, 'If it were down to just me, I couldn't have taken any one man there on my own, shut them in. It'd be like having blood on my hands.'

'But there isn't any blood.' Valmarie turns to face Kelmar and touches her cheek. 'So, stop. We wanted justice for our boys. You're just carrying guilt, and can't put it down. It's not serving you well. Come on. Get the bark in and help me strain. We've got to get on.'

I crawl back under the bush by the door and listen to the sound of pouring water.

Kelmar's white boots step outside and Valmarie closes the door. I peek through the willow twigs. Kelmar has a bag over her shoulder and a bowl in her hands and Valmarie carries three candles in glass jars. Them walk up the hill towards the circle of boulderstones, Kelmar's white boots gleam like two moons walking across a night sky.

I crawl out and watch till Valmarie and Kelmar are hunched over getting things out of the bag, thems faces lit up by the candles.

*

Valmarie's kitchen smells of some bitter plant. There's herbs hanging upside down from the beams of the ceiling. Jars stacked along the shelves. One of them is labelled 'Mad Honey – Rhododendron Bees', another has straggly leaves and white flowers tangled inside it and the label says 'Hemlock'. Another says 'Valerian, high concentrate'. I step back and bump into the table where a candle flickers. A root lies on a chopping board, sliced in half. The top half is like a screaming baby's head, but the bottom is the stump of a wizened old man's body.

I go into the room with the fireplace, it's lit by three candles. There's a wall full of shelves stacked with wooden boxes, all different sizes, from the floor up to the ceiling. The boxes all have drawings on them burned dark into the wood. There's a picture of a heart on one, an eye on another. Some of the boxes have words as well as pictures. A flute and the word *sad*, a footprint and the word *float*. A pot of honey named *revenge*, a map called *nonsense*, a cup named *company*, a cracked jug called *pointlessness*. All the things in these boxes must be what she's burglared from people's homes. A noose, a comb, a bat called *colony*, a mirror with the word *land*.

I pick the one with the bat and the word *colony* on it and open it a crack. A tiny bat sits in the corner, quivering, eyes glinting. It flits out quick. I step back, my feet bang on the floorboards.

Sitting on a box high on the wall the bat rattles the tips of its scratchy wings against the wood. It's got a picture of a key on the side. I drag over a stool, stand on it and reach up to get the box. It's jammed in between all the others so I ease it out. It's heavy and I near drop it. I shake it but there's no sound.

The bat sits on the key box, blinks up at me as I climb down. I brush it off and it flits around the room. I open the key box, but it's empty. The bat lands on my bag and crawls in.

Valmarie's fireplace is a strangeness. She's stuck shells all over it, then gone over them with a hammer and smashed them all up. On the mantelpiece is the Thrashing House key. I pick it up and it sings a high metal sound, and when I blink Mam's face is there, on the back of my eyelids.

The key starts Mam's voice over again:

I want this child I'm heavy with to come out. Too heavy for my back. It's funny to think of me being someone's Mam. Ned as someone's Da. Him will tell this child stories of the sea . . .

I want to hear her again, but I put the key in my bag and look out through the uneven windowpanes, and the ripples make Valmarie and Kelmar look like them are underwater. The candles burn bright in the jars in the grass. Valmarie scatters something from the bowl. She puts the bowl down and faces Kelmar. Them raise thems hands up to the sky. Them're dancing, spinning around in the circle. Them look like them're swimming in air.

I close the back door, quiet, crawl up the hill and hide in the shadows between two boulderstones to watch.

*

Valmarie and Kelmar spin like them can't see anything outside themselves. The dark clouds shift so fast, the night sky is spinning with them. Valmarie stops, leans over, like she's letting out all the sighs in her at once.

Kelmar stops, holds her hands up to the sky.

Valmarie calls, 'Come to us, tell us what is hidden.'

Them're trying to call up Sishee.

But Grandmam said that Sishee couldn't understand words no matter *how* them are said, so I dun know what them expect from someone in a story what can only understand pictures, not words.

Valmarie calls again, 'Come to us!'

Kelmar drops her arms and shouts at Valmarie, 'It's not working! You've missed something out!'

There's a glint of metal in Valmarie's hand. She raises a knife and dashes out of the circle. I hunch in close to the boulderstone, shut myself away in the shadows.

Kelmar flies out of the circle and grapples with Valmarie, twists the knife from her hand.

Valmarie makes a sound like a dog, howling.

Kelmar stands firm, her chin out. 'Dun break the circle, come on, if you forgot to do the knife bit, we've got to start it again!'

'No point!' shrieks Valmarie. 'If we don't *believe* she's going to come, she won't – just like I haven't believed I'm going to find what I want, for years – not for years!' she sobs.

Kelmar walks her back into the circle, talking low and quiet.

Something moves on the top of my bag, crawls out and up

my shoulder. The bat called *colony*. It flits off me, so fast it looks like hundreds of bats – peeling shadows off itself into the dark sky. It flies round Valmarie and Kelmar.

I crouch down.

Kelmar stares up at it and says, 'Try again. Something's shifted.'

Valmarie shouts, 'It's only a bat!' She slumps down on the grass and leans forwards, her fingers over her face.

I stand up and walk backwards, away from them.

Valmarie, still hunched over, moves her fingers. Her dark eyes stare at me. She screeches out, 'Mary Jared!' and jumps to her feet.

Running down the hill, my heart thud thud thuds down the valley and up to the graveyard hill. The blackthorn bushes along the edge of the graveyard fill it with shadows. I push through a thick cluster of twigs and thorns. I can't see where my feet are falling.

I trip on something,

a sharp biting pain in my shin flashes red.

I fall

into a hidden place, buried under the bushes

where them won't find me.

My eyes close.

I fall back into the fever place that is the blank dark.

Morgan

My small bed has an elaborate birdcage carved into the head-board, an empty cage, with no bird inside it, and no door. I kneel on my blue quilted bedspread and pick out a book from the shelf, sit on my bed and open it on my lap. *The Direction of Currents and a Discussion of the Contents of Glass Bottles.* I stroke the cover. Inside it has pictures of all the glass bottles that have been found with messages inside them, washed up on shores all over the world. Photographs of faded messages on parchment, paper, papyrus, tissue, cardboard, sealed in bottles and sent out to sea.

I flick the pages and open the book to see a photograph of a drawing on white tissue, found in a glass bottle washed up by a coastal town. A picture of a tree, drawn in black, in a child's hand. Below the branches – feet planted firm on the earth and roots growing from their shoes into the soil to join the roots of the tree – are two small girls, drawn simply, holding hands, identical, with a tear on each cheek.

Where was I when my parents decided on the twins' names? Probably in the kitchen. I imagine Mum and Dad discussing names, swapping each crying baby girl backwards and forwards between them. Naming them after trees, something so far away, something they knew from so long ago, far from where we have all landed. They must miss those trees, to have chosen the names Hazel and Ash for their daughters.

I close the book of washed-up messages. I've never been near the shores here to send out my message. But I've written my messages over and over again in my mind.

The storybooks have always been my favourites, even now I'm an adult. I've learned from these that: locked-up daughters *always* escape captivity if they bide their time. That mothers are meant to be good, but good mothers often die young. And fathers are tired or poor or hard-working or generally weather-worn. That beauty in young women is described using images of snow, rose petals, blood and pure hearts, but snow melts, petals dry and curl, blood turns brown, and hearts are easily punctured or removed by all kinds of sharp implements – thorns or scalpels, axes or claws. Princes arrive at the end of the stories – but princes are only ever described as handsome, which could really mean anything. In my imagination, these princes are shadowy men who bestow kisses or happy futures. Neither of these events are ever *fully* described, and then the story just ends. The arrival of the prince seems at best suspicious, and at worst sinister.

Mum's footsteps are outside in the hall. They stop at my door.

Silence.

Mum's listening to my thoughts. The handle turns.

Her silence skulks in around the edges of the door. She's in her purple dressing gown. 'You're awake. Been crying but all right now?'

I say, 'Thanks for trying.'

'What do you mean?' She frowns. 'You forgot to sweep the kitchen floor. Your father's asleep. I don't want the twins woken.'

'I'll do it, soon.'

She nods, once, and walks away. Along the hallway a door creaks open and clicks shut.

I open the ruffled lilac curtains. The tall house on the hill seems to look back at me through the dark. Tonight, it looks a different shape. Almost . . . the shape of a hand, with turrets for fingers. It doesn't look like that in the daytime.

Or at night.

It's never looked like a hand before.

One of the fingers flickers in a ripple on the windowpane.

Come here.

*

I've dropped the broom on the kitchen floor. I can't move, can't believe what I have in my hand, can't look away from it, in case it disappears.

Such a small thing, this black clunky key. And yet it unlocks the outside world. I turn it over and over in the palm of my hand. Pinch it to make sure it's real.

The key to the padlock in the pink fence.

It's fallen from Mum's charm bracelet.

This chance will never come again. When she notices she's lost it, she'll collapse into pieces and then break everything else apart to find it.

I knew I just had to bide my time. I didn't have to hack my way out. Didn't have to barter for my escape. Didn't have to cause pain.

I just needed something to happen.

The house on the hill beckoned. *Come here.*

And Mum has dropped the key.

So something has happened.

Now is the time to begin the story of my return to the mainland. Of returning to a place called home. Turn back to the first page. Can't take anything I love with me and perhaps it's best to take nothing at all, because in so many of my storybooks, the first page is blank.

Mary

In the blank dark, blue eyes open with a sound like the scrape of metal.

A tunnel of eyes, watching me. Each eye leads to another, the lids joined like fish scales, stretching further than the sky and deeper than the earth.

I've been here before. In a fever place. These eyes belong to someone. These eyes are from some other time, long before now. Pain right through me, ice all around me, and through the dark, blue eyes stare. I'm floating in this tunnel of eyes, my shin stings, two marks on it, red raised lumps. No light apart from the glints in the eyes.

Eyes filled with sky
sky filled with eyes
only the night sky.

I'm lying in a hollow, in thick grass. I'm hid in the graveyard, ivy tangled over a blackthorn bush what keeps me from view. Headstones I can't see must be all around me. Names and names and names. My shin stings like it's aflame.

A rope lies coiled in the grass like a sleeping snake.

The deadtaker said to Da when Mam died, 'If she'd been

able to get the venom out she might have survived.' I cut one of the handles off my bag, tie it round my leg just above the bite.

I grip my knife. My hand shakes. I make a cut. Only a scratch, islands of blood. I clench my teeth and plunge the blade in deep, cut right through the two raised tooth marks. The venom seeps out, runs thick pale yellow down my leg, streaked through with blood. I press down around the cut, squeeze as much poison out as I can. My legs shake like them'll never stop. Pain shoots all through me, my heart thuds my ribs, the thud spreads all over me, thudding my head, my hands, my legs, my back. The strength goes out of my hands. The blackthorn bushes and ivy move in the wind, the dark sky spins and blurs. The ground wallops against my back.

I open my eyes. Clouds scrunch up in the dark sky, like a giant hand has pinched and squeezed them into shapes.

My blood feels solid. Pins and needles jangle over the skin of my face. The only part of my body I can move is my eyes, and the night sky is thick with thorns.

A sound. Someone breathing. In and out, low and heavy, the breathing of a man.

Movement of grass behind my head, hims hand swishes the grass. Him is hid here with me, letting me lie here. I clench my throat and try to make a sound. It dun work. A smell of dust. The moon is lost in clouds.

'You're awake,' says hims low voice.

Hims hand appears.

A pale white hand, long and thin.

Him puts it over my mouth.

Can't get my mouth wide enough to bite.

Him leans in close to my ear.

It's hims eyes.

My brother's eyes in a tall man's face.

Langward.

Him hisses in my ear, 'You look so like your mother.'

Hims hand over my mouth. A scream, trapped in my throat, a pincushion with pins sticking outwards. Hims eyes crawl down my body and back to my face.

I strain as hard as I can, nothing moves.

Him slides hims cheek against mine, breathes in my ear, 'They've been searching for you. But you're not found. So here we are. In a hiding place, as if we're children. And you . . . can't speak, can you?' Him takes hims hand off my mouth.

I open my eyes wide, think *get away get away get away*, but hims cheek presses against mine and him hisses in my ear, 'Beatrice should never have ended the brief, I have to say, unsatisfying, *us*. Dying is so *selfish*.' Him sits up and stares at my chest.

'You've forgotten. Should I remind you, or would it be cruel? Should I remind you that . . . for her, it was always about trade. We agreed that I'd leave her alone, but, she said I could have *you*. And aren't you . . . grown-up.'

Hims face blurs like him is above the surface of the sea and I'm looking up from the seabed. Freezing cold, white cracks in my blood where it should be warm. This is a lie to break me open, so him can smash me up.

Him taps a finger along my eyebrow. 'I know what you're thinking,' him says.

I'm thinking: Dun say Mam traded me, for I've got a head full of blanks in my memory and I might believe you.

Him says, 'You're thinking, how did I escape from your Thrashing House, when the others couldn't?' Him waits. Hims pale face shines like polished stone. 'A door opened. They didn't *believe* they could get out. So they couldn't. Panic renders people dumb. A bit like you are now, if you think about it.' Him strokes my cheek with one finger. Him strokes, strokes, mutters, 'Belief is a powerful thing. Seeing what you *believe*, rather than what's there . . . believing there are no doors, when a door is open.' Him leans hims face over mine.

Him puts the palms of hims hands on both sides of my face. Hims eyes look at my hair, my lips, my cheeks, like him is hunting for something in my face. Him says, 'Beatrice. Of course I would meet you again, in a graveyard.' Him presses my cheeks together, makes my lips pucker.

Him shakes hims head, lets go of my cheeks and snarls in my ear, 'What shall we trade?'

I want the blank dark. Anywhere that isn't here, anywhere that isn't now.

Langward leans over my lips full of pins and needles. I think of the broideries I make. How sharp the needle is. How I jab it through the linen when I'm doing a picture I dun like. Broiderie needles coming out of my lips. Bloody hims face up with scratches . . .

I'm too young to be here, under hims hands. Too young for whatever this is.

Him moves down so him is kneeling next to my thighs. I can just see hims head and shoulders. Hims shoulders move. Him unbuttons my coat. The fabric of my dress rips. Him leans forwards, frowns at my bandaged breasts.

My head jerks.

I smash it back as hard as I can on the ground.

I'm back in the blank dark, blue eyes all around me and I'm not even scared.

*

Langward kneels next to me. Him puts hims finger on my cheek.

'You're awake. Stop crying,' him says, sharp.

My face is wet.

'You're a mess.' Him leans over me and lifts my shoulders.

A red flash. I'm sat up. The scream in my throat shrinks and hides.

I've room in there to speak.

'I'm fine,' my voice is hoarse.

Him takes hims hands off me and says, 'Tell me you're fine again.'

'I'm fine.'

'Tell me nothing happened. I'm not here.'

'Never saw you. Let me alone now.'

'And . . .'

'Nothing happened.' Him feels further away.

'Again,' him says, sharp.

The sky shifts, and shifts back.

Him nods. 'If you don't tell anyone I've ever touched you, and say "nothing happened" if asked about me, I'll trade with you.'

'For what?' I ask.

'For saying "nothing happened", I'll tell you all I know about Barney. But this trade can't be broken.'

I stare at the grass. Him knows something about Barney when everyone else just thinks him is part of a trade. Lost to the main land. If I agree to this, there's no Thrashing House for Langward. No justice for me. This night is forgotten.

I say, 'Agreed. Now tell me about Barney.'

I gaze at a strand of ivy hanging from a clutter of thorns and twigs, and wait for him to speak.

'Your father told me Barney was my son.'

'Why would him—'

'I didn't know, till the trade of the boys was first discussed. You've forgotten.'

'I know you're Barney's real Da. What else?'

'No. I don't think it *would* be right to remind you.' Hims head tilts. 'It would make you . . . more *attached*. Though it may be pointless, if it is as it seems. It was planned the same as the others. Your father knocked Barney out, and took him out of the back door while you were selling his fish.'

'Da knocked him out? Barney must've been so hurt!'

Langward frowns. 'Be quieter, or I won't speak.'

I swallow, hard. 'You can't *not* speak. It's a trade. I remember the back door slamming.'

'Your father tangled him in a fishing net. When you went back in, I carried him down to the boats. Your father hid in the cold room.'

'I looked in your boats—'

'You didn't check the fishing nets.'

Him *could* be right about this. I dun see nets in the boats. I'm so familiar with the sight of them. Always helping Da repair them. All Da's silences, him must've been thinking that Barney dun belong with us, not with Mam gone. Da got me to work so hard to keep him, but all the while, him were planning how to get rid of Barney.

Langward growls, 'Don't cry.'

'So where . . .' I whisper.

'I don't have him any more.'

'You last saw him on your boat?'

'Unconscious, when we were about to leave. But just out to sea, the fishing net he'd been tangled in was empty. He couldn't swim?'

Unconscious. 'No, him couldn't swim.' I stare up at the sky so my tears dun come out. 'That's why you stayed here so willing. Flashed the light to tell the other tall men to go.'

'I wanted to know if he'd been washed up here. Living, or dead. I've found nothing.'

My throat sends needle sharpness through my neck. I ask, 'What did you want him for?'

'I wanted a constant reminder. The others said he was too young, but I told them I'd find a use for him.'

'So the other tall men dun know him is your son.'

'I decided, best not.' Him flexes hims fingertips. There's blood on one of hims fingers. 'I thought it would be *interesting* to have a son. Make the world more . . . tolerable. He looks so like her, despite—'

'No. Him *dun* look like her. Him looks like himself.' I glare at my shin. 'You know *nothing* of what it's like to live with Barney. You never will. No matter how bad a father Da were for Barney – you'd be far worse. I can't see you *ever* knowing how to love a small boy what's sick or afraid – you couldn't even pretend to.'

Him grasps hims hand round my neck. 'I've kept my trade – told you all I know.' Him twists my face towards him. 'So, say it.' Hims eyes are full of anger and want, all mixed up together.

'Nothing happened,' I choke.

Him lets go, climbs up out of the hollow and walks away.

Now I can breathe.

If him believes my lie, that Barney can't swim, him might go away to the main land when the other tall men come back. If him dun believe me, him will go on searching, while I can't, for I've got pins and needles all through my legs.

What has him done to me when I put myself in the blank dark?

I look down at my torn dress.

My belly covered in blood and dirt.

I dun know what parts of me him touched.

With what parts of him.

But if nothing happened I can forget this.

If nothing happened I can dig a grave for it.

Throw earth all over it.

Say nothing is nothing.

Like peeling off a shadow.

Morgan

Halfway up a hill, I look across the island. Directions. Expanse, distance, danger? My head and body feel so light I could float off up into the sky, but I plant my bare feet in the cold wet grass, step around thistles and rocks, watch for brambles. I imagine I'm a farmer who tills the fields and feels the earth pulsing beneath the grass. I can smell the salt air that blows in from the sea. In the night sky clouds pile like floating islands. I could be a fisherwoman with a cloudboat that drifts me from one cloudisland to another. My eyes are used to the dark, and there is a vastness of hills, a horizon of ocean in the distance. I can pick out the shapes of walls and stiles, small cottages, a hill crowded with gravestones. Where my father must go when he buries the dead. I don't think he ever told me the collective noun for gravestones. Perhaps now he never will. I want to turn back, write him a note to say goodbye.

A woman wearing a long coat tied at the waist walks along the thick hedge at the bottom of the graveyard. I duck down behind a bramble bush and watch her. Something twists inside my stomach and tells me not to speak to this woman, in her dark coat and white boots. My mother's voice saying, *All the people here are mad . . .* flits through my mind.

I get a little nearer to the woman and crouch behind a small laburnum tree with coiled branches. The trees are stunted, some grow with their branches stretched to one side, as if the wind has taught them to lean away from coldness.

The woman has stopped – she's listening to something in the graveyard behind the hedge. If she was in one of my storybooks, what would she be listening to? What can she hear in a grave-yard? Do the dead bodies lie there at night, their coffins risen up, like blanketed beds, handing around hot milk and honey, telling each other filthy limericks?

The woman turns towards me. I crouch lower. I think she can see me, but she turns back to the hedge.

Someone else is in the graveyard, further up the hill. A woman with long dark hair and a pale face. She stands next to a grave, leaning on a spade. I shudder. She's going to dig up one of the coffins my mother made and my father buried, with its grue-some contents. Dig up someone she was in love with . . . kiss their dead blue lips.

My throat catches, an acid taste.

The woman with the white boots hasn't seen her.

Further along the hedge, a man who looks like a tall shadow walks out of the graveyard.

Everything holds its breath.

Mary

I've crawled up out of the hollow and I'm surrounded by graves. Names of dead women and thems still living children carved in beneath. Children's names under thems Mam's. The whole family is dead with the Mam gone.

If I die now, the deadtaker will carve through my name beneath Mam's. I will have a headstone of my own with just my name on it. Just like the men. Them have a headstone what speaks only of them. No belonging people. Dun know how long Barney will be missing before the deadtaker scores out hims name from Mam's headstone. Or if him needs a body first. The deadtaker carves in the names, scores out the names, carves in the names. When him buried Mam, him wore black gloves with a small tear across the thumb. Hims skin underneath shone pale from the touch of death.

Something moves in the dark.

A young woman with long coils of fair hair. She sits down behind a headstone. I dun recognise her. She leans her head back, like she's considering what to do. She's dressed in a light-coloured dress with a smocked bodice and wide skirt. Must be freezing. She could be from the cottages at Wreckers Shore. Them keep to themselves.

An owl hoots near me.

I gasp out.

The woman hears it too, looks over and crawls towards me. I pull my coat around me but can't do it up. I reach for my bag, only my arm shoots a jab of pain.

She crawls towards me, drops my bag in my lap and sits down next to me. She looks younger from close up. Not as young as me, but a whole lot cleaner.

'What happened to you?' Her voice sounds like the talk of the tall men.

'Nothing happened.' I clasp my bag to my chest.

'Yes, it did,' she says. 'I saw a shadow man leaving here – a prince? Did he kiss you – was it a *poison* kiss?'

'Him dun kiss me.'

'Have you been kidnapped? Did *he* kidnap you, or was it one of those women – are they witches? What did they do to your leg?' She leans towards the ugly gash where I cut it. She looks like she wants to touch it, her face full of hunger, like a child picking a scab.

'You ask a lot of questions, dun you. Weren't any women here. Just me. Can you see my knife?'

She runs her fingers over the grass, crawls all around me, ogles it close. Gets distracted by some insect she's found.

'It's gone then. Leave it.' I'm trying to get the blanket out of my bag but my fingers dun grip. She drags the bag to her and rummages, pulls out the blanket and asks, 'Are you a murderer? Is that why you had a knife?'

'Look. If I were a murderer, what'd I be doing in a graveyard, when everyone here's already dead?'

She pulls the Thrashing House key out of my bag. 'What does this unlock?' She holds it up, gazes at it.

'Put it back.' I reach out my hand.

Her shoulders slump, she puts the key in my bag and wraps the blanket around me. I reach down to untie the bag strap still tight around my leg. I can't undo the knot.

She watches me, her hands in her lap.

'All right. Can you help please?' I mutter.

She swoops down on my leg, unties the strap, her hands clean and soft. She asks where I live and I tell her.

'A *cottage*,' she sighs. 'Perfect. I'll help you get there, if you show me the way.'

'You *know* the way. Traders Bay. Where the tall men—' The trapped scream sends spikes into my throat.

She says, 'I'm Morgan.'

'Mary,' I gasp out.

'Pretty name.' She smiles and holds out her hands.

'Dun want anyone to touch me.'

She drops her hands down. 'Well, you won't get far without someone to hang on to.' She stands up.

I stare at her toes. 'How come you're out with bare feet?'

'I don't have any shoes.' Her dress smells so clean I dun want to dirty it. She's stronger than she looks as she lifts me to my feet. Pain shoots down my bitten leg. She holds me stood up and helps me sling my bag over my shoulder. I feel like I'm going to crumple down. The sky keels and shifts.

I step on my good leg and lean on her. It's hard to talk and walk at the same time. I ask, 'How come . . . you never been to . . . Traders Bay? Dun your belonging people trade?'

'Belonging people?'

'Family.'

'My Dad's the undertaker.'

I stop. 'The *deadtaker*?' My voice is shrill.

'You call him that?'

'Has *him* sent you for me?'

178

'Of course not. You're not dead.' She sways, catches my weight and nearly tips over.

Outside the graveyard we can see the Thrashing House, and she asks me about it. I tell her how it can be seen from just about any place on this island – look uphill and it's right there. She never heard its name before and I tell her no one can get out what's been put in . . . and I dun tell her that's not true. Langward got out.

I say, 'Look, walking hurts, distract me . . . tell me why you dun have any boots.'

She tells me she's never had boots since she's lived here, because she's never been allowed outside of her home. She tells me she has twinned sisters and them dun have any boots either. She tells me she lives with them and her Mam and Dad but that she wants to get to the main land because that's where she thinks her home really is, not here where she's lived all these years. She tells me about her books, pages tied at the sides with stories written down. That she likes insects and gets upset if them're hurt.

I feel like that makes her someone I could trust.

She tells me she needs somewhere to hide because she's just left her family. And she asks about mine.

I say, 'Da's an old worn boot. Mam's deaded. My little brother what I love the most has been took and I can't get him back. So them're gone.'

She stops walking, I sag against her. Her eyes shine with tears. '*All* gone? Just you left?'

My voice is stuck. I almost cry because the night sky is so big above us, but there's something so sad in the deep shade of blue.

I say, 'I've got no other belonging people. Them were it.'

'Your brother . . .'

'The two women you said you saw—'

'Where has he been *took* to? Have you looked carefully at animals? He could have been transformed – into a mouse, or a rat, or a bat, even a small cow?'

I say, 'Him hasn't. What did the women look like?'

'Like they didn't want to be seen.'

'Red, or dark hair, like mine?' I pull at my hair and my finger catches in a knot.

'One woman's hair was black, her skin was pale. The other's hair not as dark but nearly, like yours. Bigger than you, though. Much bigger. About Mum's age.'

'A strong girth?'

'Yes. Not unlike a baby giant.'

'Stop talking nonsense.'

'Sorry.' She nods. 'You said your Dad was . . .'

'I can't go home.'

'Why not?'

'I've thieved something I shouldn't have. I'll end up in the Thrashing House.' I stare at the grass.

'That building you said no one goes in or comes out?'

'No one comes out what goes in!'

'Oh,' she whispers.

Morgan holds me up as we stumble up the hill towards the Thrashing House. Her arm feels strong, but she's struggling with me leaning so hard. Her family dun trade. So the tall men will never have been to her house.

Stood still for a moment, red pain in my legs, I can't speak. She stands still and patient.

'Morgan.' I'm breathing too hard. 'I've got a . . . thought.'

'Tell me.'

'Can I get . . . into your folks' house? You'd be safe enough . . . to hide at my cottage. Your Mam and Da won't find you at mine. We could . . . just . . . trade homes.'

She shakes her head. 'My family will see me. I can't go back.'

'Look, I'll get put in the Thrashing House.'

She stares up at it like she's not sure it's something to be scared of.

So I lie to her.

I say, 'My little brother's been locked in the Thrashing House. I'm next.' My face burns, for she's so clean and good, she smells of soap and her dress is much nicer than mine, and here I'm lying to her, to get her to do something she dun want to.

She frowns. 'We should get him out. I don't mind if it's dangerous. In fact, it might be—'

'You *would* mind,' I growl. 'You'd mind if you'd lost someone you loved.'

Her face is pale. She says, quiet, 'This is *real*, isn't it?'

'Of *course* it's real.' My voice cracks. 'If them lock me in there too, I won't come out again. If I make you a promise when I need to trade with you this bad, I'm going to keep it, or you can wallop me yourself if them find you because of me. Course I know you're not going to trust *me* yet, but I've got to trust *you* as well.'

She smiles a little, but not like she means it. She stares at the grass. 'That building looks so grand from a distance. But sometimes it looks like a ruin. I thought it would be beautiful on the inside. A ballroom, an orchestra playing or the banquet hall of a great castle . . . But it isn't, is it?'

'No one knows.' I swallow, hard.

'So it *could* still be beautiful.'

'Shouldn't think so.'

'Why would they lock you in there?'

'I've got the key for it – the one in my bag. I thieved it.'

'You can get locked up here, just for stealing a key?'

'*That* key. Aye.'

'I could be your nursemaid. We could both hide in your cottage till you're better, till the boats come and I can get away. Then I'll go, and you can hide somewhere else?'

I lean hard against her to keep me from crumpling and speak sharp as I tell her that everyone knows I live there and that it's fine enough for her, but when she's gone, there's nowhere else I can go. I tell her she's not thinking right, and ask if her mam's a kind woman.

She says she dun think her Mam would take me in. She glances at my shin and says, 'Even your skin is torn. And your dress . . .'

The sky is lighter and the grass blows in circles in the wind.

I tell her I'll show her where my cottage is. I can't walk and talk. I say, 'Think hard. I need somewhere safe. So do you.'

We're at the top of the cliffs at the path what leads down to the beach. Stars are scattered all the way down to the horizon. The fishing boats are tied up to the cleat posts and in the dark them look like open coffin boxes.

Morgan props me up, frowning. Keeps glancing behind us at the Thrashing House. It's silent, no creaks, no groans. She's thinking so loud I can almost hear her.

I say, 'What if I just lay down outside your pink fence. Stuck my leg out . . . so your Mam can see I'm hurt.' My throat is hoarse. 'She'd have to do something then.'

'I *dun* know what she'd do.'

'Dun copy me! Talk proper. Dun sound right from your mouth.'

'I still *don't* think she'd take you in. She dun trust anyone.'

'Keep your own voice. Look, you can see my cottage from

here. At the edge of the row, nearest the beach.' I point down the cliff. My cottage looks rickety and worn, but solid. It's like nothing has happened.

Only my legs shake and my belly aches, deep inside of it.

She says, 'Are you all right?'

I stare at the empty sea and tell her where I've put the cottage latchkey. I tell her about the tall men, tell her to get herself hid in one of thems boats, for that's the only way she'll get to the main land.

Morgan turns to face me. I never seen a face so clear, like she's never seen anything she dun want to. Her face is like an empty piece of linen what's yet to be stitched on. No wonder she's copying the way I talk. Trying to make herself a picture of something, but on her it dun fit.

She says, 'I'll get you close enough so you can crawl to the fence, lie down and stay still. Mum walks around the inside of the fence each dawn to check no one is lurking outside.'

'Who does she—'

Her eyes shine. 'No one ever is. This time, *you* will be.'

There's a girl on the top of a hill in the distance spinning around in her white bed dress. We stop, the girl keeps the spin going slow then quick. A stocky man climbs up the hill to her, can't see him clear, for hims clothes are dark. Him puts hims arms around her and bundles her away over the hill.

I whisper to Morgan, 'Them should be asleep.'

'Who are they?'

'Could be Fiona, she lives on one of the farms near there, so the man's likely to be her Da, but it's too dark to see. Could be she's getting tangled from not sleeping.'

'What do you mean, tangled?'

'Just from not dreaming, not getting rid.'

'Of what?'

'Her dreamings. If you dun sleep you do get . . . Dun matter, you'll understand if you stop sleeping a while. Sends you a bit, you know . . . Crazed.'

We stop at a well. I lean on the cold stone ledge, breathing hard.

Morgan looks down into it and says, 'There's a well in our garden. I used to think I could climb down and find my way into a tunnel to get out.'

'You never did climb down?'

'Just once, when I was small.'

I stare into the well. 'Wouldn't want to get stuck down there.'

'It felt as if I was being pulled down even further. Gravity.'

'We're there in the water.'

'We're like reflections of each other.'

Our faces blur on the surface of the water, her hair light and mine dark.

'Morgan.'

'What?'

'I want to drop the Thrashing House key down the well. Then go down myself after it. See which one, me or the key, hits the bottom first. Dun let me.'

She grips my hand.

I squeeze her fingers. 'Dun know why I said that.'

'Come on. It's getting lighter.'

At a crumbling stone wall near her house she lowers me down on the grass. My legs crumple. She stands behind a gorse bush and stretches her back. She says, 'Don't move suddenly when Mum sees you. It might be good that you look a mess, but she startles so easily. I can't make you any kind of real promise.'

I take her hand. 'I know. It's up to her and me now.'

The lines on her brow disappear. 'If she does let you in, you haven't seen me. You've never met me, never spoken to me.'

She looks at my dress and crouches down on the grass. 'I can't leave you like this.' She rummages in my bag and finds the box of broiderie threads and needles. She's in and out of my bag, getting different coloured threads out, putting them back. Fumbling with her pockets, in my bag, out of my bag.

I say, 'You can't sew, can you?'

'No.'

We stitch up my dress with me stitching from the top down while she works from the waist up. The light's not yet bright enough. My hands are too cold to stitch right. There's a great jagged seam when we're done, from my belly to my neck, and all the buttons gone. I must look like a broken toy. One what's been ripped apart and stitched up.

Like the moppet.

'Give me my bag.' My voice sounds sharp.

Morgan sits back, pink in her cheeks.

'Please.'

She passes it to me. The moppet is curled up tight in the corner, right down the bottom, hiding itself. The first time I met Langward is when I found the shell what's inside the moppet. What if him put Barney's voice in there, when him pinched out my fingers . . . to trick me.

I want to tear up the moppet, shred the stuffing, throw it into the wind. Cut the shell out of it, scream and yell and cry my own voice into it and stamp it to dust. Only I can't do any of these things.

It's the only thing of Barney I've got left.

Morgan says, 'I wish I'd met you . . . before now.' She kisses my cheek.

185

I close the bag. 'Me as well.' I nod, 'I'll crawl from here to the fence and play dead. Go on, get to mine, quick.'

She nods.

'If you see a tall man with brown eyes—' My belly cramps, '—then leg it.'

'Was he the man at the graveyard – the shadow man?' Her voice shakes.

'Just run.'

A tear rolls down her face. 'He's not a rescuing kind of man, is he?'

'No.'

She squeezes my shoulder and goes.

*

Against my spine the ground feels like it's shaking, only the shakes are trapped in me. Streaks of clouds above me, spun with pale orange threads. The sea will be reflecting this same sky all the way from the horizon, in the waves what could have drowned my brother.

I close my eyes. The wind blows over me. A gap in the wind. Someone stood right beside me, blocking the wind away. Someone crept up on me so silent.

'Give. It. Back.' Valmarie's voice.

I open my eyes. There's no one here. Just the sound of the wind. I close my eyes and listen.

Valmarie's voice speaks again. 'Give. It. Back.'

I open my eyes a slit. Just the sky above me. I close them again.

I think back loud. *Get gone.*

'We need it,' she hisses.

Did she hear me?

'The bells need to ring.'

She did hear me.

I want to scream, *Get away from me leave me get out of my head you can't just walk through folks minds without knocking first . . .*

She says, 'I'll find you . . . just as soon as I . . .' The sound of digging. Digging? I open my eyes a crack. Nothing. Close them.

'Here. It. Is. It did sing back.'

Her voice is a sob. 'I thought . . . you were . . . lost to me . . .' Her voice drifts away – them words are not for me.

Morgan's Mam is peering out between the slats in the fence. I'm soaking through with the wet from the grass and a cold wind blows my hair over my face.

I think about what to say to her . . .

Love me for a short while, just because you're someone's Mam, though you're not mine. Or I could pretend she's my own Mam and say: I'm going to have to make myself believe you'd never have traded me. That though you weren't always kind, you were good. Because to believe what him said will take so much away, it'll be like it's raining inside me, not just rain, but gales and hailstones and fog.

Tears roll into my ears. I need to give Morgan's Mam something she wants. Only I dun know what that is.

She says, 'I can tell you're awake.'

I open my eyes and sit up. Pain shoots through my legs. I look at the pink fence, with her green eye in the narrow space between the slats.

I say, 'Were it you what drew the flowers all over this fence?'

The eye creases up. 'Years ago. Chalk. The rain washed them away.'

My voice shakes. 'Them were pretty, but even real flowers dun stay that way for always.' A memory comes. A broken ship, wooden planks as cargo. All strewn along the coast at Wreckers Shore. The planks this fence is made from. Me stood there, feeling small, looking for the deaded crew. Never saw anyone. Just a whole cargo of wooden planks in piles along the shore.

I say, 'That's a good strong fence. Strong planks, from ship-wrecked wood. You were clever to get that, to make such a high solid fence.'

The eye squints.

'You like flowers, then?' I ask. 'I could draw one for you in broiderie threads. If you've got some linen, I could broider you a flower with my needle.'

Her eye blinks.

I get the broiderie threads out of my bag. 'I could do a purple one, or crimson – a campion, or blue-green? Or sea thrift, the colour of your fence.' I hold the threads up. Her eye stares at each new colour like she wants it more than the last. 'If I could get warmer, I could make a pretty one for you. Just need to sit at a table by a window. I'll use lots of colours if you want. Only the rain won't wash them off. Them'll always be bright if you keep the sun off them.'

'I've got a bedspread,' she says, slow. 'I could bring it out. You could pass it through when you're finished.'

'Can't stitch if I'm shaking with cold. If I could come indoors, I'll stitch it, and when it's done, I'll go.'

Her eye stares at the bright threads in my hand. I can hear her thoughts. Pictures. A bedspread, warm dreaming, under stems, leaves, buds, flower, full bloom. Morgan thought loud as well. Must be this family's way, as them've been so locked away. Thems thoughts have got all loud, for them aren't getting them out by talking to other folk.

I say, 'I dun mean you harm,' and put the threads in my bag.

'No. I don't like colours to be in the dark.'

'I'll get gone now, see if other folks want a bedspread done.' I push the threads down, deep into the bag. 'Plenty of folks'd love to sleep under flowers what'll never die.'

'No.'

'Were you wanting one then?'

Slow, like each word saws its way out of her, she says, 'I've got a table you can use. And a chair. I think they'll like you.'

She's all off-kilter.

There's a rattle of something metal, jewellery or suchlike. She pushes open the gate. She stands fixed, like she's stuck in a picture. Hand held out, brown hair blown across her face, her bracelet chink clink clunk in the breeze. She's staring at her bracelet and she yanks the padlock off the gate. She's wearing a dress with patchwork grey and orange fabrics. It looks like a sunset what's been stitched all clumsy. The orange is a fine light fabric, the grey is thick. It hangs wrong. She stares all around at the hills with her mouth open a little, like she's tasting the air for smells.

I get up, near trip, but catch myself on the fence. I lean on it with my hands and step after step, walk my legs along.

She's stood there, eyes not settling on any one thing.

I ask, 'Is someone watching?'

Her words crack out like stones, 'The padlock wasn't locked.'

I hobble past her, into her garden. She smells of honey and sawdust.

She closes the gate behind me. Frowns at her bracelet, picks at the tangle of broken chains and clunks the padlock shut.

I'm in.

She rushes ahead of me, goes up the garden path and indoors. A door clacks shut inside the house. I hobble to the door and look inside, but she's gone. The floorboards creak as I go in. A corridor what smells of fresh sawn wood stretches out in front of me, bigger than my whole cottage. Wooden panels on the walls and two closed doors on each side are painted garish greens with orange and pink dots on them. Another door at the far end is painted with yellow and purple crescent moons. She's painted the brightest colours she can find, to make a picture of a happy home.

But the colours all clash.

I close the front door behind me. No one's going to get past that fence. No one'll get past Morgan's Mam neither, for she's as locked as that padlock.

It's rude to leave me stood here.

Maybe she's gone off to talk to her bedspread and friendly furniture. Perhaps them're all together behind one of them doors, arguing about whether her chair wants to make me feel comfy or not.

Morgan's Mam shrieks from upstairs, 'Morgan!' A wail, a thud. Footsteps cross the floor above me, muffled sobs.

I lean hard on a dotted door, it swings open too easy and I'm on the floor. Sharp pain hollers through my legs. I rub my bruised knees.

I'm in a room just for play. Toys scattered over red and blue painted floorboards; toy boats, tiny houses, bright-coloured blocks. A table, stencilled with red and gold stars fills near on half this room. Love hearts are scratched on the tabletop, H and A carved in the middle, HA HA. Love is laughing at me.

Three tall windows made up of eight panes each let in so much light. Nailed around the wooden walls and between the windows are huge sheets of paper with black and white drawings.

I dun breathe at the sight of what the drawings are of: Sishee's dress pegged to the bottom of the sea; Annie's son, Kieran; Valmarie's son, Dylan; Valmarie's sealskin; Kelmar's son, Jake . . .

I pull a picture down, hold it close to my eyes, soak the picture into them, can't blink in case it goes away, seeing hims face makes my heart thump. I know that even with the tall man for hims Da, the love I have for him hasn't changed at all.

Someone has drawn a picture of Barney.

Hims face looks up at me in black and white. My chest aches, my heart thuds. Someone in this house has seen him close enough to draw him. Barney would've had to sit there, so still. Quiet for ages, so this picture were made just right.

Not like him were at all.

Barney could have been found washed up at Wreckers Shore or in the poisons at the north shore; at some place the currents dragged him. And him could've been brought here, to the dead-taker, by someone what dun know him.

This could be a drawing of Barney, dead.

Morgan

My head is full of Mary, my heart feels stuffed full of feathers, I want to wrap her up. I don't want to feel like this with everyone I meet. I just feel like this because she's new. Everyone must feel this ache in their chest when they meet someone. How do people decide who to care about? My heart thuds. The next person I meet, I'm *not* going to care about them.

I've gone all the wrong ways, staring at every blade of grass, touching the branches of the small trees, avoiding thistles and climbing stone walls. I've passed a smokehouse and a farm with three barns, but now I'm nearing the graveyard again and can see the Thrashing House on the highest hill. I know how to get to Mary's cottage from there. My limbs ache with tiredness, I'm rumbling with hunger, my bare feet walk me forwards. There will be a bed and food in Mary's cottage, and soon I'll sleep.

But the woman with long black hair comes out of the grave-yard with her spade over her shoulder. I crouch down behind a twisted blackberry bush. Is she a witch, an alchemist, a dissec-tionist, gruesome scientist or confused vampire . . . out in the graveyard all night with a spade?

She goes towards a small house where a murder of crows squat along the gutter, making croaking sounds at the dawn.

The woman carries some kind of worn textured fabric. She reaches the house and leans the spade against the wall. She holds the fabric out. But it's not fabric, it's an animal hide. She shakes it out and earth falls in clods.

She clasps it to her. Holds it, strokes it, smells it and disappears around the back of the house. I want to know what she's found.

I knock on the back door.

No answer.

I fumble with the catch, which clicks when I push it down. The door opens into a small kitchen, herbs and spices in jars. I pick up a small bottle with a clear liquid inside it. The label reads, 'Forgetting herb'.

On the other side of the kitchen a door is ajar.

'Hello?' My voice is too quiet. 'Hello?'

I push the door open and can't speak, because the woman is naked.

She lies face down on the floor, on top of a decaying animal skin that smells of earth and of death. Her hands wrap what was once the face of the animal around her own face, she holds its earholes against her ears.

She sobs, her shoulders shake, she cries into the pelt, her body rolls against it, covered in soil, old fur sheds on the floor, almost dust. Her back is so pale, her black hair trails over it. She cries, clasps the skin around her face, her shoulders rise and fall, her shoulder blades clench, unclench, her smooth white skin is covered in goosebumps.

I can't stay here and watch, because I want to step in and wrap her up, tell her *It will be all right, it will be fine,* but I don't think it will.

*

Inside Mary's cottage I lock the door behind me. The ceiling is low, the smell of damp in the air. A pair of worn brown boots stand behind the door. Coats and shawls hang on hooks.

My feet want to dance, I spin around, my arms outstretched. Bump into the table by the window, the chair by the fireplace, the cupboard. I feel dizzy, laugh and can't stop. No one wants anything. No tea to make unless I want some. No floors to sweep unless I need them clean. No moods to understand, to placate, to ignore.

I can do whatever I want.

I twirl through each room, this one with a fireplace, a bedroom with two beds, one smaller than the other, another bedroom with a double bed, a kitchen. The furniture is all functional. Tables, a few chairs, cupboards. The only elaborate details are embroideries on every piece of fabric. On the cushions, bedspreads, pillows, curtains, blankets.

I stop spinning.

Embroideries are scattered everywhere, a tablecloth embroidered with purple clouds has been hurled over the chair, a large folded piece has been thrown in the fireplace. An empty wooden washtub in the corner of the kitchen is filled with handkerchiefs, embroidered with blue children holding hands.

A resourcefulness of embroideries.

I lie on the fabric strewn across the floor and look up at the beams on the ceiling, my arms outstretched, imagine what it would feel like to float up there, light, weightless, like a transformed creature in a storybook, a goose turned thistledown, spider turned moth, hedgehog turned butterfly. I could fly in here, float just underneath the ceiling . . . So I exhale, and float up to the ceiling. I drift my family and the locked pink fence out of my lungs. I fall asleep, curled next to a spider's web between two beams.

*

Someone bangs on the door.

I'm on the floor.

I roll over, crawl under the table beneath the window and curl up into a ball.

A voice crashes through the keyhole. 'Mary love, it's me again.' An accent like Mary's, but older. Choked. 'Please open the door. Mary, I'm so sorry. I've done wrong.'

So have I. Because I've stolen the Thrashing House key from Mary. It only brought her trouble. I bury my head in my knees.

Animals sniff at the door. I hear the sound of waves washing along the beach. Gulls wail.

The voice speaks again. 'Maybe you dun hear me knock last night.'

Scratching at the bottom of the door, dogs whine. A spider spins a web in the corner underneath the tabletop.

'I'm sorry, Mary. It's all mixed up, 'ent it.'

The spider lowers itself on a thread. It has detailed grey markings on its body, it lands on a floorboard and skulks across the floor. I crawl to the front door and a splinter gets stuck in my toe. Sitting with my back against the door, I ease the splinter out, reach for the brown boots and put them on. They're too small, but only just. I stand up and open the door.

The woman jumps back. Her three dogs growl. She's not much younger than Mum. Skinny and sharp-faced, with a shock of hair.

I say, 'Come in.'

She steps further back. 'Where's Mary?'

'She's not here.' I open the door wider and say, 'But come in.'

She purses her lips. One of her dogs whines, raises a paw. Whimpers. She walks in and the dogs try to follow her. I nudge them with a boot and shut them outside.

She tugs at a button on her dress and frowns at some embroidered napkins on the floor. 'Mary lets the dogs in.' She folds her arms. 'What you throwing Beatrice's broideries around for? Who *are* you?'

'Mary said I could stay.'

She puts her hands on her hips. 'I'm Annie.' Her cheeks are pink. 'Look, I'll come back when Mary's home.' She glances at the floor and rubs her hands together. 'You should pick up them broideries. No idea Beatrice'd left so many. Them'll be worth a lot.'

'Well, let's clean them up.' I snatch up the embroideries on the floor, pile them on the back of the chair. As I walk around, the boots graze my heels. I reach into the fireplace, fish out a large embroidery, I sit down in the chair. I smooth the embroidery on my lap, it has a picture of a grey cobweb on it, the detail is beautiful, silver raindrops hanging on unravelling threads . . . but no spider.

Annie sighs, sits down on the stool and stares at the empty fireplace. 'Mary gave me stew. Since then, I find it hard to swallow.'

'Why?'

'Can't talk to anyone.' She grasps at a small cloudy button on her dress and it comes away in her hand. 'I miss Beatrice. She'd have understood.'

'Beatrice?'

'Funny you dun know her Mam's name.' She frowns at me and drops her hands into her lap. 'Dun believe the tall man were a ghost. No need for ghost trade, passing through my hands.'

'What did you say?'

'Look, there's ghost trade all over the floor! You can see it. Help me pick it up!' She leans down and picks up something invisible from the floorboards, rubs her hand over her pockets, eyes far away.

'There's nothing there Annie. When will the boats that go to the mainland come?'

She whispers, 'Where're you from? You safe, or from a dreaming?' Her head twitches and words rush out of her mouth. 'Glass question mark. Smash!' She claps. Her hands fly up in the air. She rubs them together. 'Could be doubt. Dun know what Martyn were doubting, always seemed sure enough with me. Fragile doubt. Unsure . . . wanting reading taught . . . I never knew . . .'

'What's wrong with you?'

Outside, one of her dogs howls.

Annie leans forwards and holds out her hands to the empty fireplace. She rubs her hands and holds them out, again and again, faster and faster. She mutters under her breath, 'If the bells dun ring. Nothing goes away. Stays here.' She prods the side of her head. 'In here. In my pockets.' She slaps her hip. 'No bells in my thoughts.' She slaps her forehead.

Two of the dogs howl.

She looks at the embroidery on my lap and says, 'I were beautiful on my wedding day. Beatrice broidered my dress all over with silver cobwebs. My hair piled so high, I looked like my face were floating in a cloud. I got lost in my wedding dress, but I were sleepwalking, looking for home.' She stares at her hands. 'Not having the dreamings took. Mam died. Aw. Missed her. Aw.' She pouts her lips like a child. 'She died and I got the cottage and the dogs.'

She smoothes her hands over her hair and smiles at me, shyly.

Outside, all three dogs howl.

I say, calmly, 'I'm sorry your Mum died. When will the boats—'

'I dun know it were *the dogs* I were missing. Not really *Mam*. . . Dun say it out loud. Shhh.' She puts her finger over her lips. 'Everything were all right again, when I got the dogs back . . .'

She shakes herself and squeezes her neck. 'I miss him. Cover him in kisses. Martyn.' She cups her hand over her mouth. 'Dun doubt I loved you the most. I miss you so much I can't find words—'

'Annie, please stop.'

She jumps up and slaps her hands on her hips. She says, 'I need my dogs!' and staggers towards the door.

I follow her, grasp her thin arm and swing her around to face me.

She glares at the battered rug on the floor.

I say, 'What's wrong with you? Are you mad, or is this a tangle from not sleeping? Mary said—'

She lifts up a foot and gazes at her white boot. 'Keep-my-mouth-shut boots.' She trips, I try to catch her but she slumps on the floor, legs outstretched.

I open the front door and her dogs charge in.

She sits up. 'Here them are!' Holding her hands out to the dogs she beams like a child. Three black tails wag, three tongues lick her hands, her face. She pets them, turns and frowns up at me. 'Who are you? Where's Mary? How did I get down here?'

Two of Annie's dogs lie next to her, the other one rests its head on her lap, gazing up at her, its tongue dripping drool on her grey dress. She keeps her eyes on the dog, smoothing its fur with her hands. I'm in the chair opposite her. It's as if we met just a moment ago, and the last conversation didn't happen.

I say, 'Mary might be a while. Maybe you should come back another time. Not today. Maybe in a couple of weeks or—'

'What's she up to?' Annie frowns at me. Her fingers pinch

the dog's ears. It shakes her hands off, she kneads its jowls. It grunts, eyes glazed.

'I don't know.'

Annie says, 'Write it for me.' Her eyes gleam. 'Write it all down.' She leans over the dog and kisses the top of its head.

'Can Mary read?'

'Mary understands the letters, aye. Beatrice taught her. Beatrice liked to write things down to remember how she felt. Never knew she'd not need to be reminded, for she died too young to forget.' She strokes the dog's head and sighs.

'But you . . .'

'Never got to learn, were looking after my own Mam, weren't I? She'd gotten sick.' She looks at me sideways. 'Mothers teach daughters.'

'Why don't sons learn to read?'

'Weaving Room talk. That's the place for it. But some of the women . . .' She leans on the table and stares at me. 'You twenty-one yet?'

Three choices. The truth, a lie, or silence.

I silently nod.

'That's all right. Never seen you there. Never used to think this way. Maybe it's best to look at things upside. Or were it down . . . I dun fit no more.'

'There's a Weaving Room – if I'm twenty-one, am I allowed to learn weaving?'

'Of course there's weaving. But a whole lot of women together dun do just one thing at a time. All kinds of things, cloths, tapestries, baskets, scarves and shawls, all the cloths an' fabrics – much is woven there. And much is talked of.' She leans forwards. 'Do you know about the snake ropes, left on the shore in crates?'

One of her dogs barks.

We both jump.

She coughs. 'Never said that. Come to the Weaving Rooms. You're of age. But if you've not been there for the Scattering Up, I shouldn't speak of it to you. You might find *you* fit, though by the looks of you I'd doubt it. Bit too *clean*.' She looks at my eyes.

I look at her stained dress. 'What's the Scattering Up?'

She says, 'After your next monthly, keep the rags, dun wash them out. Take them along at the next dark moon. That's when you'll swear not to speak of the Weaving Rooms to them what dun belong there. Powerful circle, is that one. You'll not be able to talk of the Weaving Rooms to none what shouldn't hear.'

I cross my legs.

Annie says, 'Write Mary this letter then.' She rummages in the drawer. 'Ah. Here.' She takes out a bundle of sticks of charcoal and eases one out with her thin fingers. She pulls out a thick book made of rough paper, stitched down the side with orange embroidery thread. The book is blank, with a couple of pages torn off.

She frowns. 'Odd she's letting you sit in her cottage, when she's not here. What did you say your name were again?'

I slide out a chair, sit down at the table and pick up the stick of charcoal. I tap my fingers on the table. Pick at the orange stitching on the book.

Annie says, 'Right then. Mary love, I feel right bad for knowing about the trade and not telling anyone.' She stares out of the window at the empty horizon. 'The tall men dun want our men to talk, and spoil the trade for them. But them never knew Martyn had told *me*.'

The charcoal screeches on the paper – she talks faster than I can write.

She glances at me. 'Are you getting this writ?'

I nod.

'I keep thinking of my Kieran. Him is stood under a tree, after the rain has been, and the tree is still raining. Tree rain falls all over hims head, turns to pure gold and fills up hims pockets. I'm *so* proud of him.' She stares at my hands. 'You never wrote that bit.'

'I did. Just before you said it. Keep going.' I tear out the first page, to start a new letter.

She doesn't notice. She says, 'The tall men said on the main land it were important to think of the future. I felt a fool for never thinking like that.'

She glances at me. 'You're not writing.'

I say, 'So you never think about what you really *want*—'

'Me and Martyn talked Kieran's future all through—'

'I don't mean what people *do* – I mean the person you *could* be.'

'I'm myself, pet. Can't be another person later on. You're born just the once, you know. I'll lose the threads if you keep interrupting!' She presses her palms on the table. 'Get this down: I knew the tall men wouldn't want me to talk. Not if them wanted to trade for more boys.' She picks at the skin on her finger. 'I never knew a proper secret afore, not about anything.' She smiles. 'I told two of the tall men I knew. Said I'd talk unless them gave me something just for me, then and there. Them gave me a whole lot of fancy foods, and some silky ribbons the likes I've never seen before, and I traded them on for a good amount. Got the window fixed, and plenty in to last us for the winter. And then we decided to move to Wreckers Shore, Mary – you know I need more than I've had. Never have been fast at knitting and the main land folks *will* change what them want so often. I told the tall men I wanted a pair of white boots just like Kelmar's.'

'Are there only two pairs of white boots? Can you dance in them? Are they hard to take off . . . no, that was the story about *red*—'

'It's just me and Kelmar what have them, aye. Cobbler says it's showing no respect to the animal, to change the colour of its hide. But it's dead by then, 'ent it?'

I look under the table at the brown cracked boots pinching my toes. And at Annie's new boots, pacing up and down, bigger than these ones. I ask, 'Can I have your old boots?'

'Shush it. I decided to tell them next time that I wanted a new white dress, made of crushed-up spun salt. After that, I were going to ask for a cloak made of woven soot and a necklace made from the tears of flies.' She beams.

'Lovely.' I lean my elbows on the table.

She stops pacing and glares at me. 'Just write, will you! So. Write this: Them brought the white boots. Not the same as Kelmar's, as her boots *are* the cobbler's after all, just painted 'em white, she has.' She smiles at her feet. 'I kept these boots hid for a time, but I want to wear them, though them're too big. Them remind me Kieran's got a better life now, and when I doubt that, I look at them and them shine the truth of the main land back up at me.'

'Do you really want me to tell her about your *boots*?'

'Well, all folk've been talking of Kelmar's, so someone's got to speak of mine. All right. Dun put that bit down.'

'Right.'

'Say this to Mary: I'm all jumbled for I can't stop the Thrashing House calling me so loud.'

'It *calls*?' I stare at her.

'Still is.' She clasps her hands over her ears. Her eyes seem terrified. 'Maybe now I've said it, it'll stop calling. Walk down the beach when you've read this, I'll watch at the window for you – we got to stick together you and me. Let's talk soon, even if you're angered?'

'Do you want to sign it?'

She whispers, 'Just write my name. Annie. Dun think I told you that.' She walks to the front door. 'And you've still not given me yours.' Her dogs spring up, tails wagging, and follow her outside. I close and lock the door behind her and read the letter:

Dear Mary,

I knew about trading boys before other people did.

I knew I had to keep it a secret or the trade would be spoiled.

So I blackmailed the tall men and got the windows fixed and we were going to move house.

The tall men brought me some nice things (including boots that don't fit) and I had some lovely ideas for pretty things that are impossible to get, but good to dream about.

I feel guilty.

I think the Thrashing House is calling me.

Talk to me on the beach if you're angry,

Annie.

I open the drawer in the table, pick through scraps of folded fabric, stray embroidery thread ends. Taking out a piece of blue thread, I tear the letter out of the book and tie it up.

I stroke the next blank page on the empty book, sit down and write:

Once upon a time there was Annie.

Annie had three black dogs.

One called Blame.

One called Shame.

One called Guilt.

She hid behind Blame, Shame and Guilt, so no one would see her. The three black dogs snapped at anyone who came near her. Annie smiled to herself, thinking how their teeth frightened everyone else away. She fed the dogs and loved them and would never part from them. Made them blankets from the warm ash in her fire, pillows from the thickening slops in her cooking pots. Gave them soft sleep and a beach to run along.

And all was well.

No one could see who she really was because she was too busy taking care of the dogs. And the dogs were the most interesting thing about her. She was certain of that.

But one day she cut her thumb while chopping potatoes for stew. The dogs caught the scent of blood and acted like the animals that they really were.

So they turned on Annie, and Blame, Shame and Guilt killed her dead. They lived happily ever after, known only as 'The three black dogs who killed their mistress', which they thought suited them much better. They smiled with all of their teeth.

The end.

*

I might have days, weeks, here, staring through the thick glass of this window at distorted waves that wash in and pull out, with no boats blurring through, no way back to the mainland, my heart beating out, *Soon, let it be soon.*

Please let a boat come, to carry me away.

No brother, no mother, no father, but behind the door

between other coats hangs a small child's coat, a man's wool hat and a woman's shawl. On the back of one of the bedroom doors is a nightdress, an embroidery across the bodice of a tree with curled branches. Mary said her father was an old worn boot. I'm sure that's what she said. I look at the boots pinching my feet. They're old and worn. I whisper at the left boot, the one that hurts the most, 'You're not her dad in disguise are you?'

And of course it doesn't answer.

I write in the book:

There's . . .
A boot for a father.
A thrashed brother.
An injured daughter.
A dead mother.
I stole the Thrashing House key.
The wind blows so cold that it curls up the trees.
No one is here in this cottage but me.

Everyone is gone. Will I be next?

It could be this cottage itself that makes people vanish. My own disappearance could be being plotted. The fireplace could be considering how best to sneak up and swallow me. The chairs want to ambush me, break my bones with their legs. I should plan for this attack, arm myself with knives from the kitchen, hide myself underneath that trapdoor in the floor, unless the trapdoor is planning to guillotine me . . . I should run . . . but I can't stop thinking that this is a cottage where four people once breathed and slept and cried and laughed and ate and lived. And don't any more.

But it doesn't feel empty.

I'm being watched. My spine prickles. Someone else is here in this room. I spin round. My breath catches in my throat.

A woman kneels on the chair by the empty fireplace, her arms folded on the embroideries piled on the back of the seat. She stares at me, intently. From the dark hair, pale skin and the deep blue of her eyes, the resemblance is clear; it's Mary's mother.

'You're dead,' I say, before I can stop myself.

Mary

The door creaks open. I wipe my eyes and nose on my sleeve.
A little girl with a pale face and light wavy hair peers round
it. Big blue eyes. She's so pale her skin is almost see-through.
She steps into the room and folds her arms across a fancy grey
dress, clean and pressed. Another face, the same face, looks
round the door and joins her. Her dress is the same, only nut-
brown. She shuts the door and folds her arms the opposite
way, left over right. Them look like reflections. Twinned. With
bare feet.

Them stare at me, not moving.

I take a step towards them.

The twin in the grey dress backs away.

'Dun worry.' I take my coat off and put it on the table. 'I'm
Mary. Going to do a broiderie for your Mam.'

Them glance at each other. Something flickers in thems
eyes.

I pick up the picture. 'This boy, have you seen him?' I keep
my voice gentle.

Them turn away. Them each have ribbons in thems hair, one
brown, one grey. Them walk out of the room. One twin looks

back at me, smiles with tiny clean teeth. The smile dun reach her eyes.

I follow them. Them stop next to another door. I look down at my dirty dress, torn down the middle, stitched rough. Covered in brown stains, still damp. My dirty bag with just one handle and threads hanging loose. A gash in my leg, thick dark blood and dirt smeared across it. The bruise around it already blue. My hair, tangled.

'We'll clean you up—' says the twin in grey.

'—because you stink,' says the other.

My cheeks flame, 'That's rude, now!'

The twin in grey steps back.

I fold my arms. 'Do you *think* rude together, as well as talk it?'

Them take each other's hands. The one in the brown dress says, 'We always think together when we agree. And we always do—'

'—agree. Apart from when—' the twin in grey smiles.

'—we can't decide which of us is prettier or cleverer.' Thems smiles drop.

Them open a door to a steep wooden staircase leading upstairs. 'The bath's ready. We're going to clean you upstairs in our own bathroom, where we wash our dolls.'

'You have a washroom here just for dolls? Course you do.' I follow them upstairs.

In the twins' bedroom, two grand wooden beds stand side by side. Two mirrors over two sets of drawers. Blackberry-colour fabric drapes along the walls, silver trees painted over it. I follow the twins to the corner of the room. Them lift the fabric, and there's another door. It opens into a washroom with a huge wooden washtub right in the middle. It's painted with curled shapes like seeds growing, bean to shoot to root. The washtub is full of steaming water and thick bubbles froth on the surface. The twins pick up two metal buckets.

The one in grey says, 'We'll fetch more hot water, it's nearly full.'

I say, 'Dun worry. It's just right. You two wait in your room for me.'

Them hold each other's hands and stare at my dress, like them're thinking really loud that I should take it off right now.

My hands are filthy, black grime under my nails. 'Come on. You wouldn't bathe in front of me. I'll let you brush my hair after.'

The twin in brown whispers, 'Dress up dolly. We can give her ribbons in her hair, make her look like she's going—' them smile at each other and whisper together, '—outside.'

Them glance up at me, heads tilted.

'Go on, out. Guard the door so no one comes near. It's an important job. You can play with my hair after, and we'll talk about the drawing of the boy.'

Them smile. Them *might* mean it this time. Hard to tell. Them close the door behind them.

*

If I stay in this washroom as long as I can, there's still a tiny bit of hope that Barney is still alive. I can hold it in my hands, make it spark, make it glow bright, keep it hid just for myself. Not think about what it will feel like, when it goes out.

I pull my dress off over my head. It looks like a dirty dishrag on the floor. I check the door is still closed. I pull off my vest, unbind my breasts and them ache as I kick off my boots and socks. I step out of my drawers, pick them up and look at the gusset. No blood. Pinheads of light swirl behind my eyelids, I grip the edge of the washtub.

In the small rippled mirror my eyes are too old for my face. Dun want to look at my belly. From the pain tight across the skin, the smears of dried soil over it, I know that's where hims hands were. I can smell the dank dead graveyard on me. Sickness catches the back of my throat. I splash water over my face. My hands are smeared in dirt.

Can't get in this washtub, I'm too filthy.

On the damp floor in the corner I curl up, my arms around myself. I hear Langward's voice in my head . . . *You look so like your mother*. Press my cheek on the floor. And I do look like her. I curl up tighter.

Him dun see me, him wanted something of hers. Wanted to spite her, even when she's dead. Because the way him loved her is like a poison that spreads.

My head's full of thorns and spikes.

Blackthorn bush thoughts: part of me is still lying there in the graveyard, staring up at the sky through tangled twigs and thorns. A shadow of me peeled off, feeling all the things I dun want to feel, waiting to be buried.

Thorn.

Lying here thinking him might've said the truth: Mam traded me.

Spike. Spike. Spike.

The worst thing of all is that it *could* be true.

And she's not here to ask if it is.

Thorn.

My shadow, peeled away.
Sinks into the earth.   Mine.
Not mine.

Never going to let anyone
touch me.

                              Are there any hands what
                              dun want anything for
                              themselves, just to stroke
                              me into light?

Everything needs to stop.

                              Everything needs to come
                              back.

My heart judders.

                              I've got to get clean and
                              stop thinking half in half.

*

Under the water in the washtub I open my eyes and surface.

If I leave my shadow, her, in the graveyard, she'll rot like all the corpses. She's stuck there. I shout *Mary!* in my thoughts. Plunge down in the water, see her lying in the graveyard. *Stand up!* Behind my eyelids, she hobbles to her feet.

I surface.

Come here. I breathe in.

Plunge down.

I see her. She staggers. Pushes her way through bushes, hobbles over stones, her arms flail. She trips and stands and trips again – she moves like she's being tipped in waves. She crosses the fields. Threads tied from her waist to mine tug her along. She pitches, surges, tilts.

She drifts through the pink fence, sifts through the front door like she's made of black smoke, climbs the stairs, passes through the twins' room. She's at this door. I judder as she sieves through it.

I surface.

She stands at the other side of the washtub.

We stare at each other through steam. She's got my face, body, ripped dress, but she's made of grey and black twisted threads.

She's angered, hurt, crying. Tears leave pale trails on her grey cheeks. She reaches her hand into the washtub, splashes water on her belly and winces.

I stand up, all clean and clear, no pain in my body.

She stands opposite me, smeared in dirt, face dark and full of pain. She bares her teeth at me and pulls her dress open. I look at her belly. It sags from hurt, her skin hangs like folded linen. I look down at mine. Now I know what Langward did. Stretched from our right hipbones up to under our left ribs. The cuts show the letters, a deep, red word, carved in our skin with my knife:

LOVE

Love, that I dun feel and is not felt for me.
Love, a scar to heal over time.
Love can scab up, dry out, flake off.

I reach out my hands. Shadow Mary groans and it sounds in my head. Her hollow eyes scowl under strands of hair. Neither one of us wants to be attached back onto each other. This is Shadow Mary, my own twin.

What do you want? I ask her in my thoughts.

She clenches her hands. She holds them out and looks at them. Her nails have grown. Four crescents of black blood, across the middle of her palms. She sighs, like it's a relief. Her voice in my head says, *Hide me in the moppet, with Barney.*

I look down at the palms of my own hands. Them are clean and clear, wrinkled and puffed up with water.

The moppet is curled tight in the bottom of my bag. I pull it out and drop it on the floor. It sits up, raggedy ears hanging over its beady eyes, dull with steam. I turn the moppet round so it faces Shadow Mary. *Get in.* I think at her. She steps towards me, fists clenched. I think, *Hide in the moppet, with Barney. I'll look after you.*

She breaks into pieces, smaller and smaller, and drops through the steam. My heart thuds. Shadow Mary is a pile of blackness on the floor. The blackness moves like a dark fog. It gets sucked in, where the opening of the shell must be.

The moppet slumps forwards. I pick it up and put it next to my ear.

Barney's voice says, 'Mary here.'

Shadow Mary says, 'Go. To. Sleep.'

I imagine me and Barney are together, curled up for sleep, me stroking hims hair. I listen close, and say, 'Barney, I'll always keep the moppet, no matter what, because you're mine.'

Shadow Mary's voice says, 'Go. Away.'

Morgan

'You can see me,' says Beatrice, with doubt in her voice.

'Yes.' Anita told me once that ghosts didn't always know they were dead and would become offended if the living ever said it to them.

She says, 'It's taken too long to be seen.' A low wind blows in the room, and is gone. 'Am I still here?'

'As clear as anyone alive would be.'

Beatrice puts her hand over her heart. 'Dun know . . . how long . . . this will last,' she pants. Her chest rises and falls against her hand. 'No one sees me. I've lost all the names . . . the first things that went . . . I need them here, need them to think. Of. Me.'

I take a deep breath, 'Mary's hurt.'

Beatrice wails, 'She won't come home!' Her breathing is too fast.

I touch her shoulder.

She looks at my hand, as if she's unsure what it is. 'Can you feel me?'

I nod.

Beatrice's shoulder feels like a dead bird. Cold feathers. Desperately fragile bones. 'Hold me.' Beatrice has panic in her eyes as she stands up and reaches out her arms.

My arms open.

Beatrice's thin frame leans into me . . . I listen for her heart-beat. There isn't one. Mine beats hard. Dead feathers tickle at my neck. I'm holding her . . . I don't want . . . I turn my face to hers.

Beatrice has grown pale feathers all over her, apart from on her face.

Her sharp eyes gleam.

I pull away, she grips harder. Cold crackles through my arms, my heart thuds, I twist away from her, but she grasps my back, ice pushes through my spine towards my heart.

'You're dead!' I shriek.

A gale sweeps through the room.

I'm alone in the middle of the room, my arms wrapped around myself. A small white feather twists in the draught on the floor.

*

I'm freezing cold and I need to light a fire, but there's no fuel by the empty fireplace. I wrap myself up in an embroidered tablecloth and feel like a crone. Crones wear shawls, so I find one, sling it around myself and hobble into the kitchen and out of the back door. There are old fishing nets strewn around, a rusted saw and a broken wooden table. The track that leads along the back of the other cottages is empty. A dog barks and I don't think crones like barking dogs, so I drag the table quickly into the kitchen, get the saw and close the door.

The shawl and tablecloth I'm wrapped in are embroidered. Beatrice's things. I tear them off and drop them on the floor. My hands are freezing and the saw is nearly blunt. So now I'm a woodswoman, and I'm resourceful with a blunt saw. I get some good pieces of wood by sawing up the table and now there's sawdust all over the kitchen floor.

I take the wood into the other room, lay the fire and strike a match, and another and another. Poor little match girl, so cold and alone. The fire takes a while to catch. I hold the shawl over the fireplace so it sucks up the air.

My teeth are chattering. On the floor by the fire, I hold out my hands and let the warmth spread through me.

Thoughts crash around my head, all fighting to be chosen and I don't know which thoughts are mine and which are Beatrice's. I get the book, sit in the chair by the fire and write:

Once there was a ghost mother.

She was hungry for any kind of life, because she had lost hers somewhere. She thought her daughter could keep her alive, and she looked in the daughter's heart, but she couldn't make her home there. The daughter had a picture of her mother on a wall in her heart, and it wasn't flattering. The ghost mother knew that she wouldn't be able to live in her daughter's heart, staring at this portrait of herself.

The ghost mother was left homeless, seeking some other heart to live in.

My neck prickles. Beatrice is back. I keep writing.

A word of warning to those seeking friendship: if you meet this ghost mother and she holds out her arms, don't hold out your own.

She's grown her daughter's bones and blood in her womb; she remembers the warmth and the beat, how her hopes were built into the cells of her daughter's body. And how to grow a heart.

She remembers how much expectation she had to build, to pant her daughter into the world. But she realises that her expectations were unfulfilled. They were all the things that she wanted for herself and never got. So she is left wandering, seeking a heart, any heart, your heart, to make her home.

Don't ignore this advice and open out your arms – you won't know anything is wrong, till you hear a heartbeat in your breast, that just misses the rhythm of your own. By then it will be too late.

The ghost mother will curl warm in your heart while you stare through disorientated eyes, and find you don't know what you feel.

*

Beatrice is still here somewhere, hidden in some shadow, under a bed, in a cupboard, just in the corner of my eyes when I blink. She's still here because I can't stop thinking about her. I'm calling her back into her home with my thoughts. I gather up every embroidery I can find, roll them up, pack them away in the cupboard and close the door. I sit at the table by the window. The sea is empty and grey. I try not to think about Beatrice.

Instead, I think about my own parents.

In our last year on the mainland, my parents had a room they hid things in whenever anyone died. I saw them dressed in black, smuggling them in night after night and locking them in there. Valuable items – boxes of jewellery, pillowcases filled with gold coins, bundles of notes stuffed in a mattress, silverware, bronze statues, furs.

The money they had after each death can't have just been the fee for my father's services. They had a lot more money every time someone died. More than they knew what to do with. My mother ordered new clothes and jewellery. She paid young men to come and coil and uncoil her hair while she smiled at herself in the mirror. She got whatever she wanted delivered to our door in parcels. Fine lacework, designer shoes, bolts of silken fabrics, leather coats, delicate beading, fur-lined boots. Her face scrubbed plucked tweaked, injected smeared plumped.

She looked and felt beautiful. Stolen beauty.

My father would go out for expensive meals. I listened through the banisters when I heard the front door bang. My mother would rush to the door to hear him speak. He'd tell her how he drank the richest, most expensive wine, 'Like the blood of kings'. I imagined shimmering wine glasses, brimming red, that a king had dripped from his forefinger at my father's request.

'Ooh, and what did you eat . . . my lord?' Mum sniggered up at him, her hands on her chest. My father told her, 'Seventeen courses. Twenty. So many I lost count.' He'd lick his lips and smile. 'Silver spoons and forks for fingers,' he once said, as he arrived in the hallway downstairs. He glanced up, caught me watching, fluttered his fingers at me with a glint in his eye, and shouted, '*Child, back to bed.*'

He filled himself with food and wine. Stolen sustenance.

Now my mother is no longer beautiful and my father picks at his food.

What happened to make them run? My best friend, Anita, was a ghost. Proof that ghosts exist, if my parents decided to believe me. But they didn't.

'Ask them where they get their money from . . .' Anita

whispered, over and over into my ears as I slept. I'd hear her halfway between sleep and waking, her lips over my ear, holding her hair away from my face, being so careful never to let any part of herself touch me.

But I didn't ask them.

But, perhaps, one day they saw her.

Anita could have poked my mother in the face, called her . . . a thief? She might have kicked her, pulled her hair, made fear rampage through her heart for a moment, for a day, a week, a year . . . and still, now. If my parents stole from so many dead people's homes, raided their possessions, they could have thought a whole army of ghosts might be marauding after them. No wonder my mother doesn't think she's safe.

When we left, they brought bolts of cloth, seeds, cans of plant feed. They brought crates of books and clothes. They brought Mum's hammers, saws and chisels, Dad's embalming chemicals and scalpels, cloths for shrouds. Handles and hinges and fittings for the coffins. They brought his smart suits and her chalks and paints and rolls of paper. They brought themselves: an undertaker and a coffin-maker when there was no one else here to do these jobs. They grew as much food from the seeds as they could. Anything my parents need but can't grow, my father very occasionally goes out to get. And he gives the islanders 'forwards trade' for it. Forwards trade is for death: his promise to prepare bodies, provide a coffin, dig a hole. So people give him what he asks for.

Because the dead must be buried.

My parents are thieves and they stole from the dead.

My father's greed. He persuaded Mum to help him steal.

His idea, and now, his guilt.

*

A fog is coming in. The sea is settled, with the tide out, washing on the sand. I wonder who is staring out of the windows in the cottages next to this one, if their parents ever stole, and if it made them feel this kind of angry-sad, when they finally let themselves realise what they'd known all along.

So I was brought with them, made to cook and clean in a house they built themselves – a house no one had died in – a home with no ghosts. My past was denied, along with theirs. So I ended up living inside my storybooks. My favourite story wasn't in any book. It's been hidden in my head.

I write it down:

A Story of Love
A young woman is trapped in a house for too many years. One day she begs the sky outside her window to come and take her away. She cries at the sky. It doesn't listen. She shouts and whispers. The clouds look sorry, make rain, but nothing else happens.

When she tells the sky she loves it, wants to float in it, to love it for exactly what it is – an open expanse of clouds, of rain, of gales and snow, of sound and light and dark – the sky knows that she has seen it for itself, for all of the parts that make up the whole sky: she doesn't just love it for its sunshine or blue. The sky grants her wish.

The sky blows a gale that sends a witch, steering a pirate ship, to just outside her window. The witch is singing the most heart-rending soaring song the young woman has ever heard. She dances over to the witch's ship on the notes from her voice and the witch transforms her into a cat.

The witch strokes and fusses and loves her. For years the cat and the witch are content, but later, the witch sees that though the cat is a good rat-catcher and is content on her lap, it always goes into the cabin when it rains, having a dislike of water. The cat seems strangely guilty about disliking the rain. The cat remembers the promise it made when it was a young woman – to love the sky for exactly what it is.

The witch sees the cat looking sadly out of the cabin window at the rain, relents and changes the cat back into the young woman, who by now is no longer young. The witch thinks that the woman, having lost all those years to being a cat, will become angry and leave her. But the woman is not angry with the witch. 'Those years were not lost: I have experienced purring in my throat, the sweet taste of cream, the euphoria of catching rats, a taste for the warmth of fresh blood and the gentleness of your hands.'

The witch trains the woman as her apprentice. They bargain in conversations made from tumbleweed, throw black and white chess pieces backwards and forwards between their hands and the woman learns enough to become a powerful witch. They rescue one another from melancholia, laugh over the naivety of kissed toads and debate to the conclusion that power should be earned and not claimed.

They travel the skies, landing whenever they feel the desire to do so. They sell poisoned apples to the suicidal to grant them a quick and painless death, and laugh if they decide not to eat them. They offer lovesick maidens potions to cure them of unrealistic visions and then give them telescopes so they can map out the stars.

After many years of travel, when they have learned all they can from responses to both help and hindrance, they see they have become old. They land the pirate ship on a high rooftop in a city full of chimneys. They take in lost children and transform them into cats if their lives are not making them happy. Every night the two witches sing at the sky, their voices rise into the stars, are soaked clean by the rain, scrubbed by the clouds, and dried by the gales.

There they live to this day, in their ship full of purrs.

*

I wake in the chair by the fire that's gone out. A wind is blowing in Mary's parents' bedroom. I get up and struggle with the door. A gale blows it shut, but I shove, it springs open, and there isn't any wind.

The window is closed. Embroideries are strewn all over the double bed. On the bedside table there's a pillowcase embroidered with an albatross, and a bedspread stitched with crows, seagulls and owls hangs from the wardrobe door. A gale has rampaged through this room, scattering embroideries that lie where they've fallen.

Beatrice has thrown her embroideries around again, to tell me she's still here.

Footsteps thud behind me. I turn, and the door clicks shut. There in the middle of the floor is a rolled-up piece of grey fabric, the back criss-crossed with embroidery threads. It wasn't on the floor when I came in. I can't stop thinking of her, because she's making me. Poor, dead Beatrice.

I pick it up and unroll the fabric. It's an embroidery of this family's tree. She's stitched on all the names, embroidered leaves around them, stitched the trunk in ochre and earth-coloured threads. Shown all the connections with twigs.

There's another name on this family tree and it links itself to Beatrice's. Beatrice had a brother or sister. The name of their father is the same but the mother is different. The name of Beatrice's sibling is embroidered over in thick black stitches, uneven and angry.

Jig jag.

She's stitched them out of the tree. Mary has an aunt or uncle. She could have gone to them. With a small knife from the kitchen, I cut away the black threads. The name underneath is stitched in crimson thread.

The name of Mary's aunt is *Kelmar*.

Annie mentioned her. The woman with white boots I saw at the graveyard. Mary's brother is here on the tree as well, his name should be next to hers, but it's been sewn in a little untidily. Barney. The picture of a small rabbit stitched next to him. Only three years old. So little. Mary said he was locked in the Thrashing House, somewhere Annie is scared of. She's a grown woman. He's far too little to be frightened.

So I have three reasons to go to the Thrashing House:

1) I want to get Mary's brother out for her to make up for taking the Thrashing House key.
2) I really want to see what it's like inside.
3) The Thrashing House beckoned me.

And I have three choices, so when it's dark, and no one will see me, I'm going to do all of them:

1) Go to the Thrashing House and get Barney out.
2) Find stitched-out Kelmar.
3) Find Mary.

Just three things to do. Then I can come back to this cottage and wait for boats, and when I leave this island, I'll do so clean and light. Unlike my father, I'll have no guilt at all.

Mary

I'm sat on one of the twin's beds, all clean, a damp towel wrapped around me, hiding my bindings what're drying quick and getting too tight. My hair's been combed and braided. The twins unravelled the tangles I thought I'd already ripped out. Four vicious hands tugged and twisted, pulled and tweaked. I feel like I'm not really here. A red ribbon pinches the top of my head; them have fixed it so firm that it stings. Them told me, 'To be pretty, it has to hurt.' The twins said my hair is too lovely for my dress what I've scrubbed clean and left hung to dry over the side of the washtub.

The one in grey – Ash, she said her name were, when yanking my hair – has gone off to get me an old dress of thems Mam's from a dress-up box. Hazel is standing by the door watching me, kicking one bare foot against the other.

Ash comes back in with a black linen dress. I take it into the washroom where my drawers and vest are nearly dry. I put them on and pull the dress over my head. It's far too wide but it covers me from neck to ankle.

I come out into thems bedroom and say, 'Who did the drawing of the boy?'

Ash sits on the bed on one side of me and Hazel on the other.

Hazel says, 'I'll give you two answers – you have to guess the right one. My answers are: My sister. And. You did.'

'Which sister? Ash or Morgan?' I ask, quick.

Hazel says, 'We've got a question for you, so we'll tell you, if you answer *our* question first.' She goes to the mirror, picks up a pink ribbon and ties it in her hair. Ash follows her and unties her own grey ribbon and hands it to Hazel, who puts it in her hair as well. Both of them are watching me in the mirror. I hear a thump in the room. Them are thinking so loud the air feels thick.

Them stare at me.

I stare back.

No one in this house has spoke to me of Morgan yet. Them tricked me into saying her name. That will be thems question: *Where is Morgan?* We're face to mirror to face to face. Not one of us wants to speak the truth.

But I say, 'Ask me then.'

'What's it like?'

'What?'

Ash says, 'Outside. Where you saw Morgan. What's she hearing that we're not. What's she looking at. What can she smell.'

'What's she eating, who's she talking to, what can she see that we can't see—'

'You're not asking these like questions. Just saying—'

Ash says, 'Too many questions stop sounding like questions when we think them a lot.'

Hazel says, 'We can stop being friendly. Because we're—'

'You dun have any friends.'

'We've got an axe,' says Ash.

'Good for you. So?'

'We can get out whenever we want. We need to plan it—'

225

'—make sure outside is better. In case Mum hammers a plank over the hole we axe out of the fence, so we can't get home.'

I smooth my hand over the soft bedspread. 'If I tell you what it's like outside, will you tell me about the picture?'

'Are there any places we can have?'

'Houses just for us. Without a fence—'

'—for us together.'

'No parents—'

'—no sisters. Only for twins.'

'No, the cottages are all lived in. You dun want an old rotten barn, not after living here.'

'We might.'

'Are there mice in it?'

'Aye, I'd have thought so.'

'That sounds perfect.'

'It'd be cold in a barn. No toys. No food. You wouldn't like it. Smells of cow shit. You'd be dirty all the time. And the mice dun do being friendly. Them'd chew off your fingers when you were asleep. Tell me the truth about the picture.'

Hazel frowns at me. 'Why haven't *you* had your fingers chewed off?'

'I dun live in a barn.'

'Can we have your house then, since you're not in it?'

'There's a ghost in it.'

'Morgan will love that.'

'Never said she were there, did I?'

Ash says, 'You thought it.'

I glare at her. 'What do you mean, she'll love it?'

'She likes ghosts. More than she likes us.'

'Come on, she dun.'

'Does. Wants to live with the little girl one.'

I look round the room. 'She see any ghosts in this house then?'

'No, she says it won't have any, not till someone *dies*.'

I say, 'Well, you'd best keep that axe of yours safe then.'

Them glance at the wall-hanging in the corner.

I cross the room to the corner. 'Can Morgan talk to ghosts – hear what them say?' I stroke the fabric wall-hanging, run my fingertip over one of the silver-painted trees.

Hazel nods.

'So if Morgan were in my cottage, and I'm not saying she is, mind, if there were a ghost there, she could ask it a question for me?'

'Of course she could.'

'Now, in case your Mam or Da ask, we dun talk about Morgan. And if you tell me about the picture of the boy, I won't tell your Mam where you've got your axe hid.'

The twins come rushing at me, as I find the axe leaning in the corner behind the wall-hanging.

I say, 'So the picture – who drew it?'

'It wasn't me, *or* Hazel *or* Morgan,' mutters Ash. 'It was *you*.'

I tell them not to lie to me, and at least tell me something I can believe in.

Hazel says, 'No, Mum draws the picture, but you draw *on top* of it. With your eyes.'

'Load of skank,' I mutter.

Hazel sighs.

I say, 'All right. How do my eyes draw the boy?'

Hazel says, 'Because that's what you want to see the most.'

Ash poses, her face rests on her hand like she's in a drawing. 'Mum draws what she thinks she's drawing. When someone else looks at it, they see what they really *want* to see. You saw a boy you love.'

Hazel nudges her, 'Not what she really drew.'

I slump back on the bed. I thought someone here'd seen him. I thought . . . I just want to be little like this pair, and I can't. I curl up on the bed and can hardly breathe, for the bindings are tight round my chest, and them feel like them're coming loose as I sob. The stain from my tears spreads across the bedspread. Tears come out of my eyes, nose, mouth. I'm brimming with sea.

Morgan

She crawls across the sand towards the quiet waves as I approach her. Her white hands and feet shine underneath the decaying animal pelt. Underneath the pelt, her hair is tangled and thick, the colour of ink. The crying naked woman. Still naked beneath the pelt. Still crying.

I stop next to her and ask, 'What are you doing?' My voice is shaking.

She twists her face towards me and hisses, 'Get. Gone.' The pelt slips from her shoulder, her pale skin is almost blue. She pulls the pelt around herself and old dead fur sticks to her damp hands.

'You're freezing.' I squat down next to her, the pelt smells of soil and decay. I cover my nose.

The head of a seal hangs over her shoulder. Its collapsed eyehole has a fly buzzing at it.

I flick it away and say again, 'What are you doing?'

'Nothing to do with you.'

'Don't—'

'You've no right to care. Never seen you before. Won't see you again.'

'Someone has to.'

'Someone does. It's not enough. Leave me.'

'Why isn't it enough?'

'Care is *selfish*.'

'Don't do this—'

'You think . . . well, I'm not. Drowning myself. I'm releasing myself. Get. Gone.' She rolls onto her front and crawls towards the waves.

I walk beside her.

She stops, frozen, one white arm outstretched. 'I said—'

'Releasing what?'

'None of your concern. Go.'

'I don't know what to do.'

'Don't. Do. Anything.'

'Do you need—'

'I need to get into the sea.'

My chest aches as I walk backwards away from her. She crawls, her shoulders heave her towards the incoming tide. The pelt shifts and sways on her back, sheds dry fur and soil. The claws trail from the back of the pelt and leave scratches in the wet sand.

There's no wind. Far out at sea, underneath the waves, the currents twist and surge. I turn away. On a distant cliff, a lone woman stands watching.

I look back at the sea. The woman crawls into the waves. I go back into Mary's cottage, kick the door shut behind me and lock it. In Mary and Barney's bedroom I plunge myself down on Mary's bed.

I punch at the mattress, because the crying naked woman says it's selfish to care and I want to stop caring but I can't . . . and it might be that my mother was right and all the people here *are* mad, so I shouldn't care about any of them, but maybe it's all right to care about mad people, but maybe she's right and it isn't, and there might be boats coming soon but I want to stop caring so I can just stay here and watch for them, and not think about someone choosing to die, and not wanting help or care when that's all I'm able to give . . . and she doesn't want these things, so I feel like I've got no choices because she's making the biggest choice of all, and I feel as if I've been punched by her choice, but I haven't, but this is a punch, a thud, she's going to drown . . . I thump and bang my fists at the mattress till the dust clouds make me sneeze.

My heart pulses in my throat as I lean on the table and look out at the beach. A thick fog is coming in fast. A seal's head bobs in the small waves and is caught in the ripples of the windowpane, magnified and shrunk.

The crying naked woman has drowned.

A feeling in my chest, of loss, of grief, of something I don't have words for. Something that could drown me if I let it. I pick up the bottle of forgetting herb that I took from her house, and read the label:

> *One spoonful for every day that needs forgetting.*
> *Amend dosage as required. Do not overuse.*

I put just one drop of the bitter liquid on my tongue.

Through the window, the empty sea. A beach is covered in fog. I've been standing here at this window . . . how long . . . I stare and stare and stare out at the fog. What's this bottle? Forgetting herb . . . a herb to forget . . . and I've . . . forgotten I have it in my hand.

Faces come out of the fog.

Two women in shawls, their cheeks pressed against the windowpanes. Eyes uneven, cheeks twisted, lips askew. An enormous hand taps on the glass.

I shake myself, back away from the faces and bundle myself into a brown musty coat. On the table are . . . Annie's letter and the Thrashing House key. I was going to do something . . . before . . . the fog came in.

The Thrashing House.

I shove the key and letter in the coat pocket. At the window, one face disappears. The front door handle rattles, so I leave the cottage through the door at the back.

Mary

Morgan's Mam's eyes are puffed up. Her lips narrow as she looks down at the dress I'm wearing. If her teeth all fell out, she'd look like some kind of frog. She dun speak, just turns away from me, walks along the black and white squares on the corridor floorboards. I can see from the tall windows it's getting fogged up outside. She looks hunched and squat, solid.

I follow her into a room with a small bed, a table and a chair by a window with flouncy curtains. On the bed is a folded piece of lilac linen.

She nods at it. 'Do the bedspread. Flowers. Lots. Every colour you have. I want to be able to dream in flowers when you've finished. I need some good dreams, from somewhere.' She draws a square of green linen fabric from her pocket and blows her nose on it.

She says, 'I've got to make food. My eldest isn't here. *She* cooks. Get sewing. Dinner soonish. Downstairs.' She walks away.

'Dun talk like I'm just a *thing* of yours.'

She spins round. 'Did you see my eldest? Outside?'

'No,' I answer.

'Liar.' She walks off. Her feet thud on the floor.

I call after her, 'Look, I've got to—'

She's gone off behind another door.

The crescent moon door at the back of the downstairs hallway is open. I go in. Morgan's Mam is crouched, rummaging in a cupboard in a huge kitchen. There's cupboards all around the sides, a range and a great wooden table and five chairs. She gets out a handful of onions and stands up. She sees me and drops the onions. Them roll across the floor.

I bend down to pick one up and watch her under the table, picking up three at once, dropping two of them. She glances at me and says, 'What's your name, liar?'

I put the onion on the table.

She stands up and looks me up and down. She says, 'Your leg seems fine now. If my home has made you better, you owe me. I need those flowers on me.'

'I never agreed a trade for feeling better.' I bite my lip.

She picks up an onion from the floor, puts it on a chopping board, as another onion rolls off the table and bounces off her foot. She wails, 'I don't know how to do this!' She bites her hand, slumps down on a chair and folds her arms like a little girl.

'Did you make all this?' I wave at the table and chairs. 'See, there's something you're good at. It's like the wood's still living, the way it shines. And the pictures in the room along the hall . . .' My voice chokes.

'What did you see?' She leans forwards. 'In my drawings?'

'A lost boy.'

She seems lighter in her face. She strokes her hair away from her cheek. 'In one of them, I saw a sunrise on the surface of the fence, which was even higher. The sunrise shone from the

234

fence into the windows, so it looked like the sun rose on the walls inside all the rooms. I might do that. There's a thought . . . another layer of fence, higher than the house.'

'But it'll blow down in the winds!'

'I could paint on a view to see from the top windows, instead of this blasted island. Mix white paint and salt together for the sun. A white, pure light . . .' She leans back in the chair. Puts her hands behind her head.

She says, 'How much gossip is there, outside, about us?'

'Not much.'

'Well, that's something. Always thought there *was*.' She looks at me, eyes narrowed. 'Just a niggle.' She stares out of the window at the fence.

'How'd you know what's lost to folks, to draw pictures of—'

'I get such good ideas in the kitchen.'

My hands are chopping the onions. The smell makes me hungry. Morgan's Mam's eyes are far away. She shakes her head, 'What was I hearing you talk about, flower girl?'

'All the lost things in your drawings?'

'Loss. Hm. Ah well. It's an interesting process.' She wrinkles her nose and sniffs. 'You wouldn't understand.'

She tells me that she dreams every night and draws every morning. That it's something about a subconscious and how it's the place in us where dreams hide. She stands and leans on the windowsill, stares out at the fence. 'The creator of automatic drawings harvests . . . yes. Harvests the images gathered within the collective unconscious. Reaps them—' She runs a finger through the air.

I say, 'Are you saying you're drawing pictures you've farmed from our dreamings?'

She turns and smiles at the table. 'I'm just going to draw

some designs for the inside of the fence. It'll make me feel better about, you know. Distractions.' She glances at me. Licks her lips. 'How long will dinner be? Five of us if you're eating too.'

The twins come in first.

'What's for dinner?' says Ash. Them scrape two chairs back from the table and sit down.

'Do you all end up doing what your Mam wants?'

Hazel says, 'Always.'

Thems Mam walks into the kitchen and sniffs the air. Both twins beam at her. She sits down and slides her chair up to the table. She nods at me, runs her spoon around the rim of her plate and the deadtaker strides in.

Him has grey curly hair tied back. Black suit and a white collar. I want to ask him something but my voice is stuck. I remember him. Him sits down. Him took Mam's body away. Him puts hims hands on the table. The tear in hims gloves. Him is not wearing gloves now. Hims hands shine pale. I'm going to be watching him shovelling stew into hims mouth, trying not to think about hims hands touching dead bodies.

The four of them sit there, spoons in thems hands, and stare at the pot of stew in the middle of the table. I want him to notice me. Him has to remember Mam for me. Remember her from before I've been told I'm a thing of hers to trade, like a broiderie.

Them watch the pot, like the stew's going to slop itself out onto thems plates. I sigh, loud as I can, and dish up. I serve the twins first, then thems Mam, then the deadtaker. Them wait till I've filled all four plates and plunge in thems spoons.

I stand next to the deadtaker. Him has dandruff flakes on hims shoulders. It looks like snow on rocks. I blow on it, only it's stuck in the tight weave of the fabric.

'Sit down too,' hisses Hazel.

'I ate mine while I were waiting for you lot.'

'Have you poisoned it?' whispers Ash and takes a great mouthful.

'Shh,' says thems Mam, glancing at the deadtaker. She guzzles her stew down, dun think she even tastes all the herbs I've put in it. The deadtaker eats slow, tiny spoonfuls, like him has five stomachs inside of him and them all want to be fed, but no more than just a taste.

I ask him, 'Do none of you say thank you when someone's put food in front of you then?'

Him puts hims spoon down. Morgan's Mam drops hers on her empty plate. The twins stare up at me.

Him slides hims chair out, turns to face me. Hims dark eyes gleam. 'Right. Intruder. You have all of our attention. Now, what is it that you want?'

'You buried Mam. She were bitten by a diamondback. Dun know much else about her death. You must have been one of the first to see her deaded. And you would've been the last.'

'And?'

I say, shrill, 'You're freezing cold for someone what should know of grief, and how it needs a bit of warm.' I fold my arms.

'This is not the time to speak of grief.'

'You put her in the ground. I were never told much, well, not enough. Dun think she's resting proper.'

'What would make you think *that*, Mary Jared?'

'You know my name, so you do recall her. I think Mam's in my cottage. How come she's not sleeping, still and quiet in the graveyard like Grandmam? I've never thought she's hanging around the cottage, much as I'd like to hear what she's got to say about the state of her deathlife.'

Morgan's Mam gets up and her chair crashes back against the wall. She covers her mouth with her hand and slams the door on her way out of the kitchen.

The deadtaker frowns up at me. 'Perhaps in your home dinner is a time for conversation. It most certainly isn't here.'

'Well, we did chatter at teatime – there's nothing wrong in that. Only there's not much point chattering at home now, as I'm the only one left, and if I *did* talk, I'd be talking to Mam's ghost what I can't even see!'

The twins stare at him. Then me. Then him. Then each other.

I shout at them, 'Will you two stop thinking so loud!'

Him stands up. 'We'll continue this discussion downstairs, and then I must see to my wife.'

The basement is lit by candles all along the walls. The room is filled with planks of wood, stacked along shelves. There's three more doors along the far wall.

The deadtaker walks towards the door in the middle.

I stop and glance back at the stairs. 'Let's talk here.'

'As you wish.' Him turns and leans hims arm on a shelf.

'Is it true Mam never saw the snake what bit her?'

'I'm not sure. Fascinating death.'

My heart pounds.

'She was bitten. Not by any snake I saw, though she was marked by one, and filled with venom. When I arrived, three women were with her. They seemed to be chanting, or rather, as they said, singing.'

'What's wrong with singing? She were out on her own, like Annie says, and them three found her.'

Him nods. 'Ah yes. One of the names was Annie.'

'And the diamondback addersnake?'

'It's all documented, in my book. The signs of poisoning by snake venom were there.'

'So, what do you mean, fascinating death?'

Hims eyes are bright, more alive than in the kitchen. Him likes talking of hims job, even if it's a job none other would want.

'It was the way they said it. Rehearsed. "She was bitten by a diamondback, it got away. She never saw the snake that bit her." All three women used almost exactly the same words, though I questioned them individually. Not one of the three would be drawn further. It's not my area of expertise, so in the end it was, let's say, more *convenient* for me to simply document it. I have doubts. Those doubts have stayed, increased, even. I have no logical explanation.'

'But it sounds like that's what happened, like them said. She were bit and got deaded.'

Him looks at me. 'As you say.'

'You dun believe it.'

'It sounded . . . invented. And the snake—'

'Maybe them were nervous of you.' I stare at hims pale hands.

'Their behaviour aroused my suspicion. I can tell a liar, even if I'm not the most appropriate person to extract the truth.'

I ask, 'Have you still got your documentation? Can I see what you wrote down when she got deaded?'

Him says something about confidential, but I say, 'No one will care what you did or dun write down.'

Him says, 'Sadly, you're probably right. Your mother was an interesting case. One that I was unable to come to any conclusion which satisfied my personal or professional curiosity. No islander has ever asked for a sight of my documentation before. In fact, other than asking me to prepare their loved ones for burial, and all that entails, which, understandably, they have not the stomach for, no islander has ever asked me for anything other than a plank of wood. So why are *you* here, Mary Jared?'

'Are you going to show me what you wrote down then?'

Him lowers hims voice. 'An information exchange would be a beneficial . . . trade . . . as you would call it.'

'And what would you want to do this trade about?'

Him glances at the stairs, then leans forwards, whispers, 'You have a building here. You people believe it to be a place of justice. I would have thought that the person or persons concerned with your mother's death would have found themselves there.'

'Well, I dun think a diamondback could've slithered in through the keyhole.'

'But do you believe it calls people? It's the local belief in it that I find so personally interesting. That all crime can be punished, dealt with, with a thrashing. I've recently heard locals say that some men have been "thrashed". They've disappeared,' him lowers hims voice, 'and yet, I'm not called to attend to their bodies?' Him raises hims eyebrows.

'I'd say, if you're finding yourself thinking of the place so much, it's already calling you.'

Him starts, backs away.

'What have you done what's so bad, then?'

Him looks like I've slapped him.

I say, 'It's best if I tell you what Grandmam told me. That's my documentation. I've got it in my head. And you'll show me your book.'

'I'll find you some paper and a pen. I assume you can write?' Him walks towards the middle door and unlocks it.

'Course I can. How many pages?'

'What?'

'How many pages are we trading?'

'I have filled approximately four, perhaps five, in my documentation on your mother. But it doesn't matter—'

'I'll do the same.'

Him goes through the middle door, leaves the key in the lock and comes back out of the room frowning, a pen and some sheets of paper in hims hand. Him waves at a dusty chair and hands me a small piece of wood to lean on.

Him goes over to the stairs, sits down and ties and unties hims laces while I write:

Dear Deadtaker,

This is some of what Grandmam told me: The Thrashing House stands on the topmost hill. It's the tallest building on this whole island. On the main land, Thrashing Houses are said to be for beating out the grain, the wheat from the chaff. Only here it's something quite different. Our Thrashing House is where we put folks when we dun know what else to do with them. No one ever heard of anyone ever coming out again what's been put in.

The Thrashing House itself is alive, it has paddles and knives and sticks and bats what come out of the walls into the rooms when someone's been sent in. And it thrashes them if it thinks them deserves it.

The deadtaker spits on hims fingertip and rubs at hims boot. I write more of Grandmam's story:

Long, long ago, a woman killed her husband. No one believed she would have done it for she were right quiet, only squeaked instead of having proper talk in her mouth. She were a bit rodent-like in her appearance. All short and sharp with two buck teeth. Everyone else on the island were under suspicion, and she herself were so shocked at what she'd done she never spoke at all, not even to squeak, after him were dead. She locked herself in the Thrashing House one day, she couldn't stand the guilt.

She were turned into a chain, for she'd felt herself chained to him, and had no other way to get away from him, other than to kill him dead with a knife. The Thrashing House thrashed the truth from her and that chain were the truth in her, of why she killed him. A rodent on the end of a chain can be right dangerous, so that's the moral of that: make sure you never keep something dangerous chained to you, even if it's smaller than you are. Its teeth might be sharp, and if it's not of a mind to use them, it can always raid the knife drawer.

A woman burglared every house on the island and were caught one night. Caught with her hands plunged deep in a jewellery box, a shimmering green glass ring on her finger, what we all knew never belonged to her hand. She became a gleaming ring which were dull copper on the inside: it were only coated shiny.

She were looking for value: fine metals, jewels or secrets; anything she could find what would make her seem greater than what she really were on the inside. And that were the truth in her. On the outside she thought herself shiny, only the truth of her were that she were dull.

Another, a girl of fourteen, had a vicious run-in with her Mam. In a fury like a Glimmera, she cut off her Mam's hand. Showed no remorse, all she'd say were that 'It were her or me.' Neither would say what the fight started over, and it dun even matter. Something about wanting to swap colours of hair, some such nonsense what were impossible all along. She wanted something her Mam had, and her

Mam wanted what the daughter had. So the daughter took a hatchet to her Mam's hand, so her Mam couldn't get at it first. She became a glove. A left-handed one, to fit the hand what had been took. Not too much to learn from that one: just that you can cover up something what's been lost, like putting an empty glove over a hacked-off hand; but sooner or later, it'll flap clean off like a shadow and show you there's nothing really there.

The deadtaker taps hims foot on the floor. Polishes a boot with hims sleeve. I've nearly filled four sheets of paper, so I write:

People who have gone mad, or are dangerous, or done something so bad we dun know how to punish them – get sent in there. Sometimes folks seem to go in of thems own accord. Only it's not really thems own accord. The Thrashing House can seek out the truth. If it senses someone has done something bad, or is dangerous to others, it calls to them, and the truly guilty slowly and surely find thems way into it.

I say, 'I'm done. You going to show me your documentation about Mam then?'

Him stands up, quick. Strides over.

'You've left that lace undone.' I point at hims boot.

'Look in the desk in the room through the middle door. If I'm not here to see you read my documentation, you did not read.' Him holds out a hand. 'Agreed?'

I drop Grandmam's story in hims pale palm and snatch my hand back.

Him puts it in a hidden pocket on the inside of hims jacket. 'You're not as quiet as I remember, Mary Jared.'

I ask him how come him recalls my name, and him says that him reads hims documentation book a lot, that him wishes him had asked more questions when Mam died, and him had questions for Da, but Da shut the door on him.

I say, 'Well, you'll not get any answers out of an old worn boot.'

'A what?' Him walks to the bottom of the stairs.

'Nothing. But tell me, and tell me the truth.' I breathe in. 'You got the dead body of a three-year-old boy in this house?'

'There have been no deaths of late.'

I breathe out. 'So the drawing of Barney really is from your wife's head?'

'It's similar to an inkblot technique, but using a more advanced and experimental skill. I assume you've never heard of the collective unconscious, of individual consciousness? She's developed a visual language that speaks of much that is lacking in these theories. I admire her skills greatly. Her dedication.'

'Look, your family's too cooped up together, you're coming up with some dipsy nonsenses what make no sense. What's so special about your belonging people, or what's so wrong with us, that you got to keep us out?'

Him walks up the stairs. One of hims legs walks straight and the other drags a little. I hear hims footsteps step and slide across the floor above me and climb the next set of stairs, one foot louder than the other.

I walk past the flickering candles and the shelves stacked with planks of shipwreck wood and open the middle door.

The deadtaker's chair is covered with shining brown leather. A desk stands in the middle of this small room. A circle of light from a flickering lamp lights up the desk. A pen and ink bottle, blank paper and a glass jar of deep red liquid and a wine glass are lined up neat on top of the desk. I drop my bag on the floor.

Inside the drawer in the desk there's a thick leather book. I lift it out, thud it on the desk and open the cover. The deadtaker has written in neat black ink:

List of the Dead.

I run my finger down the page and find:

Beatrice M. Jared .... pages 30–34.

I open it on page 30:

Beatrice M. Jared (embroiderer)
(married to Mr Ned Jared, mother to: Mary and Barney Jared)

Report on the Unfortunate Circumstances
I was summoned to inspect and remove the corpse of Beatrice M. Jared on the southern cliffs that look out across the ocean towards the geographic anomaly which is known locally as 'the Pegs'. I was hailed there by a local man, name of Mr Martyn Spender, in the evening. He reported to me in a most breathless fashion that he: 'went after my Annie' (Wife of Mr M. Spender: Anne-Marie Spender, common name Annie, occupation: knitter) 'as I dun think she really knew what she wanted. I went to the cliffs by the Pegs to find her in a right frazzle (assume: in great distress) as she and that pair, (Mrs Valmarie Slarius: occupation: herbalist, and Mrs Kelmar A. Barter: occupation: midwife, spinner and seamstress) 'had found Beatrice unconscious, and were trying to stop the deadedness coming over her complete.' (Assume: remaining with her in her final mortal moments.)

Upon my arrival, I noted that the three witnesses were

245

chanting and were physically located around the deceased. I requested that they desist immediately, in order to enable room for the procedures required in order to check for the usual signs of life. I proclaimed that the three witnesses should avert their gazes, and wait some distance away. They persisted in their observation of me, although I repeatedly requested that they avert their gaze, considering their observations and comments at that time to be particularly distracting as they persisted in asking me what I was doing and requesting the reasons for each slight movement of my person whilst concluding my investigation. Despite this annoyance, I did rapidly ascertain that Mrs B. Jared was, in fact, deceased. The two unusual aspects of the three witnesses, aside from the chanting, was the fact that one carried a rope, and all three women were wearing gloves. This was mildly unusual in relation to my observations of local dress customs. I choose to deem it insignificant as it was a particularly cold day. However, it may be worth noting that the corpse was not wearing gloves.

The deceased presented the usual pallor of death, but I observed a blue tinge to the lips and the lower extremities. The corpse had two puncture marks upon her right ankle, which were raised and appeared to be the site of the poison entering the body.

I understood from the information I gleaned from the three witnesses and Mr M. Spender that they believed the snake responsible for the bite to be a variety of snake they referred to as the Diamondback Addersnake, which they informed me was venomous. However, when I requested one to be procured, to provide venom samples for comparative purposes, none of the local people were able to provide such a snake.

Summing up:

From conversing with all three witnesses, and from further inspection of the corpse post-mortem, I confirm that the only reasonable cause of death to be ascertained under the circumstances is that Mrs Beatrice M. Jared's unfortunate demise was caused by the bite of a venomous snake, which was not located in the moments, nor days, after the death.

In fact, for several weeks, I personally sought out any variety of local snake by conducting a thorough search of the island, and despite my most persistent efforts, I was unable to locate a single snake.

In consulting my reference material on snakes, I have drawn the conclusion that the Diamondback is in fact a fictitious name, derived from some local folk tale.

The reason for the women being present was clear, though the content of their proposed discourse remained withheld; some kind of argument which required one of the women to bring a rope to the scene seems to be indicated. I can only deduce that it was a disagreement over some aspect of craft-making, which these women believed necessitated the element of mystery, when faced with persons, such as myself, perceived to be outsiders.

The fact that they were chanting when I arrived was certainly suspicious but when I asked the women about this they all stated that they were singing and went on to imply that I was a buffoon of some description if I was not capable of determining the difference between a chant and a song.

The evidence post-mortem was clear enough to ascertain that the cause of death was by venom entering the body via two puncture marks directly into the ankle, which would imply death by some variety of snake bite, but not, as the witnesses claimed, by a 'Diamondback Addersnake'.

Them had a rope with them and there's no such thing as a diamondback addersnake. I get up and lock the door. I rummage in my bag for the Thrashing House key. Someone will have thought of Mam's death while them held this key. One of the women will know.

It's not here. No. I rummage deeper. Must be. It's not . . . no. Morgan wouldn't have took it. I spill everything out on the floor and put it back in.

No key.

Morgan were so innocent . . . but she were in and out of my bag when we were stitching up my dress, and now I've lost all the women's stories.

I flick the pages of the deadtaker's book backwards and forwards. Dropping it on the desk, it falls open at the list of the dead. The last name on the list is scratched out. I lean over it. Him has written a name in and scored over it, like the person were dead and isn't dead no more. I flick through to the last pages him has written on:

For all of this time I have lived here in this remote place, I have not yet encountered anything so strange. I was walking to the tall building on the hill, known locally as the Thrashing House, in order to confirm any suspicions in my mind regarding some rumours I had overheard. One such example that easily and rapidly springs to mind is a female voice on the other side of my garden fence, in conversation with others. This voice had clearly stated: 'The men are thrashed good an' hard. We'll not be seeing them again.'

There was no doubt in my mind when I made the decision to investigate this statement that I would be thwarted yet again in my attempts to learn more of the Thrashing House, which holds these people in thrall, but yet remains locked, day and night.

I approached the building after dark, in order to investigate, but I was distracted by an owl in the graveyard, hooting on a grave. Recalling my eldest daughter's youthful love of the description of owls as a parliament, and feeling a little nostalgic for our shared past, I took a detour into the graveyard to see the owl. What I experienced at that graveside distracted me completely from the task of investigating the building.

At first glance, the owl was of the appearance of a variety of barn owl, its feathers light in colour. However, as I approached the grave, it flew away immediately, and I did not see it return. And yet there was no one at that grave, but the soil of the grave was recently turned.

It was the grave of Beatrice Jared. And I could hear a female voice, muttering.

As soon as I heard the voice I drew close, hid myself, took out my notepad and set to recording the words I heard. I was convinced in that moment that if I did not fully document what the voice said, the sense of disbelief which was frustratingly present in my person would eradicate any information that I could temporarily understand with a later confusion and dream-like sensibility that I felt certain I would experience as soon as the voice was quiet. The following is transcribed as I heard it, copied faithfully from my notes as they were recorded, alas, with a slightly tremulous hand:

'. . . torn.

Dig soil from mine grave.

Obey two women that dig and call and form me.

Mothers now.

Give life. Not death. Not same before.

Scatter earth from grave, free mine instincts. Then release . . . fly flap fall first face smash bruises. Then. Up up up, fly, swoop.

249

Instincts drawn out.
Yes, punish.
Men with lines of thoughts, guilty. Scratch, tear thoughts.
What were names . . .
Only name, myself. Once Beatrice . . .'

Summing up:
As I recorded these mutterings, and in the moments afterwards,
the voice seemed further away, so though this is not a death
as such, the voice spoke the name of the woman who lies in
that grave. As yet, I have drawn no conclusions.

*

Mam is the ghost Valmarie and Kelmar raised up to make into
the owl woman. Using earth from her grave. My hands over my
mouth smell of soil. She were my Mam, no matter what the
trade she made with Langward were. I tap on the desk. Faster
and faster. Read it again. Them put Mam's ghost into a barn
owl and set her on the men what took the boys.

Mam sent Da mad. Scratching at hims thoughts.

When she'd done what Valmarie and Kelmar wanted, Mam's
ghost were homeless, so she must've flitted off. And come home.

I read her words again:

Give life. Not death. Not same before.

Them gave her death and then brought her back. Which means
Mam were murdered by Valmarie or Kelmar, or both of them.
Not Annie. Annie loved her. She's always been afraid of that
pair, so she must've been too scared to ever say what them'd
done.

I've read more than the four pages I traded with the deadtaker, so I open the documentation book at the front page and write in the names on the list of the dead:

Mrs Valmarie Slarius
Mrs Kelmar A. Barter

I flick forwards to the next blank page and write:

Report on the Unfortunate Circumstances
I were summoned to inspect and remove the stinking corpses of Mrs Valmarie Slarius and Mrs Kelmar A. Barter on the cliffs what look out across the sea towards the place which is known sensibly as 'the Pegs' because that is what them are.

I were hailed there by a local young woman, name of Miss Mary Jared, who hollered up at my windows from outside my garden fence till I finally hatcheted my way out. She reported to me in a most breathless fashion that: 'I dun know what can possibly have happened. Them never saw who it were what hacked them to death.'

I found the two women deceased, and realised that them had been viciously and brutally mortally wounded, and deaded good and hard, by a person or persons unknown. Them were tied up in a rope of which there are many on this island, and no one ever talks about thems teeth.

Summing up:
I now believe them to be responsible for the death of Beatrice Jared. Them got what were coming to them, for sure. All vicious cuts from some kind of blade, and the rope must have been placed there to remind me of the guilt them felt about the death of Beatrice Jared. I conclude that that pair were murderous

and venomous, which took me long enough to figure out, as I'm right simple for all my fancy talk.

I feel a bit better. Not better enough.

I put the book back in the drawer and lock it. My head is getting unravelled. I can think of Mam as murdered and feel angry at Valmarie and Kelmar, but I can't get angered at Mam, even if . . .

Something lands in my hair.

I look up . . .

White owl feathers fall in this room.

I shout, 'Stop it!'

The feathers fall thicker. Cover the desk. All over the floor. I stand up, can't see where the feathers are falling from, like a blizzard from the Glimmeras what fills the room. Feathers blow and twist all around me. Settle in clumps, curl into each other. The desk, chair and floor are covered, thick. I blow one off my mouth and more get stuck on my lips.

The feathers are all over my bag, I pick it up and put it on the desk. I rummage inside and pull out the moppet.

'What's going on?' I whisper. 'What do the feathers mean?'

Shadow Mary's voice hisses, 'Leave. Us. Alone.'

'Barney, are you here in this house, did the deadtaker lie? Are you here, in a coffin box?' My heart, thud thud thud.

Barney's voice says, 'Mary, get this Mary away. Tell her go.'

Shadow Mary hisses, 'Quiet, sniveller.'

I say, 'Dun talk to him like that!'

Barney's voice says, 'She angry you.'

I say, 'Barney, dun listen to her, you talk – tell me—'

Him says, 'Shh, dun make angry this Mary . . .'

The sound of the sea washes through the shell.

'Barney?'

The moppet droops forwards, silent.

The feathers fly around me, land all over my hair, cover the moppet in my hand, but now I'm looking at the feathers twisting and spiralling through the room, making everything white, this dun feel like anything bad.

It's quiet and still and the door is locked.

Warm snow. It's comfort.

Think.

The moppet's got Shadow Mary's voice as well as Barney's.

Think.

Shadow Mary has peeled off me.

If shadows are made when bad things happen, or feelings what are too big just tear themselves off a person, a shadow of Barney could have peeled off him. Him could have left a shadow in the net him were tangled up in. The shadow must have crept away and hid itself in the shell lying on the beach.

If Shadow Mary has peeled off me, and *I'm* still alive . . . Someone must've found Barney, washed up on the shore. Him must've been hurt bad for hims shadow to peel off, but them've kept him alive.

So I've got to get out of this house and find out who.

I fall back in the feathers, send them floating up into the room. Grab handfuls and throw them twisting over me. I blow them off my smile.

Morgan

I'm at the Thrashing House door. I pull the key from my pocket and Annie's letter comes out twisted around it. I can smell the salt in the fog that drifts through the air around me. I slide the key into the lock.

The key won't turn, it won't fit into the right parts of the mechanism. I put Annie's letter on the doorstep and use both hands to push the key in further. It fits into place – the maze on the key has found the puzzle in the lock and it clicks. I turn the handle, the door creaks open. It's dark inside.

The fog thickens in swirls around my feet. I take the key from the lock. A feeling of someone behind me in the fog, someone reaching out a hand. A woman's voice shouts, 'Stop, dun, give me the key—'

I lock myself in. The door's slam echoes above me in the dark. A creak, the sound of wood breaking. A crack. A groan.

Mary's brother's name . . . I *know* his name . . . a name to call . . .

A crack, a creak, a snap.

'Hello?' I shout.

I step forwards. My eyes can't see in the dark. Something touches my hair. I spin round, step back, feel along the wall, the texture rough like bark. The key is still in the lock. I should be able to feel the door . . .

A low thud.

My eyes adjust. Archways high above me, faint light coming through small windows high in the ceiling.

A sigh.

'Who's there?'

Another sigh.

I step forwards. A footstep, right behind me. I spin round.

A stooped woman stands, half in shadow, between me and the door. A man joins her and smiles. He has no teeth. A teenage girl appears out of the shadows, puts her hand on the woman's shoulder and says, 'She can see us.'

The girl steps forwards. Her curly hair covers half her face.

'Them dun usually see us,' the man groans. He shields his eyes from me with a weathered hand. The woman turns and knocks on the door but her hand makes no sound. Their faded simple clothes are from another time.

I say, 'You're all dead.'

The woman freezes.

She spins round. 'Can you *hear* us?'

I nod.

'You can *talk* . . .' She reaches out her hand.

I step back. 'Yes.'

Her voice is shrill, 'Tell Ailsa I'm sorry I stole it. I never meant to upset her. I knew it were her Nan's – it's just it were such a lovely green, all shiny, and I just wanted it till I couldn't think of nothing else. She made such the biggest fuss, near on got everyone there is to get all angered, and *I'm* angered for what she did, but if she'd just have took it back, I could . . .'

The man limps closer to me, talks over her voice, 'No, tell Margaret I never meant to take Billy away. I just missed him

255

and she dun let me see him. I weren't for keeping him, I never meant for her to think . . .'

The girl yells, 'I *did* mean it, but tell her it were her or me, and it weren't going to be me, an' she'd do well to understand that. I'm sure she's managed well enough without it, I mean I dun axe her *right* hand off an' she *is* right-handed—'

'Stop it!' I shout.

'No, listen,' says the woman. 'You're the only one who's heard us. The others never saw us. We've got things to say to folks. You got to take our messages . . . tell the folks we needed to tell—'

'I don't *know* anyone. I'm here to find a small boy. His sister's looking for him, but she's hurt. Have you seen him? He's three years old.'

'It were her or me, you tell her that!' shrieks the girl.

'I can't.'

The man leans on the wall, tilts his head to the side and says, 'You're not scared to be in here. The others were scared.'

The woman says, 'Apart from the tall man . . . Now him saw the face of some woman, in a broken mirror.'

I say, 'Does a cracked mirror really bring bad luck?'

The man says, 'Why 'ent you scared?'

A huge creak from the ceiling. They all glance upwards. I step sideways so I have a clear run at the door.

The girl frowns at me and says, 'Small ones dun get sent here. *I'm* the youngest. All over a *hand*. My Mam's bloody hand, right enough, but it were her or me. What've you done then?'

The man says, 'You got the main land speak. Are them sending thems wrong 'uns all the way over here now?'

A creak from inside the wall.

'What are these noises?' I ask.

He says, 'It wants to thrash you, love. It's just gettin' itself trunked up.' He grins, his toothless mouth a wide hole in his face.

'Thrash me – with what?'

A branch falls from the ceiling, crashes on the floor across the middle of the room. I leap back. Another branch grows out, spreads from the base of a wooden archway.

'With what it's made of. Its *own* truth,' says the girl, frowning. 'You're not afeart?'

'Of branches?' I shake my head.

Another branch peels from a high archway, creaks and thwacks down on the floorboards. Leaves scatter across the floor.

'Is this real?' I pick up a leaf and hold it out to the woman.

She turns away and walks into the shadows.

I turn and face the girl, shake the leaf at her. 'Is it?'

She touches my hair, whispers, 'Give me *your* colour . . .' and disappears.

I can feel the girl's fingers in my hair like tangled cobwebs.

The man mutters, 'Not like the others, you're not. Other folk what came in through that same door as you, them saw other things. Get yourself out an' just be. You got us, 'cause we got things to be saying, an' *you* could've listened. Not if you'll not do it, but. This place is full.'

There are faint faces around the edges of the room, like distant candle flames in the shadows. A whole army of ghosts. 'Who are they?'

A branch crashes down on the other side of the room. The pale faces flicker and fade away.

He says, 'The dead must be buried.'

'That's what I've always been told. My father—'

He interrupts, 'We weren't. Buried, see. So you get what's happened. We're stuck here.'

A branch thumps down, scatters twigs across the middle of the floor.

I ask him, 'Why weren't you—'

'Anyone put in here dun have anything left to bury, 'ent it.'

'What *is* this place?'

'Tree growed into this. Needed to protect itself, dun it. All trees cut down, some for the houses, barns, for weaving rooms, others for the platform and hanging pole. Punishing by death, that were. Folks liked to watch them twitch.' He cringes. 'Punished all kinds of folks for not that much wrongdoing. Dun think this tree wanted to see the wood from the others used that way. And it saw the other trees drop, get sliced, hammered, bolted. It twisted, grew itself into this place.'

A huge branch crashes, not far from where we stand.

'It's angry,' I whisper.

He glances upwards and back at me. 'Calls what's needed, gets rid of what's not. Listen, whatever you've come here for, you'll not be finding young boys. Get yourself out. An' quick. Dun know if it'll open a door for you. Opened one for the tall man, but.' He fades into the wall. He's gone.

A branch swooshes down. Twigs scatter across the floor. I back away, towards the door. A huge bough creaks, swishes, cracks down. Branches and twigs tear at each other over my head. I stumble over branches into the middle of the room, a muscular bough hurtles down. It's blocked the door and the key away from me.

I'm in a forest of trees being felled. Another branch thwacks down. I leap forwards and a sharp twig scratches my leg. It's bleeding.

The creaks and cracks are so loud I can't hear my footsteps as I jump over branches strewn across the floor, some still attached to the curving walls and archways. I call up into the ceiling but my voice is lost in cracks and creaks. Leaves grow from archways, branches push out of walls and pillars, extend between the small windows, tangled twigs spread from thick boughs that lean from the walls.

A thickening branch splits away from the tallest archway, a branch thick enough to break all my bones with one thwack. It creaks as it bends. The branch tilts, sways. It's seeking me out, creaking, twisting, the leaves churn, build up force, a storm, trapped inside it.

Along one of the walls are small curved doors. One is open. I clamber over broken branches, kick fallen twigs away, yank the door, squeeze into the small space behind it. A branch thwacks down, bashes the door shut. I'm locked in. Again.

In this tiny cramped space behind the door there's a slight glow, but I can't see where it's coming from. The wooden floor underneath me is rotten and branches smash and crash outside. I run my fingertips along the floor away from the door. The floor disappears. There's a hole right behind where I crouch. I can't see how far down it goes. The smell of dank earth seeps up from it into this tiny space. I hang on to the doorframe.

The room outside this door crashes. Twigs rip, branches tear. This building remembers the ghosts of the other trees. It wants to punish.

It's silent out there.

I push at the small door. It sticks against a pile of branches. I shove it, hard, and it opens.

I crawl out into the room and stand up.

The room stretches into high arches up above, the light coming in has faded – outside it must be getting dark. There's a strange light in this room: I can see all around me, where pillars stretch and curve around the high ceiling, the walls are wooden, solid, with curves instead of corners. The wood is moulded, and I can't see where any part of it has been joined together. No nails, screws or any kind of join. Nothing creaks or crashes, no boughs or leaves grow from the walls. The floor is hidden under a felled forest: ripped boughs, torn branches, fallen leaves. Insects fill the air; moths flicker, dragonflies flit, a hoverfly vibrates, held by wings that move so fast they blur.

Nothing falls, nothing crashes, everything is still. Whatever this building needs to do, when its branches churn, thwack and beat whoever comes in, it has finished. The only sounds left are the sounds of vibrating insect wings.

Mary lied. Her brother isn't in here.

I extract a strong branch and gather up a bundle of twigs. My hair falls over my face. That ghost who touched it has turned it white. So that's what she meant when she said, *Give me your colour*.

But right now I'm going to do the thing I know how to do the best.

I'm going to clean up this mess.

Using the thinnest twigs to bind larger ones to the branch, I make a witch's broom. I sweep the leaves into one pile and it feels like a dance. Sweeping the twigs into another pile, I realise that some choices lead into danger, and some lead out of it. I can sweep this floor, clear my mind and see stillness in a building that seemed full of danger. Danger is something that thrashes and beats and breaks itself down, and leaves calm in the air when it's gone.

I sweep the cobwebs that the spiders are spinning just over my head. The insects hover in the air. This whole room is full of green smells. I sweep up clumps of moss and bark.

My white hair glows in the dark, and that's why I can see.

Dragonflies dance around my white hair as I sit on the floor and break up some twigs and use them to make letters. Three choices:

Go home.

Look for Mary the liar.

Wait for boats.

Why *should* I only have three? I think up some more:

Open up the door and turn the Thrashing House into a school where I can teach all the boys and men to read.

Build my own raft out of the branches in this room and set off out to sea.

Knock on every single door on this island till I find someone to fall in love with.

Go to the Weaving Rooms and weave a great big web to live in.

Reinvent myself as a wise witch, sit in a cave and have people come to visit so I can hear lots of stories. Hand out magical potions that are really just seawater.

Capture all the insects in this room and make an insect circus. Charge a fortune for each showing, and become rich.

All these choices would be the best thing in the world to do. So why am I sitting on this floor not moving?

Because I'm still thinking of Mary.

This was meant to be escape. Freedom, the mainland. My real home. And even if Mary's a liar, maybe *because* she's a liar, I want to find her.

Right now I hate her.

I walk towards the mountain of branches still blocking the front door as I rummage in my coat pockets for Annie's letter.

It's not there.

It must have fallen out of my pocket behind the small door.

I crawl halfway into the dark space behind the door, the light from my hair shines on the hole at the back, wide enough to fall down. I feel with my fingertips for the rough paper of the letter. I crawl further in, my hands are on the edge of the rotten wooden floor, the smell of dank earth . . . I stop.

Remember.

I put the letter outside on the doorstep when I was unlocking the front door. And didn't pick it up. So that woman reaching out from the fog at the door might have found it.

The sound of footsteps behind me and a sharp shove. The door crashes against my feet. The sound of a girl, laughing. My hair has stopped glowing. I'm hurtling through darkness, my empty hands grasp at air,

falling

down

down

down.

*

I read of the underworld in the mythology book, but this underworld has no fire or dark pronged creatures. Here, the underworld is a tiny hole buried deep beneath the ground. And I'm stuck in it.

The underworld is made of compressed soil, and there's no way out.

Drifting in and out . . .

IN

a hole the earth is thick and the sky is so far away I can't breathe

OUT

of the world disappeared. Light. Sight. Gone.

IN

this place my lungs are insistent, demanding, persistent, my heart, a clock that will stop when the air is all gone and I'll tick myself

OUT

of hope. Under soil, more soil. Below soil is rock, under rock, more rock, then gasses, through to a fire in the centre. It pulls me

IN

two directions, backwards is upwards, lost in memories, trapped. Wind them around myself, spiders' silk and sleep

OUT

my years before now. This impossible now: no one in the world above knows I am below

IN

the earth beneath me, I plant my fingers like roots of a tree

OUT

down down down, this relentless pull of gravity.

*

I scratch cold, dank soil with my fingernails. How long will this sense of touch last, or like sight, will my senses fall away . . .

Sound.

Above me. A creak, a faint low groan. The sound of something growing. Is this movement in my mind . . . a trapped place for hope to grow in, before the gravity pulls too hard.

Smell of earth and something green . . . something growing, spreading . . . the Thrashing House has roots.

Roots split the soil above me. They could push through me, tangle me in them . . . so, is this what I have to do, dig further down, rather than up? How deep can I bury myself, when I'm not dead? The roots above me, solid and coiled, tendrils spin down from them, twist in my hands, light as fine hair, the soil falls away. Above me, the space that must lead back up, but *up* is too high, too dangerous, too steep. I walk the palms of my hands around the hole I'm in, search for a way out, some weakness in the soil. This tiny chamber, a pocket of air in a lung. Alveoli, deep underground, so the roots can breathe. The soil feels looser here. Someone's already dug at this patch and the soil feels cold and damp in my hands. I make a small hole, push my hand into it. Air moves on my fingertips. This must be a way out.

Two choices. Stay buried. Dig.

I'm a blind mole, digging deeper, digging down . . . But between my fingertips, in my palm, on my wrist, my forearm, I can feel air. My hands are tunnelling and this hole is nearly wide enough. The smell of dank air, and a faint other smell: the sea, the salt air of the outside. Escape.

Shift this dirt . . . scrabble, move the earth . . . I push soil through and make the hole wider, deeper. I shift my feet, sit on the edge of the hole, nudge myself forwards, drop through it and

land

not far below. There's enough room to stand. I'm in a tunnel of earth and roots. A way out. I move forwards in the direction that the air is coming in. My white hair lights up and gently glows, so I can see.

The sound of waves. I edge forwards, the tunnel is wider. I round a curve, and there are smashed rocks under my feet.

The tunnel has led into a cave. I move towards the direction of cold air. Salt air blows in, the sound resonates: the wind plays the cave like a discordant instrument. Rounding the next rock face, there is the mouth of the cave; the rocks are dark around the edges like enormous broken teeth. The mouth of the cave holds the whole outside world in its jaws.

The shore, the sea. Thick dark clouds in the distance over a tiny rocky island on the horizon. I slip and slide over jagged rocks. There are traces of some gleaming mineral on the rocks; here is a shore, the sea, the stars. I fall out of the cave, my body hits broken stones. I roll over, lie gazing upwards, flood air in and out of my lungs.

Swallowed back into the world, I laugh it in, cry it out, fill my mouth and eyes with sky.

Escape is possible, even from the darkest places.

I can choose to feel anything, do anything, walk away or stay. Get completely trapped, and still escape. I don't want to run away any more. I want to find something to run towards. I pick up a sharp stone and carve a word into a rock:

HOME

Mary

The stairs creak on my way up to the ground floor. I've got the keys to all three doors from the basement in my bag.

I open the door at the top of the stairs. The kitchen door is open, it's dark in there.

Morgan's Da steps out of shadows. 'This story you wrote—'

'Dun spook me like that.' I breathe, hard.

'—how real is it?'

'What she said. It thrashes out the truth. Now you know. I need to get out. You going to open the gate for me then?'

'My wife has . . . misplaced the padlock key. She wishes the gate to remain locked.'

'She's skittering in madness, for all her clever drawings. What if Morgan wants—'

'Now, how would you know the name of my daughter?' Him folds hims arms.

I clench my hands.

'So, where is she?' Him leans towards me.

I knock back into the wall. The keys in my bag clunk. 'She dun want you to find her.'

'Was she all right?'

'Well, I think she can take care of herself. If she hasn't got enough food she'll just *steal* some.'

'When you saw her. Was she—'

'She's fine.'

Him smiles. 'Good. That's good.'

I say, 'You're not going after her then?'

'No, but I'm certain she'll be back. My wife is, however, less certain. She's decided she wants you to stay, to do her bedspread and help—'

'I've got to get gone. Tonight. So, you going to let me out then, or have I got to smash your fence up?'

Morgan's Mam steps out of the kitchen. Them both take my arms, bluster me along the corridor, through a door and up the stairs. It all blurs, for thems hands grip too hard.

I'm pushed into the room with the small bed and folded bedspread.

The door is pushed shut behind me, a key clacks in the lock.

I bang on the door with my palms, shout, kick and screech but . . . I stop. I'm just fighting a locked door with no sound on the other side of it. I yell, 'No wonder Morgan's took off!'

I try to open the window but it's been painted shut with thick lilac paint, and the panes are too small to get through even if I did smash them up and find some way down to the ground what isn't falling.

Throwing my bag on the bed, I slump myself down beside it.

The bedspread lies there, folded, blank, waiting for my flowers. On a shelf are books. Morgan told me about these. All shapes and sizes. These have pages full of tiny neat words. I lick my thumb and rub at them. Them dun smudge.

Stories and stories and stories. I get some of them down off the shelf and put them on the bed. I sit down and look at the pictures in them: a girl with a mirror, another of a wise old woman and one of a jug and a blue cornflower what's crying. Maps, apples and plants. Girls in flouncy dresses, all crowns and red lips. Some pictures are crammed so full of colours, them look real. Not made of stitches at all, but of real things, squashed flat.

But them're just some place to get lost in.

I listen at the door. Silent. I rattle the door handle. Listen. Nothing. I kick it hard, and behind me I hear a quiet, slow tune being hummed.

I spin round.

Shadow Mary sits on the bed, all dark and grey.

In shadows under her hair, her eyes gleam.

She sings a slow song I've never heard before:

'Blank dark in you

a place you never cross to.'

I say, 'Get back in the moppet.'

She keeps singing.

'Stop it.' I put my hands over my ears but I still hear her inside my head.

She sings, 'You take the sun down, burn it out

bring night, right into me

but night frays

rips away

shadows rumple and tear . . .'

Stopping singing, she says, 'When Barney were born—'

'Dun you get in my head.'

'Not just your head. My head. Your head's full of blanks. I've got the rememberings.'

I put my hands over my ears. 'No no no no no.'

She reaches under the bed and picks up a pair of small scissors.

I say, 'Put them down.'

She grabs a clump of her hair. Opens the scissors.

'No!' I reach forwards but she cuts a clump of her hair off, just below her jaw.

'You got any rememberings of this, then?' she whispers, her voice hollow.

'Stop it. Please.' The tears in my eyes blur her up till she's not there any more.

I sit on the bed. A picture of Mam and Da leaps up and sticks in my thoughts. This picture isn't my memory, but I'm in it. It's come loose from Shadow Mary.

In my bedroom at home, Mam stands by the door, holding Barney, when him were just new. Me, three years younger, sat on my bed, Da sitting next to me, cutting my hair. Cutting it off, short, to my jaw. Stepping back, saying, 'She'll be wanting to be outside again soon enough. Like you said, we dun want anyone—'

Mam says, 'Dun, Ned. I'll do it. Said I would. Mary, it's for the best, you know that. Only us what knows, and only us what will. If you dun look nice, no man'll try anything you dun want them to. You know that.'

Da says, 'Kelmar'll talk.'

Mam says, 'She'll not.' She holds Barney close to her, her tears fall on hims head. Mam rocks him, says, 'It's best this way, Ned. I've got more of the tincture from Valmarie. I'll keep on giving it her.'

I watch myself, sitting on the bed in my bedroom. Not speaking. Looking just like Shadow Mary.

Da steps back, nods at her hair. 'Well, I'd best finish. Can't leave it half-done.' Steps up to her, cuts the rest of it. Him steps back again. 'It'll grow.'

'And be cut again,' Mam says, her face sad.

Mam and Da are stood by the door with thems new baby.

Shadow Mary sits on the bed in her pale blue bed dress, staring out of the window.

Them are frozen in a picture.

This picture makes my legs shake. I pull the moppet out of my bag. Whisper in its raggedy ear, 'Mary dun make up rememberings.'

Barney's voice says, 'Mary, it's too dark. Cradle me . . .' and the sound of him stings me right across the chest, as waves wash through the shell and carry hims voice away.

I bury the moppet in my bag and my hand touches one of the basement keys. I stare at it while I cry away the sound of Barney's voice. I think of Grandmam. Her arms around me, my eyes closed, feeling her soft shawl on my cheek.

I started thieving keys not long after Grandmam came to live with us, for she'd told me she liked thieving bits of broken plates. She had a locked-up box under her bed, and she kept her growing collection in there. My hands had wanted metal, so the first thing I stole were the key to her box. She thought it were a good game, but made me give that one back to her. When I did, she told me about thieving. This is what she said:

When you're a thief and you believe what you're doing is right, you can get away with it, without anything bad happening by way of consequence. If all you ever thieve is keys, and you believe that keys are belonging things for you and you alone; no trouble will come your way. You remember what I've told you about believing you are right in whatever you do. Watch out for the call of the Thrashing House.

Others seek out guilt like spiders darting after a tangled-up fly. So watch you never let yourself feel guilt about what you're thieving. Guilt gets tangled, and that will be that. You'll get blamed for sure, and the tangles will tie you in knots – you'll believe you're guilty, so you'll be punished. And all you needed to do from the start were – to believe you were not.

So, if you're a thief of keys, believe that the keys belong to you and only you. You're only taking back what's already yours. And if it's already yours, you're not doing wrong and have no room for guilt.

Keys unlock things, so if that's the thing you've chosen to thieve, know there's something in you what calls out to be unlocked. Whatever folk choose to thieve, it is something to do with what is missing in them. So if you meet a thief who steals everything them comes across, and them are indiscriminate with thems thieving, it means them believe them have nothing of worth in themselves. If you meet a thief who only steals tokens of love – rings and posies and jewels – it is because them needs to be loved, and has either not enough, or too much, love to bear. Think careful about what it is you thieve, because that will tell you what is important to you, and that is the truth of all thievery.

Thinking of Grandmam's voice reminds me that I've got good memories what've been stitched so firm them can push away anything from Shadow Mary. Grandmam said:

We live on an island of thieves, Mary. No one else will tell you that, but that is the truth of this place. So, watch what is precious to you, keep it close by and thieve only what belongs to you.

Me and Grandmam talked, then I rested my head on her shoulder and picked at the threads in her shawl.

'Keys unlock things.'

'Them do that, Mary.'

'I want to keep them so I can unlock things with them.'

'What kind of things, pet?'

'Doors. Hidden things.'

'What's to be unlocked in you? Think on that, pet. Might make sense when you're older. But you got to believe in what you thieve. If keys are what you want, mind you think loud an' clear them all belong to you.'

'No guilt, Grandmam?'

'No guilt, pet.'

She showed me all her bits of broken plates. We spread them out all over the floor, some were painted with flowers and some were blue, green or white. Mam got back from her walk and looked at them all as well. We decided Grandmam liked thieving broken bits because she'd spent so many of her years fixing and mending things. Mam made the three of us valerian tea and told Grandmam not to break her cup.

I asked Mam what *she* liked to thieve. She said she dun ever remember thieving anything, apart from the last spoonful of honey in each jar. Grandmam said that meant that Mam wanted some sweetness just for herself, but it had to be a sweetness what dun last too long, so it'd be special each time. Mam said she thought Grandmam might be right.

I look through the keyhole. Morgan's Mam and Da have left the key in the lock on the other side. Well, that were careless. I take the basement keys out of my bag. Lie them all on the floor. The longest key should do it.

I find the book with the biggest pages. The first page has a picture of a great black shaggy dog what's drooling blood. 'Sorry Morgan, I know this is yours,' I whisper, 'but you thieved the Thrashing House key from me, so this makes us even.' I tear out the picture of the dog, and another page, and another.

I push the torn-out pages under the door and shove the longest of the keys into the lock. It bashes against the key what's in there, pushes it out, it clanks on the floor. I lie down and pull on the first piece of paper, but it comes through empty. I use both my hands and slide the other two pieces towards me and feel a bump as the key hits the bottom of the door. I slide the paper along, towards the hinged side, where there's a bigger gap. The key passes through, on the picture of the dog. I grasp it in my hand and unlock the bedroom door.

*

I step outside into the night and close the front door behind me. The moon is a grey glow, trapped in a cloud. The clouds scrumple up to the north, thickening. This fence is too tall to climb over. The earth is thick with grass roots so I can't dig under it. I look round the garden for a stone to smash the padlock. No stones. No rocks. Nothing sharp or heavy. Someone's already thought of this.

My hands are swollen with cold. At the gate, I pick at the thick iron padlock with a broiderie needle. The workings inside of it click twice. The needle sticks on the next one. I ease the needle to the left, down, up, right. Can't find the next clack. The metal of the padlock hums in my hand.

Behind me, the windows of the house stare at my back. My shoulder feels frozen, sharp, from holding the needle so tight and firm. The padlock sends a pulse through my fingers.

'Go on, tell me,' I whisper. I can feel the touch of Morgan's

Mam in the padlock, feel that she comes and goes through this gate. Often. But the metal sends a sharp zing through my fingers. It dun want me to know.

There's a bitter smell caught in the cold still air. A smell of metal. Like blood. I move the needle, listen close for the next click in the padlock, and the next one. Just a couple more clacks will unlock it. I listen, my hands numb, white. My hand feels like a fat moon, my fingers grip the needle like it's going to pull down the stars.

Right up, left down, click. Further in.

This smell of metal in the still air.

Blue eyes opposite me, between the slats in the gate.

A round face hangs there, pale in the dark. Her black coat locks away the rest of her body in shadows. I let go of the needle and lose all the clicks.

I gasp out, 'I dun have the Thrashing House key!'

Kelmar says, 'I know.'

I step back from the gate. 'Murderer.'

She whispers, 'You could only be here. I've looked everywhere else.'

I'm here face to face with her, the gate between us, but I'm somewhere else, locked in a room, ice all around me. Somewhere inside me, not yet in my mouth, a scream is storming up . . . only my hand reaches out, wants to touch hers. I pull it down.

I whisper, 'There's something you want to say. So say it.' I put my hands over my mouth.

She stands like a tree, her feet planted like them have roots. 'I'm the only one what knows, Mary. Know more than you do, an' that's not right—'

'No, stop it . . .'

'It were too hard.'

I stare at her face, a pale moon behind the fence. She can

274

help me. I pinch my hand and can't feel it. I want her to go away. I want her to keep talking. I want to grip her hand, for her to pull me out of here. Kelmar's face is a floating moon, it's the only real thing I can see in this dark. Flashes of pictures flicker in my mind. Ice in the cold room. Soot on the walls. Pictures from Shadow Mary. Barney, newborn, screaming in Kelmar's arms.

My voice says, 'Help me.'

'Mary, I know.' She reaches a finger between the slats in the gate.

'This is . . . no . . . no . . . dun want this.' I shake my head. 'Dun . . . just say it.' I put my hands over my ears.

'It's best you remember.'

'Why?'

She leans her hands on the fence, her mouth talks in the gap. 'Because it were that tall man and him got out. I saw Barney in hims eyes when we took him to the Thrashing House. I saw, as well, you dun remember him.'

'Dun say . . .'

'I've searched east and west for you . . .'

Clouds pile up high. Black underneath.

Kelmar says, 'Come on.' She draws out a bright metal knife from her coat. Sticks it in the gate hinge. 'You're coming home with me.' She twists the knife. Wood cracks.

I sink down in wet grass. Look up at the clouds what bunch, scrumple, bundle, spin. The gate splinters, cracks, her knife twists it open, the planks break, crack.

Kelmar, in the garden, with me. Her voice, 'Can you stand?'

She pulls me up on my feet. The ground shifts. Ice through my legs and hips. Kelmar's strong hands pull me through the broken gate, my bag knock knocks, the keys inside clunk.

Kelmar pulls me, fast walking.

Keys unlock. Rattle. Turn in my head.

Fast uphill, her arm, strong under my shoulder.

The cold air unravels twin hairdo.

Red ribbon, child's play, falls away.

She pulls me along. Her mouth talking, telling me Mam said I were contagious, she took everyone in. She says, 'I know what the shape of a baby is like, and her belly, it just weren't the right shape.'

Unlocked.

A picture from Shadow Mary. Mam makes cushion bump, stitches it for her belly. Ties wadding around, makes belly big, bigger. Wears bump dress. Pretends pregnant. Me indoors for months. Belly swollen like moon. Not allowed outside. Doors locked up. Mam saying, 'Mary's terrible sick, get away, you'll catch it.'

Kelmar's voice, saying Mam locked us in the cold room so I'd be numbed with ice and not scream. Her words scratch the inside of my head. I'm remembering screams, trapped in my throat. My voice whispers, 'The blank dark. Full of *your* blue eyes.'

Kelmar pulls me up the hill. The ground is too fast under my feet.

'Stop.' I stand still. 'I'm not here.'

Kelmar lets go of me. 'It's shock. It'll pass.'

I stand dead.

The lie I've been telling myself for three years . . .

'Move!' Kelmar's arm around my shoulders.

I fall. The grass tilts. Washes me down a hill and up another in Kelmar's arms. Track cuts through grass. Sand path. Low gate. Pebbles.

Front door opening.

Indoors.

Blanket chair softness. Think warm, but shaking cold. More blankets. Kelmar's hands wrap and wrap and wrap. Her voice, saying there and there and there.

Kelmar's blue eyes in the cold room.

The screech of a baby.

Mam saying him were hers.

Him were only ever mine.

Not my brother, my son.

Morgan

The clouds pile up in the night sky above the rocky island in the distance. Every hair on my body is raised. My fingers are covered in dirt and scratches.

At the edge of the water I reach out my hands to rinse them, but the water glows bright blue. Too bright. I snatch back my hands. Just beneath the surface there's seaweed, entwined and tangled. The seaweed is threaded through skeletons of fish, their eyes dissolved away to blank holes. The seaweed frays on the surface, the ends of it are dead strands. The small waves wash over it, fizz and bubble, change colour from blue to white to cream to brown. Strands of the seaweed move, coming out of the water, rippling over the stones, the strands are moving towards my feet, thickening . . .

I step back. The seaweed twists and coils, thickens, advancing towards me. I back away, clamber over broken rocks, my heart thudding, towards the caves, over sharp stones and cracked rocks. This is a poisoned shore. The broken rocks around me gleam along the waterline. A decomposing gannet lies in a rock-pool of green water. Streaks of bright colours, the algae is stained pink. I lean down to lift out the dead bird, I want to bury it. But something pulls my gaze away, to a path next to the caves.

A tall male figure stands at the top of the path on the hill. I blink, and he's gone.

I climb the path, wipe my boots on the grass, which lightens in colour, thins and withers underneath them. I reach the top of the path. No cottages huddle near this shore. Just scrubland. I can't see the man anywhere.

The Thrashing House stands tall in the distance. A long walk, but from there I can find my way back to Mary's cottage. Perhaps it's just the stillness in the air, perhaps it's relief that I saw the seaweed before it reached my feet and dragged me into the poisoned waters, but my breathing has slowed, and as I look up at the sky I have this feeling that something's changed. That Mary might have come home.

*

My hair glows so brightly, I must look like a walking candle as I step along a narrow path in between two peat pits, mounds of peat stacked like bricks, and gashes in the earth. A couple of wooden sleds lean against a stone wall. The air is thick and still.

I hear distant voices, I take off the coat and use it to cover my hair.

Too late.

A woman's voice calls out, 'You. Hidden daughter.'

Walking towards me is the woman who asked my father for the plank, wrapped in a warm coat, a ragged grey shawl over her hair. There's a younger woman with dark eyes with her. They both have empty round baskets strapped to their backs. They stop, blocking the narrow path.

The plank woman says, 'I'm Camery. This one's Chanty. Where you going?'

Chanty folds her arms. 'Dun you mean, where's she come from?

I say, 'Let me pass.'

Camery says, 'You went in.'

'Where?'

'Thrashing House, 'ent it,' says Chanty.

'You've got the key,' says Camery, holding out her hand. 'Give it to us.'

Chanty says, 'How'd you get out?'

I open my mouth to say, *Through a door, down a hole. Digging. Then tunnels. Caves.* But my voice doesn't speak. I try again. I look over my shoulder at the clouds thickening, closer still. 'I can't say. Let me pass. There's a storm coming.' I step towards them.

'Give us the key.'

'I don't have it.'

'Well, where—' says Camery.

Chanty glances at my coat, still over my hair. 'Course she's got it.'

I try to say, *I left it inside the lock*, but I can't. 'It won't let me say.'

Camery says, 'No—'

'How do you know I was in there?'

'Kelmar tried to stop you going in, only you slammed the door in her face.'

'That was Kelmar? Running at me through fog, I thought—'

Chanty yanks my coat off my hair. Both of them step back, stare at my glowing hair, their eyes wide.

'Must've been fearful in there, to do that to you. And you not able to speak of it,' whispers Camery.

Chanty rummages in the coat pockets. 'Nothing. What about her dress?'

'It's not in my dress.' I snatch back the coat.

'We need that key.'

I try to say, *It's inside the Thrashing House, still in the lock.* But all I can choke out is, 'I haven't got it.'

'We need it.'

I say, 'You can always go in—' and my voice won't say, *the way I came out.*

'Dun talk chicken shit,' says Camery. 'Not going in there. Not done anything wrong.'

'Neither have I. Well, if you want the key back that badly, maybe you should take—' My mouth opens and closes – I think, *the door off its hinges.*

They're both frowning. 'What's she trying to say?'

Camery puts her hand on my arm and whispers, 'What did you see in there? Were it paddles and bats, knives – all them kinds of things?'

'I saw—' I can't say, *ghosts.*

They step back, pale.

Camery says, 'Poor thing. You can't even speak it. Were it *fear* did that to your hair?'

I try to say *no*, but it won't come out.

Camery whistles. 'Terror did that. So young, to have your hair turned white with shock. How old're you?'

'I think . . . I'm twenty-one, that's the right age, isn't it?'

'You dun know your age?'

'I must have lost count.'

'Come to the Weaving Rooms. Tell all us women what happens—'

'It doesn't want me to say—' *how to get in or out, what it's really like inside, or where the key is now.* Again, my mouth won't speak. 'I could try to write it down.'

Camery pulls her shawl tightly around her. 'Do that. Come to the Weaving Rooms. Soon.'

Chanty says, 'She can't come to the Weaving Rooms yet. We women have other things to talk of, she knows nothing—'

Camery interrupts, 'You seen a tall man up this way?'

I turn away and point in the direction of the poisoned shore. 'There was a man – on the cliff—'

'We'll have to walk into the storm then.'

'No – take shelter – I only saw him for a moment. He could have been any man.'

'Well any man's not good enough.'

'No,' I say. 'They probably aren't—'

'What's she meaning?' Chanty says.

'Sorry. I wasn't thinking.'

'You were. Heard you, I did.'

'If the men can't read or write, does that make them more . . . like beasts?'

Camery says, 'Than what? Dun see the deadtaker getting hims hands dirtied over a cow being down. Getting that cow up on its feet again, saving it, instead of sitting indoors waiting for folks to die. Our men take care of what needs taking care of.'

'Don't they want to read?'

Chanty says, 'Read what?'

'Oh.'

'What?'

'No books. You don't write stories down.'

Chanty says, 'We've plenty stories. Tell them to each other.'

Camery tells me that women read and write – the spinning and knitting stitches they've found to work best, about the length of threads it takes to make a cloth, getting the right recipe for lye and about the temperature needed to boil colours into yarn. She tells me that women's trade has kept all of the islanders alive for generations. She says, 'You shouldn't listen to your Mam.' She folds her arms. 'Nothing wrong with our men.'

'You've met her?'

Chanty says, 'Not able to talk about her.' She opens and closes her mouth. Camery nudges her and they step to the side.

I walk past them, turn and say, 'It might have been your tall man I saw. All the way down there at the shore. It's a long walk. Hope you find him.' I throw the coat over my hair and tramp along the path through cold, still air.

*

I didn't realise how long it would take and how far it was – the distance from the peat pits to the Thrashing House, down the path from the cliffs to the beach, and through Mary's cottage door. The view from my windows at home told me nothing of measurements. Neither did maps or geography books. They talked of inches and miles, gradients and heights, but not how long it takes to cross such a landscape in boots that don't quite fit.

Mary hasn't come home.

But someone's been in here since I left, and they've turned over these rooms. The drawers with threads and needles are tipped under the table, the back door is open, knives and forks are mixed in with dry rice and sawdust on the kitchen floor.

In Mary's bedroom, clothes from the drawers and cupboard are strewn across the floorboards. A box of keys has been scattered all over Mary's bed.

On top of the keys, a scrawled note on rough white paper reads:

Key thief.
Give it back, Mary.
We know it were you.

Those distorted faces at the window when I ran out must have come in here, searched the cottage and left it like this. I know how I'd feel if someone had broken into my room and torn up my books – I'd feel rummaged. But these are not *my* things.

I tie back my dimly glowing hair and gather up clothes, small jumpers, socks, trousers in a thick blue fabric, vests. Mary's underwear, rags, dresses, about five rolls of bandages and a small mirror.

I clean a pot and make porridge, eat a huge bowl of it and it burns my mouth, but I don't stop eating till the bowl is empty. I wash up the bowl, the spoon and the pot and all the knives and forks from the floor, and sweep up the rice and sawdust.

In the room with the fireplace I put everything away as it was, and sweep the floor behind the front door. Putting the broom down, I open the door to the room with the double bed – Mary's parents' room. Nothing's been touched in here.

A small carved cupboard in the corner holds a jar of buttons, a pair of white gloves, thick fabric covered in patches: they've been repaired over and over again. There's a dusty glass bottle. I take out the stopper and the bitter scent of the forgetting herb coils out into the room. I steady myself and clink the stopper back in.

Flat on one of the cupboard shelves there's a raised piece of wood. I try to move it. It won't shift. I take everything out and feel around the edges. I push on it. It clicks down, then opens. A secret compartment in the shelf. Inside there's a small book with a black cover tied shut with string.

I touch the string around the book, and my fingertips sting – they feel like they've been cut, but there's no blood. I look closer at the string, at the coppery colours twisted through it.

It looks like the moving seaweed from the poisoned shore. I get the white gloves out of the cupboard and put one on, stroke the string and look at the fingertip. It's tinged yellow, smells of sulphur. I tear off the string.

Two choices. Read. Don't read.

I sit on the bed and flick through the pages, entries in a tiny, even script.

This is Beatrice's diary:

Him is too close. Him is never going to have me. Him comes begging with them eyes of hims, tells me him is 'in love' with me. I've told him I dun feel 'in' anything for him. Not 'in love' or 'in hate', not 'in anger'. How can him talk of love like it is something to drown in, like being 'in waves', or 'in the washtub'? Or perhaps it's more like being caught. 'In mousetrap'. Sorry. I'm 'in birdcage' with you so I can't do anything but peck. Now I'm just being 'in stupidness'.

Not that I'm fearful, only perhaps I'm a bit in disgust.

For it's disgusting the way him pants at me from inside hims eyes, like there's a stray dog living inside him.

I flick forwards, to a few months later. I read:

I came home to find him by Mary's bedroom door. I'd only been outside, to talk with Annie, for she'd been sick and I'd wanted her well again.

But him were here in our home.

My daughter crying in her bed. Blood all over her.

Not long thirteen.

I went for him, scratched hims face and him grabbed my wrists, still got the bruises, for him is stronger than him looks. I

285

screamed and cried — how could him touch my daughter how could him touch her how could him.

But him said I should've let him have myself. But I never could have. Him said, what did I expect when she looks so like me?

But though I cried fit to break, him said him would come again for her till I gave him myself.

I said never never never and said I'd tell the whole island, and that him would be punished.

Then I said I'd tell all the other tall men, and only then, him spoke less angered.

Him said on the main land them do prisons and all kinds of torture in prisons and is that what I want for him?

And I said yes. I do want that, I want you to be tortured, I want you to die for what you've done to her.

Him said if I'd let him have myself, him would never have touched her, so that's what him would say to others if I ever spoke out — him would say that I traded my own daughter.

So if I speak out, or him speaks out, we will only speak against one another. And where is my daughter in this: she has no words to speak it.

I have sworn him my silence, so him will let both of us alone, and I never will let her alone again, never when the tall men are here.

But it weren't him what had to wash the blood off her. It weren't him what had to tell her over and over, it were safe to go to sleep. It weren't him, it won't ever be him, what has to make her forget it.

But a trade is a trade. Him dun know anything else, and perhaps I dun either.

I don't want to read this, but still my hands turn the pages.

Him has kept to the trade, came in the boats with the others, but him stayed away from our home.

Valmarie has given me the forgetting herb. It works. Thankful it works, I am, for Mary were in a terrible way. But she is forgetting.

I told Valmarie the tincture were for me, something terrible had happened I needed to forget. She could see how pale I were, and I couldn't hardly speak, though she said she'd keep silent. I were shaking myself. Dun want anyone to know. Dun want him to come back for Mary or for me, not ever again.

My eyes feel stained, clouded. This crime was never punished. It was buried. I shouldn't know this. Just one more page and I'll put this book down. One page. Then I'll stop.

I choose the final page:

K and V have talked Annie round – she were always too easy swayed. She's got too many folks giving her thoughts she talks up into storms. I could change A's mind as quick as stick a pin in a cushion if I wanted to.

She's been swayed to thinking that us weaving the snake ropes is wrong.

If it were that bad to be sending the snake ropes off to the main land, for sure the Thrashing House would have called all of us women. The north shore is full of the Glimmeras' hair, more and more comes, it creeps towards us, for it is full of thems poisons. But we cut it away, and contain it in the snake ropes. What the main land folks do with crates of snake ropes, well, that's thems choice.

I'll put my own hands on a snake rope. Be the first to touch them bare — women have always been gloved. But not all the things we believe are as true as our mothers and grandmothers might have taught us. I'll prove it to them. I'll take my gloves off. Wrap a snake rope round myself, on my bare skin, my ankles, my wrists — prove to them the effects aren't as bad as them're making out. We're not spreading poison by weaving the snake ropes and sending them away, we're containing it.

The last entry in a dead woman's diary, where she had something to prove that I don't understand.

This book isn't a story. It doesn't have a beginning or an ending. It's not teaching me anything or making me feel I could become someone else. I can't think about what Beatrice has written in here. But I do have to think about this feeling, curled deep in my gut, that this book wanted to be found. That it needs to be read. I feel sick, knowing that a book can be a place for such painful secrets to be written onto pages, so Beatrice's mind could be unburdened, and this crime concealed. Closed away inside a cover, placed in a hidden place, forgotten.

I hear a sigh. Beatrice's faint breath mists up a windowpane. Her translucent finger writes in the condensation:

TELL HER

I say, 'I can't tell Mary anything. They're *your* words . . . I shouldn't have read them.' But there's an ache in my chest. When Beatrice was alive, she chose silence over justice. A choice I've never had to make. I couldn't have played my game of three choices for this.

I lay the diary on Mary's pillow and whisper, 'Beatrice, I'll look for her. Somehow, I'll find her and bring her home. But your diary . . .'

Breathing another fog on a windowpane, I write:

IT'S MARY'S CHOICE

A cold wind blows around the room, and stills. For the first time since I've been in it, this cottage feels empty.

Beatrice has gone.

*

Just a feeling, but there is something certain. It feels solid and sure, right in the centre of me, that in this empty fireplace soon there will be a burning cracking fire and two pairs of hands, mine and Mary's, to warm at it. She'll teach me embroidery, I'll bake potatoes and thick stews and honey puddings. We'll never go hungry. We'll know each other well. Not family, not tied together. Not trapped.

Choosing this. A choice for both of us, and it's the only one I want.

A woman's shrill wail from outside. I open the curtain and a draught creeps in through the window frame. On the beach, Annie's three dogs bolt past, turn, sniff the air and tear towards the path that leads up to the cliffs. They've caught a scent. There is a crowd of women, one carrying a wide-brimmed hat, following the dogs, slipping, sliding after them through thickening snow.

Chasing towards something . . .

Annie's wail grows louder, a grief inside it like the sound of high winds. Large flat flakes of snow spiral from the grey and pink sky. I bundle myself into a coat, hide my hair with a scarf and follow the women.

*

The women's footprints lead around the side of the Thrashing House. It stands tall above me, half-white and half-dark. The snow flurries horizontally.

I stop at the door. The key will still be there in the lock, on the inside. It should be out here, so it can be used.

The wood of the door creaks. A sound in the lock.

Clickclickclack of the key.

I turn the handle and push the door open.

A creak, a crack from the shadows.

The ghost of a man steps from behind the door with the key in his hand. He's wearing a woollen jumper and a thick pair of trousers.

He says, 'Tried to get you to see me. But them were louder. Them'd waited far longer.'

'They were old ghosts. The people they wanted me to give their messages to wouldn't even be alive any more.'

He nods. 'Long gone.'

'But you're from now.'

He holds out his hand. The Thrashing House key lies across his palm. 'Dun give this to Mary. Too much for her. Give it to someone older. But you tell Mary, her Mam did her best. Might be right. Might be wrong. But she tried. Me, I were all kinds of useless.'

I take the key. 'How were you useless?'

'Talk of trading boys made me think to tell the tall man Barney were hims son. Him'd never known. Thought Mary'd remember what him done to her, if she still had Barney. Dun think that would've been good for her. But I dun know. Takes a Mam to know these things.' He stares down at his feet. He's wearing only one boot. 'See – useless.'

'You're Mary's father.'

He nods, his eyes are tired. He glances up at me and back at his feet. 'Relics.' He lifts up his bare foot and puts it back down. 'You tell Mary, I'm sorry about Barney. Thought it were right. Thought she'd be best without him. Over time.'

I say, 'I'll tell her.'

He nods again. Glances up at me as he pushes the door shut.

I lock the door and put the key in my pocket.

*

I watch from a hill as the women and Annie's dogs flounder around the graveyard. The gravestones are coated in snow. The bushes are dark and twisted, like black-inked lung diagrams, the coiled branches and sharp twigs thicken up from the ground and disappear under piles of heavy snow.

It's silent.

The dogs have no direction, they scamper, shake snow from their coats. One woman catches a dog, holds its nose to the wide-brimmed black hat. She whistles and it cuts though the air. The other dogs collide with her, and they relearn the scent.

The dogs sprint towards a dip in the hill under the Thrashing House where a small house is covered in snow. A woman was crying. But I can't remember her face . . . fog . . . the waves on the beach . . .

Barks crack through the silence. The dogs are at the house. Other women from all over the island are closing in. I move closer and watch from behind a small tree, push a branch out of the way and snow drops wet on the shawl that covers my hair. A woman reaches the house and peers through the window. She lets out three shrill whistles. The dogs howl, bark, scratch at the door. Five women reach them, one of them opens the door and the dogs charge in, the women behind them.

They drag out the shadow man.

He doesn't respond to the women's pushes or shouts. The women form a circle around him and release his arms. He stands up, towers above them. He doesn't move. A woman reaches in her pocket and pulls on a pair of white gloves, several of the others do the same. One woman carries a large round basket, she walks around the circle. The gloved women reach in, draw out a length of thick rope, and another and another. They wind the ropes around the man. The other women stand back, watching.

He gazes at the sky. The women tie his arms to his sides, bind his legs together. Still, he stares up at the sky. They wrap him in thick ropes from his neck to his ankles. One of the women, wearing a black shawl, stands in front of him, leaning on her walking stick.

A shrill whistle, she pushes him backwards with her gloved hands. He falls, slowly. Three gloved women break his fall. Four others move in and pick up his legs. He is laid flat on their hands. The woman in the black shawl leads the way. Seven women carry him, three at each side and one at his head. The others follow behind in single file. They march away through the snow. A silent funeral procession with a living body, and no flowers.

A low groan, deep underground. The procession of women moves along the centre of the island, over a small hill. One woman splits off in another direction, taking the dogs away.

The procession is going to pass my parents' house.

I wonder what Dad would say if they asked him to bury a living body. Or what he'd say about this snow, still falling so thickly. A silence of snowflakes. I draw the coat tightly around me and follow the procession.

*

Thieves. I can't live with them again. Their stolen food would taste like dust and decay. The clothes I've left there would feel like shrouds on my skin, and the sound of Mum hammering would be the sound of bones knocking under coffin lids.

But the pink fence is covered in blue-white snow, the sky above it glows pale pink and floats in the windows. A whole landscape of pastel colours. A picture of some sugar-coated home in a winter bedtime story: a house that tastes of sugared almonds and marzipan. But anything in a storybook that is as sugar-sweet as this always gets destroyed.

If this were a picture in a story, it would be an image of a home that waits for change. Waits for a wolf to come calling, asking for a new red coat, or for bears to break in and eat all the oats, for a baby with a squirrel's face to throw a hazelnut at a crack in the wall. The whole sugar house would collapse, dissolve itself. The sweetest story would change into a darker tale, where there's no sugar left anywhere in the whole world and real bears roam, armed with teeth, claws and killer instincts. Where the dead lie voiceless in their graves and criminals are never caught.

A story that lasts longer than bedtime. Longer than the final page. Longer than a kiss. Longer than a lifetime. As long as ever after. And right now, that seems like the worst thing that could happen.

The gate in the pink fence is off-centre; it's been broken.

Inside that sugared house is the only family I'll ever have. They'll want the gate mended, locked up. I want to shut them away safely behind it.

My heart clenches in my chest and I think of my mother and how she looks like a child when she eats the food I cook for her, and how my father has given me a respect for all living things. And the twins, secretly plotting their escape.

My parents made sure I had so many books, and taught me to read and write. I think of all the games of three choices I've played, when I thought I had none. My parents had choices as well. They chose to bring me here with them. Other children are left behind in the world, when their parents run away from something. From wars, from tragedy, from shame, pain, loss, from losing control or will or hope. Or called towards something else – a bottle, a missed opportunity, death, a second family, a hospital bed, a new lover . . . So many choices. Many people have children, but they can't always keep them.

But mine kept me. Nothing bad has ever happened to me. I think of Mary having had no choice at all.

The procession of women trudges away over the hill through the snow in another direction, away from my parents' home.

My parents wouldn't know what to do if danger came and hammered on their door, demanding a cup of tea. But perhaps it's time it did. Maybe sugar only tastes sweet when it's been stirred.

I keep out of view of their house, and follow the women.

Mary

Darkness behind my eyelids. 'What happened to me?'

Shadow Mary's voice inside my head, *You have forgotten. Forgotten everything.* Over and over, her voice cuts my belly like metal.

The tall man walks towards me in bed.

I call out for Mam but hims pale hand closes my mouth.

*

I wake under thick blankets. A fire. A box of matches on the hearth. A basket of peat. A room I dun know. Silence. My hands fidget, wool scratches my fingers. Samplers in frames on the walls, a cross-stitch of a woman's face. A crimson rug on the floor. The fire burns bright, only I can't feel the warm. Through the window, the sky's thick with grey clouds.

A doorway with a heavy black curtain pulled across it, a woman's voice humming behind, low, quiet.

Kelmar's voice, louder. 'Dinnertime, keep them teeth sharp.'

I'm inside Kelmar's cottage.

Bright colours light up everywhere; the floorboards gleam

brown and ochre, the crimson rug has flecks of red, orange, deep blue.

Sound. Claws scrape. Something thumps in my head, a pulse. The sound of crunching. My jaw too tight. A bump, a low growl. I lean forwards; my spine aches.

A bark. 'Hoy. Settle.' Kelmar's voice. Her boots thack thuck across the floor.

My heart thack thuck in my chest. I move my arms, shift my hips forwards in the chair and sharp pins prickle down my legs. My voice cracks out of me, 'Is Annie here?'

Kelmar calls out, 'No. Just her dogs.'

She comes through with two green cups, puts one in my hands. The warm tea smells of honey and cinnamon. The chair opposite me creaks as she sits down.

'How're you feeling?' She sips from her cup like it's easy.

'Sore.'

'You're in shock. You understand that?'

Not far away from this cottage, clifftops. Just a walk. Just one step, and another, and another. I will see the Pegs, watch how strong and brave them are to stand so solid while fierce waves wash all around them.

Kelmar's voice, 'Mary, come back.'

Is everything old, like the Pegs? The Pegs hold on tight, dun let nothing wash them away. I've always wanted to see Sishee's dress under the waves. Sishee's drowned dress. Inside the teacup, in the tea, the sea swirls around the bottom of the clifftops. Such a long way down.

'Mary?' says Kelmar's voice from somewhere.

I'm swimming in the sea in the cup because I'm not yet drowned.

'Wake up.'

I surface.

Kelmar leans forwards, 'Do you want to talk, or do you just want quiet?' She seems huge.

I stare into the tea. The rememberings are floating in the cup. Pictures. Watching something from a long time ago . . .

Mam stood in my bedroom holding the baby wrapped in a blanket.

Hims fingers twitching.

Mam said, 'A baby needs a name, and with a name, him will know who him is.'

My voice, 'Call him Barney for me.'

She took him to the door, said, 'All right. Mary, this is my son, your brother, Barney. You get up out of bed soon. Folk're talking.'

She walked away with my brother, Barney.

My breasts bound beneath a heavy bed dress. Mam'd bound them the day after him were born, showed me how. It were to stop the milk. That were the first time. Three years ago and now there's no milk, but I still bind them flat.

Mam pretended the baby were hers. A woman in to wet-nurse him, who'd lost a baby of her own. Blank over her face. Mam must've got up to him in the night, changed hims nappy, weaned him quick off the wet nurse's milk and onto warmed cow milk. I held him close when she weren't watching. Whenever she caught me with him she never said a word, but she looked so sad when she took him from me.

It always were my arms him wanted.

I always wanted him in my arms.

And then,

'She died,' I whisper.

Kelmar says, 'I'm so sorry Mary.'

I lift my cup to my mouth. Eyes float in the tea. Kelmar's blue eyes from the blank dark. The blank dark is the part of me what kept all the things I forgot inside of it. I drop the cup. The eyes spill all over the floorboards. Them close and are gone.

*

The space between me and Kelmar is dark and warm. I breathe hard. I lean away from her, and the space grows bigger. She moves back to her chair. I wipe my nose on my sleeve.

I've got ghosts in my eyes she can see.

'Where's Valmarie?' I ask.

'Gone.'

'For good?'

Kelmar frowns down at her hands. 'She won't be back.'

'What happened?'

'Found what she'd been looking for. No need to stay in a place if you're not tied to it.'

'Did you tell her about me and Barney?'

'No.' Her face is open and clear.

'But you pair were close.'

'It weren't anything I wanted to speak of.'

My throat cracks out, 'Dun believe you're the only one what knows. You must have told even just one person, got it off your chest.' I stare at her large breasts and up at her face, quick.

She dun notice. 'A midwife knows what's going on. If I were to speak to just one person, I'd lose trust. Not just trust from people, neither. Me, the birthing woman, and life and death stood watching from the corners. Always four of us there, keeping hope high, all possibilities considered. All waiting to see what the next contraction brings. These things are not for the chattering of. Trust's too easy broke.'

'So you never told anyone?'

'Your Mam wouldn't let me near you after. Not even to check

298

you were healing right.' Kelmar looks at the fire, she's still talking, telling me she came round for days, then each week, then a month later, but Mam never let her in. She tells me she saw me out and about but always with other folks there, or I'd walk away, sometimes look right through her. She tells me she thought about talking to me, but then she thought I were coping the best way I could.

'Dun understand forgetting.'

'You were too young. Sometimes folk *can* remember the hard stuff, other times them have to blank it out.'

'I kept drinking a tincture. The whole year is blank.'

'The forgetting herb. But your Mam . . . there's coldness in that.' Her teeth bite her plump bottom lip.

'So, is that why you and Valmarie killed her, for the sake of coldness, for what she did or dun do right?' In the grate the flames dance.

'We?' Her face is flushed. 'Oh no, you dun think that. *We* never killed her.' She spills a splosh of tea on the rug and stands up. 'I'll get a rag.'

'Are you telling me it were Annie? She can't have. She loved Mam and she's been there for me all this time since Mam got deaded. Were it all three of you?'

She goes out through the curtain. One of Annie's dogs comes in, sits next to me, whimpers as Kelmar comes back in, kneels down and mops the rug. She says, 'I can see how you'd think that, but it weren't like that.'

'What *were* it like?'

She sits back on her haunches and tells me it's too much for me to talk of Mam, and I tell her I'd best get back home then, so I can ask Annie. The dog stalks off, slumps on the rug by the fire and sighs.

'Mary, it's too much shock, you're to rest.'

'Since when did you care so much for me?'

'Since you were a terrified girl too young to give birth.'

I double over, my chest aches like she's kicked it.

She says, firm, 'Mary, there's something you need to decide.'

'Dun want this.' I cover my eyes with my fingers.

Kelmar pulls my hands down, gentle, and says, 'I need to know if you'll let me speak out about Barney, about what that tall man did to you.'

'I dun want—'

'Him is held at the Weaving Rooms.'

I sag back in the chair. 'Him is caught,' I whisper, 'so I dun need to think—'

'You *do* need to think.' She grips my hands. 'And I've needed to think an' all. The Thrashing House must've let him go because there's a truth needs to come out, outside of its closed door. We need to deliver the justice.'

My heart thuds in my throat.

She says, 'You've no Mam in the Weaving Rooms, so I want to speak for you. I need to know what you'll let me say.'

My hands shake.

She squeezes them. 'Tonight, the women meet to decide what's to be done with him.'

I ask how them caught him, and Kelmar tells me Annie's dogs tracked him. She says the women need hims name to call him out from the silence him is surrounding himself in, that him won't speak any words at all.

'So Annie and her dogs found him?'

'Not Annie.' Kelmar stands and goes to the window. Folds her arms and looks out. I get up slow, walk over and stand next to her.

Outside the light in the sky is bright, with grey, green, blue and pink colours spun through the clouds. The sky seems darker than the land, though it's daylight – for all across the hills, the fields, rocks and bushes are covered in snow.

I say, 'Warm snow . . . a storm from the Glimmeras.'

'Aye. A storm from the north,' says Kelmar. 'The moment you fell asleep, it started to snow. While you were sleeping, the snow came in flurries and sweeps and covered everything up. Like you were meant to wake and see everything all new again.'

She puts her strong hand on my shoulder. 'Now, what do you need to do, to help you decide?'

'I want to go out in the snow.'

She smiles. 'Then that's what you'd best do.'

*

I wear Kelmar's missing son Jake's black coat. The snow glistens as I walk out of her cottage, like the island's been stitched into a different picture. Kelmar's cottage is covered in snow, with the chimney smoking. I thought I shouldn't speak to her all this time, since Mam dun want her near.

That were another lie I told myself.

I stamp my feet. The snow flurries up in the air. I kick it and it scatters like flour. Kelmar wants me to think about Langward. I think about Morgan and wonder if she's still in my cottage and if she can see Mam's ghost. If she can ask Mam's ghost if she really traded me. Or if Langward lied. I wrap my arms around myself. Because it matters.

Too much.

I kick up the snow some more. Can't feel anything. I think about how Grandmam could tell me how warm the snow were, if she were here with me now. How if Mam were here too she'd laugh, for she only ever half believed anything Grandmam said. The snow's bundled all the noises away, tucked them up for warm sleep. Like Barney would be, if I had him here with me. I wipe my nose on the coat sleeve. I put my arms around myself. My heart burns warm. Not my brother. My son.

My son, Barney.

Barney *is* mine. Nothing can take that away. A half of him is mine, so I can make that half fill him up, warm him through, warm away anything what belongs to Langward. I can make Barney *all* mine far easier than him can. For him dun ever know Barney. I've always known him. Always loved him. And Barney has always loved me back. Langward can never ever have that.

Kelmar told me to think. So I have.

I flail my arms like I'm fighting whoever has Barney. I rage and punch at the sky, like these punches will pull down the clouds and get Barney back in my empty arms.

I stop.

What if it were Valmarie what has him. And she's gone. How long ago? How long could him survive, hid away in her house when she's left it? That animal what lived inside her black eyes. Animals want young. Animals breed. Her son Dylan were took. She loved him so fierce.

With the heart of a seal.

What if she took Barney for new young? A new seal cub from out of the sea she thought she could love . . . The snow is thick white dust. My feet go deep, sink and slide up to Kelmar's front door. Inside, I pick up my bag.

Kelmar comes into the room.

I gasp, 'When did Valmarie leave? How long ago?'

'Not long, why?'

'Where's your storm room?'

'Down there,' she waves at a hatch in the floor. 'But what—'

'Give me a candle.'

'Mary—'

'If you want me to trust you, just—'

She gets a candle and lights it.

I surge across the room, open the trapdoor and climb halfway down the ladder. She passes me the candle and I climb down and put it on the floor.

'Let me alone.' I climb the ladder, close the trapdoor, bolt it, hear her call out, 'Mary!' I climb down again, squat on the floor, open my bag and get out the moppet.

'Barney, are you still there?'

Listen close.

'Barney?'

The sound of waves.

I look around the tiny storm room; shelves with candles, fire-lighters, pickled cabbage in jars. The sound of the sea surges in my ear. 'Barney?' Nothing but the sea. Wash in, wash out . . .

I say, 'Mary?' The sound of waves dies down. 'Mary, is him there?'

'Go. Away,' she hisses.

'Just tell me – has hims shadow gone?'

She says, 'I'm too young to look after him.'

'You dun have to. I'll do it.'

'You can't have him for a son.'

'Is him still in there?'

'You have to look after me.'

'I can take care of the both of you.'

'Dun believe you. You pushed me into the blank dark, and then when you were hurting again, it were me you left in the graveyard, me you let him carve on. Him has cut me across where hims baby grew in me, and you won't show anyone.'

Kelmar's footsteps walk across the floor above me.

Shadow Mary's voice cries in my ear, 'You dun see, even on all that white snow, you dun have a shadow. I'm going to give you back all your murdered memories. Every. Single. One.'

I say, 'Please, we got to get him back. You love him, dun you? You want him back too, though you're angered with me?'

The sound of the sea.

I say, 'Let him talk if him is there. It might be too late, if hims shadow's not there with you, it means him could be dying – or dead. Please Mary, him could be—'

A small sigh breaks through the sound of the waves.

'Barney?'

Hims voice says, 'Mary, this Mary not let me talk.'

Kelmar knocks on the trapdoor, rattles it.

'Be up soon, just leave me!' I shout.

Kelmar knocks again.

'Not long!' I holler up at the trapdoor.

'Barney—'

Shadow Mary says, 'So you heard him.'

Kelmar shouts, 'Mary, come out. This dun feel right – what're you locking yourself down there for? Unbolt it!'

I push the moppet back in the bag, climb the ladder and undo the bolt. I blow out the candle as Kelmar wrenches the trapdoor open.

'What're you up to?' Her voice is sharp.

I climb out and wrap my arms around myself. 'Barney fell out of the tall man's boat. Him is here somewhere.'

She shakes her head. 'You can't know—'

'I do. Langward told me.'

*

Kelmar's put two bowls of thick chicken soup on the table. I sit down as she clatters in the kitchen. Annie's dogs are asleep by the fire – a breathing pile of furry heads and legs.

Kelmar comes back in and hands me a spoon. 'You decided what you want said?'

'You're asking me like I'm to choose a colour of thread.'

'Snow did you good then.'

'Maybe.'

She looks at the spoon in my hand. 'The punishment—'

'You decide it.'

'But after what him did . . .' mutters Kelmar, her eyes shine with tears. 'And you're thinking Barney's still here somewhere. Look Mary—'

'You loved Valmarie, dun you.'

'Right. Food.' She goes into the kitchen.

When she comes back in, her eyes are shining and she's got a basket of bread in her hand. She slides out the chair and sits down opposite me. She says, 'Getting upset for what's gone and not set to come back dun make it easier.'

I swallow a spoonful of the chicken soup, my throat clenches. 'You're sure the women have the tall man? If him got out of the Thrashing House, how do you know him won't—'

'Course we'd be careful of that. Now stop asking me questions. You're just talking me all over the place, but I've got questions for you. What's got you thinking Barney's still here, and who's this Langward? I'm not talking of anything else till *you* get to talking.'

'Dun want to.' I put down the spoon.

'Well, you got to tell someone, and I'm the only one you got to listen to you. Not like you bothered much with folks once your Mam died. You've had no one there in her place, little use that she were.'

'She were my Mam, no matter what she did. I loved her, even if—'

Kelmar's voice is sharp. 'She only let me help you after I swore on my own life I'd not tell anyone. If she'd let you die giving birth, I'd have—'

'You dun care for me that much.'

'I always cared for you, and just because you dun know it,' she takes my hand, 'it dun mean I stopped. You've gone and done it again, we're talking of something else. Come on. Who's Langward?'

I mutter, 'You need the name of the tall man, dun you?'

'That's *hims* name?'

I nod. She squeezes my hand and lets go. 'Mary, that's it. We'll get him out of hims silence. Oh Mary, that's the best thing you've done, telling me—'

'You want me to talk, so stop up yours!'

There's a smile hiding in her mouth. 'Him *can* speak, then, just won't. Sorry.'

'You're sure him is held firm?'

'Him'll not get out.'

There's a shadow in the corner of the room, but when I look at it, it's gone. I swallow hard and say, 'Think I need to show you something.' I unbutton the waist on the black dress. Hold it open so she can just see my belly.

Kelmar gasps, and comes round to get a closer look. 'Oh Mary. Did him—'

'No. Just this. It's nothing.' I button it up.

'That's not nothing. Can you not feel it? I'll get a poultice.'

'Dun need anything, it's fine.' I eat some more chicken soup.

Kelmar sits down. 'You're not feeling anything, are you?' She puts her hand on my arm. 'Might be that you're right, maybe you *do* need to shut it away, for a while at least.'

She asks me what I'll let her say tonight at the Weaving Rooms.

I say, 'I want them to know Barney's my son and that I'll get him back off any one of them what's found him. Tell them if anyone's seen him or thinks someone them know might have him, them have to tell me. So, say whatever else you want, as long as you say that.'

'Look Mary . . .' Her voice is soft.

'Dun say—'

'It's been a long time. Dun fix your hope too high.' She pats her chest.

I dun pat mine. 'I have to.'

She takes my hand. 'Anything else you want to tell me?'

'Him said Mam let him have me in her place.' I frown at her. 'A trade. Do you think she'd have done that?'

Her eyes have tears in them. 'I know she weren't always right in what she did, but even so, I can't see her doing that. Him is trying to hurt you even more, blaming her. Harm even your memories of her. You've got to hang on to what you know.'

'But I dun remember *enough* of her . . .'

Kelmar smudges a tear off her cheek. 'What him did to you, him did for himself, even if it were to spite her. She couldn't have made him do anything him dun want to.'

I stroke the rough weave in the fabric of the dress. 'Tell the women never to talk to me of him. Not ever.' One of Annie's dogs comes over and leans against my leg. I stroke the dog's head. 'I'm so tired.'

There's a drawing of shells on Kelmar's bedroom wall. A patchwork quilt is spread over her bed. I kick off my boots. The smell of lavender makes me heavier. She lifts the quilt and I lie down.

She says, 'You'll need clean clothes for when you're up. Ones what fit you, not like that piece you got on. You'll fit better Jake's clothes than mine.'

She goes and gets some folded black clothes, strokes them and lays them on a chair. She presses the quilt around me with solid sure hands.

I tell her I've never been in a bed this big. She smiles at me so warm, I say, 'Can you tell me a story?'

She sits on the bed next to me and the mattress sags as she shifts her weight back. My eyelids close. Her pillow is so soft it sinks under my face.

Kelmar says:

This is the Story of the Stone Crow.
The crows stood along the rocks, talking and gossiping to one another, thems voices like croaks. This were many many years ago, when the sky were so low, if them flew upwards them bashed right into it. It were never thems intention, although them did fly and get bashed often enough, for birds are made to fly.

To the crows, it were a hard life, with the sky so low. Thems beaks got dented, thems feathers ruffled, sometimes them'd get pure knocked out by the sky, depending on how hard and sudden them took off into it. Some got killed, others got broken beaks and had to learn to eat in a whole different way, and the rest just felt giddy a while, till them recovered.

Crows are clever birds. Them watch and learn all kinds of things from one another. One crow never took off at all, but watched all the others bashing and buffeting against the sky. For weeks it sat on the edge of a rock, for months, for years, some say. This crow knew that if it stayed still, right where it were, it would never get hurt by flying. It sat and thought all the time about the sky and how it were so close, just hanging there above its head, waiting to damage it.

Over the years it turned to stone, this crow. A solid rock shaped like a crow, so you'd never have known it had ever been all feathers and made for flight. You'd have thought, if you saw it, that it were the stone carving of a bird.

The other crows knew though. Them pushed and tapped and rolled it off the rock with thems dented beaks, and used thems claws and wing tips to push it all the way across the hills to the edge of a cliff what looks out over the sea.

You can still see that stone crow to this day, though the weather has worn it so it looks like a rock with a sharp beak shape that points out at the sky over the sea. The other crows laid it there so it could always see the horizon, and all the clouds above it. Them wanted it to see how far the sky has risen to now.

So the stone crow can always imagine, even if it can't feel it in its stone heart, what it could feel like to fly and not be afraid.

*

The bedroom is almost dark when I wake, the light from the window is strange – the night sky twists with blue-grey clouds. I get up, quiet, and put on Jake's jumper and hims thick warm trousers. Never have worn trousers before, but my legs are so warm in them. I walk round the room, smiling at how I can sit down and stand up and lie on the floor and I'm all covered up from head to foot. I watch the door and loosen my bindings under Jake's jumper, just a little.

Kelmar clatters in the kitchen.

The moppet crawls out from under the quilt. I pick it up, quick, and get back in bed.

'Barney?' I whisper. 'Why's the moppet out of my bag? Did Kelmar—'

Barney's voice says, 'Dun go to Weaver . . .'

'I'm going to follow her so I can—'

'This Mary say Weaverroom bad bad.'

'I need to see the women all together, see who might've found you and got you hid somewhere it's dark.'

'She says keep away tall man.'

'I could leave you both here. Hide the moppet somewhere.'

'She say no no bad man. She make for cry.'

'She makes you cry?'

'Not Barney cry. Mary cry.'

A loud crash outside in the kitchen. I push the moppet under the pillow.

The dogs' claws clatter behind the door.

I pull the moppet out again. 'Barney . . .'

The sound of the sea. Him has gone.

In the kitchen I listen at the curtain to the women's voices in the other room.

Nell's voice says, 'Can't put him back in without the key.'

There's muttering and Camery says, 'Poor girl.'

I hear Chanty's voice saying, 'Him can't stay here and, well . . . like Nell said . . .' One of the dogs growls.

The voices speak again, them're talking about Langward and how them each dun want to choose, and if them kill him, whose hands would do it and still be able to keep working on the cloths and weavings when them'd deaded someone. Camery's saying she couldn't step up for it.

Kelmar interrupts her and says, 'We've got to decide on levels.'

'Levels?'

'Of punishment.'

Nell says, 'Him deserves worse than anything.'

'Well, that's death with no truth left behind, 'ent it?' says Camery.

Kelmar says, 'I guess him'd be pretty much considered punished if him is dead.'

Nell mutters, 'Nothing from before and nothing to come—'

'Shall I take the dogs back down to Annie after?'

'No. Let her sit with herself for a bit. See what comes.'

Chanty pitches in. 'So is it death we're decided on? We could row him out to the island of the Glimmeras, let thems poison hair kill him. No, we could put him in a boat, tow him out to sea, far as we can get him. Then tell him to go back to hims home . . . if him can find it.'

Camery shrieks, 'Him *raped* her!'

I back away from the curtain, cold all over, I crash against a cupboard and thems voices keep talking, but so far away . . .

Kelmar comes into the kitchen, closes the curtain behind her, puts her arm around me and says, quiet, 'We're off soon, but you dun want to be hearing any of this, you said—'

'I've changed my mind. I do want a say in this. Punish him with what him *is*. That's worse than being punished for anything him has done. If you're looking for hims truth, like what the Thrashing House should've done, I can tell you of that. Him is a trader through and through. Him dun give anything unless him takes something away. So trade him.'

'Trade him for what?'

'The three boys them took to the main land. Make the tall men bring them home. Make the tall men agree that Langward is never to come back here. If the tall men refuse . . . keep him away from me. But do what you want with him.'

She hugs me and says, 'I'll speak well for you. You'll be all right here?'

'Aye.'

Her big hand squeezes my shoulder. 'You sure?'

'I'm fine.'

'You're not, but we'll talk of that later. We're heading off now. Keep the dogs in, or them'll head straight back to Annie. I'll leave my door unlocked, but I'll be taking my key with me. Just so you know.' She smiles at me. 'You'll be . . . all right, given time.'

*

The fire crackles in the grate. There's paper and charcoal sticks on Kelmar's table. I stare at the blank paper, my hand clasps the charcoal like it wants to write something down, but it dun know what.

So I get the moppet and whisper, 'Mary, write what you want.'

I put the moppet on the table next to the blank paper.

In the kitchen I give Annie's dogs some water. In Kelmar's bedroom I make her bed and sit down. I stare out of her window at the night sky and bright snow. Think how still and quiet it is.

And I think of the word Camery said. The women will speak that word to each other tonight, when them talk of what Langward did to me. The women will always think of that word now, whenever them see me. Whenever them speak my name.

I'm sitting at a wooden table,
near a fire in someone else's
home, writing words I dun
ever want to speak.

I'm here in another room,
looking at warm snow out
of the window, stroking
patchwork with my fingers.

I warm my hands by the fire, stroke the dogs so them lie down
quiet and I walk over to the table. Shadow Mary has written
on the paper.

Or it might've been me:

*I've no language for hims force, unwanted. No compass to
measure it on my body, no map to chart where it were, or a
clear injury to show what him took from me.*

*So I'll not name it. It's not mine. It's nothing I can speak
of.*

*Other people want to name it so them can choose a
punishment for some damage them can't see. But without a
name for it, I'm myself. I refuse it. I'll not let this word attach
itself to me. If it does, people will only see damage when them
look at me; them will meet this word, for it is a terrible word
to meet.*

Unspeak it for me.

Dun speak to me of a punishment for this crime.

*The justice I need steps in my footprints and lives in a
shadow. Let your eyes see the shadow what's always beside
you, for the shadow needs to be cared for, to be mended,
repaired.*

Dun let your eyes see what has been done.

Let your eyes see the things I do, and do well. Let your eyes see the shadow what can't speak, and help it mend.

And that will be some kind of justice.

*

Annie's dogs watch me. An ache in my chest. Enough being a child in someone else's home. I have to go back to *my* home. Find Barney and bring him home too. That's everything. And that's enough.

Annie's dogs jump at me as soon as I pick up my bag. I push them away and look around the room.

There's something in the air in here, something missing, not noticed, forgot . . .

One of the dogs barks.

I sit down by the fire, hold out my hands and stare at them. Is it about Mam, about what Kelmar wouldn't say, about Mam's death . . .

No.

About *Annie* and Mam's death . . . no. Still dun believe Annie would ever hurt Mam. But she's never told me the truth about her death, for there's more to it than what she's said.

Not that.

Think.

About everything Annie's been keeping to herself. That she knew about the boys being traded before anyone else did. She's not been lying to me. Just not telling me the truth.

Not just that.

Firelight flickers over my fingers.

It's the truth. I feel it like a secret glow in my hands.

Think.

Something about my hands.

What have them touched that them know is true?

Something here in this room.

Think.

It's her dogs.

Pacing, by the door.

Think.

She loves these dogs more than anything else. Is never apart from them. So why weren't she out with the women, tracking Langward with them? Why hasn't she come for them?

Think.

I haven't been inside her cottage since before Barney got took. Because each time I saw her, she said she'd come round to mine . . . and I never even noticed her do it.

Think.

She were talking of moving house with Martyn, all the way to Wreckers Shore, and that were decided quick and quiet, not long after Barney were took.

Think.

Whenever I asked the moppet, 'Where are you?' Barney said, 'It's dark.' So him is so well hid, no one would ever see him outside.

Think.

If him needs to be hid indoors and kept in the dark, it must be because all around him, outside in the light, or looking through the windows, are all the folks what know exactly what him looks like.

Think.

If Barney untangled himself from the nets and fell out of the boat just as the tall men left, him wouldn't have had to swim far at all. Him could've been washed up on the beach.

Think.

The beach where Annie walks these dogs, every single day. Think.

That's it. That's truth.

I scrawl a note for Kelmar and leave it on the table.

*

The bright light from the pale moon splashes off the snow. As I shut Annie's dogs inside, a shadow moves next to me.

The shadow flits over the snow, the same shape and size as me. Shadow Mary is beside me. We run towards the cliff path what leads north. My feet slip and slide in the snow, catch on the stones hidden under it. Shadow Mary leaves no tracks.

I stop and breathe hard. Shadow Mary stands a few feet away. Waits. Watches me with her hollow eyes.

We're running again. I hear her voice in my thoughts, *Can't even remember, can't even remember, can't even remember*, her voice, the beat of a drum.

'Stop it.' My feet slide and slip, she runs faster than me. My legs are too weak, I trip, fall and sit up, rubbing my shins.

She leans over me. '*You* called me back. I'm not going away. Unlock the blank dark.'

'Dun know what you mean.' I try to get up, but stagger and fall again.

She leans down and hisses in my ear, 'Stop taking keys from other folks, and unlock the blank dark.'

'Dun know how to.'

'I'm giving you all the memories back. Keep doing it, till them're all just yours. For I dun want them neither.'

'I were made to forget them. The tincture.'

'You could've looked for them, you knew them were missing, knew you had blanks in your head.'

'I dun want them! I should get rid of *you* – done it before, and I can do it again!' I stagger to my feet.

She snarls at me. 'Then you'll be half of yourself.'

'I just want Barney back.' I walk away from her, fast as I can.

She's next to me. 'So you're going to shut me away again, pour all your love into him—'

'Aye, I am,' I say. 'Him needs it.'

She keeps up with me. 'And when Barney grows up and leaves you, and you're left staring at yourself in some mirror, what will you see if I'm not there? Ever seen a face with no shadows on it?'

'No.'

She hisses in my ear, 'It looks just like a ghost.'

Morgan

Hidden behind this long black curtain that covers a high window and the wall beneath it, I can't see anything. The window has gone light and dark again in the time I've been still, listening to quiet talking, footsteps, the sounds of doors opening, doors closing.

And now, just my own breathing, and beyond the curtain, thick silence.

I walk along the wall behind the curtain and find a white door. I open it and step into a small room. The walls are painted cornflower blue, and in the middle of the room a long cabinet houses a collection of objects behind rippled glass. There are small pieces of white paper beside each object, covered in handwritten black words.

On the paper next to a left-handed glove:

MEGAN BROOK
To be learned:
Never want something that
you know you can't have,
until the impossible
becomes possible.

A strand of my white hair has come loose and I tuck it away under my shawl. I wander the length of the cabinet. A scratched ring, a mirror, a necklace made from glass beads. A chain. A glass question mark. A stone with a hole through it. A pile of salt. A small rusted bell.

An old worn boot. The paper next to it reads:

NED JARED
To be learned:
Never let a sense of uselessness
lead you in a direction
you are unable to retrace
your steps from.

Mary's father. In the corner of the room is a small table and chair, on the table is a pen and a pile of small pieces of blank paper.

I write on one of them:

THE THRASHING HOUSE
is full of ghosts.
The dead must be buried.
These objects are relics of ghosts,
so bury them in the graveyard.

I close the door quietly behind me and listen. No sound. I crouch down and crawl out from under the curtain, the black fabric heavy and thick with dust.

I stand up in a huge room, filled with looms and woven fabrics. This room is lit by candles, flickering along the far wall. In the middle of the room are solid frames, looms made of wood and metal. Half-woven fabrics of wool and thick threads, patterned and plain, tweed and twill. On a much smaller frame, an embroidery with the trunk and roots of a tree and leaves every possible shade of green. Notes on a small book on a table next to it, of the colours and stitches they've used.

On one side of the room are baskets piled high with matted seaweed from the poisoned shore, nets slung over them. There are three machines in the centre of the room that have a much simpler shape than the looms: each made from a wooden frame with a handle on one side and a geared wheel that turns. The strands are fed through a small wooden dome shaped like a spinning top. The spinning top must turn, to twist the seaweed into rope. There are white gloves with stained fingertips on the floor next to some crates stacked against the wall. To make the ropes, the women must twist the seaweed and walk the width of this room.

I look in the crates where the muscular ropes are coiled like sleeping snakes, the strands held in place by double-pronged pins, to stop even one strand unravelling. Some of the pins are sticking outwards as well as inwards. One of the ropes moves.

A shrill whistle from outside.

I spin round. The arched front door is closed. I turn back into the room. Along the walls are other doors. Silent rooms, closed away.

A high platform at the back of the room has a circle of chairs that surround a tall wooden box, an oval object on top of it. I walk past the frames and looms towards the platform.

The oval object on top of the box is the shadow man's head. My stomach twists. The women have beheaded him.

His eyes move to mine. His body must be standing inside the box beneath that head.

Still attached.

He says, 'You've been hiding.'

I say, 'You've been caught.' There's a yellow tinge to his pale face.

I climb the steps onto the platform. A creak and groan in the wooden planks underneath me.

Three whistles from outside.

His voice is a groan. 'Quick—'

'I'm not going to help you.'

His breathing is laboured. 'Trade.'

'You haven't got anything I want.'

I walk past him to the long heavy curtains at the back of the platform. I step between two curtains and hold them shut just beneath my eye. I can see the back of his head and the whole circle of chairs.

A loud clack and the arched door creaks open. A crowd of about fifty women, young and old, stride in, their footsteps thud on the wooden floor. They're wearing thick coats and shawls flecked with snow. They stride towards the platform, gazes fixed on the man's face. They come up the stairs. Candles are lit and placed around the outside of the chairs. Their feet echo on the floorboards.

The chairs creak and shift as they sit down in the circle around the man. Only one or two of the chairs are empty. The women's faces on the far side of the circle glare up at him, focus and determination in their eyes. An old woman with a black shawl over her hair raps her walking stick on the floor three times.

A woman wearing a purple shawl walks around the outside of the chairs, sprinkles salt on the floor. Encloses them all in a white circle.

The old woman stands, her sunken eyes gleam as she takes out a small hessian bag from a hidden pocket, moves towards the man and sprinkles another circle, in earth, around the box.

She announces, 'The Thrashing House delivers justice. We have just been told of hims crime, and the length of time it has took to bring it to light. The Thrashing House has released him. This is because the truth had to come out, and could not, if him were thrashed. We've to deliver justice ourselves.'

From under the floor a loud creak that sounds like the Thrashing House roots.

A woman's voice clangs out, 'I've been given hims name. We can pull hims voice from out of hims silence. Pull off hims name; the one word him can hide behind.'

A low hum. The women close their eyes. The hum rises in volume. Their bodies are still, their mouths open wider as the volume increases. The notes are a discordant sound that fills the room, the lower tones a dirge, the higher notes a lament that soars through the air.

One woman stands, her white boots gleam as she advances towards the man. This must be Kelmar, Mary's aunt. All the other boots are brown. She walks around the edge of the circle of earth.

'Laang . . . waarrrd,' she sings, her voice is a chant. 'LaangwaarrdLaangwaarrd Langward.' The sound is vivid and rich, I almost close my eyes, the hum of the women, this voice that chants above them, makes me drift, I'm pulled both out of and into myself, something inside me waking, another part falling asleep. Drawing out and pulling back, drawing out . . .

All the voices pick up the word, their tones and pitches the same, the letters are unimportant, the order is rearranged. My eyelids droop. I shake my head to wake myself. A word without beginning or end becomes a word with no meaning.

The shadow man screams.

His scream is like the scream of a horse. It cuts through the chant and the women's voices increase in volume. His scream gets louder and louder, his scream, no, more than his scream, some *part* of him is tearing. They are ripping his name away, leaving him with nothing to hide behind.

The old woman lights some herbs she holds tightly in her fist. She walks around him, sunken eyes closed, but sure in her footsteps. She feels her way in the sound, still chanting, smudges the air with the smoke, which coils out, rises, thickens. The scent of lavender and some other herbs . . . sage, valerian . . .

The women chant, their eyelids closed.

His scream fills the whole room, jars through the smoke, the chant, all his anger, lust and confusion, all the things he's ever felt and kept hidden. His scream fills my head, and I can see why the women's eyes are closed. Scratches zigzag through the smoke above the man's head – his scream tears. Rips through anything his eyes see – his scream splits the air that he breathes, the air we're all breathing.

I fall forwards onto the platform and my head hits the floor. The others still have their eyes closed, one of the women blusters down to me, clamps her hand over my eyes, hisses in a distorted voice, 'Hum. Just hum.'

She yanks me up, my feet scuff over the salt into the circle and the man's scream seems quieter, one hand shoves me down onto a chair, while her other hand tightens across my eyes. She takes her hand off, I keep my eyes shut and feel her pull my shawl up to cover my hair. She pushes my head forwards so it's bowed.

I hum. The scream grows quieter, seems a long distance away. With my eyes closed and a hum in my mouth, I've stepped into another room, empty and clear, where I stand alone, looking at blank walls. A room that exists just alongside this room where my body sits. A room with dust around the cornices, a thick lilac carpet and no doors. A room where I can still hear everything that's going on, but nothing touches me. In a room next to me, some women chant, and some man screams, but I'm not there any more.

My hum is too loud.

I don't know what note it should be. The chant around me is lower, I lower mine . . . the scream has stopped. I blink hard, the sounds around me drop to silence.

The box has split open. The man is slumped on the floor. Puddles of ropes around his ankles and wrists. He raises his head. I keep my head bowed, glance round at the women from under the shawl, they're all watching the ropes that snake around him, slowly tightening.

The old woman stands over him, just outside the edge of the earth circle. She says, 'Unpunished Crime,' and stretches out her arms.

The women's expressions are angry, faces flush, spittle flies as they shout one name: Mary Jared. Their voices shouting are stones smashing, winds howling, the deafening crash of waves. I tilt my head and listen hard, it's not just Mary's name, but her name followed by words . . .

Kelmar stands, walks towards him, I pick out her voice, 'Mary Jared . . .' she shrieks. She leans over him, fists clenched, feet still, not stepping over the earth circle. I catch some of her words . . . but I don't want to hear them.

I try to cover my ears but the woman next to me grips hard on my wrist. Her face is hidden under her shawl. So I hum and can't hear their words any more. The women, still shouting, all stand. The woman's hand yanks me to my feet, her palm is sweaty. I can't hear her voice. The woman to my left screeches out, 'Mary Jared, can't even remember, can't even remember, can't even remember!' over and over again with a rage like a storm in her voice.

We advance towards him, I'm pulled along in this circle of shouts. The circle closes in, our feet stamp as beads of sweat cluster on the man's pale brow. The circle reaches Kelmar and includes her. The old woman thumps her stick on the floor three times.

The shouts stop.

The air between us feels solid, thick with anger. All around me, the women's breaths are fast and heavy. The ropes twist and coil around the man's legs.

'Speak, Langward,' the woman with the walking stick says in a cracked voice. 'In your own defence. We will listen, without interrupting.' She glances around the circle of women. 'You have one chance to tell us what you want to be took into account for your crime. Then we will leave you, talk, and return with our decision on your punishment.'

I want to back away, behind the curtain. I pull my arm from the woman's hand, but she grips even harder.

The old woman speaks again. 'We will hear your defence. Begin.'

The women lean in to listen.

Sweat drips from his clammy skin. He says, 'It is old, what you speak of. There's no proof in silence.'

Kelmar's eyes flash. 'There's proof in that boy's eyes! There's proof in my hands. Proof in the memory I have of bringing that child into the world. I know whose belly that child grew—'

The old woman thuds her walking stick on the floor.

He replies, 'A lost child has no proof in his eyes.'

Kelmar says, 'We've all seen them. As we see yours.'

He laughs.

A murmur passes between three women opposite me, their faces flush pink. The old woman silences them with a thud of her stick.

He glares at the old woman and there's anger in his voice, 'You can't punish me for something I've no control over. Her daughter reminds me of her . . . always has.'

All around me a low murmur.

He says, 'Traders are always between places.'

Everyone is silent as he talks about maps, distance, water, nothing being fixed, and how he has never been settled enough anywhere. He tells how he gave Beatrice more trade for her embroideries than he gave to anyone else, and she didn't tell him not to.

'Enough.' The old woman's voice slices sharp through the air. Her face is raised to the ceiling, scored with lines like old bark.

He continues, 'Beatrice should have refused the extra trade I gave her.'

'Did she ever offer you anything other than her broideries?'

'No. I wanted more.'

'You gave Beatrice trade for trade. You can't blame her for something you *wanted*. You show no remorse, so are not worth the listening. You treated Beatrice's daughter like a ploughed field, some ditch to shovel your dirt in. Worse than that, you're still a danger to her. We'll be keeping you bound.'

She steps back and the women return to their chairs, whispering. The hand on my wrist yanks me down onto a chair.

Three women step towards the man, pull gloves from their pockets and squeeze their fingers into them, watching him. One woman kneels, clears three gaps in the circle of earth and the three women step through and bind him tighter with the thick ropes. The youngest of the three glares at him as she yanks the rope. The women step out through the gaps in the circle and shift the earth back into place.

His eyes roll up to the ceiling above the platform. It's painted with a mural. Birds and animals all over an island, seagulls, crows, owls and dogs all painted in a rough simplistic style. The sea around the corners, seals splashing in the waves. A painted woman sits cross-legged in the middle of the mural, in a long white dress with white flowers woven through her hair like some kind of deity. A garland across her heart, with the word 'Sishee' painted in faded blue letters. Her hands, outstretched, full of small clouds. This painting of a young woman, at peace and full of wonder, watches us all from above.

The old woman looks around the circle, her eyes stop at Kelmar. She says, 'You're the only mother here of a boy what's been took. So. Ask him.'

Kelmar stands up and says, 'Are the boys what were took to the main land still alive?'

He says, 'We are not killers.'

A sigh sweeps around the room. Kelmar slumps down and puts her head in her hands.

The old woman walks back to her chair and sits down.

'We're not done yet,' says another voice. A chair scrapes the floor as Camery stands up and walks over to the man.

The old woman leans forwards on her stick.

Camery asks him, 'Why do you take the crates of snake ropes?'

He replies, 'Poison spreads. Isn't that what your island stories say?'

'What are the snake ropes used for on the main land? It's not just me wants to know this,' Camery says, glancing at the other women. Her voice is strong. 'The men – them've seen them there in the crates on the beach for years. Them want to know why you take them.'

The old woman's voice cracks out, 'Camery.'

They glare at each other like cats. Anger crackles between them.

I lower my head, the woman's hand squeezes tight on my wrist. I keep my face hidden under the shawl. The old woman settles back in her chair.

Camery spins round to face the man. 'I'm not wasting this. Not if we can get more out of him. What are the snake ropes used for on the main land?'

The old woman's voice is tight. 'We *have* to get them gone. If them folks have a use for them, it's not for us to consider. Them are away from us, an' that's all we need concern ourselves with. Remember Beatrice. It's for the good of all.'

The man gazes up at Camery. 'They're of value . . .'

A voice shouts, 'So how come we dun get anything for them then? We should be trading them, not twisting them in secret and dragging the crates to Traders Bay at night, like we're doing something wrong!'

'Shut up!' Camery yells, her eyes fixed on the man. 'They're of value to what kinds of people?' She looms over him. 'Torturers? Murderers?'

'Among others,' he says.

'Others?' she spits.

'They are used to kill.'

The women in the circle are silent. They stare at him, cheeks pale.

'Who do you kill?' says Camery.

'*We* don't. We trade them on.' A rope squeezes his neck.

'So them're for death.'

'People all over the world pay for death. Always have. Always will. A punishment with no . . . repercussions . . . no further evidence. Just. Death.' A rope around his ankle loosens, coils back and moves along his foot.

Camery says, 'And the snake ropes kill some folks more quickly than others. You're not yet dead. Just poisoned. Now that tells me the snake ropes can't help but cause harm. It's in thems nature. But them move and twist slow when it's to be a long, slow kind of harm, and them move too quick to see when it's to be just one bite. Them are venomous, full of thems own evil, and them're feeling for the evil in you, curling round you, squeezing, poisoning you slow . . .'

He doesn't speak as Camery goes back to her chair. The woman next to her nudges her arm, nods her head. Camery points at the old woman, who glowers back at her. '*Now*, we're done, Nell.' She slaps her hands on her knees.

The women stand and I bow my head. The women talk in clusters, while the circle of salt is swept up. Nell approaches the man, whose eyes flick around, glazed. She leans down and says to him, 'We'll be taking our discussion on your punishment to another room. You're to be kept here bound, till we've fixed on a decision.'

She glances round and catches my eye, steps towards me and pauses. I watch her feet and walking stick come closer to me. 'How old's this one then?' she asks, quietly.

I don't breathe.

The woman next to me grips hard on my wrist. Her voice whispers, 'Twenty-one. Just.'

'Well, soon then. Bring her again, for the Scattering Up.' Her feet walk away.

I exhale and whisper, 'Thank you,' to the woman next to me. I can hear her rapid breathing, she grips my wrist so tightly my hand has gone numb.

The other women walk away in groups of threes and fours, down the steps from the platform and through one of the doors on the side wall. I wait for the last cluster to move away. I try to follow them, but the woman yanks me across the platform and back behind the curtain.

Her voice hisses; 'You're not going with them, stupid girl, you're not a part of this!'

'Mum?'

She pulls her shawl down. She's got fury in her crimson cheeks. The footsteps disappear. A door bangs shut.

'Now,' she says, and drags me out from behind the curtain, across the platform, past the man in the circle of earth, pulls me down the platform steps and past the looms and baskets and ropes. At the arched front door she pushes me ahead of her out into the night. She steps outside, her feet deep in the snow, closes the door behind us, turns to me and grips my arm again, her eyes furious. 'Did you leave for *this*? You're coming home.'

'I'm not.' I yank my arm away.

She stumbles. I reach to steady her, but she steps back.

Her words hammer out, 'So help me, you *are* coming home. The gate's smashed, the twins went outside and they want to be allowed out again, and this *filthy* girl made dinner and stole all the keys. *And* she didn't do the flowers I needed.' She wails and bites her hand. 'You *are* coming home.' She sobs.

I say, 'That old woman knew you. All those nights you locked me in my room – you came here?'

She turns away.

'You lied about my age, so they wouldn't get angry—'

She answers over her shoulder, 'With *me*. For bringing you.'

'But you didn't bring me.'

Her feet are planted in the snow, even with her back to me I can tell her arms are folded.

I say, 'Mum, you remember that story, the one about the girl who took care of everyone she lived with, and more and more people kept moving in, because they wanted to be looked after?

She got three choices from a visiting witch. Her reward came when one of her choices resulted in the whole household dying in a firework accident. After that, she gave herself all kinds of new choices – she let herself be wicked, to play with fire, torch houses, burn down entire cities. She danced in the ashes and had never been happier. You read me that once, when I was little.'

She doesn't turn round. 'I did not.'

'You tried to change the ending, and said that the girl was happy when she'd used her last choice to please other people. Her mother, I think it was. The girl had scrubbed so hard, she'd worn the skin from her hands, so her fingers were made of bones. You said she could clean so perfectly because having bony fingers meant that she could scrub and scrape even the tiniest corners with incredible precision.'

'I was clever, I was teaching you to keep your feet on the ground. You were seeing ghosts, hearing voices—'

'I knew you made up the ending. I'd already read it.'

Flakes of snow fall on the back of her heavy dark coat. Her silence thickens around her, like a fence with no gate.

I ask, 'Did *your* mother read you stories?'

Her back stiffens. I reach out my hand but don't touch her.

'You saw Anita, didn't you?'

She finally turns round and glares at me.

'You stole—'

'Quiet,' she hisses. 'She was an imaginary thing, some phantom you dreamed up. The thought of ghosts, they rage through my dreams even now. Is that what you'd have wanted, to let your mind just wander off, to find more imaginary friends to haunt your own mother's nightmares with?'

'Perhaps I needed a ghost to play with. You and Dad living like kings and qu—'

'Quiet! This island needed an undertaker, it needed a coffin builder. We're needed, even if the people are all mad, the dead must be buried!' she cries, her hands over her ears.

'The Thrashing House called you here,' I whisper. 'You weren't just running away. You were running towards.'

Wiping her eyes with her hand, she turns and walks away.

She looks like a small child, lost in the snow, looking for a home with a fire inside it and a mother who can smooth out her hair and warm her with baked bread, steamed puddings. I wonder what stories her own mother told her, if she ever talked to her at all. I imagine her in a story with a happy ending, with a fireside that's always warm.

*

Outside the Weaving Rooms, I sit on the steps leading to the door that holds behind it a man tied in poisoned ropes, and a crowd of angry women discussing justice. On the ceiling, a painting of a woman with white flowers in her hair.

Some time soon I will move, and something will begin. I'm waiting for the moment when the door opens, like the cover of a book, and I will step up, introduce myself to Kelmar and she'll take me to Mary.

The snow spirals and flickers through the pink and grey sky. The whole island is silent and white. An empty page, waiting for someone to write a new story on it.

I look at the footprints of the women that lead up to the door of the Weaving Rooms. They had a reason not to wait. They had a reason to move.

To make these footprints. To chase after something they want.

I think of the ghost of a father who feels useless. And the ghost of a mother who wrote, *Tell her*, before she was blown away.

Kicking the snow off my boots, I go through the arched door, cross the room with the looms and open the side door that the women went behind.

They sit around a great wooden table. Their faces swivel and gape at me.

I say, 'I'll give any one of you the Thrashing House key, in exchange for being told where Mary Jared is right now.'

A clatter of loud voices, chairs shifting against floorboards.

Kelmar stands, says, 'Keep talking,' then walks around the side of the table. Some of the women rise to let her squeeze past, she pushes other chairs out of her way. Mutters and mumbles scuttle around the room between paler faces, frowning up at me.

Kelmar reaches the doorway, turns back to them, says, 'The matter in hand. Justice.'

She takes my arm, closes the door, glances up at the man and says, 'We'll go outside.'

I follow her. 'Does Mary know you're her aunt?'

'Outside.' She opens the arched door.

We step into the snow.

She turns to face me. 'You got her out of the graveyard, and got her somewhere to recover. So I'll be trusting you to take care of her till I'm there. And no, she dun know I'm her aunt. Fell out with Beatrice when Mary were born. She thought I should've told her how bad the pain were to be. Said she'd never have chose to have a child if she'd known. Never forgave me for it. So, no. Mary never has known me as her aunt. So let *me* tell her that, and dun think it's your business.'

'I won't. Where's Mary?'

'At mine. Look.' She walks a few feet from the door and points at a funnel of chimney smoke behind a small hill. 'Follow the smoke to that fire and you'll find her there. Watch you take care of her. Dun give her any shocks. She's had enough.'

'Thank you.' My eyes blur.

'The key, then. Give it here.' She holds out her hand.

I pull it out of my pocket. 'Her father said to give it to someone older than her.'

'Her father's thrashed. An old boot.'

'You'll take care of this.' I put the key in her hand.

Kelmar nods, watching my eyes. She says, 'I'll look after it as much as you'll look after Mary. Take turns, that's how we take care of this key. And that's what it'll be for you and Mary. Not have one care more than the other, but both have to care just enough. Be yourself first.' She reaches out a hand and strokes a strand of my white hair escaping from the scarf. She says, 'You've got a lot of hope glowing in you. And she's found some way to keep going. Might not always serve her, but it's got her this far. You're as light as she's dark. Tell her I'll be home, soon as I can.' She walks back into the Weaving Rooms and closes the door behind her.

I knock on Kelmar's front door. No one answers. I open the door and Annie's dogs crash out, knock me over and charge away. I brush off the snow, go inside the cottage and call Mary's name into every room.

She's not here.

A note lies on the table.

> *My Barney is hid in Annie's cottage.*
> *Come and find me as soon as you get this.*

334

I'm not sure which direction to go in. But the dogs know, and the dogs have left paw prints.

So I chase after them through the snow.

Mary

I slip and slide on the path down the cliffs, fall and get up again.
Bash my feet on buried rocks, stagger and yank myself on.

This snow on my face feels cold.

But Grandmam said the snow here is never cold.

But this snow is.

It melts on my cheeks.

My feet slide the last distance and I fall onto the beach.

Grandmam lied. Not a lie. A story.

I pull the moppet out of my bag. Yell at it, 'Are you real? Just
answer me, *are* you my Barney's voice, or some story I've made
up in my head?'

I listen close, to nothing.

I push and shove my freezing thumbs at the seam across its
belly. The stitches hold firm. I tear at them with my teeth but
I can't feel my mouth. I sob at the moppet, 'I only *think*
Barney's alive, because you've been talking when I listen – are
you real? Am I chasing after something dead?' I listen close,
to nothing.

The moppet dun speak, so I drop it in the snow.

*

I lie at the bottom of the path. The sea is black and the sky is thick with snowflakes. The snow falls over me. Annie might not even have Barney. This could all be me needing to believe I can find him alive, that I can have him back so I can keep myself so busy taking care of him that I've no need to think of how to take care of myself.

So I can be a ghost for him. A face with no shadows.

If Barney really is drowned out at sea and dead without being buried, without me able to stroke hims hair for the last time before him is sealed in a coffin box, lowered into a grave with only hims name on that I sit at till flowers grow over him in summer and snow falls over him in winter, then there'll just be me crying till the sky goes black and my eyes dun see.

And it'll be my name the deadtaker carves into a headstone. Kelmar might make him carve Barney's name beneath mine, but then hims name will be scored out as soon as it's been carved in.

That will be the end of my belonging people.

The moppet is buried in the snow. I whisper, 'Did I made you real?' Tears freeze on my cheeks as I pick the moppet up and rub them away with its cold scratchy fur.

I whisper, 'Even if I did, I can't let you go,' and put it back in my pocket.

There's my cottage, the windows dark, the curtains open. No one inside it. So Morgan has gone.

If nothing else, Annie's someone what knows me. Someone I thought I could trust, but now dun. But at least I know what I'll see when I look at her. I'll see someone what's got her shadow still attached.

I drag my feet through the thick snow, past my cottage and up the path what leads to Annie's worn wooden door.

I bang on the door. Rattle the handle. It's locked.

In all these years I've known her, I dun remember Annie ever locking her door. Dun even know she had a key for it.

For if I had, I'd have thieved it.

The sky spins around.

I hammer on the door, scream Annie's name over and over. I look in the window. The kitchen is full of shadows. I dig out a jagged grey stone from her path.

I hurl it. The window shatters.

Reaching in, I find the catch, open the window and climb through.

In her dark kitchen the broken glass is scattered across the floor, there's a crack in the floorboard that leads to a doorway, and Annie sits on the floor in the doorframe, hunched over. I scream at her, she curls up, arms over her head. I flail, angered tears all over my face, slap her head, pull her hair, shout, 'Why've you got your door locked?'

She dun fight back.

'Why've you locked it? Tell me!' I pull her hair, hard.

I stop. Let go.

My heart thud thud thud in my throat.

I squat down next to her. My voice, cold, 'Annie, have you got Barney? Give me him now.'

She looks up at me, dark under her eyes. 'Oh Mary,' she whispers. 'Them took the dogs . . . why did them have to take the dogs?'

I put my hands on her shoulders. 'Give me him.'

She raises a limp hand, points to a cupboard at the back of the room, I near trip over her getting to it. I open the cupboard door. Inside is a heavy wooden box. I drag it out. It bangs on the floorboards.

Annie yells, 'No! Dun take him. Them took mine. You're still

338

too young to care for him right. It were milk of one of the lost ones – my baby's milk what kept him alive, for Beatrice, her shame when her milk wouldn't come for him.'

The back of my throat stings. '*You* were hims wet nurse,' I whisper, my hands on my flattened chest. 'You made him live, and now you've . . .'

Inside the box,
a black cloth covers a lump.
Barney is here, dead, in this box.
I close my eyes and reach in.
Grip the cloth. Pull it away.
Open my eyes.

Ropes coil and twist around each other. I throw the cloth back in over them. I yank Annie up and push her against the doorframe.

'That trap dun work on me. I've been bit twice by them ropes. I've not been deaded. That's your doing, for taking what's mine. Where is him?'

Her eyes flick at the floor. I fly down, pull back the rug, there's the trapdoor to her storm room. It's padlocked, with a small key still in the lock. I turn the key and wrench the padlock open. My fingers grip the key, want to take it, but there's Shadow Mary's hand over it.

So I leave the key in the padlock.

Annie stares at me, her hands over her mouth. A low wail comes out of her. She walks to a corner of the room, slides down on the floor. She sits there hunched up, mutters against her knees, 'Kieran sold. Martyn gone. Kieran sold. Martyn gone . . .'

I lift the trapdoor.
A ladder leads straight down.

'Barney!' I shout loud into the dark.

Nothing.

My voice echoes, 'Barney . . .'

'Annie, did you starve him?' My belly clenches as I listen to the silence in the storm room.

She stares at me and says, 'I want my dogs back.'

'If Barney's dead, you'll not be needing your dogs. You're going to want to be in the Thrashing House rather than take what I'll do to you.'

She buries her head in her arms. 'Calling calling calling . . .'

I climb down the ladder into the dark. I climb as far as I can and the ladder ends. I can't feel the bottom rungs. It's broken. I call again, 'Barney . . .' and the echo sounds hollow around me.

Silence.

Footsteps above me, Annie's face looks in.

She pushes the trapdoor shut. The padlock rattles and clacks.

She's locked me in.

I breathe in and jump down from the ladder. I land on something soft. Light shines in from a tiny sun in the corner of the room.

The whole floor of the storm room is thick with owl feathers. Bundles of candles and matches on high shelves, a stinking bucket on the floor, some dry bread in a basket on a chair. In the far corner there's a small wooden bed. On the bed a ragged brown blanket. Under the blanket the curls on the back of hims head are just as I remember them.

Barney.

Is him breathing?

Let him be breathing.

I move towards him,

time is slow, the sun moves across
the storm room, it hangs in the air
over him, shines warm light on hims hair.
Him lies so still. The sun shines,
brighter, lighter. A whole day passes as I
cross the room
him sighs in hims sleep, rolls towards me,
alive.
I cry out.
Wrap my hands around him. Him reaches hims arms around
my neck. I pick him up. My arms are full.

'I've got you, Barney, I got you,' I whisper. My tears fall on
hims hair. Him puts hims hands on my shoulders, leans back
and looks at me. Hims brown eyes have my reflection inside.
Him slumps forwards against my chest and hims arms hold on
tight.

I look around the storm room.

Light shines from the sun, burning so bright, everything has
come alive in here. The air is full of tiny floating pieces of cloud.
Blue and purple butterflies flit everywhere – from Barney's
dreamings.

I cradle him. Him breathes in deep, smells me, sighs. My
cheek strokes hims hair.

The storm room floor covered in tumbles of white owl feathers
looks like warm snow.

'That's better, Mary,' him says, 'better now.'

We sit in the corner of Annie's storm room with a candle burning,
casting shadows on the wall. I watch them flicker. Barney is
asleep in my arms, holding the moppet tight to hims chest.

Above me, the sound of barking dogs. Annie shrieks, her
footsteps stamp over the floorboards.

The front door slams.

Silence.

I carry Barney to the bottom of the broken ladder. See how far it is to get onto the first rung.

I look up at the locked trapdoor.

Soft footsteps cross the floor above me, and stop.

The sound of a key, turning.

Acknowledgements

I'd like to thank my agent Lucy Luck, for her editorial advice through early drafts, and her constant support and wisdom.

My talented editors, Jocasta Hamilton and Suzie Dooré; Carole Welch and the team at Sceptre.

With thanks to the hardworking team at HarperCollins, Canada: Jennifer Lambert, Iris Tupholme and Jane Warren.

The staff at Sussex University CCE: Mark Slater, Susannah Waters, and especially Catherine Smith for always being right and Anna McGrail for her invaluable questions and for demanding a weekly word count. My writing group: Anna, Gra, Lucy, Noel and Woody for their feedback and friendship, David for his expert advice and kindness.

Alan for his knowledge of birds and plants, and Anne for not reading the ending first.

Andy, Ben, Caspian, Fiona, Kate A, Kirsty, Orlando, Rachel, Sophie and Tom for reading early drafts.

Ros, for her help with echoes.

Rosie and Sue, for their faith in dreams.

Jac, for believing in hard work and magic.

Paul and Sarah for cake, hugs and emergency coffee.

And Kakey, for reminding me 'it's time to take the red shoes off; stop writing and get some sleep', and then giving me a pair of bright red shoes for Christmas.

An exclusive, unedited extract from Jess Richards' second novel

COOKING WITH BONES

coming soon.

My sister is a formwanderer: she is a mirror of want. Each person she meets sees what they want, when they look at her. And she changes for each pair of eyes. Though Maya's three years younger than me, when I was really little I'd desperately wanted a twin. I'm the one who's closest to her. I've cared for her, brushed her hair, fed and comforted her. I've given her games and stories and pictures to imagine. I've slept in the same room as her, borrowed her clothes and watched her wear mine.

But now we're grown.

She's grown for sixteen years.

As I've grown, what I want from Maya has changed. Now, part of me desperately wants her to be herself.

But she doesn't know what that is.

This morning Maya sleeps in curtain-sieved sunshine. I perch on the edge of her twin bed and blur my eyes. Her dark hair streams over a pale yellow pillow. She dreams. I don't. So within her somewhere, something is separate to me. I look at her face and see mine. With a want, strong as marble, I force her to show me how other people have seen her.

Different faces flicker on hers like masks. Her expressions distort with a thousand reflections. She murmurs, cries, laughs, cries again. Whispers. Shouts. Whimpers. Smiles. Her fingers grip the rosebud duvet, she scratches, touches the fabric.

She's dreaming away echoes of what others want.

Some of these faces are beautiful; a child: a boy, a loner. A woman hunting miracles, an old man hankering for faith.

We all hope we want good things, but this isn't true.

That face, yes, that one. I'd swear that's a face of a killer.

It wavers away, becomes wider, sweeter, the lips mouth the whispers of someone newly in love.

If I let my sister go everywhere and anywhere and no-one cared, I could learn the secret desires of everyone in this city. These faces show me that many people who Maya's met are seeking hope.

Maya wakes as if she's inhaling the sky.

She sees me and her face shifts into a mirror image of mine. Her hair twists back into long dark layers, her pyjamas, as she sits up, are made from the blue satin fabric I'm wearing.

She blinks her eyes into sight. 'A dream of death. Something's about to change.'